THE
VERY MARROW
of Our
BONES

CHRISTINE HIGDON

a misFit book

Published by ECW Press
665 Gerrard Street East
Toronto, Ontario, Canada M4M 1Y2
416-694-3348 / info@ecwpress.com

Get the
eBook free!*
*proof of purchase
required

Purchase the print edition
and receive the eBook free!
For details, go to ecwpress.com/eBook.

Library and Archives Canada
Cataloguing in Publication

Higdon, Christine, author
The very marrow of our bones :
a novel / Christine Higdon.

Issued in print and electronic formats.
ISBN 978-1-77041-416-7 (softcover)
ALSO ISSUED AS:
978-1-77305-186-4 (PDF),
978-1-77305-185-7 (EPUB)

I. TITLE.

PS8615.I368V47 2018   C813'.6
C2017-906188-7   C2017-906189-5

MISFIT
Editors for the press: Michael
Holmes /
a misFit book
Cover design: David Gee
Author photo: Peter Higdon

PRINTING: MARQUIS   5   4   3   2   1
PRINTED AND BOUND IN CANADA

The publication of *The Very Marrow of Our Bones* has been generously supported by the
Canada Council for the Arts which last year invested $153 million to bring the arts to
Canadians throughout the country, and by the Government of Canada through the Canada
Book Fund. *Nous remercions le Conseil des arts du Canada de son soutien. L'an dernier, le
Conseil a investi 153 millions de dollars pour mettre de l'art dans la vie des Canadiennes et des
Canadiens de tout le pays. Ce livre est financé en partie par le gouvernement du Canada.* We also
acknowledge the Ontario Arts Council (OAC), an agency of the Government of Ontario,
and the contribution of the Government of Ontario through the Ontario Book Publishing
Tax Credit and the Ontario Media Development Corporation.

Ontario
Ontario Media Development
Corporation

ONTARIO ARTS COUNCIL
CONSEIL DES ARTS DE L'ONTARIO
an Ontario government agency
un organisme du gouvernement de l'Ontario

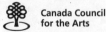
Canada Council
for the Arts

Conseil des Arts
du Canada

Canada

RECYCLED
Paper made from
recycled material
FSC® C103567
www.fsc.org

For

my father
my brothers
my sons

I used to think of marriage as a plate-glass
window just begging for a brick.

JEANETTE WINTERSON, *Written on the Body*

It was under the milk jug on the kitchen table. A wet ring cut across the centre of the paper, a lined sheet she'd torn from one of our scribblers. Mine probably. The ink had run milky blue, veins emptied onto the page. Why I hid it, I can't say. Why I didn't say anything about it to anyone, even when the police came, even years later, when my brother Trevor hammered a little wooden cross with her name on it into the garden, like for a dog's grave, and I kicked it over, I will never know.

The note said: *Wally, I will not live in a tarpaper shack for the rest of my life. Love, Bette.*

None of us knew about pain. Not the kind that leaves you shattered and speechless. I had watched Trevor fly from the tree fort once—a graceless trapeze artist—and heard the sharp, unexpected snap of his wrist against the moss and cedar blanket of the forest floor. I'd seen my twin brothers Alan and Ambrose knocked bloody and unconscious in a dirt-bike crash at the gravelly corner of Forward Road and Hemlock Street. And when Jed was a puppy he ran headlong into the moving wheel of Mr. Tenpenny's half ton. But no one had died. No one had left us. Not even a dog.

Once, my eldest brother Geordie and I came across the carcass of a freshly killed young possum in the back woods. Its arms were raised above its head, as if in disbelief. Beseeching. Whatever killed it had ripped open its belly and eaten all its tender bits. My mother's disappearance left us all like that. Gutted, hapless creatures flung unceremoniously into raw isolation.

Sometimes pain brings people together, helps them to cross the grand abyss of human discord. The lost are found. Sons reach out to fathers after years of silence. Sisters forgive brothers. Sometimes it's too late.

TOWARD *the* END

My brother, he could use some mercy now.

MARY GAUTHIER, *Mercy Now*

I was early and Trevor would be late. When the rain came, I took cover under the awning of the Sylvia Hotel with half a dozen others. The sky had been overfilled and resentful, waiting all day for its moment, and the rain pelted down, kicking up puffs of sand on the beach. Then, almost as suddenly as it had begun, it stopped. The sky had told us what it was feeling. Now it was ready, like a lover, to lie serenely above us, purged.

Not me. I don't know what set me off. I was regretting having agreed to meet Trevor, so maybe the heavens and I were commiserating. Or maybe it was just my turn to glower and the sky's tantrum had given me permission. Whichever, I walked along the beach path, away from Stanley Park, my mood matched by the tossing sea.

A young man skated by, then another, chasing. Grace on wheels, shoulders forward, arms back, rainwater spraying up behind their calves. Their lithe bodies flew away into the distance and I sighed. My most recent romantic encounter—a middle-aged American theatre critic—was still causing a commotion in my heart. Never again. I kicked a rock on the path and watched it fly off the seawall. I found a bench. It was dedicated to a dead person. This one read: *Mac Clifton and Nippie. Beloved Husband and Father. 1920–2006. Nippie. Faithful Companion. 1995–2007. Playing fetch in the greatest field of all*. Poor Nippie. I sat on the wet bench, covering the plaque with my back.

The tide was now as out as it could be. A knot of small children and a couple of women were combing the beach for shells and bullwhip kelp and other sea treasures. Another pretty young couple skated by hand in hand. I watched them, feeling even more irritable, until the boy tripped and the pair of them flew hands first to the wet asphalt. The Good Samaritan got the better of me, but not before an agreeable if completely uncharitable wave of score-settling washed over me. Enough, Lulu, I told myself. Pull yourself together. It's just Trevor.

●

Trevor was loping down Bidwell then waiting to cross Beach Avenue. Too thin, and always the same—receding hair in one of those pathetic pencil-thin ponytails, skinny jeans, his ancient leather jacket. He was carrying two motorcycle helmets, one the kind you might as well not wear—a skid lid, Dad called them. I hadn't been home for a year, hadn't seen Trevor in longer, but he hadn't changed. A little more gaunt maybe, if that was possible. He hadn't noticed me yet. For a moment I considered slipping into the public washrooms at English Bay, pretending I hadn't shown up. I'd done it before. That way I'd be sure of ending this stormy day without an argument. I should have.

He saw me. His arm went up, a long slow salute, a cool cock of the hand. Right on, Trevor. A car swerved, honked. Trevor gave the driver the finger and danced, Mick Jagger, across the street, pretty spry for a lifelong addict.

"Hey, Lulu. Little Sis. How are ya?" His hug was hard. No meat on his bones to make it sweet. Not that women seemed to care. Trevor, of all my brothers, had always had the gift with women. They fell for him. Smart, interesting, ought-to-know-better women left boyfriends, husbands, other countries for Trevor. And he unfailingly left them for some cherished wisp of freedom, or one of his other addictions.

We walked toward a big driftwood log on the beach; already we had nothing to say.

After a moment he said, "Remember Great-Aunt Nellie's story about Joe Fortes?"

"No."

"Old Joe, she called him. He lived around here somewhere, in a little cabin. He taught all the kids in English Bay to swim. Her too. Nineteen oh seven or something. The city gave him a friggin' state funeral when he died. Don't you remember her telling us about him?"

I shook my head. Trevor often remembered things I didn't. And I had memories of things he didn't. Even the stories we both remembered seemed authored by two different pens.

"What did you want to see me for?" I said, foot, as usual, in my mouth. It was not the kind of question I had intended to ask nor the ones I had rehearsed in the car on the way into town. But Trevor was well defended. He turned to me, no sign of injury in his eyes.

"A guy's got a right to say hello to his little sister every once in a while, don't he?" He smiled and leaned into my shoulder. "Besides, I wanted to talk to you about something."

At the same time, I said "What?" and he said, "You're never home, Lulu." Surely that wasn't what he wanted to talk to me about.

"Sorry," I said. A dog ran past hauling a stick longer than itself. A stout woman in her seventies, her hair covered by an old-fashioned chiffon kerchief, shambled past shouting after the dog. Mum would have been seventy-six, but nothing, I imagined, like this woman. More so than with any of my brothers, being with Trevor made me think of her.

"What are you sorry for?"

I shrugged. "Do you ever think of Mum?" I said, nodding at the woman with the dog.

"Mum? Kind of weird to call her Mum, don't you think?"

"Well, what do you call her?"

He didn't say anything for a while, then, so forlornly I grimaced: "You bet, Bette?" It was Dad's phrase. "I don't know," he said finally. "I don't call her anything. You kind of forget after forty years, don't you?"

He looked down at his hands, examined his knuckles. His fingernails were dirty. I looked at his face in profile. He'd never had acne but it seemed pocked anyway, and his beard had never grown in well. He was only fifty-five, but he looked haggard and lost. I turned away and counted the freighters anchored way out in the bay. Seventeen. There were two big motorboats too, probably ferrying ships' crews to the shore—those Russian and Turkish merchant sailors who would stagger back up Granville or Burrard at two in the morning as the bars and clubs emptied, their toques askew. I never bothered to count the sailboats. Even on the grimmest days there were plenty. Vancouver is one stinking rich city.

Trevor might have been counting the freighters too, like we used to, way back when. I had a memory of the seven of us spilling out of the car at the foot of Cypress Avenue, down by the Maritime Museum. Summer camp for the poor. I must have been eight and Trevor thirteen. Mum had a picnic basket. Alan and Ambrose were cool fifteen-year-olds, skipping stones on the little beach. Dad was trying to teach our eldest brother, Geordie, to fly his homemade newspaper kite. The string got tangled around Geordie, and Dad had to cut it with his jackknife and let the damned thing soar away. For a minute it jerked up into the sky, its tail made from one of Mum's nylon stockings. Then it stalled and plummeted into the water. Geordie bawled and paced back and forth along the shore but Mum lured him to her with an egg-salad sandwich, the last one, and called him her big boyo, which he was. The rest of the world called him other names back then—retard, moron, halfwit, dunce. Then Trevor dropped his sandwich in the sand and Mum told him there weren't any extras—there never were—and he stormed off.

I suppose all that could have happened on one trip to the beach, or Trevor's egg salad could have been peppered in the sand one day, Geordie's kite flown the coop another. Whichever, it was probably one of the times Trevor and I climbed out onto the rocks together and counted freighters in the bay, always a rare moment, a truce between us. That was a long time ago.

"You're coming tomorrow, right?"

"Wouldn't miss that wedding for a million," he said.

"Wear something nice."

"What for? You really think anyone would care?"

"Well, you could do it for Dad." I laughed as soon as I said it. It was nonsense.

"Dad, schmad," Trevor said, and he laughed too.

Dad wouldn't give two hoots about what anyone wore to a wedding—including the bride and groom—and we both knew it. He'd likely walk through the doors of Fraser Arm's Legion Hall and sit in the front row, proud as punch, in goat-milking overalls and steel-toed boots.

"Let's go climb a tree." Trevor poked me in the ribs.

"What the heck are you talking about?" He was avoiding something. I could tell.

"Remember that damn climbing tree. Twice as high as

the Smallwoods' house wasn't it? Four storeys at least. Is it still there?"

I remembered Trevor talking me branch by branch up the big fir in the woods behind the Smallwoods'. I was only five, and he caught hell from Mum when we got home and I told everyone about it, but I'd never felt anything so glorious and free as being that high.

"I'm not dressed for climbing," I said without enough sarcasm to change the smile on his face.

"Okay, then let's go for a ride," Trevor said.

"Can't. I've got to get the bloody wedding cake. That's why I came into town. Trust him to want a cake from somewhere in Vancouver. Some baker friend of his."

"Come for a ride first. I'll get you back here before rush hour."

Trevor must have read my mind because he held his hands up in the air then pushed at his sleeves. "I'm clean, honest. Been totally clean for thirteen months. I'm off everything. Even booze. These are next." He tapped the pack of cigarettes in his shirt pocket. Then he waggled a helmet at me and smiled seductively. I wanted to say, You can't use that kind of smile on your sister, but ironically—and the realization made me squirm—his tactic seemed to be working.

"Where?" I asked.

"Squamish."

"Squamish? Jesus, Trevor, that's too far."

"Just up the road then. To Horseshoe Bay. No. Lion's Bay. The route's a beauty."

"I've got to get the wedding cake."

"Come on. The bike's just up at my place on Harwood."

"Since when do you live on Harwood?"

"Since I met Julia. Who I'm bringing tomorrow, by the way."

I gave him a look. "What happened to Barbara, or was it Amanda? How old is this one?"

He gave me a look. "You're one to talk, Lulu Parsons."

I wasn't. And didn't.

"At least I hung on in my marriages for a few years," he said.

"What, like two and a half years each is an admirable record? And half of one of them spent in jail."

"Well, better than three months. And better than leaving a poor bastard at the altar."

I kicked at the sand. "I had a dream the night before."

"Must have been some dream."

"I dreamed that someone left a bag of shit on my doorstep. Besides, he didn't like dogs."

"And you couldn't live without a dog."

"No, Trevor, I couldn't."

He didn't say anything.

"At the time I thought I couldn't," I said. A weak defense, I knew.

We were both silent for a long time, mired as always, immovable siblings with a million words to say but no will to start a conversation that wouldn't bruise. I felt Trevor lean toward me and then, when I wouldn't take my eyes off the ocean, when my mulish soul refused to respond, he turned back to the bay. Later, I would regret my coldness, but I was caught by stubbornness, and by something else: the angry part of the sky had moved north and suddenly it felt on my skin the way April should—fresh, green. That spring should be such a surprise to me—that I never expected it to return—tied a knot in my stomach.

Finally Trevor said, "I heard one of your tunes on the radio last week."

"Where?"

"I don't know. Some middle-of-the-night show in Wyoming maybe. I gave you a blast on my air horn when I heard it, though. You must have some old-time music fan down there."

"Which song?"

"'Beside Billy Babcock's Grave.' A bright subject if ever I heard one, Lulu," he said with a laugh.

All I knew about Billy Babcock was that Dad kept a photo of Billy and himself in uniform in his top drawer and that they'd been best buddies until Billy's eighteen-year-old body was blown to bits on Juno Beach in 1944. Seemed as good a subject as any for a lament.

"How's the fiddling going, anyway? You playing at their wedding tomorrow? Taking a break from the road?" Trevor closed his eyes and feigned a fiddle in his arms. I believed Trevor was actually interested in my music about as much as I believed God was rooting for one football team over another. He nudged me with his elbow then his eyes moved to my throat and the silver chain I wore around my neck with the tiny silver fiddle on it. "Still wearing that, eh?"

I raised my hand to my throat, annoyed. "Well, I won't be playing 'Billy Babcock.'"

Trevor picked up a stick and scribbled a few of his own personal hieroglyphics in the sand—a truck, a heart, a curvaceous woman. Then he stabbed the stick into the centre of the heart. Not viciously, just matter-of-factly. Christ, I thought, are we that simple?

"I wrote them a new song," I said. "It's called 'Finally.'"

Trevor stood up and rubbed his hands together like he was cold. With so little meat on his bones, maybe he was. He turned to the sound of a pair of motorcycles droning past. His own language—trucks by necessity, born and bred to them, but motorcycles for release.

"Finally," he said. "So that's how you feel."

It wasn't a question so I didn't reply.

"Why don't you come home, Lulu?"

"Where's home, Trevor? Fraser Arm?"

"How about Canada, for starters. Doris Tenpenny's got a room for you."

"Doris? Jesus. That is not going to happen."

"I like Doris."

"When was the last time you saw Doris?"

He just grinned at me.

I turned away and said, "I'm home enough. Besides, I've got a home down there."

"Four walls, someone else's furniture, and a bottle of wine does not make a home, Lulu."

I would have said 'you're one to talk' but we'd already exhausted that old standby.

"Don't forget the wine glasses and my books." I forced a laugh. I wasn't up for a fight though I'd been both willing participant and instigator a thousand times. I'd been lugging a box of books around with me for ages. Some moves I never even unpacked it, but I knew exactly what was in it. I also knew that my apartment in Nashville was just that— an apartment in Nashville. I'd had apartments in Louisiana,

Florida, Arizona, California, Oregon, Massachusetts, and New York. I'd lived a year here, two years there, and then back around again, always in towns where music was king. Festival organizers invited me, and I went wherever they asked. Folk, bluegrass, country, indie, sometimes the blues. I had somehow managed to cross all kinds of musical borders, which mostly just made it difficult for reviewers and music stores to categorize me. I guess a fiddler can do that. Someone who'd never met me wrote a review once saying the fiddle suited my turbulent personality. I hate music critics.

Trevor was silent for a while, then he said, "Beware the Aeolian Winds."

"What?"

"Odysseus. Look it up."

"Odysseus."

"He got so close to home and then he made the mistake of taking a nap. His crew decided to open some bags he'd been guarding. They thought it was gold or treasure, but it was the Aeolian Winds and they blew the ship away from shore for another twenty years."

"Did you see that in a movie or something?" I don't know what it was about Trevor that made me cruel. "Anyway, I like being away."

"Like mother like daughter," he said.

"What the hell is that supposed to mean?" I was at least conscious of a 'Here we go again.'

"Nothing." Trevor flung the stick away. "I kissed Mum once," he said. I saw an angry fifteen-year-old in his face.

"So?"

"I mean I really kissed her. Slipped her the tongue."

The knot in my stomach cinched tighter. If I could have

moved, my feet would have jerked out for solid ground, my arms would have snapped up to prevent the fall.

"The morning of the day she disappeared." He was staring out at the bay, his hands in his pockets, shoulders hunched. I could feel his hopelessness, or maybe it wasn't his.

"I had my paper route, and when I got up she was sitting in the kitchen drinking coffee. Dressed. It was five-thirty or six in the morning, for Christ's sake. What the hell was she doing up at six in the morning? I don't think she'd gone to friggin' bed."

I watched a shudder pass through him. He looked at me with eyes that both warned and pleaded. I didn't move. I didn't want to hear more.

"Do you remember how she set the laundry on fire the night before she disappeared? Do you remember that? You were so little," he said.

I did. I'd been ten. I remembered. She'd put the laundry basket on our wood-burning cookstove—absentmindedly, we'd figured—and it'd burst into flames.

"Lulu, she looked so sad, sitting there with that empty pot of coffee." He was fumbling in his pocket for his cigarettes, and then a lighter, and his hands shook.

I stood. I wanted to hug him but nothing in our history included any kind of comforting.

"How come you never told anybody?"

"Like I'd tell you," he said, without rancour.

He leaned toward me and I put my arms around him. His body was rigid. He muttered something. I wished I'd never come to town to meet him. I wished I'd never heard.

"Lulu," he whispered, "she kissed me back."

●

The signs on the highway say *Watch for Falling Rock*. It's like the grisly warnings on cigarette packages—you know it happens but you don't expect it to happen to you.

On the beach Trevor leaned into me for a long time. I would say he cried except there were no tears, just the sound of him taking short sharp breaths, trying to get control of something he never would. Eventually he pulled away, not looking at me, and wiped at his eyes with his yellowed fingertips. He took my hand and we walked up to Harwood Street. His old white Ducati was parked out front of a three-storey stucco apartment building. He put the better helmet on my head and went inside for a minute. When he came out, he handed me a leather jacket.

"Your lifesaver, Madam."

"What don't I touch again?" It had been a century since I'd been on the back of one of Trevor's motorcycles.

"Don't touch that." He pointed to the muffler and mimed a sizzling finger. "Hold on tight."

In seconds we were moving very fast down Denman then along Georgia Street into moss-fragrant Stanley Park and past the lone monkey tree at the entrance to Lions Gate Bridge. The bridge buzzed under our tires. I tightened my grip. Once, when we reached the Upper Levels Highway, I closed my eyes, but an intense vertigo threatened my balance and I opened them again. The wind roared past us, or we roared past it, bringing childhood memories of schoolyard swings flying on their own, teeter-totters moved by violent invisible ghosts. North of Horseshoe Bay the ocean was aquamarine. We passed a creek, and its dank green smell flooded me. A few minutes later there was the scent of fresh-cut cedar, pungent, orange, like an exclamation mark. The sky seared blue.

By then I had more or less surrendered; any speed would kill us if we had to brake suddenly. Wiping out at a hundred and thirty would be no more dramatic than crashing at the speed limit. We'd be rag-doll dead either way, despite the leather and the helmets. Trevor rode as though he knew I had silently given him permission for speed and we bent in synchronicity, leaning tight into each curve, as I had learned to do before I was a teenager.

Trevor must not have seen it until it was in front of us. He had turned his head and was shouting something but his words were carried away by the wind. I was leaning to catch them and I saw the spray of rocks—just a little spray of falling rocks—bouncing on the asphalt like something in a slow-motion movie. Maybe I instinctively jerked the wrong way; the thought haunts me still. The Ducati wobbled slightly and Trevor swerved, a tiny swerve. Then the bike slid out from under us. I remember thinking: *we're crashing*. For a moment, Trevor's jacket was still in my hand and we were sliding side by side, a single pair in a school of fish. Then coloured lights were flashing and a woman in a uniform had her face close to mine and her mouth was moving but I couldn't hear her. I remember brown, brown eyes and some wisps of black, black hair escaping from a ponytail. And Trevor, lying still ten feet away.

PART ONE

Daughters

1967, 1968

But you were looking for an orchid
And I will always be a dandelion

ANTJE DUVEKOT, "Dandelion," *Boys, Flowers, Miles*

LULU

My parents had one last short argument the night Mum set the laundry on fire. It was late, and the house still stank of smoke. All the windows were open despite the November rain and the living room was cold. I heard the sharp tap-tap of Mum's kitten-heeled mules and then the slap-drag of Dad's old corduroy slippers. I don't think Mum knew I was behind the couch until the argument was over. I remember praying that she didn't—given what she had said—and wishing I'd gone to my bed instead.

The narrow spot behind our battered green couch probably satisfied some animal instinct in me—a safe place to hide—but something else too. Occasionally, while lying there, I'd hear Mum come into the room and stand still in front of the couch. Those times, she must have known I was there, each of us listening for the other's breathing, but I would hold my breath, and maybe she did too. Then I'd hear her kneeling on the creaking springs. I'd look up and she'd be looking down, peering one-eyed through the gap between the wall and the couch. "All right?" she'd ask. "Just want to be alone? Want your rooster pillow?" She'd stare at me as if she didn't know me, or sometimes, as if I weren't really there. Sometimes I'd wake there in the morning, a crocheted blanket dropped over me from above and the tattered rooster pillow—a cross-stitched thing I loved—tucked under my head.

We each had our defenses, Mum and I. Mine was solitude. She didn't stay around long enough for me to know what hers were.

That night, my mother's voice was all harsh whispers. Dad was his pleasant, level-headed self, until the end. Even then, at ten, I had begun to understand that she found his evenness exasperating. Like me, she must have wanted something to smash up against and feel some resistance, someone pushing back.

"For Christ's sake, Wally. I can't take care of him anymore," my mother said.

"Geordie's a good boy, Bette. You don't have to."

"He's not a boy. He's twenty years old. And I do have to take care of him. He called on Frankie today to play skip with Lorna. She's six, Wally. Lorna's six. Frankie said the girl was terrified."

"Bette dear, how could anyone be terrified of Geordie?" Dad laughed a little, coaxing. "You've said yourself that everything Frankie says has to be taken with a grain of salt." He paused, then asked, "Why would you let Geordie play with Lorna anyway?"

"I don't, Wally. I can't control where Geordie goes anymore. He's big. You know how stubborn he is. Have you looked at your son recently?"

"He looks all right to me," Dad said.

Mum didn't reply for a minute. Dad must have reached out to take her hand or touch her because she hissed *Don't*. When she finally spoke again, she sounded like she was choking.

"Verna says we should think about Woodlands."

I thought I'd be sick behind the couch. Woodlands School was where the "mentals" were sent. It stood on a hill near the B.C. Penitentiary. Essondale, the asylum, was a few miles down the highway. But in my mind they were all the same forbidding fortress overlooking the Fraser River. My brothers had filled my head with images of bleak dungeons and long, dark corridors lined with tormented men, raving women, and abandoned children.

"You can't mean that," Dad said. There was such a silence I imagined I could hear their hearts beating. Mum said nothing. When he spoke again, his voice, for the first time in my life, sounded strangled. "He'll go to Woodlands over my dead body," he said.

I waited for her to say something, but it was Dad who broke the silence, with relief in his voice. "Besides, Geordie's too old for it," he said. "They'd never take him now." There was an even longer pause and then Dad said softly, "What has changed, Bette? You love Geordie. He's our boy."

Mum didn't answer. She must have waved him off because he left the room. I listened for the sound of my mother's heels. Go, I pleaded silently. *Go*. But she bent down to move the end table beside the couch. As she knelt, I saw her in the light and shadow cast by the floor lamp behind her, her face dark and a halo of light around her curly hair. My mother lay down on the floor and reached her arm toward me. She made a guttural, suffering sound that terrified me. I pulled away.

●

We only knew she was missing when Dad got home and our hungry stomachs brought us all together in the kitchen at the usual time. For a while Dad insisted we wait. "She's been late before at suppertime," he said. But it was Tuesday. She never did anything on Tuesdays. And it was rare that she wasn't home for supper. When she was out, we'd know about it; there'd be instructions for one or all of us on the counter: *Casserole in cooker ready at 6. Needs salt. Lulu, make sure Geordie drinks his milk. Back at 7. Mum.*

We ate peanut butter on toast that night—a restless group in the kitchen's glare, oddly peaceable together for the last time I can remember. Around the time Dad decided that it was no longer usual for Mum to be that late, someone knocked at the front door. In Fraser Arm, front doors were for pallbearers, Jehovah's Witnesses, and the police. Friends came to the kitchen door. But there was Martin Currie, one of Dad's former Boy Scouts, standing on our never-used front stoop in a spanking-new police uniform.

He stood up tall like Dad taught his Scouts to, and said, "Mr. Parsons, Captain Smallwood asked me to tell you to get your friggin' goats off the road. Sorry, sir. I'm quoting."

We must have been a sight, the six of us crowded in the doorway looking at poor Martin. I don't suppose anyone knew whether to be relieved or more worried. Our little posse stepped past Martin to the corner of the house and looked across the side pasture. Even from there we could see that the gate was wide open. I went cold. I suddenly knew why she'd reached behind the couch, caught hold of my wrist and squeezed it hard. "You'll always take care of Geordie. Promise," she'd said. The note under the milk jug wasn't a warning, it was a farewell. My mother hated our goats, and the hanging gate should have tipped Dad off that she'd run off with what even my ten-year-old mind knew was one spiteful goodbye.

Then Martin said, "Besides, we've got enough on our hands with the disappearance of Mrs. McFee," and the kind of hell no one ever wants to talk about broke loose.

DORIS

She wants to be able to speak. Surely here, in the henhouse, she could. The hens bock-bock as Doris Tenpenny, wearing muddy rubber boots, hooks back the chicken coop door. They squawk and flutter. They hurry on yellow or black or red feet down the ramp and out the door. But even here, she cannot sound the words. In her twenty-four years, not one word has ever come out of Doris' mouth.

Why do you squawk? I am here twice a day. I know I invade your sanctuary and steal your eggs, but I have done this for eighteen years. I knew your mother, and your grandmother, and her mother before.

Doris reaches into a straw-filled nest. The egg is still warm. This one is brown. She rolls it in her weathered hands, wiping bits of straw and guck from the shell. How wonderfully essential and simple an egg is. A perfect oval, smooth, containing either one breakfast, eaten many ways, or the gestational home of a chicken—twenty-one days, sooner if it's warm or the hens are particularly broody, longer if she leaves the door to the henhouse open to the breezes. How many thousands of times has she placed eggs into the rough cardboard cartons: half a dozen, any colour or size, for Mrs. McFee; a flat of thirty smooth brown eggs, perfectly symmetrical and clean, for Mrs. Parsons. *What does she do with so many?*

But Bette Parsons has disappeared. And so has Alice McFee. The police have been here. Doris examines her hands. *How can they be so worn?* It is the hard work she does. Washing, cleaning, tending the garden. And the chickens.

When the police came, they asked when Mrs. Parsons and Mrs. McFee usually bought their eggs. Had they been here that week? Had she noticed any strangers about? Doris watched her own rough hands write Tuesdays and Thursdays and No and Yes, on the piece of paper they put in front of her. Which strangers? Three strangers. No. Ten, she wrote. An old couple in a rare red Rambler Rogue convertible, *the top up, of course,* with Oregon plates.

"You know your cars, eh?" The older policeman smiled. "You wouldn't have caught the plate number by any chance?"

She nodded. Doris had never seen a Rambler Rogue before. Why would she not remember the plate? The policemen exchanged a look, not believing.

"Really? Write it down, please. Who else?"

A woman with seven children in her car, a speckly grey Ford Falcon, 1966. The woman driving it said her cousin said she should buy her eggs at the Tenpennys'. She was from Wesleyville. She talked a lot.

"That's three. What about the other seven strangers you mentioned?" the young policeman asked.

Doris took the pencil and circled 'seven children,' tapping the words impatiently. *Are they not listening?*

"Oh, that's a passel of kids," he said. "No one else?" She shook her head. "And Alice McFee. You saw her last Thursday?" Doris felt a flush creeping up her neck. The younger policeman frowned at her. "What?" he asked. Doris shook her head.

"Thank you, Miss Tenpenny," the older policeman said. He took the pencil back when they left, a yellow HB, freshly sharpened, with an unused eraser.

On Monday nights Doris makes sure there are thirty browns ready for Mrs. Parsons. Or until this week, she used to. They're no better tasting, and no better for you, but they're prettier. Most hens lay brown eggs, but some people like white. The Crèvecœur hens lay the big browns Doris gives to Bette Parsons. Sometimes the little girl, Lulu, and the big boy, Geordie, come with her, and Mrs. Parsons lets Lulu carry the flat back to the car, though never Geordie. There were too many accidents. And sometimes she just waits in the car for her children and waves at Doris. Mrs. Parsons looks like a movie star in her fitted coat and slim slacks, and her curly hair pinned behind her ears. She pretends to be happy and she smiles when she buys her eggs, but she smiles with her mouth only, not her eyes. She has iron in her soul. *What will happen now?*

Doris goes into the henhouse and closes the door. It is just warm enough inside. She reaches up above the top row of roosts and brings down a brown paper bag. She sits on the old wooden chair against the back wall, under the coop's dusty window—she must remember to clean it—and takes a book out of the bag. There is barely enough light to read by, *which might account for my poor eyesight*, Doris thinks, but it might be hereditary as well. Both Mother and Father wear glasses, after all. The heat lights are on but they are red. Doris doesn't like to make the hens lay when they do not want to, but Father insists that she light the hen house through the winter. She will not fight with him over it. That is for her little sister Joan to do, and Joan does not care about chickens. When she has done her reading she will leave the lights on. She does like the chickens to be warm. Warm enough. It has been a cold November.

Mr. Cray, Fraser Arm High School's librarian, is the source of Doris' books. He comes weekly and buys a dozen whites or browns, greens or blues—he doesn't care which and has said so. While Doris puts a red elastic band around the grey carton with the perfect checkerboard of eggs she has chosen for him, Mr. Cray lays a brown paper bag with a book in it on the egg stand and tells her about the author he has chosen. He gives her a brief synopsis of the book while he is getting his change out of his pocket, counting out the required forty-seven cents. Doris hands him a bag that contains his eggs and the book she is returning. They have read more than one hundred books together in the past five years without exchanging a word. Not a spoken word from Doris, at least. On a piece of typing paper taken from the room in which her father writes his sermons, Doris has written the names of every book Mr. Cray has brought her. The first ten books Mr. Cray chose for their secret reading club were books written by women. Though not without their own risks, Doris knows these books reflected Mr. Cray's initial tentativeness about Doris' appetite for controversy or spice:

Pride and Prejudice
Wuthering Heights
Jane Eyre
Sense and Sensibility
Emma
Martha Quest
Klee Wyck
Swamp Angel
The Stone Angel
A Jest of God

She thinks of their list. She knows it by heart. Since their first ten, they have read Whitman and Ginsberg, Thoreau and Hesse, Mitford and Lindbergh, Brautigan and Solzhenitsyn, E.M. Forster and D.H. Lawrence, Salinger and de Beauvoir, Jacob and Wilhelm Grimm, and more.

"I propose we read Sartre next," Mr. Cray said several weeks ago, and yesterday he left *Iron in the Soul*, the last of the trilogy, on the egg stand.

Doris wipes the cover with her hand and ruffles the pages looking for his note. She takes out two pieces of light onionskin paper. On one he has typed his comments on their last book, a reply to her comments; the other piece is blank, for her. She rereads Mr. Cray's meticulous notes and feels the tiniest sensation of satisfaction, like someone else is smiling in her throat. She reaches up and pulls a manila folder from its hiding place. She adds today's piece of paper to the bottom of the pile and carefully writes 'Iron in the Soul, J.P. Sartre,' on her book list, hesitating only slightly over whether to hyphenate J.P. The chickens are calmer and a few of them have returned to the henhouse, pecking at the ground around her feet. She shh-shhs them and holds her palm out to Mary-Magdalene and Elizabeth who strut away, ignoring her. Then she opens the book. When she looks up again, Doris is on page 113.

She feels her glasses slipping down her nose and pushes them up with a tickle of annoyance. Tomorrow is Thursday. Will Mr. McFee come? *Please God, don't let him come. Please, dear Lord, don't let him come.*

LULU

Through the rest of November and into December everyone was betting on the chances of stumbling upon the proverbial shallow grave in the farmer's field. Two shallow graves. Fraser Arm's pastures and forests were combed for fresh piles of dirt and the words drifter and murderer were tossed around as confirmations. Despite my secret knowledge of Mum's flight, I conjured a vivid image for my schoolmates—a man with cigarette-stained teeth, sallow skin, treacherous red-knuckled hands, and a cruel sneer he'd worn since birth. This made-up monster lurked with me at night, and the weather seemed to collaborate with everyone's fears and brought us endless days of cold rain and sleet and a merciless wind. Dad sat with me every night until I fell asleep—I presumed as much out of his own anxiety and grief as mine—but he didn't say much. The schoolyard parking lot was packed with cars mornings and afternoons as panic-eyed parents dropped off and picked up their kids who were now too precious to walk to and from school alone.

And Aunt Kat came.

We all drove to the airport on a foggy day at the end of November to meet her flight from England. None of us had set eyes on her before, except for Dad, twenty years earlier, and she'd been just a kid then. But when we saw the woman with the violin case strapped across her chest coming down the escalator Geordie ran toward her.

"That's not Mum," Alan shouted after him.

Crawling home in the fog, Dad kept apologizing to her for having brought all of us to the airport. I had to sit on Aunt Kat's bony knees in the front seat with the violin. She wasn't all that much bigger than me. The boys had a silent elbows-and-knees fight in the back seat until Dad turned around with another Mum-like glare. Geordie reached over the seat and took Aunt Kat's hand and wouldn't let it go.

Aunt Kat made a small sound when she got out of the car on Forward Road. I saw our embarrassing wreck of a house through her eyes. A muddy yard rutted with truck tread marks, two dead delivery vans rusting away to nothing, a crazed dog barking and straining at the length of its chain, tarpaper covering the house's exterior as though it was newly built and in the process of being finished, except it wasn't. She seemed game enough as she went up the kitchen steps and crossed the threshold. I could smell the goats from there and hoped she couldn't. At that point I was liking the idea of Aunt Kat.

"Right, then. Who can tell me where I'll find the tea?" she asked.

●

No one paid Geordie and me much attention that winter. I suppose they all thought that if I wasn't asking any questions they wouldn't try to give me any answers. Who can blame them for not knowing what to do with me? Everyone was a mess. I was numb, anaesthetized, stone cold. God knows what was going on inside my brother Geordie. He and I roamed indifferently around the neighbourhood in our rubber boots, cracking thin layers of morning puddle ice and playing games that included discovering secret passageways through the rain-soaked forest to where Mum had disappeared, and sometimes, if my best friend Nadine Ogg was along—being with Nadine made me braver—stumbling upon a rotting corpse.

How is it that we forget? How do we turn what we know to be true into lies and the lies into new truths? For a few months I carried her note around in my coat pocket, fingering its softening folds, rereading it endlessly, looking for something more than the blunt truth of it. I hated her. I wanted to betray her to the policemen who cruised as aimlessly around the neighbourhood in their black and whites as Geordie and I did. I wanted to tell the men in suits who'd set up camp in the field across from the McFees' place. But I was more afraid of what breaking my silence would cost me. Finally, I read the note one last time. I dug a hole in the cold hard earth beneath the tree fort and buried it, shut tight in a jam jar. And then I forgot. Or thought I forgot. Or dreamed I remembered a milk-stained note on a kitchen table.

It was easier believing she was dead.

●

Come February, everything in the world outside our house was normal again. The visits from the undercover cops ended. People went about their business. I wasn't catching anyone wiping a smile off their face the moment they saw me anymore, and everyone stopped being extra nice. At school I took my turn skipping rope in the gym again, and parents quit asking me, in their pitying voices, if there was any new news. I stopped telling the kids that my mother had been murdered and that if they knew what was good for them they'd stay in at night. My grade five teacher did call Dad at home one night to say she'd overheard me saying that the one good thing about my mother's murder was that we didn't have to eat liver anymore, but pretty well everyone stopped talking about Mum and Mrs. McFee. Their disappearance had lost its cachet, and like everything in life, time slid along, taking with it the appalling sting.

At home it was another story. We were frozen, or angry, or just mechanically soldiering on, all different-sized wheels on the same dump truck. Trevor, Ambrose, and Alan fought incessantly, and Geordie just seemed bewildered and kept asking when Mum was coming home. Dad took to blaming himself, muttering out loud as he puttered around the house fixing things, busy doing everything but being my dad. Aunt Kat mostly wept. She would stand over the big old cookstove every morning, holding her hands to its black cast iron until the second it was too hot to touch. I figured Dad would ask her to leave because it was so upsetting, but he seemed oblivious. So I spent most of my time outside, in Fraser Arm's ditches, poking through the ice and, later, the mud for pop bottles.

Pop-bottle picking is an art. I should know. Apart from the time I took a dime off Dad's dresser and he asked us all at supper who took his pocket change and I had to fess up, I rarely had any money unless it came from picking bottles. Picking was best in the spring, just after the snow was gone and before the grass got green. Then you could find them easily, lying glinting in the open. Wait a little longer and you'd have to take a guess as to whether someone might have tossed one there—which in Fraser Arm was one in five—or get scratched up by the salal while checking, which wasn't so bad, or in the blackberry briars, which was. In certain ditches, you'd always find either a pop bottle—a Coca-Cola, a Dr Pepper, an Orange Crush—or a beer bottle, the stubby brown ones. They'd be clean or dirty, filled with cigarette butts, or covered in big green slugs.

Nadine Ogg and I were tireless pickers. As soon as we each had ten, we'd make a penny candy run up to Mr. Chen's Food Market on Cypress Street, a bottle hanging from each finger, clacking and chiming their glass sounds. Even better than a trip to Chen's, picking bottles that winter and spring carried the new promise of something sinister and exciting. I'd started having dreams in which Mum spoke to me. First it was from the ditch in front of the McFees' windbreak. "Lulu," she said in a flat voice, "never walk alone in Raven Ravine." A few days later I dreamed of her again. "Lulu, you'll find my body in the Logging Trail," she said from the dark woods. Then her mouth and ears grew wild with ferns and her body sank into the undergrowth and I saw something glittering where she'd been: a pop bottle. By the time the pussy willows had begun to show their catkins and the world was revolving toward green again, I'd begun to write new nightmares while awake. Mostly, I had her rising from ditches and sloughs, and speaking to me, a detached voice from deep within blackberry thicket cages, offering clues as to where she might be found.

Our pop bottle route had always been the same, with few deviations, but that spring I made Nadine cut through the Logging Trail with me again and again, even though we were forbidden to go there well before my mother and Mrs. McFee disappeared. Sometimes we took Geordie along for protection. He couldn't outwit anyone, but he was a bit like having a big dog along; no one bothered you. We zigzagged beneath the power pylons, keeping a watchful eye out for the child molesters that were supposed to be lurking in the salmonberry bushes, and I looked for my mother's grave. Behind a big old stump in the bushes one morning, Nadine and I found a blond wig and a pair of pantyhose tied up in knots, which scared the pants off us and made the Logging Trail even more alluring.

There were three biting dogs along Willow Street— Blackie, Kip, and Zeus—and they were never tied up. Passing their houses required sticks or stones, just in case. It was safer up on Portland Road where the Cottingham brothers would drunkenly toss us their empties from their second floor deck—if they were out of jail. We'd check in the tall grass along the electrified fence in front of the Jones' shack up on Arbutus Street and sneak through Dangerous Old Man Montgomerie's hazelnut orchard, the very edges of it at least. Occasionally, we made hurried skirts along the top of Raven Ravine. We wouldn't have admitted it to each other, but its long shadows and dank fern smells made us both truly fearful. Most of the time we'd end up down on the

T-road that had a real name but was known to us all as the Glassy Road.

No one lived on the Glassy Road. It had been tarred and pebbled for years, but a house had yet to be built on the marshy land that some developer had hoped to pass off as habitable. Everything had grown over with weeds and every spring both the ditches and the ponds of surveyed lots were thick with tadpoles and frogs and Jesus bugs which we captured and kept in jars until they died. On higher, drier ground, sparse alder saplings twenty feet high grew up where the old forest had been cut down, and in summer, foxglove, bull thistle, buttercups, and red clover covered the piles of bulldozed dirt. The older boys had made a motocross circuit over the manmade hills and rode their dirt bikes through the wildflowers and the mud. That spring, the sound of their high-pitched bee engines keened through the nights.

The Glassy Road lived up to its name; it was an anti-playground strewn from top to bottom with shards of broken glass—green, white, clear, brown, and the occasional bit of Milk of Magnesia blue. There was some art to the practice of smashing bottles too. Nadine called it glass graffiti.

One Saturday near the end of March, Nadine and I were out picking when we saw the red flash of a police car cherry at the dead end of the Glassy Road.

"They found her," Nadine said.

We dumped our bottles in the ditch and I grabbed Nadine by the hand and pulled her toward the crowd gathered around the cruiser. This would be it. Mum would be there, in the frog pond, her body weighted with stones and tied with a skipping rope that had finally rotted. Or she'd be in a green garbage bag, like Nadine had said she would, unrecognizable.

Or behind the pile of abandoned culvert pipes, half-eaten by coyotes. When we pushed into the circle of kids, we saw that Martin Currie—who no one took seriously as a cop until he beat the hell out of one of the Cottinghams later that summer—had Perry Gladish and "Meddlin' Edwin" Milton up against the cruiser. Martin looked nervous. Perry and Edwin would have been in grade ten, same as Trevor, if they hadn't both dropped out. Some called them stupid, but I knew they were wily as tomcats.

"Whaddya mean you ain't sayin' nothin'?" Martin said to Perry. He pointed at something on the ground, which I quickly identified as Edwin's two front teeth, glittering like rubies among the glass shards at their feet. Martin looked at the other kids who'd gathered round. They were working on their own screw-you-cop postures. "Who did this to Edwin?"

"Nobody."

"Nobody who?" Martin reached for Perry's hand but Perry pulled away and slid it behind his back. Edwin had a weasely little face and anxious eyes. He ran his tongue over his red gums and spat blood beside Martin's foot. Martin lost it. He grabbed Edwin by the front of his shirt and shook him.

"What the fuck is wrong with you? You wanna end up in jail? Don't you get it, Eddy? Don't you get it?" When he finally dropped Edwin, Martin lost his balance and lurched sideways. He looked right at me and I saw his chin tremble like he was going to cry.

"Get the hell out of here, all of you," he shouted and he staggered to his cruiser.

When the police car left, scraping its chassis in the weeds and wildflowers beside the road to avoid the glass, Perry wiped his bloody knuckles on his jeans and said, "You're all right, right?" Edwin nodded and the two of them climbed onto Perry's dirt bike and they rode off. The littler kids and their snot-noses went back to collecting tadpoles in the ditch. Nadine and I walked away, my stomach aching with what I saw in Martin's face. Someone smashed a beer bottle behind us and its brown glass sprayed all around our feet with a *thock* and a *chshhh*.

"Never mind, Lu. Just guys being stupid," Nadine said. "Let's go cash in our bottles."

●

The only thing modern about Chen's Food Market was the air raid siren perched on top of a shiny steel pillar out front. Even the parking lot was just dirt rutted with holes big enough to drown a child in the rainy season. Mr. Chen had built the store himself, everyone said. Even new, it had apparently looked like a shack, all plywood and tarpaper and great, dusty windows held in place by two-by-four trim and pasted with huge hand-lettered advertisements. The building leaned hard to the left and some people refused to shop there for fear it would fall on their heads. The dark façade made Chen's look small, but when you swung in through the wooden door with its peeling paint and its little porthole window you'd find yourself in a big, clean, drywalled room lit by bare light-bulbs hanging just above head height. Row upon row of tidily stocked plywood shelves rose from the floor and disappeared into the shadows above.

Mr. Chen carried the basics: margarine, milk, Campbell's soup, saltines, Dad's cookies, toilet paper, Dutch Cleanser, toilet plungers, macaroni, Spam, canned tomatoes, canned peas, pork and beans, clothes pegs, Kotex, cigarettes, pop, and candy. He gave credit and kept accounts in small bound books, each with its own sheet of carbon paper, in which he wrote, in time-consuming detail, the date, descriptions of the purchases, and the new tally. From the looks of the little books filed on their sides in a wooden drawer near the cash register, about fifty Fraser Arm families ran tabs at Chen's. My parents never did. My father always said he'd sooner throw eggs at the queen than buy on credit. He lumped grocery store credit-users in with shoplifters, people who clipped coupons, and men who couldn't hold their liquor, which was ironic.

Taking bottles into Mr. Chen's was tricky business. Mr. Chen didn't like dirty bottles, old bottles, or ones that were chipped. He wouldn't take beer bottles either. We had to go up the road to Wilkie's Wrecking for that. Anyone bringing bottles into Chen's knew the drill: we loaded them into cardboard carrying cases at the poorly lit back of the store under the watchful eye of his mother, Old Mrs. Chen. We waited while this woman, the tiniest and oldest we'd ever seen, lifted each bottle, carefully inspecting it for slugs, which she hated, and rubbing her dry, crooked fingers around the rims, feeling for chips. If we'd been careless enough to bring a chipped bottle or a slug in with our cache, she'd toss the bottle into a metal garbage can where its bang accused us of deceitfulness. Then she'd chase us to the front of the store with a torn slip of butcher paper on which she'd written our tally. Old Mrs. Chen would wave the tally paper around, frown, and purse her lips before she put it safely in her son's palm. Then she'd give him an adoring smile, which I never saw Mr. Chen return, and disappear into the shadows at the back of the store.

We had twelve bottles between us that day. Two cents a bottle, when penny candy was a penny and a chocolate bar could be had for a nickel. Nadine was already outside with her choices: a Wagon Wheel, a five-cent bag of salt and vinegar potato chips, and two Double-Bubbles. She always took the same thing, the number of Double-Bubbles the only variation.

"No loitering, Lulu," Mr. Chen said. He waved his hand over the candy counter. "Choose."

I don't know how he thought anyone could choose quickly. Mr. Chen had the biggest candy selection in the world. And my decision was being hindered by the fact that Lance Chen, my classmate, was behind the counter. I picked five licorice babies—one of my favourites—and put them on the counter along with my Pixy Stix, caramels, and red licorice whips. Mr. Chen always put the candy in tiny brown paper bags. I liked them almost as much as the candy.

A hand reached over my shoulder and snatched the bag from my hand. My brother Trevor. "Licorice babies," he said sticking his fingers into the bag and pulling one out and popping it into his mouth. "Yum."

I screeched and jumped for the bag Trevor was now holding over my head.

The words were instinctive. "I'm telling Mum!" I shouted.

Trevor's face went white. He shoved the bag back into my hands. The silence was so sudden I felt as though we were all, momentarily, being suffocated. Every ounce of air had surely been sucked from Chen's. My mouth opened and closed like a fish dying on the wharf.

"Hey, Lulu." Mike Tenpenny put his hand on my shoulder. The warmth of it was like something I'd forgotten existed. I floated into his dark brown eyes. I had the time to inspect Mike while we all drifted in the silence of the outer space I'd created with my words. Dad called the Tenpennys the tidy farmers, and looking at Mike I understood what he meant. Mike was in grade ten like Trevor, and they were both in Dad's Scout pack, but their similarities ended there. Next to Trevor's faded grey t-shirt, holey jeans, and Beatles-length hair, Mike's short-sleeved white shirt, belted trousers, and crewcut made him look like he was ready for church, and he might have been. His dad was the Baptist preacher. When he took his hand off my shoulder I wished he hadn't. But I was finally breathing air.

For a second Trevor's gaze flickered across my face. Before he learned to temper them, I used to be able to read in his eyes whatever was going on in his heart. That one fleeting glance was enough to cinch my heart in a vice and spin me into the hollow of my own feelings, which at that moment was rage. He was leaning against the pop cooler, his arms crossed. Mike stood slack-handed beside him. Trevor, tamped down and boxed up, was an asshole.

"Enjoy your crappy candy," he said sourly, not looking at me.

I flew at him. I might have landed my own punch had Mike not put his hands back on my shoulders and turned me toward the door.

Outside, Nadine asked, "You okay?"

"No. It's Trevor."

"Yeah, well, you should have sisters. That's worse," Nadine said.

I started walking. I was filled with fury and loathing but another feeling was seeping in. In that brief second in the store when my brother's eyes met mine I'd seen a flash of misery. He was like something wounded, an animal in pain. It left me wretched.

●

Nadine and I always ate our loot in our secret hiding place just inside the entrance to the forbidden Logging Trail. In our respective houses, between Nadine's five big sisters and my four brothers, even a lowly caramel was fair game.

"What do you think Mr. Chen's mom is saying?" Nadine asked me. She had Wagon Wheel crumbs all over her mouth.

"I know you committed that murder." I imitated Old Mrs. Chen's scolding voice and waggled my finger at Nadine. "And I'll prove it one day."

Nadine stared at me with her serious look. "Maybe he did kill someone, Lulu. Maybe he murdered Mrs. McFee."

"No, no, no. Not Mr. Chen. He wouldn't. I know. Listen. She's saying, 'One day I'll run off and leave you. You'll pay for making me count pop bottles all day.'"

"Maybe she will run away one day, Lulu." Nadine hesitated, practicing her best pregnant pause, I suppose, while she measured the potential impact. "Like your mom did," she said, looking me straight in the eye.

I stared at her while my feelings sorted themselves out with my body. I guess my feelings must have talked to my fist because I punched Nadine hard in the nose, just like Trevor had taught me, with my thumb folded around my knuckles, not tucked inside my fingers. It was a boy's punch that Trevor might have congratulated me for and I was pretty pleased with it, except that two seconds later Nadine fell limp off the log. She was bleeding all over her new pop top, the pale turquoise one with the string fringe around the bottom, and a huge pink wad of bubblegum was glowing in her open mouth. I thought I'd killed her. I ran, screaming like I'd stepped in a wasps' nest, through the bushes and out into the middle of Richardson Road. I waved my arms at the red car coming toward me. I knew the rule about getting into cars with strangers, but it was Mr. McFee in his convertible who stopped.

Everyone knew Mr. McFee.

DORIS

Mrs. Puttkammer is fussy about her eggs. She likes to open the carton and turn each one over in case Doris has hidden a crack at the bottom. Mrs. Puttkammer doesn't know Doris would never do such a reprehensible thing. Mrs. Puttkammer might have guessed that this would be so, after buying her eggs from the Tenpennys for seventeen years and never finding a cracked one. Still, she checks every time and Doris lets her, as Mother did before her, waiting silently. *What else is to be done?* It is while Mrs. Puttkammer is turning over the eleventh egg that Doris, looking over Mrs. Puttkammer's shoulder, sees Mr. McFee's red Chevrolet Impala pass the farm on Reifel Road and turn onto Hemlock Street. Lulu Parsons and the youngest Ogg girl, Nadine, are both in the convertible. And Nadine, it looks, is covered in blood.

Doris opens her mouth with a slight pop of air, and Mrs. Puttkammer looks up in surprise, as if she might spy a word sitting miraculously on the end of Doris' tongue. Doris shuts her mouth sharply and holds out her hand for the money. *The weather is too unpredictable to be driving a convertible.*

"All right, Doris," Mrs. Puttkammer says. "They all look fine." Doris gives her a well-honed stony look, and as soon as she drives off, pulls the large red CLOSED sign out from behind the egg stand and hooks it on its nails. She leaves two flats of eggs on the stand, one brown, one white, that will soon be exposed to the afternoon sun. If it is too warm, she will have to give them to Mother to hard boil later. She hurries behind the house to the back driveway that lets out onto Hemlock, regretting her choice of footwear. Rubber boots and woolen socks are fine for the chicken coop or the garden, but not for running. The McFees' house is six houses along Hemlock from the corner, if you count the Wheatleys'.

A hundred years ago, Mr. McFee's grandfather, Havelock, built the big farmhouse, and his wife, Hattie, made him plant a windbreak of Douglas firs and cedar across the front of the property and down the sides. Now, that hedge has made a hidden fortress of the house. Blackberries have twined through the lower parts of the trees like Grimms' fairy tale vines, and already Doris can see the tight green berries that, at the end of August, would have made Mrs. McFee's purple jelly. *If she weren't lying dead somewhere.* Doris rushes halfway up the long driveway, a narrow double-rut grass path. There was, they say, a more welcoming time at the house when the first McFees invited neighbours to dine and were said to have eaten off imported English china. Now the untended boughs of the great trees have grown so low that only a smallish car can pass under without being molested. But no car is there.

Doris crosses Hemlock and walks as quickly as she

can down Forward Road. The Parsons property and the multi-daughtered Oggs' improbably small house are about halfway down the road. Doris is pink with heat but she won't remove her sweater; she is wearing only a short-sleeved dress. There it is, Mr. McFee's car in the Oggs' driveway. Mr. McFee—"Please call me Aloysius," he'd said that morning in the church basement—must be inside. Doris stands across the road in the loose pebbles that escaped the tarring, her hands clasped at her breastbone. The Oggs' never-used front door opens, and Mrs. Ogg, stout and in slippers, comes out on the steps with Mr. McFee. She's laughing and shaking her head. Mr. McFee takes a few steps down the stairs, stops, looks back, then laughs, too uproariously, Doris thinks, for a man who lost his wife not five months ago. Lulu skips out the front door and down the stairs and Mr. McFee waggles his finger at the skinny little girl, who is now running across the Oggs' front yard and slipping through the barbed-wire fence into the Parsons' goat pasture.

When Mr. McFee finally notices Doris, the laugh in his mouth vanishes. He gets into his car and turns west, the wrong direction if he's thinking of going home. She sees his face, ill at ease and flushed, as the car turns. He is not the confident man who, with a friendly smile, blocked her way up the stairs from the church kitchen a year ago where she had burned the peanut butter cookies for the Sunday School class. He is not the man who stepped closer and pressed his middle-aged body against her, lifting her dress with one hand and sliding his fingers beneath the cotton of her underpants.

Doris thinks of the two flats of spoiling eggs on the egg stand. She jumps across the ditch, green with frogspawn, and steps into the woods. The trees open onto the Grantham's orchard, which ends at the fence she will have to climb to reenter her own backyard. In the orchard, she becomes aware of the softness of the warm spring air and remembers Mr. McFee's sigh and his minty breath as he pressed his face into her neck and rubbed her gently between her legs. The hardness against her hip was his penis, she knew this much from the books she had read, though she was still surprised by the suddenness of it. She remembers how still she stood in her shocking, silent rage. "You won't say anything, will you?" he asked, vaguely penitent, as if there were more than one answer to that question. What soul in Fraser Arm would have believed that Mr. McFee would do such a thing?

LULU

I turned eleven on April first. It was a dismal event.

That morning, Aunt Kat had come home from the SuperValu with a store-bought cake.

"Just look at this lovely cake, Lulu," Aunt Kat said, and she opened the box to show me.

Its dripping maraschino cherries had stained the white icing and made it look like a ghoul had gummed it all around its edges. I hated it. I thought of the tall angel food cakes Mum always made with the Tenpennys' eggs. Aunt Kat looked proud and excited, and I didn't want to disappoint her, but I was shocked that she didn't even know that the birthday girl wasn't supposed to see the cake until it was brought flaming to the table with its requisite number of candles. Aunt Kat was supposed to go back to England, but now she'd called long distance to quit her job and was staying on. Indefinitely, Dad said. I decided then that Geordie and I needed a new mother, and that Aunt Kat wouldn't do.

Mum had been missing for four months and eighteen days. We were studying sharks at school and I felt like one—a creature that had to keep moving just to breathe. My need to find a new mother was confirmed as I stared down again at that miserable SuperValu cake at suppertime. I made my wish and blew out the stubby, reused candles. Aunt Kat sawed the cake in eight with the bread knife and the seven of us ate it like we were starving. Then we all stared at the last piece until Dad, who I'd never witnessed wasting a speck of food, picked up the silvery cardboard plate with its stained wet doily and dropped it in the garbage.

I waited for Saturday morning to launch my plan. I found Geordie lying on the living room floor on his belly, chin on his hands, watching cartoons. It didn't make much difference that Dad refused to get a colour TV. I figured Popeye was in black and white anyway. I lay down beside Geordie and watched Popeye and Bluto dancing together in an elaborate fight over Olive Oyl. Geordie laughed every time they hit each other, which was constantly.

"Spinach!" Geordie shouted, when Bluto sent Popeye flying under some barrels. Sure enough, Olive Oyl had the can.

Geordie could get ornery if someone interrupted his cartoons, so I waited until the spinach-fortified Popeye had turned Bluto into a punching bag before I tested my idea on him.

"Geordie. I've got an idea." I rolled onto my back and looked up at his full-moon face.

"Will it get us in trouble, Lulu?" Geordie was no slouch. He knew me well. He hadn't taken his eyes off the television.

"How come you're so smart?" I jumped up and turned off the television before the advertisements started because Geordie liked them as much as Popeye. He sat up in protest and I sat cross-legged in front of him. I shook my head. "No trouble." Then I whispered my plans. "I think it's time we found us a new mom."

His eyes opened wide. He was a master of dramatics, Geordie. That was probably my fault. For as long as I could remember we'd played a game we called Geordie Gets Mad. I'd call out an emotion and Geordie had to show me with his face what it meant. Right then we were somewhere between worried and sad. "We've already got a mom, Lulu. I don't want a new mom."

"Mum's dead, Geordie."

"No she's not. You're lying. Mum's not dead. Uh-uh." He shook his head, slowly moving it from side to side as far as his neck would turn.

"OK. Maybe she's not dead, but she's gone for*ever*." Geordie's head turns were getting more exaggerated and speeding up, a bad sign. "OK. She's not here now, is she?" I asked. I was a fool not to have anticipated that he'd balk. "Come on. Come with me." I wanted to get Geordie outside. The last thing I wanted was for the boys to overhear, especially Trevor.

"Popeye's not over, Lulu. Turn it back on, OK?"

"It is over. And this is more interesting, Geordie. I promise." I took both his hands and leaned back to pull him up. In the laundry room I helped him get his jacket and rubber boots on. Everything but the wind was saying that winter was over. The brown pasture was tinged everywhere with the quickest green. Mum's little patch of daffodils had come up around the tool shed and all of their yellow trumpets had opened.

"Look, Geordie. Daffodils." I could taste the word—daffodil—and felt it waxy on my shark tongue. Then, wondering whether a shark had a tongue, I said "narcissus" out loud too. That's what Aunt Kat called them. It felt wrong. It wasn't big enough for these trumpeting flowers.

"I hate daffodils." Geordie was the king of weighty declarations.

"Me too," I said. No point being on his bad side.

"I like dandelions."

"I *am* a dandelion." I cracked Geordie up with that.

"Where are we going, Lulu?"

I didn't reply, and as always, he passively followed me, the cartoons only half forgotten. Geordie could be lured away from anything but dessert by the promise of an adventure in the woods, and we'd had plenty of those. There was a place on the property line, at the east end of the goat pasture where, come summer, the yellow broom shrub was so thick I could hide, sitting on the split-rail fence someone had erected decades before Dad decided to bring his family back to Fraser Arm. Even before the broom had blossomed, its mass of tangled brown branches hid me from the rest of the world, which is what I most wanted. Often, at suppertime, I'd hear the clack of the back screen door and Aunt Kat or Dad would call my name into the dark—anxious, pleading voices carried off by the wind. I would sit on my fence in the broom ignoring them until I heard the level of concern or annoyance in their voices rise. Then I'd skirt around to the front of the house and saunter down the driveway. In my heart, I knew it was cruel, but someone had to pay for my fury. The only person I spared was Geordie. If he could have pronounced the word, he might have said that was debatable.

I led Geordie across the goat pasture, then we crept, bent over, under low-hanging salmonberry bushes until we came to the fence and my hiding spot. A day earlier I had picked most of the pale white-green lichen off the fence rail. There was a darker, wet spot now, where the lichen had been. I poked at a multi-legged pill bug with a twig until it curled up armadillo-like and rolled off the rail. We watched it disappear in the dry grasses. I could hear Ambrose and Alan chopping wood, the axe blows cantering a doleful rhythm. From the top rail I could see the apple trees. They wouldn't blossom for another few weeks, but their buds were a ready-to-burst red.

I wasn't thinking of finding someone new for Dad's sake. I had decided that my father would be forever washed with despair, pining for Mum for the rest of his life and building shrines to his dark-haired beauty and to her ability to pressure-cook a good pot roast. Pot roast, I missed, unlike her weekly shoe-leather liver offering. Alan and Ambrose, I figured, didn't really need a mother. They'd be turning eighteen soon. Alan would be graduating from high school, and Ambrose, who had only got through grade eleven—not for lack of intelligence—had a job at Beaver Lumber and a girlfriend as tight-lipped as he was. Trevor, as far as I was concerned, didn't deserve a mother.

"What do you think, Geordie? Wouldn't a new mom be so nice?" Sitting on the fence, I was face to face with him. I was hopeful that he'd agree, but instead I could see he was working up to something. Geordie never just cried. He wept the uninhibited, noisy tears of filterless mourners, shrieking and thrashing the way the rest of us want to but learn much too early to control. He had moved his hand to his mouth and begun a low moaning and his eyes were filling with tears.

"Geordie, Geordie," I whispered, a selfish terror of my own rising up as I imagined his howls giving away my hiding spot to the twins. "It's just temporary. Just 'til we know for sure."

"Mum's not dead." He stood there taking deep breaths, making his best, exaggerated scowl. I waited. Finally his breathing settled and he said, "I like Mrs. Ogg."

I slid off the fence. "I love Mrs. Ogg, too, but I think she's kind of busy." Geordie was right. Nadine's mom, Mrs. Ogg, was the most logical candidate. She lived next door and we already knew her because she had been having coffee with Mum every morning for as long as any of us could remember. But with six girls of her own, and a surprise grandchild growing in Nadine's middle sister's belly, I doubted Mrs. Ogg would be willing to take on Geordie and me. "What about Mrs. Puttkammer? She's nice. Wait. She's not nice. Strike her off the list. Mrs. Tanner."

"Mrs. Ogg."

"Mrs. Smith."

"Mrs. Ogg."

"Mrs. Royal."

In a few minutes we had a list of twenty-two contenders—sixteen neighbours, three teachers, our doctor's receptionist, and our dentist's wife. Geordie suggested only Mrs. Ogg.

"What about the lady who drives the Bookmobile," I said.

"I don't know, Lulu. We don't know her name. What's her name, Lulu?"

"Doesn't matter," I said, though the thought of her short hair and her gravelly laugh made me nervous. "We can ask her."

"Just until Mum comes back though," Geordie said, giving me his doubtful look. "When's Mum coming back, Lulu?"

"Just until." I felt a flood of anxiety; could Geordie learn to love the Bookmobile lady or Mrs. Tanner? Until that moment, I hadn't ventured much further than thinking about who we might choose to replace Mum, but I could already feel the details of it wreaking havoc with our lives. I pulled a box of wooden matches and a safety pin from my jacket pocket.

"Don't play with fire, Lulu," Geordie wailed.

"I'm just going to sterilize the pin. Don't go all hither and thither," I said, quoting Mum.

"Why? What are you going to do with the pin?"

"We're going to swear, Geordie."

"Mum says not to swear. I'm not allowed to swear."

"This is a different kind of swearing." To sterilize them, Dad always burnt the needles he used to pry summer slivers from our feet, but the wind blew out three matches before I decided that a little spit would do the job just as well. "Give me your hand, Geordie."

"No way, Lulu."

So Geordie stared wild-eyed as I poked the pin into my own finger. I should have checked the pin for sharpness. It took a grim prodding to break the skin and when it did the pin pushed much farther in than I'd expected. The pain was brief but shocking and I yelped. We both looked down on the bright bubble of red that beaded up and dribbled over the edge of my finger. I would have recognized his expression as a herald of certain disaster if I'd been one ounce wiser, because Geordie, as he had never failed to do at the sight of blood, fainted dead away in the long grasses.

I confess that I thought of poking Geordie with the pin while he was unconscious, but I knew it was going to be work to get him to keep our secret and I was no longer sure what I'd intended us to swear anyway. Some kind of oath of allegiance had seemed appropriate but as I squatted there in the grass I couldn't think of anything but our daily school recitation of the Lord's Prayer. I took Geordie's limp hand and pushed my bloody pointer finger up against his. Something I'd heard about lying down in greener pastures came to mind, but seeing that Geordie was already lying there in the grass, I gave it a pass.

•

The Habs swept the series that year, and in May, when hockey season was over, Béliveau and Esposito, Mahovlich and Mikita, and their TV black-and-white jerseys gave way to our very own *Don Messer's Jubilee* show. Aunt Kat stopped playing her fiddle in the bedroom we shared and started playing in the living room instead. Until then, the sounds that held me spellbound had been once removed. For months I'd been sitting outside the bedroom door, my head pressed to it, drinking in each plaintive note. Why she emerged from the bedroom was never clear. She might have been troubled by the lack of focus in the house that came with the end of hockey season. If that was her reason, it didn't work. Dad wouldn't have admitted it to Aunt Kat, but he wasn't enamoured with the fiddle, and it never took long for Alan to slink off after supper with various excuses, or Ambrose and Trevor with none at all. But Geordie and I stayed, transfixed by the swift movement of Aunt Kat's fingers and bow and by the music that flew out of her beautiful brown fiddle. Eyes closed, mouth set in a line, her head moved slightly with the beat and the muscles in her arm were sinuous beneath her pale skin.

One evening Aunt Kat called from the living room, "Would you like to try, Lulu?"

It was Scout night. Dad and Geordie were at the Legion Hall, and the boys had disappeared to their own various haunts right after supper. Which left me alone in the house with Aunt Kat. Without the buffer of others, I'd been sitting at the kitchen table pretending to do homework to avoid a one-on-one with her. Though Geordie was infatuated with our aunt, I had been maintaining a wary distance that she mostly respected. But the possibility of being able to produce such beautiful sounds was too grand a draw for me to refuse her offer, and she likely knew it. The only other musical option in my life that far had been the recorder. Once I'd heard Aunt Kat play the fiddle I realized that the recorder, which had before then brought me some minor thrills, was a miserable little creation.

Aunt Kat tucked the fiddle against my neck. My chin settled comfortably into the rest. She moved my arms into position and straightened my left wrist. Before I'd even made a sound I felt transported.

"Keep the tension," she said, "arms up and out. Position is often utmost."

When she showed me how to draw the bow up then

down again across the strings I felt a sigh of pleasure in my body, despite the caterwaul that resulted.

"Put these fingers here," she said. "Now try." A new sound resulted, not quite the wail I'd first produced. "Good. Determination is all you'll need, Lulu. Music is the food of love."

I tried note after note, my fingers shadowing Aunt Kat's on the strings, until I heard Dad's truck in the yard.

"Tomorrow?" I asked, quickly taking the already beloved instrument from my shoulder.

"Tomorrow."

●

I figured the boys secretly liked the Don Messer show. Otherwise they would have just left the rest of us alone to watch the sweet-faced Mr. Messer play his fiddle and the old couple, his sidekicks, belt out their songs each week. Geordie called the show *Got My Dancin' Boots On*, after a line in the opening song. I wasn't willing to provoke more mocking, so I kept my tapping feet to myself, but Geordie shook the house with his lumbering attempts at square dancing. Dad would have had the boys' heads if they'd teased Geordie but I was fair game. The boys sprawled back on the couch, their long, indifferent legs tripping hazards for their dancing brother. They snorted with laughter, not at Geordie, but at the dancers who pranced around on the stage. But they didn't leave the room until Don Messer had played "Till We Meet Again," the show's closing song.

Once I'd had a few more lessons, I disappeared every afternoon with the fiddle case under my arm, feeling Aunt

Kat's approving gaze on my back. I practised in my hiding place on the fence behind the blossoming broom or in the tree fort if it was raining. From memory I picked the notes out of the air and found them on the strings. I knew when the note was true by the smooth sensation in my body. Off notes were as irritating as clichéd fingernails on a blackboard. One evening, about a month after Aunt Kat first put the fiddle to my shoulder, my love of the instrument overshadowed my fear of being derided; I picked up the fiddle and stood with my back to them just as *Don Messer's Jubilee* was ending. I played along perfectly with the closing song. Geordie was the first to clap, but they all did. Even Trevor. Aunt Kat's eyes were glossy. I ran from the room, chased by an excruciating joy.

DORIS

Doris hears the police cars before she sees them. For a moment she cannot tell whether they are coming or going. They pass the farm in a black and white blur and Doris imagines she can feel the whoosh they create. *Whoosh.* She likes the word. Lewis Cray says the Fraser Arm police force is corrupt. People have talked to Doris about the newspaper article in the *Vancouver Sun.* The article said several policemen were on the take, which, Doris understands, means they were taking bribes. Not many of the egg stand customers believe that. "If they were *strangers* . . ." Mrs. Currie said, but the men on the force are Fraser Arm boys. "Some hippies called my son a pig," Mrs. Currie said. "Poor Martin."

What a pig has to do with a police officer, Doris does not know. Father has always said that the police are our friends, but Lewis Cray has been right about many things. Lewis Cray says you would not like to be a boy in trouble with the police in Fraser Arm. Edwin Milton is a fine example. Edwin has gone to Essondale. Lewis Cray says Edwin Milton just needed someone to believe in him. The police don't believe in troubled boys. That, Doris might believe.

Doris is practising calling Lewis Cray by his first name because the last time at the egg stand he dropped off *One Hundred Years of Solitude* and said, "Call me Lewis." Then he blushed and said, "In your mind." He blushed even redder after that. It didn't change Lewis Cray's colour in Doris' mind. Lewis is still just a little darker than robin's egg blue. It is not going so well with *One Hundred Years of Solitude*, though. The word *impractical* has come to Doris' mind, but she is not sure of herself. What, Doris thinks, gives her the right to literary sureness?

One by one, things stop after the police cars go by. Father has been working on the old Massey-Harris tractor, but he turns it off. There is a rattle then a clunk as it stops. Father casts a wary eye at Doris, which says, *stay here.* She will not, of course. Lulu Parsons has stopped playing the fiddle. Doris feels that stop most acutely. Lulu plays in the woods behind the Tenpenny farm where she must think no one can hear her. Doris does not know the songs that Lulu plays. There is no reason why she would. The Tenpennys do not have a television or a phonograph. Father forbids music in the house, even on the radio. Doris' little sister, Joan, asked Father if he thinks music leads to dancing. Joan is only twelve years old but she is already Father's burr.

Doris puts the CLOSED sign up at the egg stand and follows Father at a careful distance down Reifel Road. He is striding around the corner onto Cypress Street as if he has been called by God to do so. Doris looks up into the trees.

Everywhere are splinters of red light. The crackle on the police radios is not its usual humdrum. It sounds red too. Then Doris hears the sharp report of a gun being fired and there is Father running back around the corner and into the woods. Father never runs. She sees the sound; it is a crashing red.

Doris knows the gunshot has broken the rules by which she and Father play; he waves a frantic hand at her and she goes to him. They stand together, ready, in the trees across from the Osmond house. "Dear God in Heaven," Father says. He grabs Doris by the shoulder. "Dear Lord, Dear God," he says, for young Gregory Osmond has come out the front door with a calico cat under his left arm and a gun in his right hand. He puts the cat down on the front steps from where it does not move. It licks an unworried paw. Gregory shoots it. The cat falls forward and is still. Its dark blood floods out. Doris feels an unfamiliar sound deep inside her, like a wave coming all the way from the other side of the ocean. Father makes the sound for her. It is a hard, instinctive grunt.

Gregory waves a slow, defeated circle in the air with the gun. "They're all dead." He shouts it. "They're all dead." This time it is a scream. Gregory's mouth opens wide again but nothing comes out. Silence is waiting to see what Gregory will do next. Even the police radios say nothing. And Doris cannot think for a minute. Then Gregory arches back, swings his arm like a baseball player, and throws the gun in a powerful overhand pitch over the policemen and the police cars, into the trees near Doris and Father. Gregory falls to his knees and bends to sob into the cat's fur and shattered bone. Doris' hands rise to cover her ears.

They don't have to surround him with their guns or push his face into the ground; Gregory isn't moving. There is no reason to yank his arms behind his back to put on the metal cuffs; he is not resisting. They don't have to drag him by his armpits to the cruiser. Doris is sure he would have gone politely. These policemen are his friends, after all. Martin Currie. Les Webster. Peter Babiak. Doris' remembrance is so clear: she sees four little boys riding their bicycles along Reifel Road—Gregory in the lead, Martin, Les, Peter. Mustang bicycles, heel to toe, their arms crooked around a long wooden ladder. Going blackberry picking. Here's another memory: Gregory at the egg stand with his freckled face and cowlick. Gregory holding his mother's hand.

Death brings a crowd. The ambulance parts it like the Red Sea. Shannon Ogg is peddling up Cypress on her bicycle. She stops beside the police car in which Gregory sits. She ignores the policeman who tries to shoo her away. She raises her shoulders and hands as if to say to her friend's big brother, Gregory, what are you doing in the back of a police car? And Doris sees it from the trees: Gregory smiles at Shannon, Shannon smiles back.

LULU

Quite a lot happened that summer in Fraser Arm. On June first, Gregory Osmond killed his parents, his married sister, his little sister, and his parents' cat with a Colt 45 in the middle of the day, and famously, he smiled at Nadine's sister, Shannon, who saw him sitting in the back of the police car. Edwin Milton got sent to Essondale for dancing on top of a police car down at the Royal Bank Plaza, shouting, "Go ahead, kill me," which they very nearly did according to Janet Smallwood, whose mother, Ruth, was watching from the window of the pharmacy. The rumour went around that Brianne Bowdley had been having sex with her uncle. And Mr. McFee asked me if I would be up for a really big adventure.

For a long time, I thought Mr. McFee took me over the Pattullo Bridge because really big adventures didn't happen in your own backyard. They happened in other places, like

Africa or New Westminster. I was looking for pop bottles in the ditch in front of the McFees' house, and he came sauntering out his driveway.

"How's the picking, Lulu?"

"Okay, I guess." I had five pop bottles laid in a row in the grass on the edge of the ditch. "Ten cents."

"Not bad." Mr. McFee was tall and skinny and had a way of turning the edges of his mouth down and furrowing his brow and smiling with his eyes at the same time.

"How's Nadine's nose?"

"That was a long time ago, Mr. McFee. It's better. She's not mad anymore."

"That's good. I thought you'd killed her with your right uppercut. Was that a right uppercut or a left hook?"

I laughed. Mr. McFee made everyone laugh.

"I heard you're learning to play the fiddle. Actually, I hear you are very good on the fiddle. Somebody told me you were a prodigy. Music is the food of love, Lulu."

Aunt Kat had said the same thing. I didn't know what either of them meant. "My aunt's teaching me," I said.

"You like her?"

"She's all right."

"Any news about your mommy?"

I squinted at Mr. McFee. Nobody called Mum *mommy*. "She's dead," I said.

I liked the way people reacted whenever I said that. Mr. McFee raised his eyebrows but didn't say anything and I lay down in the grass to reach under the trees for a bottle I could see way in by the trunks. Then I had the bottle in my hand and raised it up to show him.

"Slug," he said, pointing and grimacing comically.

I flicked the slug off and put the bottle on the grass with the others.

"Anyway, I'm thinking of getting a new mom," I said.

He laughed, "How do you propose doing that?" Then he frowned when he saw I was serious.

"We have a list."

I hadn't actually made any progress on this front. In fact, it wasn't just Geordie's reluctance that was holding me back. I had been having second thoughts. So I wasn't sure why I was telling Mr. McFee.

He raised his eyebrows again. "I could maybe help you with that," he said. "You and I have a special link, Lulu." I was standing in the ditch wondering what exactly he meant by a special link when he said it: "Would you be up for a really big adventure?"

I thought about it for about ten seconds while I sorted my pop bottles by kind and height. "A good one?" I asked.

"Yup," he'd said.

"Where?"

"New Westminster."

I nodded. He seemed like a clever man, standing there with his hands in his pockets, whistling nonchalantly. Or maybe it was just the promise of crossing the Pattullo Bridge.

I said yes.

"What's your favourite colour?" He'd stepped forward and, crouching down, pulled a quarter from behind my ear.

"Orange," I said.

"If you had to be one kind of candy, what would you be?"

And then there we were, driving over the orange Pattullo Bridge on a sunny Saturday in the middle of June, a bag of

Licorice Allsorts beside me on the seat, half of them already in my belly, my hand out the window resisting the warm wind, the tires going clickity-clack on the bridge, and Mr. McFee singing *Nothing could be finer than to be in Carolina in the mo-o-o-or-ning.*

It wasn't my mother's fault that I ended up on the other side of the law at the age of eleven, but she wasn't there to stop me, either. And she didn't know about Mr. McFee. Nobody did. Nobody would have believed me, anyway.

From the bridge, you could see forever. To the left, the railway tracks followed the river in front of New Westminster's old wooden buildings—a bunch of fat dusty old ladies, I always thought. To the right, Woodlands and the B.C. Penitentiary loomed on the hill over the river. I'm not sure I knew which was which back then. They were just hulking shadows that brought up shreds of disquiet and a memory of my mother that made me look away.

The wide Fraser River rolled beneath the bridge. Tugboats pulling booms of logs and fishing boats hung with heavy nets churned up the brown water, leaving white swaths behind them. Speeding motorboats stitched the big boats' trails together with their own thin wakes. Sometimes, if you were in the narrow right-hand lane heading into New West, you could hear a train clacking along on the railway bridge that ran underneath the Pattullo.

"You a Brownie?" Mr. McFee asked.

"Nope."

"How come? You look like the Brownie type. Your dad's a Scout leader."

"I'm too old to be a Brownie. I'd be a Guide by now, if Dad would've let me."

"How come he didn't let you?"

"I think he didn't like the Brownie leader. He said she looked like a man."

"Well," Mr. McFee said, "how'd you like to be a Brownie today?"

I started to doubt his cleverness. I felt the first whiff of anxiety, the thought that maybe I shouldn't be all by myself in Mr. McFee's car, eating Licorice Allsorts.

"Look in that bag," he said, nodding over his shoulder. "Go on. Have a look."

I knelt and stretched to reach the airline bag in the back seat. Inside was a Brownie sash covered with badges someone had sewn on with yellow thread. I fingered the bumpy little symbols and my old friend, envy, leapt up in my chest. My brothers were Scouts and I had always sewn on their badges, a task both bitter and sweet that my mother couldn't or wouldn't do and that I wouldn't have given up for anything.

But they had given everything up. Earlier that summer, after a rainy weekend in Garibaldi Park, my brothers had informed Dad that they'd attended their last jamboree, all three of them. They said it just like that. At supper, Dad had said something like, "Well, boys, wasn't that fun?" Ambrose had looked at him deadpan and said, "We've attended our last jamboree, Dad."

My father was utterly dejected. He looked from Ambrose to Alan to Trevor, hoping to find a crack in their armour. There wasn't any. It was 1968. They'd already begun to grow their hair long. That they'd hung in that long was only because Dad believed so fervently that a boy schooled in the Scouts could do no wrong. My father told the boys that it was a decision they would regret for the rest of their lives. Geordie agreed. He said he wasn't ever quitting Scouts. Their defection that day left another deep cut in our father's heart.

"What's this for?" I asked Mr. McFee, sliding back down onto the front seat and holding up the Brownie sash.

"How good are you at talking to people, Lulu?"

"Pretty good, I think."

•

I listened to Mr. McFee's plan and before I could ask too many questions, I guess, I was standing on the front porch of a fancy-looking house on Primrose Avenue in New Westminster. Mr. McFee's empty car was parked around the corner—I don't know where he was—and I was doing exactly what he had told me to do. I rang the doorbell. A nice-looking old woman came to the door and looked at me and my Brownie sash so indulgently that I realized I'd missed out on more than just hanging around other uniformed girls and leaping around fires. I gave her my biggest smile. It was one percent genuine, ninety-nine percent fear.

"I'm a Brownie," I said, "and we're doing a button drive." The woman looked perplexed. Never one to leave well enough alone, I explained that though I was older than the usual Brownie, I was still allowed to be one because I was an immigrant.

"From what country?"

"From Scotland."

"But don't they have Brownies in Scotland?"

I froze.

"What are the Brownies doing with the buttons, dear?"

Mr. McFee had given me the answer to a few questions, but oddly enough, not to this one. "For the poor," I said.

She looked at me a few moments. "Well, I do have an old button collection. I always think I'll use them someday, but there they sit. Let me see if I can find them. They're in my sewing box somewhere."

About two seconds after she'd turned her back, leaving me at the open door, Mr. McFee brushed past me, with his finger to his lips, and ran quickly up the stairs. I could hear the woman talking to herself down the hall. A few seconds later, Mr. McFee was back, halfway down the stairs, mouthing *OK?* I nodded, my heart pounding in my ears, and he skipped out the door faster than I imagined any man could. I waited for the woman to come back, which she did, with a little cloth bag filled with buttons. I said "Thank you, ma'am," and then I ran down the road and around the corner to Mr. McFee's car.

Mr. McFee was in a fine mood.

"By God, Lulu, you're a natural," he nearly shouted, messing up my hair. We drove off quickly, back over the Pattullo. But instead of driving home up Reifel Road, Mr. McFee drove into Wesleyville, past the tavern with the animated neon sign of a bucking horse and the Chinese restaurant with the neon rickshaw's spinning wheels and the pigtailed boy pulling it whose knees flew up and down. When Mr. McFee deposited me down by the undeveloped lots on the Wesleyville side of Hemlock Street, I had to pee so badly I went in the bushes. But I had a two-dollar bill in my pocket and a thin silver bracelet, too big to stay on, sliding along my arm.

DORIS

Where is the Parsons girl coming from? Three times now Doris has seen Mr. McFee's Chevy cross Reifel Road and each time, a few minutes later, Lulu crossing from the south side too. *God forbid. God forbid.* Who is there to warn? Not Wally Parsons. She has no truck with men. Bette Parsons' sister then? The woman has come to the egg stand many times. At first, her curly brown hair and pointed chin, so like Mrs. Parsons', turned a few heads and provoked a wicked amount of tongue-wagging. Some thought at first that Bette Parsons had returned. There were no end of places people said she'd been. Old Melvina Mitchell even said she'd come back from Hell. *Of all places.* Eventually the gossip mill brought the truth about the woman who looked like but wasn't Bette Parsons. Then people told Doris other stories about the sister.

People tell Doris the queerest things. She is the stranger with whom everyone shares his life story, even the most pitiable details. Their confessions will go no further, of that they are sure. Mrs. Hatley has had an abortion. Mrs. Powell's frail old mother was in the hospital over Christmas, not because of gallstones, like she had said, but because Mrs. Powell beat her. Eleanor Plaskett has been having an affair with a man from Vernon, and the man's name is Vernon. *Fancy that.* Laura Carney went away to Alberta for eight months and didn't come back with a baby. And everyone says that fifteen-year-old Brianne Bowdley has been having sex with her uncle.

Doris has never been farther than Hope, B.C. *Such an expectant name for a town.* She went with the church group once, when Father decided he was being called to minister to the Indians. Lewis Cray's books, though, have taken her everywhere, and she is sure that people in the world past Hope are more remarkable if not more charitable than those in Fraser Arm. Even Father had something sour to say about Bette Parsons' sister last week. "She seems fancy," he'd said at breakfast the morning after he'd made his friendly call. The Parsons aren't believers, but a new soul must always be approached and encouraged. Father had given them time. "The good Lord knows they have been through an ordeal and rushing them would be inappropriate," Father said. "She calls herself Kat."

"Cat? C.A.T?" Mother said.

"K.A.T. From Katherine," he said, with an unusual twist of his lip. He had just cut the top off his egg and was looking down at the too-firm centre. Doris remembers the disappointed look he cast at Mother and the little twist on his mouth, as if there were something particularly contemptible about Mother, or about Kat, sister of Bette Parsons. She is not Kat *Parsons*, but Doris has decided she will call her that, just to avoid confusion, until she knows. Doris still does not know, because no one has told her; her name is not what people wish to gossip about.

The first time Kat came, driving Mr. Parsons' pickup, Doris knew it wasn't Bette. Even before she got out of the truck, Doris could see that the set of her jaw was different. She is more feminine somehow, though it has nothing to do with the clothes; perhaps she walks finer. But Doris can see how, out of the corner of one's eye maybe, one could make a mistake. Kat Parsons' grief has settled now. The first times she came, she was raw. It made Doris want to touch her, which is not something that Doris feels very often. Doris likes to touch the chickens, and the dog, and the barn cats. But she doesn't like the feel of human beings. Perhaps it is their smell, or their colour.

Doris knows there is something wrong with her brain. She's not sure why, but people and animals and names and places have colours. Even if she were able to speak she couldn't explain it. Who would understand that Father is burgundy and Mother a pale yellow, like the inside of a lemon peel? The dog is turquoise, the biggest barn cat is purple, and the chickens are each their own colour. Mary-Magdalene is black, and Ruth, maroon. Martha is a brilliant green. So was the rooster, who once was Moses but whom Doris has renamed because he has never seemed as pious as he should be to have the name of the prophet. *How could any rooster be pious, given his job?* He's Heathcliff now and a slightly different shade of green.

Lulu, as she crosses Reifel Road, has a colour too. It is a

murky beige that makes Doris' insides squirm. There is an uneasiness in her body, a creeping at her feet and fingers, as her own colour—dark red—seems to be giving way to this same unpleasant beige. The way the beige is taking over has been making Doris not at all sure of who she is anymore. What feels queerest to Doris is that it has never occurred to her to pay attention to who she is, 'til now. She, and the others just . . . were. Everything was once quiet and familiar and not to be examined. But now there are two colours and two Dorises. Earlier she imagined that it was Lewis Cray's latest book choices that were causing the colour changes. This morning, reading *I Heard the Owl Call My Name*, Doris discovered a flash of beige in her black hair and she thinks there may have been some on her shoulders as well. The way the beige clung, so tenaciously, distressed her. Today, though it annoys her to admit it, she knows what is causing the beige. It is Mr. McFee. She has had to break her life into two parts—before Mr. McFee and after Mr. McFee—red Doris and beige Doris.

Doris turns away from the egg stand and walks back to the garden where she can see over the peas that need picking right onto Hemlock Street. Lulu is passing the Wheatleys', skipping along in her turquoise shorts without, it seems, a care in the world. Doris opens her mouth and "I . . ." sits on her tongue but will not come out.

LULU

I knew what Mr. McFee and I were doing was wrong, especially when he started asking me to duck down in the front seat so I wouldn't be seen, but whenever he rolled past in his convertible and stopped, waiting, half a block down the road, I would saunter up to the car as though all this was new. He'd nod and say, "Well, if it isn't Lulu Parsons," and I'd get in the car. We'd drive to one of the towns nearby—New Westminster, Coquitlam, Maple Ridge, Vancouver—and we'd do our routine, me at the front door playing the innocent Brownie, and Mr. McFee inside pawing through jewellery boxes or underwear drawers. Sometimes, without my knowing, he'd slip out the back door and I'd be left guessing how much longer to engage our patsy, my heart shuddering in fear. Finally, he'd make his way around to the front of the house again and stroll whistling past and I'd know my job was done. People closed doors in my face. Or asked me to come in. Every time, I'd swear I'd never do it again. But back in the car Mr. McFee would be jubilant, almost drunk on the experience, and I'd get my reward. It was something different each time—some money, a bangle, a pair of pierced earrings I couldn't wear. It was my own early addiction; I knew I should say no, but I loved it.

"Lulu," he said one sunny morning in August, after another heist in Vancouver, "I want to show you something."

He looked excited as he reached into his shirt pocket and pulled out a fine silver chain. I felt a surge of pleasure as he dangled the chain and the little silver violin that hung from it.

"Thank you, Mr. McFee," I said.

"You're most welcome, Lulu. But that's not what I want to show you. Just wait." The car started with a roar that seemed to please him. "Stanley Park, here we come. Let's sing," he said, swinging the convertible onto the road.

"I have to be home soon, Mr. McFee."

"Well, I thought you said you just have to be home when your dad blows the whistle, Lulu?"

He'd caught me there. In the summer, we left the house in the morning and often only came back if we couldn't find lunch somewhere else, or if we could, when Dad blew the Scout whistle at six. The Oggs had a whistle too. Mrs. Ogg blew theirs. They had supper at five, though, before Mr. Ogg went off to his night shift at the Coca-Cola factory. Our family ate at six.

"I guess so." I felt a tightness creeping into my gut again. "What's in Stanley Park?" I'd been to the big park in Vancouver many times before with Mum and Dad, and loved it, but I didn't want to go there with Mr. McFee.

"Well, there's Siwash Rock, and the hollow tree. Shall we go drive right through the hollow tree?" He turned toward me, pretending he'd forgotten he was at the wheel. The car swerved right and he jerked it back into our lane. "Oops," he laughed.

"I don't think we'd fit in the tree," I said, but my child heart was, as always, captivated.

"Well, I'd be willing to give it a try. What say you?"

I laughed. "No way."

"And he saith unto them, Why are ye fearful, O ye of little faith?"

"What?"

"Clearly, you don't know your Bible, Lulu. I think the moderns have made a mess of its interpretation, but we'll read it together sometime and I'll show you the best parts. The Bible's full of gems you'll be able to use all your life. Most people don't know the origins of the sayings they use. Either the Bible or Shakespeare. Do you know Shakespeare? Of course you don't. So many wonderful things ahead for you, Miss Parsons. So many wonderful things. What are we going to sing?" Mr. McFee launched into "The Bare Necessities," without waiting for my suggestion, mimicking Baloo's voice perfectly. "Sing it, Lulu."

We'd sung this song together so many times I knew the words by heart. Mr. McFee had even driven me into New Westminster one day and made me stand in line by myself at the Columbia Theatre, following me in the idling convertible as the line inched toward the ticket booth. I'd gone in alone and watched *The Jungle Book*, the first movie I'd ever seen. He was still idling outside, listening to the blaring radio and smoking a cigarette, when I came out, ecstatic.

As we drove into Stanley Park, we finished singing "Jimmy Mack" and "Georgy Girl" and moved onto "Soul Man," Mr.

McFee doing the horns perfectly. Anyone watching us would have laughed at our antics and wondered how that blond man could have such a dark-haired daughter. Mr. McFee had a tale for every spot in Stanley Park: he knew of a man who'd killed a thief and tossed the pearl-handled revolver into Lost Lagoon. Lumberman's Arch was on Indian burial ground. Brockton Point used to be a graveyard too, for white people only though. The Lions Gate Bridge wasn't named for the lions at its gate.

"No siree. It was named for those two big lions lyin' at the top of the mountains. See 'em Lulu?"

I knelt on the seat and looked out the back window. "Not today."

"I climbed the lions once."

The lions were great snowy peaks at the top of the mountain. I couldn't imagine any man climbing that high, but I didn't doubt Mr. McFee. He smacked his steering wheel and launched into "To Sir with Love."

He interrupted himself. "Hey. You know the girl who sang that was called Lulu too?"

He gave me a big smile and chucked me under the chin as we came to the great hollow tree. Mr. McFee pretended to pull the car up on the curb and over the grass. I screamed.

"What? Are you chickening out?" He winked and parked the convertible and we both hopped out without opening the car doors. We stood inside the tree, looking up. We had all done the same thing once, Dad, Mum, the boys, and me.

"This tree is about one thousand years old. A western red cedar. They put an elephant in here once," Mr. McFee said.

I was trying not to be impressed. "You can't drive through," I said smacking my hand against the back of the tree.

"True enough. Then we could just park the car in the tree and live here. What do you say to that? We could catch raccoons and fish in the lagoon and roast them on a bonfire. You know how to light a fire by rubbing two sticks together, right? I could have the back seat and you could have the trunk."

"What if it rains?"

"Well, we can always put the top up."

I considered this. I wasn't sure I'd ever seen the top up on Mr. McFee's convertible. He only drove the red car in good weather. During the winter or when it rained, he drove a baby-blue hard top Mustang.

"I think I should go home, Mr. McFee."

"As Ralph Waldo Emerson says, 'Adopt the pace of nature: her secret is patience.' You know Emerson, Lulu? No, of course you don't. But you will. I'll tell you all about him. C'mon."

He held his hand out to me. I didn't take it but I followed him, my stomach as hollow as the big tree.

"What's this one, Lulu?" I looked up through the canopy to the top of the tall evergreen and found its drooping crown.

"Western hemlock," I said. "Not the hemlock that killed the philosopher guy."

"Socrates. Excellent."

As we walked, Mr. McFee tested me, as he always did. Over the summer, we'd progressed from the simple identification of the trees, plants, and wildflowers we encountered to what Mr. McFee called "the salient facts"; everything had a name but also a story to go with it. Why did the Indians chew the bark of Sitka spruce? For vitamin C. Was the Douglas fir a *true* fir? No. When I asked him why not, he laughed and said, "I don't know. Find out, will ya?" What other name was the western red cedar sometimes known by? *Arborvitae*, tree of life. We touched bark, feeling for smooth or rough, scaled or shreddy. He plucked leaves and needles from the trees and held them in his palm showing me their veins and mid-ribs or how the needles were four-sided or flat. Dogwood, arbutus, horsetail, deer fern, huckleberry, devil's club—I'd been learning all about the flora of our neck of British Columbia.

We reached a clearing where the forest floor was carpeted with mosses and lichens and small yellow flowers and littered with fir and hemlock needles. Mr. McFee got down on his hands and knees and stared at the ground. Then he picked up a stick and said, "Here, draw a square foot. Anywhere you want. Go ahead."

I drew a lopsided square, lifting the stick to avoid, and include, a big green banana slug. The slug crawled across the area, cutting a diagonal line with its silver slime.

"One square foot. Let's look and see what's in one square foot of Stanley Park." Mr. McFee sat down cross-legged on a patch of moss and peered into the square I'd drawn. "I see our friend the slug, a pill bug, two pill bugs, some ants, some ants carrying eggs, some lichen, moss. Two or three kinds of moss, actually. Look Lulu." His arm reached up and he pulled me down by my shirttails. "There's an ant carrying a dead ant on its back." He pointed at it with a twig.

"Will they eat it?"

"I do believe they will eat it. Not very nice, but very practical if you think upon it. You'll have to come over to my house and peruse the *Encyclopaedia Britannica* for the answer to that."

Mr. McFee had never invited me to his house before. I

was curious about what lay beyond the great wall of trees that blocked the view of the house, and I'd climbed them many times, but I'd never even walked up the long driveway. There were tales of someone drowning in the well there, even before Mrs. McFee disappeared. But I felt excited about the encyclopedia. Other than Aunt Kat's *History of Art* that she brought from England and the books I borrowed from the Bookmobile, we had very few things to read in the house. Sometimes I read the ingredients on the Dutch Cleanser container. The encyclopedia set we had in the school library had to be read under the watchful eye of Miss Siry. Our neighbour three up, Mr. Brunning, had tried to sell Dad a set on installments but Dad said it was too expensive even though Aunt Kat said gaining knowledge was invaluable at any cost. Dad had asked what the difference was between valuable and invaluable and then replied that there was always the Bookmobile. He also said that by the time he'd paid for it I would be married and all the information out of date.

Mr. McFee lifted a rock and a centipede scuttled out of our square. "Wait, Mr. Bug. You're ruining our game. You know, Lulu, we can't even begin to imagine what actually exists in this square. There are organisms so small we can't see them, and they're all doing their job."

"What's their job?" I asked, poking with a twig at a few small, deep-red worm-like bugs. They uncurled and recurled a few times then lay very still.

"They're decomposing this soil here and making the nutrients for the trees so they can grow as tall as they are. The soil here is just as rich as it gets."

The longer I stared the more it seemed that the world in our square foot was teeming with creatures. I could even imagine the invisible ones—the bacteria and microbes and organisms Mr. McFee was talking about. A daddy-long-legs crossed the frontier into our square then changed its mind and scuttled back into the forest. We laughed at its gangly legs and imagined it had been wandering along not thinking and had only at the last minute seen us two giants.

"Smell," Mr. McFee said.

I put my nose to the ground and inhaled. Our square had a rich, loamy smell that felt familiar, like my father.

"How're you doing with the search for your mother?"

"Not my mother. A new mother." I took another deep inhalation. I hoped Mr. McFee would stop talking about Mum if I just kept my nose low to the ground, but instead he put his hand on the back of my neck and made his fingers curl up into my hair. I stood up so fast I fell backwards onto the ground.

"Easy girl," Mr. McFee stood and pulled me up with his hand in my armpit.

"I guess we'd better get back. I told Nadine I would play with her later," I said.

"Nadine. She's a nice girl."

•

"Our little secret, right?" He said that every time he dropped me off. I stood beside the ditch until he drove away, his tail lights tapping red for just a second at the stop sign and then crossing Reifel Road. I pushed into the bushes on one of the deer trails and squatted to pee. I would never have talked to anyone about it. I already knew that I was as guilty as he was. If Mr. McFee got into trouble, I would too. I didn't even tell

Nadine about it. But I had told her about the idea of finding a new mother, and that afternoon I found myself standing at the Oggs' kitchen door thinking that, just maybe, a new mother could save me from Mr. McFee.

●

I had hoped not to involve Nadine in my plans. I was wobbly enough in my convictions that I should even go ahead with them, and Nadine had a bad habit of taking things over the top. But I had to confide in someone other than Geordie. If I was going to do it, I'd need some help.

"I wouldn't mind a new mother, either," Nadine said.

I scoffed and reminded her that she already had a perfectly good mother and that Mrs. Ogg had actually been one of my choices.

"My mom's pretty good," she said, "but there are some difficulties."

"Like what?"

We climbed up into the tree fort and surveyed our backyards through the window. Both laundry lines were heavy with drying clothes, and in the Oggs' yard, a cat was stalking something beneath one of the old rusting cars. Shannon was smoking on the back stoop.

"Like having to share a room with *her*," she said, pointing at her sister, "and having to be quiet all the time because Dad's sleeping."

"That's not your mom's fault. And your dad works nights. He has to sleep sometime."

Nadine flipped her hand at me and ignored my argument. "What about at church?"

"We don't go to church," I said, missing the thread.

"We *could*. There's lots of possible moms there."

•

We turned our sights on the Reifel Road Baptist Church, Nadine holding the reins, and me dragging along behind wondering what I had done in my short life to deserve the chaos that was turning it upside down. I didn't actually want a new mother. I didn't want anyone or anything but my brother Geordie and Aunt Kat's fiddle. I just wanted to stop feeling. But at that moment, Nadine was our momentum and she had a team of horses ready at the top of a hill.

Neither of us had ever been to church, but our classmate Janet Smallwood had. Her mother couldn't believe her luck that a couple of unbaptised girls were ready to meet the Lord. I agreed to go on the condition that we would sit at the back, which suited Nadine just fine. "The better to see who's there, my dear," she'd said, grinning like a wolf. I sat stone still between Janet and Nadine, my eyes riveted on Mr. Tenpenny, while Nadine covertly scanned the pews. I had never liked the looks of Mr. Tenpenny, but the passion in his voice was peculiarly enthralling.

Janet's mom had sent along fifty-cents for each of us—correctly anticipating our ignorance of church things—to put in the offering envelope. While Mr. Tenpenny shouted about the prince of demons, I was confronted with another moral dilemma—those quarters sweating in my palm. Mrs. Tenpenny, the preacher's wife, smiled at me as we left. It was a wan smile, parting her lips just enough to show nearly translucent teeth, that seemed to say, "I know you've got our fifty cents, dear, and I know you'll give it back." Nadine took my hand once we were out the church doors and we ran, leaving Janet behind. When we stopped, out of breath, outside of Chen's, she held out her palm to me. Fifty cents. What fool would have imagined that two hard-up girls such as us would give up a windfall like that?

●

"Mrs. Tanner," Nadine said as we came out of Chen's with our loot.

"Who?"

"Mrs. Tanner. Over on Dempsey Road."

She had a mouthful of licorice babies and was having trouble speaking. Her teeth were black.

"But they've already got a slew of kids of their own and a few foster kids too."

"A couple more kids won't make any difference to the Tanners," Nadine said.

I turned away from her black mouth, remembering the look on Trevor's face the last time I'd bought licorice babies. Mrs. Tanner had been at church with a baby on her lap and had left when it started crying. The Tanners lived in a small pink stucco house. The front stairs were missing, so Nadine reached up and knocked on the bottom of the door. Mrs. Tanner and four or five kids answered.

"Jesus has sent us some new friends, children," she said, handing the baby to a kid who couldn't have been much older than five.

One of the bigger boys jumped out the door and pulled a wooden crate over, and we climbed up into the house while

Mrs. Tanner shooed her own children out into the toy-strewn dirt yard. Nadine was right. Mrs. Tanner would have taken in any child she could to please Jesus. We sat on the edge of her tattered brown couch in our Sunday clothes while Mrs. Tanner shut the door, turned on a little lamp with a golden shade, and pulled the dark brown curtains closed.

"I saw you girls at church," she said in a tired voice.

Mrs. Tanner was thin and had a worn, determined look about her. I recognized it. My mother had had it, too. Nadine must have known that the Tanner's world was no better than ours—that their house was no less shabby, that there were worse things than living with Shannon or Trevor—because she didn't bring up the reason for our visit once during the hour we sat in the golden glow of that small lamp. We were poor, but the Tanners were something else; Nadine and I both knew the difference between their lives and ours.

Mrs. Tanner pulled a kitchen chair up close to the couch and showed us a picture postcard of a long-haired man—Jesus, apparently—holding a lamb.

"That's you," she said, pointing to the little white lamb curled in his arms. She told us the streets of Heaven were paved with gold, and God and Jesus had side-by-side golden thrones up there. Mrs. Tanner didn't have a picture of God—"Only the redeemed dead can look upon the face of God," she said—but she had pictures of the golden roads of Heaven.

"Is it the baby Jesus or the man Jesus that's on the throne?" Nadine asked.

"They're the same man. It don't make no difference," Mrs. Tanner explained. I noticed that the worn look on her face had been replaced with a kind of flush.

Mrs. Tanner gave us each a small book of Bible stories

and games. With a stubby gnawed-on pencil, I traced a maze while she told us a story.

"Samson was a gift from God to his mother and father, who couldn't have no children. An angel of the Lord went to a field where the wife of the man whose name was Manoah was working. The angel told her she'd have a baby boy named Samson and that she should never cut his hair."

"What was her name?" Nadine asked.

"We don't know. The Lord never mentioned her name."

"But she was the one that had Samson," Nadine persisted.

"That part's not important. You just have to trust in the Lord, Nadine."

"My mom said I took twenty hours to be born 'cause I came bum first and I just about killed her. I wouldn't want to go through all that birthing and not get my name mentioned in the story."

Mrs. Tanner looked like she was thinking about that for a second. "We'll just call her Mrs. Manoah for now, okay? Anyways, so, Samson grew up and he was very, very strong. He killed a lion. And he tied three-hundred foxes together by their tails and put torches between each and set them in the wheat fields of the Philistines so all their grain was burnt up. But then he fell in love with a temptress named Delilah. That Delilah, she plagued Samson with questions 'til he told her the secret of his strength. And then while he lay sleeping in her lap, someone come and shaved off his hair, and with it went all his strength. He couldn't fight his enemies no more and he was captured by the Philistines and they put out his eyes and made him a slave."

Nadine had a few more questions about Delilah and about how cutting your hair might take away your strength and about how you might catch three hundred foxes, but Mrs. Tanner stood up and suddenly tucked her Bible under a cushion on the couch.

"Here's Mr. Tanner home now, girls. You take them exercise books and study them." She took the pencils from our hands and whipped open the curtains.

Mrs. Tanner called us lambs and told us to come back any time. She disappeared into the kitchen as we jumped down into the dirt from the front door.

I knew Dad wouldn't be too keen on the Bible books, so we climbed up into the tree fort and tried the crosswords.

"One across, Cain's brother," Nadine said.

"Who's Cain?"

"Some other godly guy, probably. Okay, two across: he built the Ark."

"I know that. Noah. Does it fit?"

"How d'you spell it?"

I spelled it and Nadine wrote it in. "How'd you know that?"

"Everyone's heard of Noah's Ark, right?"

"Who's everyone?" Nadine looked like she was trying a few other clues, but I could tell she was just thinking. Then she said, understated as always, "So, that wasn't so great."

"No kidding. Scared the heck out of me when she closed the curtains."

"She was just creating a golden feeling, I think. Like Heaven."

"Well, I'm never going back there again."

"Me neither," Nadine said. "And I don't think I want to go to Heaven anyways."

"We better burn these books, 'cause Dad's not going to like stories about a guy who ties foxes tails together."

Aunt Kat let us take the garbage out to the burning barrel and when the fire was blazing we tossed the little books in and watched the pages curl to black.

"She doesn't seem very happy, does she?" Nadine said.

We each had a plastic dish-soap bottle on a stick and were roasting them over the fire in the barrel. Mine had already started melting.

"I don't think anybody in Fraser Arm seems very happy."

"Oh, Lulu." Nadine put her arm around my shoulder and we stood watching our bottles melt, the sizzling fat drops of plastic falling in fantastic colours into the fire.

Though she hadn't thought so at first, Nadine decided the Bookmobile woman was an exceptional prospect for a new mother.

"I don't really want one now, Nadine. I've really kind of changed my mind."

"You just got thrown off by Mrs. Three-hundred-foxes," Nadine said.

"I think Aunt Kat's good, and Dad."

"Well, I think we should just go down and see Mrs. Bookmobile. She might be smart like you and me. And she's got a lot of books."

I thought about Mr. McFee's hand creeping up the back of my neck and I shivered. "Okay," I said. "But that's the last one."

We had to wait until Wednesday, and then we had to wait until every borrower had returned their books, picked new ones, offered to pay their fines and been let off the hook, chatted sufficiently with Mrs. Bookmobile, given me one last semi-commiserating pat on the head, and left. We'd brought Geordie but we made him wait outside. Mrs. Bookmobile looked at us expectantly. Then that team of horses named Nadine started galloping. Before Nadine had finished explaining what we were after, the woman put her hand up to stop her. She laughed.

"I could never, ever, ever be a mother," she said, putting more emphasis on each 'ever.' "I like kids, don't get me wrong. But I am not the settling kind. I'm not married and I don't ever intend to be." Then her eyes took on a sorrowful look. It wasn't pity. It was a look that said I've got something terrible to tell you and there's no getting around it. She sat down on the driver's seat. "You're Lulu, right?" She held out her hand and I shook it. "I'm Raylene Dubé. Pleased to meet you. You've got a dad, don't you, Lulu?"

I nodded, already close to tears in anticipation of what I was reading in her eyes.

"Sooner or later, we all lose our mothers. Even if you lose your mother as an adult, you're still a motherless child." She touched my shoulder, just for a second, and let her hand drop. "You, Lulu, have just had some dumb tough luck."

Whatever pain Raylene Dubé had of her own that made her eyes so sad, whatever story she might have told me if I'd been older, I felt the truth of her words, the staggering physical weight of them, sink into my body. I followed Nadine down the Bookmobile steps. Geordie was sitting cross-legged in the grass on the other side of the ditch, waiting. I shivered. In one brief moment, the cold hard stone I'd been carrying in my heart for nine months shifted, and with it, my invulnerability cracked away. Bleak, shattering pain took its place. Geordie took hold of my hand and kneaded it. I stood on the edge of the road in the dust kicked up by the departing Bookmobile, wanting my mother with a ferocity I never felt again for anything or anyone. Nadine took my other hand and she and Geordie gently pulled me along the road as I sobbed. Finally, I felt Geordie's big arms pick me up. He swung me over his shoulder the way my father used to but couldn't anymore and carried me home. I could feel Nadine whispering in my ear. I think she said, "Everything's going to be all right."

DORIS

Unless Father is reading the *Royal Bank Monthly Letter* aloud, it is always quiet at the Tenpenny supper table. The Tenpenny children even move their knives and forks without scraping. Scraping is forbidden. Spilling is forbidden. Talking about frivolous things is forbidden. Tonight, Father is reading the July mailing aloud for the second time: *Wood in the Mechanical Age* is not frivolous. Doris' siblings, James, William, Mike, and Joan must listen carefully; there are often questions afterwards. Doris is exempt, of course, from the questions, but not the listening. Sometimes it is hard to tell which words in the *Letter* are Father's and which belong to the author because Father edits the *Letter* with a red pen before he reads it to the family. Doris has seen that Father removes words such as "liberal" and "evolution." Doris, however, is not paying Father much attention. She is thinking about her own editing skills and wondering what she might have written that would have had more of an impact on Kat not-Parsons-but-Fenwick.

"If we interfere with Nature's way in the forests then we must use our talent to maintain them," Father reads. He smacks his hand on the table—to add emphasis or to make sure they are all listening, Doris does not know which. The *Letter* is very long and everyone has finished eating, even Mother, who chews very slowly. Doris thinks Mother chews slowly so that she will have something to do while Father is reading. Father follows up the thump of his hand with the word "thriftlessness." There is such a long moment of silence that Doris raises her eyes from her plate. Father is glaring at Joan and William as if they are responsible for the country's unsustainable forestry practices. William had better not slouch so; Father will make him pay for his sloppy posture. Though Doris is looking down again, she knows when the *Letter* is finished and when Father's summation begins. Father's tone is orange peaks and valleys while the *Letter*'s is gray plains. In a few minutes Father will go silent and one of Doris' siblings will ask to be excused. Mother will say, "You are," and she will rise, put on her apron, and do the dishes. Doris cannot wait to be free to think with dissatisfaction about her experience with Kat Fenwick this afternoon.

She'd said, "Well, I think she's safe with a religious man, don't you, Doris? Mr. McFee even came to the house and asked permission to take Lulu to church." Doris spent a whole afternoon in the chicken coop composing the note and that is all Miss Fenwick had to say. Perhaps she should have been more forceful. Perhaps she should have said: It is *not* safe for Lulu to spend time with Mr. McFee. Instead she had written: Do you think Lulu should spend so much time with Mr. McFee? Doris has learned how to make her face say I'm listening, go on. And the opposite: I've had enough of your malarkey, go away. But she does not know how to start an important conversation, even on paper. Miss Fenwick gave her a what-a-queer-thing-you-are look. Doris is used to that. Miss Fenwick took her dozen eggs and said, "Lulu spends most of her time with Nadine Ogg, anyway, Doris. I really don't think you should worry." She petted Doris' arm and left the note lying on the stand. If Lulu Parsons is going to church with Aloysius McFee, it is not to Father's church.

James finally asks to be excused. Doris had not noticed the silence; her thoughts were too noisy. Everyone rises except Doris and Father, who eye each other indifferently, each lost in their own thoughts. Miss Fenwick did not say whether Mr. Parsons gave permission for Lulu to attend church with Mr. McFee. Non-religious people often do not want their children going to church. Father has mentioned this fact with annoyance, though it seems most logical to Doris. There is some hope. Perhaps Wally Parsons said, No, I would rather she not. Go to church. With you, Mr. McFee.

Alone has never been an unwelcome state. But this aloneness—this alone with her worries for the safety of Lulu Parsons—is making Doris ill at ease. What Mr. McFee did to Doris should not be done to anyone. There are not many churches in Fraser Arm. But what if Mr. McFee is taking Lulu to Wesleyville? Or beyond? None of this is the right colour. Doris leaves the table and goes to her room. She thinks some cross-stitch will help. It does not.

LULU

Mr. McFee took me across the Pattullo half a dozen more times before fear and something else kicked through and made me vomit my Licorice Allsorts out the car window.

"I have principles," Mr. McFee told me on our last trip of the summer of 1968. "I never take more than one or two things. Even if there's a diamond sitting next to a ruby, I choose only one. That way they'll think they lost it." He passed me a badge-festooned Girl Guide sash. Where he got it, I didn't know, but some very talented girl was likely furious to have lost it.

"You've graduated from Brownie to Girl Guide," he said, which indicated to me that he thought this arrangement of ours—a couple of dollars and a trinket for being his assistant—would go on forever. "Have you ever seen an emerald, Lulu?" He was smiling an odd, nervous smile that sent something cold spiraling through me. "They're as green as . . . your eyes."

I looked at him coolly. "My eyes are hazel, Mr. McFee."

"Who cares? They're very pretty. Did you know that, Lulu?" Mr. McFee had curly blond hair that he slicked down with some kind of pomade and the comb marks showed like rows in a cornfield. He patted it carefully, hoping not to disturb the pattern. "They go really nice with your black hair. You should grow it long."

"My hair's not black. It's brown."

"Looks black to me." He wasn't looking at me anymore. He was checking his teeth in the rearview mirror.

I nervously fingered the last licorice in the cellophane bag. I'd left one of the nubbly blue ones for last. I popped it into my mouth but its little bumps made me think of the big beef tongues Mum used to stew in the pressure cooker, and I spat it into my hand.

"I'd like an emerald." Mr. McFee was talking to himself, paying attention to traffic. A blue vein pulsed rapidly at his temple. He wiped a trickle of sweat that had reached his sideburns, with the back of his hand. "That would be so nice."

We pulled up and parked on a tree-lined street near the Royal Columbian Hospital where Geordie had had his tonsils taken out. I could see the big ivy-covered building behind the row of houses as Mr. McFee and I walked up one street and turned onto another.

"You know why I go to church, Lulu?"

"Nope."

"So I can sing. No other place in the world that you can sing your heart out."

We stopped in front of a sparkly stuccoed house.

"We're doing it different today," he said. He looked as nervous as I felt.

I followed him up the steps. He held my hand awkwardly, a man unpracticed at fatherhood, while he rang the doorbell. It played a fancy song that could be heard from inside the house. He pulled two boxes of Girl Guide cookies out of his bag and put them in my hands.

"Sell her the cookies, then tell her you've got to pee. Find the master bedroom. One thing only, Lulu. Don't forget."

When the woman answered the door, all yellowy pearls and a pale gray sweater set, she and Mr. McFee shared one of those indulgent smiles and he patted my head. The woman said she'd buy two boxes for her grandchildren.

"Now, where did I leave my purse? Those kids don't deserve cookies, the little hellions," she said, staring at me, this scruffy girl in shorts, as if my Girl Guide sash was a true measure of my worth. "You must be so proud of your little girl."

I felt Mr. McFee nudge me, then he pinched my back hard and I twisted out of his hold.

"Can I use your bathroom?" I said.

Their voices followed me upstairs: "I'm sorry to say it, but my grandchildren are brats."

"Surely not."

"It's not their fault, I suppose."

"You're darn tooting about that."

"It's my daughter's fault, which means I didn't raise her right either."

"Oh, I didn't mean, no, don't blame yourself."

"I do, I do."

"They'll grow out of it."

"I'm waiting for the day."

I found the bathroom and pulled the door closed with a loud clack. Then I crossed the hall into the master bedroom. I stood over that padded red leatherette jewellery box, my sweaty hands leaving excellent fingerprints on the long, sleek dresser, pondering the rings, brooches, and necklaces all tucked neatly into the velvety partitions. I was suddenly conscious of the tidy luxuriousness of the room—the plush of the carpet under my feet, the wide bed with its shiny gold bedspread, the tasselled drapes, the long dresser—and a rough jealousy seized me. I plucked three rings from their orderly slots and jerked up the top layer of the jewellery box. In the hidden compartment was a treasure trove—strings of pink pearls, old watches, locks of baby hair tied with satin ribbon, letters in yellowing envelopes, birth certificates, a wad of American money, some old silver dollars. I shoved the bills in one pocket and the coins in another. Then a silver bracelet with a thousand charms peeked out from underneath the letters and said *take me*, so I did. I looked up at my reflection in the dresser's perfectly matched mirror. The small pale face staring back at me looked confused. This kind of house, the unfamiliar softness of it, was whispering some language I had never heard. I felt incapable of moving, until I heard Mr. McFee calling.

"Honey," he shouted in a sugared voice. He and the woman stood there talking, not watching me descend the stairs. I might as well have had live hedgehogs in my pockets, bristling as they were with stolen goods. I could hear each little charm on the bracelet calling out to the woman to be saved, like that harp at the top of Jack's beanstalk.

Mr. McFee was as furious as the Fraser River through Hell's Gate. "What the hell were you doing?" he shouted after we turned the corner. He grabbed me tight by the arm and pulled me roughly to the car.

I said nothing and felt less. I could still see my face in that bedroom mirror, like a painting in Aunt Kat's history of art book. I was thinking about the cream-coloured carpet in the bedroom and the way the light had filtered through the gauzy curtains casting a rectangle of brighter cream in the middle of the room. Did a man live there too? Did he sit on that tightly made bed at the end of the day feeling that soft carpet under his bare feet? Maybe the man and the woman would sit side by side rubbing their feet on it and talking about their terrible grandchildren and eating the Girl Guide cookies themselves. Crumbs would fall on the carpet and the woman would bend to pick them up and she'd say, "That's all right, dear."

Halfway across the Pattullo, curiosity or greed must have gotten the better of Mr. McFee because he stopped glaring over at me and said in his regular Mr. McFee voice, "So, Lulu, what did you take?" Then he put a big warm hand on my bare leg and slid it forward so that the tips of his fingers lay between my thighs, not too high up, but not too low down either. I stared at his hand, thinking about the hedgehogs in my pockets. Mr. McFee was keeping his eyes on the traffic—important on the Pattullo because the lanes were very narrow—but he had to lean a little to the right to keep his hand where it was. His Adam's apple was bobbing up and down in his thin neck and the sun was glinting off the hairs poking out of his shirt collar. Then he slid his hand farther up and pulled my thigh so that my legs came apart and his fingers were inside my shorts and then they were inside my underpants. Mr. McFee smiled another one of those peculiar smiles and I started to think about how those Licorice Allsorts might look in my stomach, their colours swirling. I jerked up and was sick out the window, all down the side of Mr. McFee's car and onto the Pattullo Bridge.

I thought Mr. McFee would be furious again, but he laughed, a relieved kind of laugh. He handed me his big white handkerchief. When he pulled up at the usual spot in Wesleyville, he just held his palm out, and I reached into my pocket and gave him the first ring my fingers found, a small diamond with two little rubies on either side of it.

He let out a long whistle and said, "You done good, Lulu." When I tried to give him the handkerchief back he said, "You keep it," and "You won't tell anyone, will you? Our little secret, right?" His eyes flicked away from mine.

I waited until I saw his tail lights come on at the corner stop sign to look at the things in my pockets. The charm bracelet had been around the world, or at least to France and Egypt. I peered at the intricate Eiffel Tower and the Egyptian pyramids. There was a Scottish bagpiper, and a cowboy boot with a spur, and a heart in the form of a peace sign. Its weight was satisfying in my hand, and when I shook it, the bracelet both jangled and rang. I pulled the rings from my pocket. One of them was a diamond and the other one was, well, as green as grass.

1974, 1975

Now use your silver tongue once more
There's one thing that I'd like to know
Did you ever believe the lies that you told?
Did you earn the fool's gold that you gave me?

LHASA DE SELA, "Fool's Gold," *Lhasa*

LULU

I sure as hell hadn't been thinking I'd be caught in the ditch with a beer bottle hanging off my finger, but that's exactly how Joey Tanner found me on what turned out to be an oddly memorable day. All I can say is, even at seventeen, you don't give up picking bottles when it's been your main source of income all your life. Joey was out cruising, as usual, in his souped-up old Mustang. For all I knew, it had once been Aloysius McFee's. He pulled up fast and his mag wheels spat gravel as he twisted onto the shoulder.

"Did anyone ever tell you you're pretty cute, Lulu Parsons," he drawled, swinging the passenger door open from the driver's seat, "in your sexy little jeans." Joey was the twenty-year-old offspring of Mrs. Three-hundred-foxes. By some miracle that Mrs. Tanner had surely prayed for, Joey hadn't turned out at all like Mr. Tanner, at least not in the grouchy department.

"Little jeans, huh. What would you know about sexy, Joey?"

"Well, I'm not sure." He scratched his neck for a second as if he really wasn't sure. "Aren't you getting to be a little old to be bottle picking? Why don't you leave them to the Scouts?"

I stepped up out of the ditch, my finger still in the neck of a beer bottle. He was leaning across the seat, all tight t-shirt and jean jacket and cocky grin. Joey was working hard on his bad-boy style but his wavy sandy-coloured hair wasn't helping. Despite the aviator sunglasses, mustache, and long sideburns, he was what you might call pretty. He pushed his sunglasses down and his lazy green-eyed gaze lingered on my mouth. For a boy who'd grown up sucking religion from his baby bottle, the look he was giving me was decidedly ungodly. I gave him back just as good.

"I don't know, Joey, I don't seem to be able to stop. I see a bottle and I just have to have it."

"That's how I like my girls, Lulu. Come for a ride? No charge. Unless maybe that's not just an empty bottle you've got there."

Joey and I had been flirting for months. I realized that getting in the car would most likely mean one thing. I was nervous but didn't want to look that way, so I stepped up to the car and looked him up and down.

"Now why would I share my beer with you?"

Joey reached out and slid his finger up my midriff under my sweater. "Because you want to?"

The electric shock that spilled down my hips and between my legs made me dizzy. I couldn't think of anything else smart to say, so I slid into the passenger seat, ready, willing.

We drove to the foot of Portland Road where it dead-ended. When we got out of the car, Joey took my hand, inter-twining our fingers sweetly. I could feel rough calluses on the inside of his fingers. The firm feel of his hand, the maleness of it more than anything, was the thing I remember most from that afternoon. And the smell.

It was September and everything was still green. We followed the path in through a young alder copse 'til it split in two directions. To the south lay Beeton's Bog, an open, hundred acres of rolling peat and wildflowers. To the west it was more forested, with vine maples and alder trees giving way to cedars, hemlocks, and firs. Someone's ancestors, probably mine, had logged there seventy-five years ago, and then again, fifty years later. Stumps the size of elephants still stood, their tops graced with huckleberry bushes.

A memory floated in: Nadine and me making pies with their round red berries, like fish eggs, in her Easy-Bake Oven. Mr. McFee and I picked huckleberries too. He'd told me stories of how the old-growth trees were cut at the height that men now long dead had been able to reach with their axes. I could imagine the lumberjacks standing on boards wedged into the bark, in pairs drawing the big cross-cut saw across the colossal trunks until the tree crashed to the ground.

The path Joey was leading me along cut beside a big tree that had been felled long ago and left where it lay, its sienna-orange length nearly crumbled into the earth.

"Looks like a Douglas fir," Joey said. I must have gaped at him.

"You don't think I'm stupid, do you?" he said, and squeezed my hand. "When I was logging up in the Queen Charlottes this summer, this old log scaler told me that when you're at the beach and someone points at a log and asks you what kind it is, even if it's just a piece of old driftwood, never hesitate, just make something up and sound confident."

We came to a clearing I'd been to just once, years earlier. It was a magical kind of place. The trees were coated in mosses of every shade of green. Everything smelled familiar. I knew the birds from their songs. Then Joey kissed me and I felt that I was slipping out of my body and climbing high into the trees to watch from above. Everything I'd ever learned, everything I'd ever wanted, everything I'd ever resisted, seemed tiny and nameless. The way the sun dappled the maple leaves above where Joey lay me down in the cool moss, the blue sky filtering through, made me think of rocks in a clear stream. When he unbuttoned my shirt I thought of the straightness of the rows in Kat's vegetable garden. When he removed all my clothes and stood up to look at me lying in the moss, I remembered a dream I'd had in which I tried to put high-heeled shoes on over a pair of grey work socks. He touched me; his tongue between my legs, a surprise. I thought of oceans and mariners navigating by the stars at night. I felt peculiar, as though someone was pouring tea, the cup overflowing, while someone else practiced scales with my fingers on a violin. Then Joey yanked off his sweatshirt and undid his jeans. I put my mouth to his bare shoulder. When he kissed me again and I tasted myself for the first time, smell and taste got confused. Then he pulled me to sit on top of him and I watched as he shut his eyes and shuddered, calling my name three times. I didn't bleed and it didn't hurt. The air smelled like salmonberry bushes and deer trails and dandelion sap on my hands.

"My God, Lulu, you're a natural," Joey said finally, taking my hair in his hands and pulling me down to his warm body.

Joey and I found places to go for a month or so, including the double bed in his mother's Jesus-filled bedroom, his car, the tree fort, and a few other places in the woods. But then he decided he wanted to introduce me to his mother and I laughed.

"Like bringing your girlfriend home to meet Mum?"

He looked hurt. I didn't mention that long ago I'd spent an hour or two with Mrs. Tanner in the golden light of their scary living room.

"Yeah, like my girlfriend," he said. "Like you. Like the girl I'm sleeping with every day. My girlfriend."

I stopped seeing him.

●

I can't say exactly what Joey whetted my appetite for, but I can say that it wasn't to be part of some new domestic arrangement. For the better part of that fall and winter, and the next spring, I churned through my share of local boys, looking for the feeling that lying down with Joey had given me. I wasn't interested in any sweet-talk from the boys. That confused them; they knew from experience they weren't likely to get into most girls' pants without making some kind of promise—about love, about the future, about not coming inside of them. I never asked them for any of that.

What I was looking for was simple: when I lay down under them a parade of such pure and uncomplicated images would march through my head and take me far away. I saw a colourful stone I'd lost as a child. A flock of blackbirds flying straight toward me, then their shadows on the wall in the golden morning sun. Twin ruby cherries hanging on thin stems over the choke in a friend's pickup truck. My emerald.

A green frog skimming the ditch. Geordie's nose. A calf being born. The pat of butter melting on Dad's cream of wheat. Peeling arbutus bark. They were images without feeling, without anger or hollowness, sorrow or regret. No matter how fumbling or self-focused the boys were, the press of their warm bodies and the smell and taste of their sweat would send me off to a world in which everything was reduced to its most basic elements. I felt joy in that nothingness that I sought as fervently as the boys sought their climaxes.

And it took me away from a shadowy memory of the first hands to touch me that way. Mr. McFee's creeping hands in the car. Always in the car. Too long ago to be clearly remembered. But still coloured by shame.

●

Inevitably it became more complicated than that. The images became fleeting, wisps of morning dreams disappearing as quickly as snakes off warm rocks. I felt as desperate as an addict. Guilty. I figured there was something wrong with me. I wondered why I couldn't just be happy to have a boyfriend, to have nearly finished high school, to have a job at the SuperValu. Instead, that spring, I was drifting peevishly around Fraser Arm with my latest—TJ Thiessen—wondering if anything at all made any sense. I hadn't been thinking about such mundane things as my reputation.

One Sunday, in the midst of all this angst, I went with TJ to his basketball game on the court behind the new Boys and Girls Club. A bunch of boys had gathered already and as TJ joined them I realized with grim alarm that I'd slept with four of them. It was too late to sneak off without looking like a Tenpenny chicken so I watched from the grass as they negotiated positions, teams, and colours, hoping to hell that they hadn't been talking about me.

There weren't enough common-coloured t-shirts so it was shirts versus skins. I watched as a number of the boys stripped off in the cool air, pulling their t-shirts up by the neck. I was experienced enough to know that men remove their t-shirts that way, but there was something about it that sent a shiver through me, an addict's quick understanding of how different they were from me. Darcy Hughes—I'd slept with him— caught me looking and stretched his arms over his head, swiveling his hips and smiling. My face went red. Jonathan Enright—I'd slept with him—was taller than Darcy, lean and boxy, and very white with a pretty face. Chris Weiss—I'd slept with him—was smaller and soft all over, with a pudgy belly pouting over his pants. He was cute, freckled, with a few curly hairs sprouting between his pink nipples. Stick insect–thin Lanky Jay seemed to be sizing me up through the fence. I hadn't slept with him, thank God. He said, "I'm skin, but I'm wearing my shirt." I figured the boys would tell Jay to be shirt then, but there was no dissention. Everyone knew Jay was skin.

TJ caught my eye and slowly removed his jean shirt, a smile in his self-conscious eyes. I was trying to make myself concentrate just on TJ, but Darcy was strutting back and forth behind him. TJ caught me looking and turned and wrestled Darcy out of the way, their strong bodies grappling. Finally, Darcy grabbed TJ in a headlock and pulled him over, and then someone shouted and the game began. They were fast, and they were good. Hands slid along sweaty naked backs, bodies bounced off each other in the air, the boys fell and were offered hands up. Their hair was wet with sweat, their faces red. They had all perfected neat little jumps before they shot and I envied the happiness reflected in that precise, slow-motion leap.

I'd watched boys playing basketball at school countless times, but this time I was mesmerized, as if my knowledge of men's nakedness—in every sense—had transformed me. I knew I ought to feel embarrassed knowing that four of these boys had pressed their naked bodies against mine. I also knew that by some unwritten law, in their minds I'd now been claimed as TJ's, at least for the time being. He'd kissed me, touched his tongue to mine, and he'd slid into me, quickly, and was done in a minute—with no apologies. Just that, and I was his. I sat there plucking the petals off the tiny white daisies in the grass, one after another. I couldn't care less whether TJ loved me or loved me not.

I shouldn't have been surprised by the insistent horn honk—I'd told Mr. McFee where I was going. There he was, parked at the curb in his new Mustang. I tossed the pile of yellow daisy centres onto the grass and crossed the soccer field to his car.

"Lulu," he slurred.

"Shit, Aloysius, you're drunk."

"Lulu, you have the perspicacity of a crow. Can you drive, sweetheart?"

"Shove over," I said.

Aloysius lifted his knees to shift over to the passenger side and the car bucked forward. I jumped away from the door.

"Brake, clutch," I shouted. "Jesus. Take it out of gear."

"Sorry, Lulu. Sorry."

The inside of the car reeked like a gin factory.

"Jesus, Aloysius. Did you puke in here?"

"No, I did not. And when did you start calling me

Aloysius?" He put his hand on my arm and I shook it off. He was speaking and moving in slow motion.

"When you asked me to," I said. A week earlier, when I'd turned eighteen, Aloysius told me he'd decided I was old enough to stop calling him Mr. McFee, but I knew he'd probably never remember that when he was drunk.

I put the car in gear and gave a quick glance over at the basketball court, hoping that no one was watching me. I'd call TJ later. Tomorrow, maybe. The McFee house wasn't far from the Boys and Girls Club, but given Aloysius' state I couldn't believe he'd made it there without killing someone, or himself. When he leaned over and turned on the 8-track the booze smell on his breath made me gag.

"It's the *Barber of Seville*, Lulu." He spoke each consonant separately.

"Yeah. I know this. Rossini wrote it for Bugs Bunny, right?" I was being perverse. I knew he'd hate it if I put Rossini and Bugs Bunny in the same sentence. But he didn't say anything. He was too drunk. We'd listened to the whole opera several times, slouching on the couch in his front parlour. I could practically hum the whole thing, thanks to Aloysius.

"Don't ever go to war, Lulu."

That was out of the blue. "Why would I go to war, Aloysius? I'm a girl."

"It was the worst thing I've ever seen. Horrific." He shook his head slowly and swallowed painfully, like he might vomit. "Nobody comes home . . . nobody comes home the same."

We'd had this conversation many times before, but not recently. Aloysius claimed to have been in the Seaforth Highlanders during the Second World War, and at first I'd listened to his heartbreaking war stories with trusting ears.

I had no trouble picturing an eighteen-year-old Aloysius helping to gather the dead, or having to kill another boy just because he was Italian. But I'd long since figured out that Aloysius McFee was an incurable liar. For all I knew some real veteran at a Legion supper or a Wesleyville bar had told him those tales of soldiers losing their feet to rot and starving to death in Italy. He did have a kilt and a set of bagpipes I'd heard him play a few times when he was drunk. He didn't play particularly well, a fact he hated. He hated the McFee tartan too. He cried every time he heard someone else play the pipes. But truth or lies, for Aloysius, there was no glory in war.

"I wept, Lulu. The day the Seaforth Highlanders came home, a hundred thousand people were out to welcome us. I just wept. You can't imagine."

I could imagine something: Aloysius standing with the hundred thousand, dreaming up a story of being one of the Highlanders, and eventually believing his own lie. I pulled into his driveway and Aloysius wiped the tears off his cheeks with his handkerchief and got out of the car. He went up to the front door with the gingerly steps of a drunk who knows exactly how much too much he's had. Aloysius wasn't ever sloppy; it was as though his fully alert self was just a quarter of an inch below the surface and could be called upon when necessary. He always got the key in the hole on his first go.

"Come in, Ada. Come in. We'll have coffee."

"Um, I'm Lulu." He'd called me Ada before when he was drunk. I stood in the grass and swung the key ring around my pointer finger, hesitating for only a moment before I followed Aloysius inside.

We usually hung out in the front parlour or in the kitchen. Aloysius would put a record on the stereo and we'd listen to whatever he was in the mood for that day. Today it was Sonny Terry and Brownie McGhee, loud. Aloysius sank onto the couch.

"Listen. Just listen to this." He passed me the album cover and hummed along to the first cut, "People Get Ready." "He's blind, you know."

"Which one?"

"Sonny Terry."

Eyes closed, head back, he patted the couch cushion. I gave in and sat beside him and he took my hand and held it tight. I didn't try to pull it away. He'd set up the pair of giant speakers so that they faced the parlour couch. We were being blasted by the blues. I examined his profile. He'd aged. At fifty-two he was only three years older than Dad but he looked older and much wearier. I felt a little thump of affection for him, looking at his worn face. I'd been tangled up with Aloysius McFee for a long time.

After the first song he sat up and said, "Turn it down, Lulu. I have something important to tell you." His speech was clearer now. He took his cigarettes from his shirt pocket, lit one and passed it to me and then lit one for himself. "Pass me that," he said, pointing at the Kleenex box beneath his stereo, which was where he stashed his drugs.

"I'm not sure why I should be the one to get up," I said, but I did it anyway.

"And turn that damn thing down," he said curtly, as if it was me who had turned the stereo to blasting in the first place.

Aloysius pulled out ten or so tissues and smoothed them neatly on the couch between us. Then he poked around in the box and pulled out a small bag of cocaine.

"Yeah?" he asked.

I nodded.

"I think we should put this long chapter behind us, Lulu." He laid four lines of coke on the album cover and snorted two of them. He passed me the rolled-up twenty and I snorted my lines.

"Which chapter would that be, Aloysius?" I ran through the number of things it could have been: the stealing, the smoking, the drinking, the drugs?

"All of it. I'm thinking this is the end. I don't want to corrupt you."

We both laughed like hyenas over that.

"Too late."

"Remember that house in Coquitlam with the dogs?" he asked.

"The one that said guard dog on duty and you said it was just one of those signs people put up to keep the riffraff out?"

"And you said Rottweilers are as gentle as lambs." Aloysius was laughing hysterically.

"They usually are. I can still see you high jumping that fence."

"Didn't know old Mr. McFee had it in 'im, did you?" He laughed, then he sighed. "I'm serious, Lulu. You're eighteen now and that's serious."

"What do you mean serious?" I laughed. "You mean I could go to jail now and not just juvenile detention?"

"Well, that. Yes. I wasn't really thinking about you. Mainly, I'm thinking of packing it in."

"What do you mean by packing it in?" I felt a wash of sadness roll into the room.

"Just stopping."

We sat without speaking for a while, listening to the music.

"But I wouldn't want you to go to jail," he said. An after-thought, obviously.

"You're the perp, Aloysius. I wouldn't."

"Well, you're the abettor."

"Innocent old me? Who'd believe that?" I leaned back on the couch and closed my eyes. "What happened to your wife, Aloysius?"

"What happened to your mother?"

"I don't think Mrs. McFee is ever coming back."

"Well, your mother certainly isn't."

I sat up. "How do you know that? You think she's dead?"

"Well . . . Yes. I don't think your mother would go away for that long unless something had happened to her. Maybe they were killed by the same person. Or maybe they ran away. Maybe they ran away together."

"I can't imagine that. Mum didn't know Mrs. McFee well, did she?"

Aloysius scanned my face then lay back and looked up at the ceiling, ignoring my question. "She was crazy, Lulu."

"Mum or your wife?"

He didn't say which. He just sat up and tucked the Kleenexes back in the box. "Even if we stop working together, you won't ever leave me, will you, Lulu?"

Working. Ha. But would I leave him? I thought about it. Weirdly, I couldn't imagine life without him. I didn't answer him, though.

"You're my girl, Lulu. You're my girl," he said and patted my hand, as if I'd given him the answer he needed to hear.

DORIS

Silent spring.

Not so silent spring. For twenty-seven minutes Doris has been imagining opening the door of her bedroom, walking down the hallway in her pyjamas, taking three steps down the stairs so that her feet can be seen from the front hall—where they are arguing—and saying *shhh*. That is all she would need say. It is such a smooth, green sound, *shhh*. Doris imagines the letters coming out of her mouth; she can almost feel them slithering between her teeth. Wouldn't Father and Joan be shocked out of their states of inter-intransigence? She considers another less practical but more possible option: she could fold her *shhh* into a paper airplane and fly it down the stairs.

Doris doesn't at all want spring to be silent. But she would like Father and Joan to be silent so that she can hear spring. There. The front door has slammed, which means

Joan has gone out and it will be quiet now, if Father does not find someone at whom he may fume about Joan. He will not find Mother; she has gone to bed expressly so that he may not fume at her. The boys know to avoid him now. All the doors are closed against him, though he has been known to fume aloud to himself some days. Doris thinks the increase in Father's fuming is to blame for the change in Mother's colour. She is almost pith white now. If Father comes into the kitchen when only Doris and Mother are there, he leaves with a sniff of vexation, as if she and Mother, just sitting at the kitchen table, were surely sent by the Lord to try his patience. Doris suspects her father actually enjoys having his patience tried. Father prefers fighting with Joan to not fighting with Doris or Mother.

The white-crowned sparrows. That's who she's listening for. The *Birds of North America* book says they sing at night. Doris went to the new public library to look at the bird book. In truth, Doris went to the new public library to look at the library and saw the big bird book on display. Doris would have liked to go to the Bookmobile, before it stopped coming, but Father forbade them to set foot on the bus. It was not just the preponderance of immoral books on the bus, Father said, but the woman who drove the Bookmobile was ungodly. When she saw the Bookmobile lady behind the front desk at the new public library, Doris wondered what Father meant by ungodly. She said her name was Raylene Dubé and she made Doris a library card without asking for any identification or expecting her to speak.

In the post-Joan silence, Doris lies back on her bed, her arms at her sides. She must close her eyes to open her ears. The frogs are noisy tonight, too. But there is that bird. *It is lovely*. If she could be any animal she would be a bird, though perhaps not the white-crowned sparrow. A crow, perhaps. If she could be any *person* other than herself, Doris thinks she would be Rachel Carson, the author of *Silent Spring*. Doris is as worried about the birds as Rachel Carson was. After Lewis Cray brought her a copy of the book, Doris' reply note began with a question: why did you wait so many years to give me this book? She even added an exclamation mark. Doris liked science class. Lewis Cray should know that. *Silent Spring* was published in 1962, the year Lewis Cray brought Doris their first book. When Doris was nineteen. Doris is nearly thirty-two now.

Doris concentrates hard on the white-crowned sparrow's song but there are other noises she cannot drown out: car tires on the wet road—*Where does Joan go in the rain?*—the ping-ping of the bell ropes at the gas station, young people talking in the 7-Eleven parking lot. Its buzzing neon sign. Doris has spent many weeks trying to decide whether all the new streetlights really do make a sound or whether her annoyance with them makes her imagine they do. Doris misses the dark and the silence. Never mind, she thinks. Never mind. She must honour the white-crowned sparrow by listening, and pray it won't be killed by pesticides.

LULU

Bringing anyone home was always chancy, so I rarely did. It wasn't just the rubble of a house I was embarrassed by, it was the equally mortifying rubble of its inhabitants. Either my father would ask the poor soul's opinion of the trade union movement—the support of which he considered nearly the only indication of a person's mettle, even though his dry cleaning delivery job wasn't unionized—or if Trevor was home, she'd have to deal with him checking her out. And then there was gorgeous Geordie. In his case it was a two-way worry. I'd have my hackles ready for the jerk who disrespected him, but I had to be ready to drag him away from anyone with long hair, which he took every opportunity to stroke lovingly. Alan and Ambrose had moved out. Alan had married Naomi and all three of them were living on a farm in Langley, though Dad was constantly—and happily,

I think—setting a few extra places at the table because they came home to Forward Road half the time.

I'd been to Janet Smallwood's place a few times since she quit the church and started smoking dope. She'd finally got up the gumption to ask me why I'd never invited her to my house. Apart from the obvious—the mud, the trucks, the dog—I couldn't think of any excuse to keep her out forever. Janet's hair was short, thank God. But I had forgotten about Aunt Kat's zeal for the company of strangers.

"Do you take sugar in your tea, Janet?" Kat asked while we were still on the porch.

I swear, Janet's foot stopped, poised over the threshold.

I'd picked up another package wrapped in brown butcher paper and tied with kitchen string on that very doorstep that morning. I didn't know who, but someone had been leaving library books on the porch, addressed to me, for months. Each one had a typed note saying "Please return to library." This morning's was *Silent Spring*.

"I'm not sure. I've never drunk tea before," Janet said, looking around the kitchen.

The look in Janet's eyes said she'd never seen anything like it in Fraser Arm, and I knew there wasn't. Everyone else's kitchens were plain and white—white refrigerators, white stoves, pale linoleum, silver-speckled arborite countertops, a cookie jar, a clock on the wall, and a knick-knack here or there. Nothing like ours. About six months after she arrived, Aunt Kat had started decorating, starting with the kitchen. She'd tsk-tsked Dad's lame protests and turned every wall and sur-face into a trinket repository—knick-knacks, paddywhacks, give a dog a bone—a kitsch collector's delight. In the eight years she'd been with us she'd been able to do a lot of damage. She alone kept the junk shop on Reifel Road in business.

Janet ran her finger along the backs of a pair of greasy porcelain salt and pepper wiener dogs and nodded at another set, white and black pugs. "It's cute."

Kat looked pleased. I groaned inside, because this was only the beginning. My aunt proudly drew aside the velvet curtain that divided the kitchen from what used to be the twins' bedroom but was now her parlour. Kat ushered us in and proceeded to turn on the many dim lamps perched on small tables, then she sat on the low burgundy velvet couch she'd found at the Salvation Army Thrift Store and patted the cushion beside her.

"Sit, sit, Janet. Lulu doesn't bring friends home very often." Janet sat beside her, sinking down and then falling backwards into the low cushions.

Kat held out one of her skinny hands to pull Janet up. "Silly girls. Now, tea."

She left us in the still room and we burst into stifled laughter, mine nervous. Janet prowled around. She sniffed the little bowls of potpourri and flipped the fat tassels on the homemade curtains. She picked up a crocheted antimacassar from the back of a plush chair.

"Weird," she whispered.

"Really weird." I agreed.

"Yours?" She picked up my fiddle and plucked the ukulele song we'd all learned at school, four simple notes: *My Dog Has Fleas.* "Who lives here?"

"We all do."

"Play us a tune, Lulu. Play that one you're working on," Kat called from the kitchen.

"I mean, who's allowed here? Does she let your brothers in? I can't imagine them in here. Sipping tea." Janet put on a stagey English accent, her pinky finger sticking out.

My face flushed thinking of Geordie stretched out on the couch. He was the only Parsons boy—other than Dad, of course—Kat allowed in the parlour, which was certainly a special dispensation given that Geordie was prone to spilling things and wiping his nose on the curtains. Janet pulled back the drapes. The glass in the big, plain window was streaked with rain. Outside, Jed was madly barking at some boys riding by on bikes. At twelve, you'd figure the degree of Jed's fury at boys on bicycles would have abated, but no. The trucks Dad and my brothers drove left long, snarly ruts on what might have been a front lawn, so, apart from a miniscule patch of grass below the window and a few flowers that Kat tended as though her life depended on it, everywhere else was thistle, weed, and mud. Why Dad didn't just give up and tether the goats out front was beyond me.

Janet raised her eyebrows at me. She had pulled the floor-length curtain all the way back and revealed the room in all its desperation. The nail-studded gyproc wall below and around the window was waiting as always to be finished, waiting since before I was born, in fact. No reason to spend a lot of money on the finishing details if you're going to cover it up with a curtain, Dad had told Kat, and however desperate Kat was to make it all nice, her secretary job at the welfare office wasn't about to pay for any major renovations.

"Good reason to keep the curtains closed," Janet said, pulling them back across the window.

I felt a confused wave of defensiveness rising as the motes disappeared with the sunlight. The Smallwoods now lived in one of the new subdivisions in Fraser Arm, a two-storey with a bright green, pesticide-induced lawn and a tightly edged black asphalt driveway bordered by uniform beds of orange marigolds. There were a dozen identical houses on either side of them and across the street. The subdivisions were attracting a different sort of person to Fraser Arm, better off, mostly. Or changing the lives of some, like the Smallwoods, who were selling their big rural lots to developers and moving into these homogeneous homes.

"Why doesn't your father finish it?" Janet asked.

I shrugged. Dad didn't see class jumping as an enviable thing but I was annoyed by how much I liked the tidy simplicity of the Smallwoods' house. No thistles, not even in the ditch, which Janet's dad, the police chief, mowed every week. The Smallwoods were probably the richest people in Fraser Arm—which wasn't saying much; they just had real jobs and only two kids. They parked their two big identical sedans in a drive-in garage. They had white shag rugs upstairs and down, and a big colour television that was in the recreation room, not, like ours, in the living room. Mrs. Smallwood made the beds so tightly that for a long time I thought she changed the sheets every day because our beds had never looked like that, except for maybe on wash day, and not since Mum had disappeared.

Kat came back with one of our metal TV-table trays, the ones with the paintings of King George V looking like a poodle. She'd hauled out the good stuff—the fancy teapot, dainty teacups, and the chocolate-iced digestive biscuits reserved for visitors.

"Shall I pour? The violets cup for you, Janet, and the gold and burgundy for Lulu," she said, beaming at our guest. She held out the sugar bowl to Janet, who plopped two white cubes and then a third into her cup with a pair of silver tongs.

"Thank you, Mrs. Parsons."

"Oh, it's Miss Fenwick, Janet. My sister is Mrs. Parsons."

Aunt Kat never said "was" about Mum. She filled her own cup then sank back on the couch with a sigh. Even when she was relaxed, her jaw and the tendons in her neck were tight. Slowly, her hand came up and she pulled lazily on a curl. I looked at her lean face, trying to remember my mother's in the powder and pink lipstick. I was reminding myself to never bring anyone home again when Trevor stuck his head in through the curtain. Kat jumped. It was one of the marked disadvantages of a doorless parlour—no one could knock.

"Sorry to interrupt, Aunt Kat. Lulu." Trevor looked Janet up and down. "Hey, Janet," he said.

Janet smiled flirtatiously at him, which made me doubly regret bringing her home. But Trevor didn't respond. He looked stoned and manic, which was the signal for my own anxiety to put its finger on the trigger.

"Dad'll be home in a minute, right? I made something. Come and see. I called Alan and Ambrose. They're coming too."

Tea time was sacred for Aunt Kat, but she recovered her composure. "Of course, Trevor. We'll come. What is it?"

He'd timed it perfectly: Dad and Geordie were just pulling up outside in the delivery van and the happy Langley three-some—Alan, Naomi, and Ambrose—pulled into the driveway from the opposite direction in Ambrose's old pickup.

"Hey," Trevor said to everyone. He wasn't looking anyone in the eye, and that made my heart thump again with dread. He even unhooked grey old Jed from his chain and then led us all around to the back of the house. There, just on this side of the fence at the edge of the pasture, was a freshly turned patch of earth about a foot square, filled with wilting flowers transplanted from God knows where. Stuck in the middle of the dirt patch was a handmade wooden cross about three feet tall. Trevor's eyes were steel and his mouth was set in a grim line. He jerked his chin toward the thing. On the cross bar he'd written *Elisabeth Margaret Fenwick Parsons* and, below that, *February 10, 1931 – November 11, 1967.* Running down the stem were the words *Bette, Mum.*

"Now we can all just move on," he said.

Dad looked like someone had stabbed a shiv in his back. Aunt Kat started crying and the rest of us stood there speechless.

Finally, I turned to Janet and said, "You can go," and she did.

I heard Jed whine, probably aching for those crossed sticks to chew on. A dozen thoughts flashed through my head, including that the cross stood exactly where I'd buried my hamster. I took one long look at Trevor and my foot flew up and I kicked at the cross until it came out of its mooring. Then I stomped on the flowers. No one moved while I destroyed Trevor's ridiculous headstone. Not even Geordie. Jed snatched up the cross and loped off across the yard where he lay down to gnaw on it. No one would get near it now.

"Sorry," I said.

Trevor's smile cut me like a saw blade.

"She's dead, Lulu." He looked over at Dad and his eyes were imploring. "Dad?" he said, then he fell to his knees, weeping.

Dad knelt down beside Trevor and wrapped his arms around him. He put his own greying head in the crook of Trevor's neck and sobbed. Seeing Dad on his knees finished the job Trevor's smile had started. I was gutted. I ran. I don't know what everyone else did after that, but when I came home from Aloysius' in the wee hours of the morning, stoned and manic myself, all the souls I'd offended were gone or asleep.

DORIS

Bette Parsons is dead.

Doris Tenpenny was among the likely two hundred people down at the Smallwoods' house on Sunday. A huge gathering because people like Wally Parsons. And people like to show their respect, even if Bette Parsons is only 99.999 percent likely long dead. *And nearly forgotten.* It has been almost eight years, after all. They say that Wally Parsons will have to go to court to have her declared legally dead. Some say that it is about time. Some say he should have done that before he had her memorial. And some people are saying that Wally Parsons must have someone waiting in the wings, because otherwise . . . though no one knows who. Doris hasn't heard anything. Nothing credible anyway. Melvina Mitchell says that it's the devil's concubine, whoever that might be. When Melvina Mitchell told Doris that, Doris thought, Melvina Mitchell can go to Hell. Wally Parsons has always been nice to everyone; that's why even Doris went to the memorial service.

They didn't have it in a church. They had it in Roy and Ruth Smallwood's new backyard. They couldn't have had it at the Parsons' because their yard is always full of either trucks or goats or cows and there wouldn't have been a spot to set up the tables of food, and people would have been in a quandary as to whether to wear their good shoes or their gumboots if they were going to have to walk around in the muck. Doris wasn't in a quandary—she almost always wears her gumboots. Father and Mother and Mike went too. Father said it wouldn't be seemly if they didn't, and it wasn't as if it were a private event. The newspaper notice said it was open to everyone who wanted to celebrate the too-short life of Elisabeth Margaret Parsons, which made everyone think that maybe Bette Parsons' body had been found. It hasn't.

Doris' father had his share of critical things to say when they got home—including that if they were planning a *picnic* they should have billed it as such and that a funeral like that was a travesty and mocked the dead—but, Doris noticed, he shook a lot of hands there, trying to multiply his decreasing flock. And Doris liked watching the Ogg girls running after the giggling swells of May Ogg's grandchildren, and seeing the Parsons boys, all men now, and Charlotte Puttkammer's and Doretta Fyshe's devilled eggs—Tenpenny eggs—going like hotcakes. Everyone loves a devilled egg, except, perhaps, Melvina Mitchell, who disapproves of anything devilish. Doris had been thinking about all of it as she watched Wally Parsons step forward and make a very short speech about Bette. His "beloved wife," he'd called her. He'd looked shy. No one cried, although Lulu looked a little sour standing along-side the Thiessen boy. And, from under the trembling aspen tree where Doris had positioned herself, it looked as though May Ogg's mascara had run. Afterward, everyone stood talking and laughing—*why not?*—in their fine clothes, and Doris thought it was a fitting farewell party for Bette Parsons.

Today, Doris is in the moveable greenhouse amongst the green beans, which are early and resplendent this year. Why *not* use a word like resplendent to describe a bean? She has hardly moved her stool from where she first set it down and she has already picked nearly half a bushel. She will sell them at the stand. And whatever is not taken, Mother will give to the families at the church who can't afford beans. She takes a bite of the one she has been holding in her hand. She feels the slight roughness of its skin on her tongue, hears the crisp sound of it between her teeth. She squints closely at the bitten end of the bean—*are her eyes getting worse?*—at the smooth little bean seed inside, the different greens of each bean layer, the way her teeth marks look like darker green bruises.

A car horn startles her. Mr. McFee is at the egg stand, and behind him, his new car, a coppery-gold Ford Mustang. He's leaning, as casually as a man can, against the stand, as if he were not a murderer and a molester of women and girls. And there is the screen door squawking open and Doris' mother coming down the side stairs, smoothing her apron. Six years ago he'd leaned up against the stand in the same way he is now, and said, "Have you burnt any peanut butter cookies lately, Doris?" Doris wrote Mother a note that night. It said: I do not like Aloysius McFee. I will no longer serve him. Mother looked at Doris more carefully than usually, folded the note six times, placed it deep in the garbage can where it would not resurface, and put her apron on.

Doris pops the rest of the bean in her mouth with satisfaction, just like Melvina Mitchell furtively did three devilled eggs while Wally Parsons gave his speech.

LULU

I was at work at the SuperValu and there was Mrs. Ogg
pushing a grocery buggy with nothing in it yet, coming
toward me. Seeing her, I suddenly had a memory: It was the
first day of school—it would have been 1963—my mother
and I walked down through our pasture, avoiding the cow
patties and our big black bull, Taurus, whose feral eyes I met
frequently in my dreams. Ducking low under the fence's electrified wire, we climbed between the second and third strings
of barbed wire—something we were both skilled at—without
catching our sweaters. Then we walked hand in hand along
Willow, safely past the mean dogs, to the edge of Raven
Ravine. There was a narrow trail along the top of the ravine.
We walked in single file and in silence, my mother ahead.
It smelled of ferns and salmonberries and fallen cedar and
something prehistoric as well. The ravine trail opened onto
the far end of Fraser Arm Elementary's soccer field which,

though still green on that September morning, was no longer particularly lush, and showed signs of summer's feet—boys and soccer balls and parents on the sidelines, stamping—and of a dry spell.

Mum had insisted that I wear a dress that morning. I don't think she really meant it. She probably just didn't want to be thought of as less of a parent by all the other school-yard mothers, or for me to be less well-turned-out than the girls in their fancy first-day-of-school dresses. The outfit she made me wear was an odd little jumper she'd made out of brown wide-wale corduroy, buying the cloth and a pattern at Woodward's and borrowing Mrs. Ogg's sewing machine. She hated sewing; when I put the jumper on, I thought of it as stitched with curses. She wanted me to wear a white blouse under it—the one she'd bought at Woodward's after she decided that making one would be too difficult—but I chose a greying black turtleneck instead, Trevor's hand-me-down. She hung the blouse back up in my closet where it gathered dust long after she'd gone. She didn't comment on my running shoes.

That first day of school, I caught sight of Mrs. Ogg in the schoolyard. She was surrounded by a bunch of neighbour-hood mothers. There was something about Mrs. Ogg that made us all want to be near her. Mum had said something about it being important for a mother to walk her daughter to school on the first day, but even I'd wanted to walk with Mrs. Ogg and Nadine. Mrs. Ogg saw us and waved, and Nadine ran over. I remembered her dress, a pale yellow A-line with a yellow polka-dot blouse, and patent leather shoes. All I could think was how she wouldn't be jumping ditches with me on the way home in that outfit.

"Don't ever take the ravine route by yourself," my mother said. She bent and kissed me, flicked one of Nadine's pigtails up with her finger, and then she was gone, her pale lipstick trace sticky on my cheek. I watched her walk back toward the ravine. She turned once to wave, lit a cigarette, then pulled her sweater tight around her. I felt a hand on my shoulder and Mrs. Ogg was standing beside me, following my mother's movement along the trail. When she looked down at me, she had not quite banished the worry from her eyes.

Twelve years later, there were Mrs. Ogg's worried eyes in the SuperValu, reminding me of that day. Nadine and I had drifted apart after elementary school. She was more social than me and running with a sporty crowd by the time we were in grade eight. I was hanging, as surreptitiously as possible, with Aloysius McFee. By grade nine our streams had deposited us on opposite banks. I rarely saw any of the Ogg sisters anymore. The older ones had married and Mrs. Ogg was a grandmother several times over.

"Guess you're surprised to see me here, eh, Lulu?" Mrs. Ogg said.

I was. Mrs. Ogg always grocery shopped in Wesleyville at the mall where she worked. This was Geordie's supermarket, as we liked to call it. And my supermarket too. I had a job behind the bakery counter, which mostly consisted of squeezing the pink or blue or yellow rosebuds of chemical-flavoured icing onto birthday cakes and writing the squirrely messages people wanted on them. I was granted this honour because of my steady hand, apparently, although I think it was more because the boss' son had some high hopes about me than how great my *Happy Birthday Sweetpea* looked on the ghastly cakes.

Mrs. Ogg told me that Nadine was getting married because there was another grandchild on the way, and, as an afterthought, that Mr. Paris—our fickle cat who'd adopted the Oggs—was fine, even though he was going on twenty-one. But I still wasn't sure what she was doing looking so sad in our supermarket. I was just thinking how all of it was very un-Mrs.Ogg-ish. Her dark eyes looked across the éclairs at me and she said, "You look so much like Bette," and she had the exact same worried expression on her face as she had that day twelve years earlier in the schoolyard.

Everything about Mrs. Ogg's visit left me shaky. I realized that even though Mum was my own flesh and blood, Mrs. Ogg probably knew more about her than I did. When my shift was over, I walked down Cappon Road toward the bog. Memories of my mother kept surfacing until I felt I was going to be washed out to sea to drown. I remembered squeezing into the old upholstered armchair beside her to watch *The Wizard of Oz*, her hand clutching mine during the flying monkey scene. I could feel the strength of her skinny arm flinging out and whapping me in the chest to stop me from going through the windshield whenever she braked for a forgotten stop sign, and the way she laughed nervously afterwards. I swear I could see her standing on the stoop, hanging laundry and crying after that great horned owl flew off with the Oggs' orange kitten.

I walked to the edge of the bog, wishing Dad hadn't decided to revive everything by having the memorial for Mum, then turned back and found myself knocking on Raylene's door. By that time, Raylene Dubé was living with her girlfriend, Birdie Feather—obviously not her birth name—in a silver Airstream in *Snyder's Dun Roamin?* trailer park. That question mark in the name had met a whole lot of commentary, but Mrs. Snyder insisted that she wanted to keep her options open. She didn't look like the kind of woman who might just pick up one day and leave her husband, Alf, surprised, but who knows what that kind of woman looks like anyway.

"Raylene's down at the burning barrel, darlin'," Mrs. Snyder shouted out the window of her double-wide.

Then there was Raylene coming around the corner, toting her empty garbage pail and a big handful of daisies. Birdie was out, thank God, probably at some "wimmin's" group howl. I definitely wasn't in the mood for a feminist re-education of any sort. I hadn't developed much affection for Birdie, and it had taken me some time to get over the fact that she and Raylene were an item. Raylene and I had become the kind of friends that calamity brings together, at least from my point of view, long before Birdie had flown in. Why Raylene became friends with *me* was probably a little more complicated; once I met her, I just never let go. Every time the Bookmobile came to town, I was first in line. At eleven, I figured Raylene was the first adult who'd ever told me the outright truth, and I'd clung to that fact like a dog would its bone. She drove the Bookmobile for eight more years after my mother disappeared, until the new library was built down by the high school and the township "took away her wheels," as Raylene liked to say. She got a job behind the circulation desk in the big new building where she said she felt like a marble in a bowling alley after so many years in the Bookmobile.

"What brings Miss Lulu here?" My face must have been doing some talking, as usual, because she gave me a once-over and said, "Uh-oh. Come on in, girlie."

Half of what I loved about Raylene was the Airstream—all twenty-two feet of it. There was a double bed that sighed when you sat on it, where she and Birdie slept, a kitchen with perfect miniature appliances, and a snug sitting room all done in 1970s modern. Pretty well every spare space on the walls was devoted to books. "Don't think I stole them," Raylene said the first time I went to her trailer. She might as well have; the whole place looked like the Bookmobile.

"Speak," she said. At eighteen, I was still her dog, and she my best bone. But evasion was one of my better-honed tendencies.

"Oh, I just thought I'd come over and say hello."

"Speak, Lulu." She had her hands on her hips, still clutching the daisies, and her look, as always, said, Don't you lie to me, girl. You'd think I'd have chosen someone sweeter to offer succour to a motherless child.

"I feel like I'm imagining things."

"What do you mean, imagining things?"

"Not imagining things, really. Remembering things that I couldn't possibly remember."

"Like what?" She pointed at the low orange couch. I sat, obediently. I could have used a good hug, but never, not in all the years I'd known her, had Raylene hugged me or even draped an arm across my shoulder.

"I remembered my mother on my first day of school."

"And?"

"Why would I remember that? I was only six. I remember what I wore. What Nadine wore."

"Christ, Lulu. It was a special day. We always remember special days like that."

"Do *you?*" I asked, suddenly curious about Raylene's

beginnings and trying to picture her in a skirt. "Remember, I mean?"

"As a matter of fact, I do. It was the worst day of my life and I don't want to talk about it, all right?" She jammed the daisies into a vase and held it up. "How's this look?"

Raylene was always picking bouquets for Birdie, but she needed a flower-arranging course. I stood up and traded places with her, holding out my hand for the scissors. I told her about what I'd remembered on my walk.

"So, what'd it make you think, all this remembering?"

"That she was sad." Raylene gave me her "go on" look. I felt embarrassed. Suddenly there it was, hitting me on my dull head like the proverbial hammer. "And that she was probably depressed. Why's it so important to me to know whether she loved me?"

"Lulubelle, everyone wants to be loved, 'specially by their mother."

"How could she have left us?"

"Well . . ." I could tell she was hedging. No one wanted to be put in the position of saying she didn't run off, because the alternative was that she was a murdered, hollowed-out skeleton lying somewhere beneath the dirt. "How many *dads* do you think have run off and left their kids? Seems like every third kid these days' got a runaway dad. No one raises much of a fuss. But when a mom runs off, well, everyone thinks its way worse, that she must have made a pact with the devil or something. And you never know what drove them off anyways."

"She had five kids. That's extreme."

Raylene gave me one of the few looks she had that didn't say, Just pull up your bloody socks. She'd had it that day in the Bookmobile and I'd only seen it a few times since. Otherwise, Raylene was pretty hard line.

"Anyways," she said, "you don't know what happened."

"Yes, I do." I knew. She wasn't murdered. She wasn't lying in a chilly grave somewhere. She'd left us. It was as close as I'd ever come to telling anyone that I knew the truth. Then the door flung open and Birdie flew in. I watched a shy smile flicker across Raylene's face as Birdie kissed her.

"Oh. Flowers, for me?" She kissed Raylene again and then looked at us both. "Uh-oh. What's up, girls? Why so serious?"

"Lulu's remembering some things about her mom."

I made a face at Raylene. She was pretty good at ignoring privacy when it came to mine, especially around Birdie. Birdie's face crumpled into a sad Raggedy Ann–doll frown. She tilted her head and put her hands on my shoulders.

"Honey," she whinnied.

She tried to hug me, but I sat down instead. I hated the way Birdie's arrival in Raylene's life had changed everything. She'd turned Raylene's straight-rowed vegetable garden into a tangled jungle. She considered every weed her friend and told us a million times a day how every one of them had some reason for their presence on Earth. She wouldn't let Raylene mow their tiny bit of lawn and screamed out in mock pain when Mrs. Snyder pushed her gas-powered mower over to what she called the offending side of the lane. Birdie planted the cabbages in a spiral, and she wrote her name in leeks and Raylene's in green onions. She had offered to plant my name too, but I told her the vegetable I wanted was zucchini. "That's just like you," she'd said, "so wild and free."

The worst part of it all was that Raylene didn't seem to

be particularly bothered by any of it. Birdie'd pretty much converted Raylene to vegetarianism along with all the other isms she was practicing—feminism, Buddhism, animism, quietism, empiricism, pantheism to name a few she blathered on about. She accused me of cynicism. That was after I snorted orange pop out of my nose because she told me that the Goddess was in the green beans we were eating. She was serious. God was in everything, she said, and she'd do everything she could to surround herself with God's beauty.

"Forget it," I said, grabbing my bag and heading for the door. I'd get more sympathy from Aloysius. Birdie stretched her arms out toward me, probably trying to catch me in her "positive energy net." She'd be performing some kind of cleansing incantation with patchouli incense in the Airstream after I left, for sure. Raylene followed me out the door.

"Wait," she said. She went back in the trailer. I waited. The stars were out, hanging in the sky like some kind of promise I could never hope to benefit from. At eighteen, I felt betrayed by everything, even the stars. Raylene's porch light flicked off and the door squeaked open. We stood there in the dark.

"You know you're not alone, Lulu."

I could see Birdie peering blindly out at us, her hands cupped around her face against the window. "As far as I can see, I am the only one here going home alone," I said.

Raylene handed me a book and said nothing more. I took it and ran out of the trailer park. At the next streetlight I stopped to look at its cover. *Surfacing*. "Jesus," I shouted and flung it into the bushes. I'd read it. Someone had already left it for me at the kitchen door.

DORIS

May Ogg. No one has prettier, darker, more mysterious eyes than May Ogg, and few people have an odder name. In fact, *Mr.* Ogg has the strangest name. It's not at all Mrs. Ogg's fault that she has one too; she only married him and had to take his name. Doris might not have married Mr. Ogg—not that she is the marrying kind—because then she would be Mrs. D. Ogg. She laughs. Mr. Ogg is Osbert. Osbert Ogg. That hardly seems fair. Doris imagines Mr. and Mrs. Ogg Sr. looking down on their little baby Ogg and deciding that he is an Osbert. Having a name like that makes one unforgettable, true, but how do parents know their child wants to grow up unforgettable? And the initials. OO. What if his middle name was Xavier? OXO. Or he was an Anthony George? A.G. Ogg. Doris laughs out loud at that.

Doris is not prone to laughing, but these days she has begun to laugh, sometimes, once in a while, now and then.

Lewis Cray has been giving her funny books. "To tickle your funny bone; you do have a funny bone, Doris?" Doris thinks she must develop one, though she worries that it might be genetically impossible. Mother and Father don't laugh. But her brother Mike does. Last week she conducted an experiment: she waited in the kitchen for Mother, she thought of the scene in Lewis Cray's latest book, *Excellent Women*, and she laughed. Mother smiled at her, a worried smile, and turned her back on Doris with her apron strings hanging low. In truth, Doris had tried it on the hens first. They liked it. Or they did not like it. It is hard to tell with hens. Indifferent maybe.

Mrs. Ogg is at the egg and vegetable stand. Most people buy their eggs now at the SuperValu where they are cheaper. Thin-shelled and blue-white, but cheaper. Mrs. Ogg still comes to the stand though she buys her eggs irregularly. Why that would be, Doris can't understand; she believes that every-thing should be done with some degree of regularity. Mrs. Ogg has been standing for a long time at the stand, blinking her beautiful eyes and staring out across the pasture, as if the answer to her worries might be resting like noisy blue jays in the pear trees out back. Doris doesn't mind that. She likes to just let people think. She never hurries anyone, except the people she doesn't like much. These days those people are amounting to a higher hill of beans than they used to.

Mrs. Ogg is standing there, and then, "What do you think, Doris?" she says.

Since these are the first words May Ogg has spoken, Doris cannot begin to imagine what it is she should be thinking about. It is possible that Mrs. Ogg is going through the change of life. They say that women are often forgetful then. Come to think of it, Mrs. Ogg's colour seems a little bit off.

Mrs. Ogg has always been a dusty purple, but she's a slightly paler purple-grey these days. Perhaps, Doris thinks, Mrs. Ogg is having one of those mid-life crises people talk about. Doris feels some apprehension because no one has told her that this can happen to women too. Doretta Fyshe said that Mr. Fyshe bought a 1972 Corvette Stingray with front and rear chrome bumpers and managed to run off with a woman half his age— for three weeks—during his mid-life crisis. Doris steals a quick look at Mrs. Ogg's car; it is still the blue Chevrolet Belair station wagon she's had for ten years.

Mrs. Ogg's sorrowfulness has bruised her eyes. If it isn't the mid-life crisis or the change of life, then something awful must be making Mrs. Ogg so sad.

"Do you ever think of Bette Parsons?" May Ogg has turned her eyes on Doris.

Doris does think of Bette Parsons. She has never stopped thinking about Bette Parsons. It isn't just the memorial last week; it is also that Doris can see the McFee house—or at least the lights burning at night behind the trees—from her bedroom window. That Bette Parsons disappeared the same day as Alice McFee still makes Doris suspect Mr. McFee of murder most foul. And now that Lulu Parsons is the spitting image of her mother—right down to her dark expression—everyone in Fraser Arm must be thinking about Bette Parsons. So Doris nods.

"I can't believe that Bette is dead," Mrs. Ogg says. "Bette and I, we had coffee nearly every morning for twenty years. You'd think I'd know if she was dead."

Doris wonders what about having coffee would make a person think she knew God's truth. But Doris is learning that illogic is sometimes the only salvation people have.

"I think she ran off. I think she simply got fed up. Or tired. Lord, she was tired," May Ogg says. She is running her fingers over the trays of eggs, and the eggs are following her, sliding sideways in their cardboard pockets. Doris will have to straighten them later. May Ogg suddenly looks like she's on fire.

"Do you know Doris, I bet you there's not a mother on this earth that hasn't some time or another wished she *hadn't* lain down with her man just when her egg was ripe." May Ogg looks for a moment like she might be embarrassed for having said such a truthful, irreverent thing, but then she looks Doris right in the eye with a defiance that makes Doris Tenpenny feel like looking for blue jays in the pear trees too.

May Ogg leaves without buying eggs. As she drives away in the Belair it occurs to Doris that May Ogg knows something about Bette Parsons, something that would have made her run off. And then Doris thinks, with a huff of gladness, that this is *exactly* what May Ogg is saying.

LULU

"I saw a bird throwing up yesterday, Lulu."

"Birds don't throw up, Geordie."

"This one was throwing up. It was on the sidewalk throwing up. How do you know birds don't throw up? Dogs throw up. Remember Taffy? Taffy threw up."

I stretched a little and watched a white cloud change from a dinosaur into a horse. The sky was brilliant. On top of the freight car, lying side by side on our backs, the sky was all I could see. No telephone wires, no trees, no buildings, just sky. The metal roof was hot on my neck and back and smelled like wet nickels. There was another smell in the air not quite identifiable. It wasn't warm enough to have been tar bubbles boiling up through the cracks in the patched tarmac, but it had that oily scent.

"What kind of bird was it?"

"A robin."

We lay silently for a while. Taffy was one of Alan and Naomi's dogs, and he did throw up a lot. I listened to Geordie's unusual breathing pattern, remembering the sound from when I was little. Sitting on his lap watching television I used to fall into a trance. Each breath came in an audible three-step—in, in, out, in, in, out—as though he hesitated mid-breath, not trusting himself or the air. Then I would press my ear against his chest and listen to his heart, thinking I'd catch it beating the same pattern. But its thump thump was as regular as everyone else's. I sat up and bent to put my ear against his heart. He put his arms around me as willingly as he always had. Geordie's hugs both calmed and caused my ache.

"I'm in love, Lulu," he whispered.

"You been watching your soap operas again, Geordie?" I laughed. Geordie was forever telling us he was in love, a new woman from around town every few months.

"Really in love," Geordie whispered again.

I sat up to look at his face. He turned away and shut his eyes. A pink flush had swept his cheeks.

"With who?" I shook his shoulder, laughing.

"With Mike." He turned to face me with a look of defiance, but his chin was trembling. When I lay my head back down on his chest, Geordie's heart was thumping violently. My own heart had skipped a beat as much out of fear as surprise.

Except for Doris Tenpenny, who surely never would, Mike was the only one of the five Tenpenny children who hadn't married and moved away. He worked on the farm with his dad, who was still preaching fire and brimstone down at the Reifel Road Baptist Church. Mike also delivered chicken manure—reeking tons of it—in his father's old Chevy pickup. Earlier that month he'd helped Dad and Geordie spread some on our vegetable garden. In the evenings lately, he'd been hanging around our place chatting with Geordie on the stoop. He'd bring a couple of bottles of pop and the two of them would sit until the sun went down, their legs dangling, their heels banging a rhythm against the wall.

People said Mike had sacrificed his life to stick around and take care of his sister, Doris. Everyone said it was a waste because Mike was smart. And Doris was strange. Her silence had set many tongues wagging. And I think there were as many tales about her as there were tongues in Fraser Arm. I'd heard, among other things, that she was schizophrenic, that she'd been raped and never spoken since, that she'd drowned once and was brought back from the brink of death, that she fell off the stoop when she was a baby, and that she'd tried to commit suicide and failed. Our neighbour, Mrs. Barker, said she was just born under an unlucky star. There could have been an element of truth in every one of the stories. Or maybe they were all just a load of bull.

Mum used to take me and Geordie to her egg stand. Later, after Mum disappeared, Dad would send me up alone for a dozen or two. Doris would point at her little cardboard sign: brown or white; small, large, extra-large; half-a-dozen, a dozen, a flat of thirty; green or blue Araucanas, premium. I sometimes went up to the farm just to look over the fence at the bizarrely beautiful collection of chickens poking around in the weeds. Dad was still buying our eggs there.

I lifted my head from Geordie's chest. His eyes were closed and he was wearing a sweet smile, dreaming maybe, of unlikely possibilities. He'd worn the same fuzzy hairdo, the same style of Wrangler blue jeans, and winter or summer weights of a blue plaid shirt since the 1960s. Every few years Geordie reluctantly broke in a new pair of jeans. I'd patched the ones he had on many times, but they were getting a little tight around the waist. He'd always been chubby, but that spring—he was nearly twenty-eight—he'd packed on a few pounds. His shirt was riding up a little and his skin was a vulnerable fish-belly white.

"What's Mike say about that, Geordie?"

"Mike says I'm his special friend. He told me."

I stood up, worried, and changed the subject. "Let's paint some more, Geordie."

"Yeah. Let's paint."

"What do you want to write?"

"Somebody to love."

"What do you mean?"

"Don't you want somebody to love?" Geordie sang.

"Oh, that somebody to love. Can you get that lid off for me then?"

Geordie had, as always, a multi-head screwdriver in his backpack. He set about finding the right head and carefully opening the can of paint. He placed the can in front of me. "Make it really big, Lulu."

I counted the letters out on my fingers, Geordie counting on his own beside me. "Thirty-one letters, Geordie. We've got sixty feet of boxcar and thirty-one letters. That's too long. They'd be some skinny, those letters, to fit."

"Skinny's okay, Lulu."

I laughed. This was our fifth weekend of what I thought of as poetic disobedience of the necessary kind—writing love notes on the top of boxcars. It had even hit the news. "Look at this," Dad had said at breakfast one morning.

He handed me the paper and I read it aloud. *"Lovesick vandal. Vancouver's traffic helicopter pilots are finding themselves distracted from their work by some unusual graffiti that has been springing up in the Lower Mainland, all of it on the roofs of trains. The boxcars are painted with slogans by a seemingly lovesick individual. Popping up last week were such slogans as 'Love is all you need,' 'Love me do,' and 'Love to love you baby.' Vancouver's baffled police are reporting that the vandals have painted at least four dozen boxcars. 'This is a new brand of graffiti,' said Constable Carey Reinholcz. 'We haven't seen this kind of vandalism before.' Reinholcz admitted that the lovesick vandal might be difficult to apprehend."*

What's a vandal? Geordie had asked. Dad explained and Geordie said, but it isn't vandals, is it, Lulu? He gave me a conspiratorial wink and I winked back. Geordie loved secrets.

Now he squatted beside the paint can. "Tell me the story again, Lulu."

"The story about the lovesick vandal? Only they aren't vandals, and they aren't lovesick? Well, maybe one of them is." I knelt down beside him. "Mike doesn't touch you, does he, Geordie?"

Geordie blushed again. "No."

"You're sure, right?" He nodded. "Just checking, 'cause that would be wrong, Geordie. You understand? Okay, give me a shorter sentence and I'll tell you the story."

"Don't you want somebody?"

"That *does* sound lovesick. But it is shorter. They're still going to be pretty skinny letters." While I painted, bending low in the warm sun, Geordie sat cross-legged, hopping backwards from each letter as it was written. "So, the story goes like this," I said. "When people are flying in and out of Vancouver, they look down before they land and they see these trains snaking along. Only now there's things written on them. Like, Love me do. Or Love will keep us together. And they think of the people who've loved them."

"And what about the lady?"

If I'd been asked right then, I would barely have understood that my train-top poetry was my own message-in-a-bottle to the woman who was unlikely ever to grace the streets of Fraser Arm again, so it was unfathomable that Geordie had put the two together. I looked at him, his eyes full of hopefulness, and wondered why I had ever told him this story.

"The lady. There's this woman in an airplane. And she's flying overhead, coming to visit Vancouver because she hasn't been here for a long time."

"But not at night. Mum wouldn't be able to see at night."

"Geordie, Mum's not coming home, not ever." I said it bluntly and quietly, looking him in the eye. He turned away.

"Yes, she is."

"I think Mum's dead, Geordie."

"No. Tell the story, Lulu."

There was no point in arguing. He'd insist until he broke me anyway. "This woman, who is *not* Mum, is looking out the window. They're flying over the mud flats and the railway tracks, and she looks down and sees this train chugging along beside the Fraser. She thinks she sees something on the top of the train, but she's not sure. But they have to circle again because it's so busy at the airport, so they fly right over top of the train again. And the lady looks down and sees one that says Love is all you need. And right behind that one there's another one that says We love you, call home."

"Does she call, Lulu?"

"I don't know, Geordie." And as usual, the hope in his eyes broke me. "I suppose she might."

DORIS

Father has not told Doris where they are going. About forty-five minutes ago, he pulled up beside the garden fence in the half ton and honked the horn, which was certainly unnecessary, for Doris, who was in the garden, could not have missed the sound and sight of him. But then Doris saw his hand wave. Get in, his hand said. Doris stood up. *How unusual.*

Father mostly meets Doris' silence with his own, or with hand or head signals. In truth, he rarely speaks to or with anyone. "At" would be a better word. Doris thinks that perhaps all pastors are like Father. But Father waved again and Doris got in the truck. They turned off Wesleyville's main road onto a side road twenty-two minutes ago. Thirteen minutes ago, without signalling, Doris noticed, Father turned the truck onto a dirt road. Twelve minutes ago Father started whistling. Doris does not know what to think. Father whistling is as unknown as this dirt road, which, to the best of

Doris' knowledge, is in the southernmost end of Wesleyville. This very bumpy dirt road is far too far from the Tenpenny farm for Doris to know, even if she did explore Wesleyville, which she does not. Doris does not drive. Reifel Road, which separates Fraser Arm from Wesleyville, is her boundary. For all Doris knows they are no longer even in Wesleyville; she can see Mount Baker in Washington State as clear as a bell. Doris ponders this figure of speech for a moment. As clear as a bell is an unclear simile. A bump in the road lifts Doris off her seat and out of her thoughts. Father stops whistling and laughs. "Going to need new shocks after this," he says.

Doris looks at Father in the driver's seat. He has a short-sleeved shirt on and his elbow is out the window, which is causing the shoulder of his shirt to puff up in the wind and ripple across his chest as though he is as muscled as Tarzan. Only Father's tie is preventing the wind from blowing out the neck of his shirt. He smiles at Doris and Doris thinks, with mounting alarm, that something must be terribly wrong. She looks past his whistling, smiling mouth, out his window. Green wheat. Green potatoes. Green corn. Green soybeans. White geese. Red barn. Brown road. Blue sky. "Here we are," he says.

Doris is not sure she wants to get out of the truck. Father is strange, she has never been here before, and there is a large dog barking beside one of the out buildings, of which there are many. But Father is stepping out of the truck with the confidence of a friend. The large dog has stopped barking and is whimpering and wagging its tail low, as some dogs do, to show it knows Father is the Alpha male. Father scratches the dog behind its ear and shouts a name: "Bramwell?"

"Tenpenny?" comes the response from behind a screen door.

Doris is curious to see who might be calling Father Tenpenny when the rest of the world calls him Pastor. Bramwell, a small man with a long beard, is leaning over the porch railing and shaking Father's hand.

"My daughter Doris," Father says, "the quiet one I told you about."

Bramwell shakes Doris' hand too.

"I hear ya like chickens," he says in a loud voice, and he waves too, like Father, as if Doris were deaf.

Bramwell's chickens are magnificent. White and Buff Chanteclers, Rhode Island Reds, Cochins, Wyandottes, Plymouth Rocks, Leghorns, Red Shavers, Jersey Giants, Welsummers. The beautiful creatures, many of which she has seen only in library books, have the run of a large grassy area.

"This here's a moveable fence," Bramwell shouts. He gives the wire fence a shake. "Just moved it yesterday. Don't keep out hawks or climbing vermin, but the hens, they go in the coops at night anyways. Coop is moveable too, Doris." Bramwell is very proud and Doris thinks he has good reason to be; the moveable pen is as extraordinary as the chickens. He waves at Doris again and opens the gate into the moveable yard. There are four coops and they all have wheels at one end and wheelbarrow-like handles at the other.

"All you got to do is wheel these coops over to the far side or wherever you want them, then move these fence posts here." Bramwell kicks one of the posts. "Just held in the ground with a spike, see? Needs a little manpower is all, then Bob's your uncle. If you're worried about hawks just put over some netting. Works really good."

"I thought you might like this moveable fence contraption," Father says. "Pick a few chickens too if you want,

Doris." Father nods at the chickens. Doris does not hesitate. She takes her notebook and pencil from her sweater pocket. Twenty by twenty? she writes. Bramwell and Father look at her notebook.

"No problem," says Bramwell. "I can make it bigger. Thirty feet by twenty's good to start with. Lots of space for your flock. You want a coop too?" He asks Father, not Doris.

"Yes. One coop," Father says. "Mike and I can make a chicken run from the moveable fence to your old coop too, Doris."

Doris wants all of the chickens. She writes their names in her notebook, excluding the ones she already has—the Rhode Island Reds, Jersey Giants, and Leghorns. She points at a small hen scratching in the grass then draws a question mark in her notebook. Bramwell squints at the notebook and then at the hen. "Hamburg," he says. "You like that little feller, eh? She's a beauty. Tiny eggs, mind you, but loads of 'em."

Father refuses a coffee and they are back in the pickup with a few chicks in a crate between them. Doris has shaken Bramwell's outstretched hand goodbye and now is nervously tapping her pencil on her notebook. She has never had occasion to thank Father for anything other than her daily bread. Mother does that. Actually, Mother thanks the Lord, not Father. But Father does not seem to be waiting for Doris' thanks. He's whistling again. "Come on, Doris, try it. It's called 'When the Saints Go Marching In.'"

Doris purses her lips like Father's and blows. She makes a surprising, glorious sound.

LULU

I was sitting cross-legged on the kitchen table looking out the window at Mike and Geordie. They were sitting shoulder to shoulder on the clothesline stoop watching Dad hanging the washing, handing him clothes pegs one by one out of old Imperial Tobacco cans, Mike to Geordie, Geordie to Dad. Maybe it had something to do with the fire, but after Mum disappeared, Dad developed a real knack for the laundry. The drying part, at least. He was an anarchist when it came to the washing; he never gave a moment to thinking about separating the darks from the lights, and seeing as it was mostly men's work clothes he hung out, there was always a decidedly grey-blue cast to almost everything on the line.

Dad had two categories for hanging the washing on the line: length and colour. Length came first—underwear, socks, tea towels, t-shirts, jeans, our worn bath towels, coveralls— pegged taut along the line. Within the length category, colours were sorted from light to dark, something that seemed illogical to me. I thought longest went with darkest, shortest with lightest. We argued over it once, and Dad held the peg can out to me. "You do it then," he'd said, his look wavering, the can of pegs not quite within my reach. Once, after he'd hung a whole load, I'd watched Dad hang a stray tea towel at the end of the line. He'd pegged the towel up and then stood on the stoop, hands on his hips, looking at his carefully arranged work for a silent two or three minutes before reeling the line back in and taking down the offending towel. He hung it over the back of a kitchen chair to dry, a relief, even to me.

"Happy as a grig, isn't he?" Kat said.

"Who? Dad or Geordie?"

"I don't know. All of them, actually." Aunt Kat pushed me and I slid off the table.

"Hey," I said. Kat hated anyone sitting on tables. "What the hell is a grig anyway, Kat?"

Kat pulled the latch back and slid the window wide open. Sweet spring slid in, a breeze and a scent, making me restless. "What's a grig, Wally?" she asked.

Dad turned as if startled from some reverie. He'd been looking a bit myopic lately, squinting down the end of his nose at the newspaper, his head tilted back.

"I believe it's a bird. A happy singing bird or something like that, Kat. Bette used to talk about all of us being happy as grigs."

For a moment we were all silent, everyone's memories of Mum no doubt floating between us. The laundry flapped, a soft, dull sound. Geordie's curls flattened and rose in the invisible hand of the breeze. Kat flipped a cigarette from her pack on the counter and lit it, leaning a little farther out the window. I stretched my hand out to take the cigarette from her and she leaned back, blowing smoke from her nose, and shook her head.

"What? Don't smoke or don't take my cigarette?" I asked. She ignored me.

"I saw a bird throwing up," Geordie said.

Everyone laughed. Dad mussed Geordie's hair. Geordie looked over at Mike, but Mike was looking at me, smiling. A trill riffled through my belly.

"I did." Geordie said.

"Ready for work, Geordie? Lulu, can you run him down to the store?" Dad asked.

Geordie'd been at the SuperValu for ten years, ever since Dad had asked his friend Tom Balfour to hire him. I remember the look on Mr. Balfour's face. "Do what?" he'd asked, shocked. But Mr. Balfour had finally agreed to give Geordie a job helping to carry groceries out to the cars. On the way home, Dad gave my knee a charley horse and said some ringing words like "See, Lulu? Never give up." Mum was furious and said that people would tease Geordie. And Dad's joy was short-lived, anyway, because after Geordie's first day at work Mr. Balfour called and told Mum he had to let him go. There'd been complaints. Too much talking, he said. I remember Mum in the kitchen, smug as a cat, saying I told you so to Dad. And then Dad was on the telephone— begging, Mum said—and later, equally smug.

"Your job will be to wheel in the shopping carts," Dad told Geordie. "Just leave Mr. Balfour's customers alone." Then he said to Mum—or maybe it was later; I can't remember because they fought endlessly over Geordie's job—"Bette dear, I defend any man's right to earn a living."

Now, Mike stood up. "I'll take him," he said.

"Wait for me!" Geordie ran down the stoop stairs.

I climbed quickly out the window. If there was something untoward going on I wasn't going to let him be alone with Mike.

Geordie rushed into the kitchen for his SuperValu apron. Mike slid into his own pickup and swung the passenger door open. He stretched his arm along the back of the seat, his fingers tapping to some rhythm of his own, and then ran his hand up into his hair. He'd abandoned the brush cut. Curls no one knew he had were making him look like a different person. I wondered what his life was like at the farm. His two big brothers were long gone. William, to Fort McMurray and work in the oil sands—as far away as his imagination could take him, Mike said. And James just across the bridge in New West, married, and preaching just like his dad. Even their little sister Joan, who was only a year older than me, was married and gone. That left Doris and Mr. and Mrs. Tenpenny. And Mike. I never saw Mrs. Tenpenny out anywhere. She was like a blank sheet of paper—nothing written on it and no pencil handy, either. I looked at Mike again—a small sweat stain in the armpit of his black t-shirt, khaki-coloured trousers that no one his age wore, and worse, pressed with a decidedly uncool front crease. Maybe that's what Mrs. Tenpenny did. She stayed home and ironed.

Geordie burst out the kitchen door. "I'm ready."

He looked so happy. I sighed thinking of how I'd have to burst another of his love bubbles. He took my hand and pulled me to Mike's pickup. I slid in next to Mike, and Geordie leapt in, bouncing on the seat. He slung his arm up on the back of the seat where Mike's arm had just slid down brushing along my bare shoulder and leaving an electric trace. I gave Geordie a two-handed charley horse, as hard as I could, and we all laughed.

"You know where my dad practices his sermons, Geordie?"

Geordie held an imaginary steering wheel in both hands and looked straight ahead, turning the wheel as Mike turned, shifting when Mike did. "Nope. Where?"

"He's got a really appreciative audience, Geordie. It's the ladies in the chicken coop."

"How come there's ladies in the chicken coop?"

"The hens, Geordie. Those ladies."

"Oh, I get it," Geordie said, bewildered still. "But there's roosters in there, too."

"Not in the hen house."

"How come?"

"They all keeled over from boredom," I said. "And the ladies are next." I blushed because it just popped out, but Mike was laughing, a big, joyous, open-mouthed laugh. My embarrassment was chased away by a flicker of annoyance. As if Geordie wasn't teased enough already.

"I get it." Geordie was still pretending to drive, concentrating. "We're turning here, Mike." Geordie chose a parking spot, shifted into park, and pulled on his imaginary parking brake before Mike had even made the turn into the lot. "Safe and sound." Geordie smiled at us.

I kissed him on the cheek and he leaned his head on my shoulder for a second.

Geordie could wave goodbye forever—his version of "You hang up first." "No, you hang up first"—and Mike must have known that. He honked the horn and pulled the pickup out onto Cappon Road, me waving until I was sure Geordie couldn't see us anymore. I had been in Mike's pickup dozens of times, alone with him even, but there was a new kind of energy in the cab. I was relieved not to be pressed up against him, having my thigh touched with every change of the gearshift.

"Don't be a stranger, Lulu," Mike said.

"Just trying to give you some space, Mike," I said, my mouth dry.

"What if I don't want any space?" He waggled his elbow at me, the muscles on his arm moving nicely.

I sighed. I shifted up a little and pulled at the hem of my cut offs. I wished that I didn't like the looks of Mike in his stupid clean-cut outfit and that he would just drive me home and go back to his mother and her iron.

Mike turned onto River Road. "Want to go for a drive?"

"Looks like we're already driving."

River Road was a narrow, potholed road running for miles along the wide brown Fraser. The muddy river was on one side. On the other side, overgrown yards were filled with rusting machinery, giant cogs, pumps, and barrels, and dozens of boats tilted on dilapidated wooden racks, in a million stages of repair. Peeling buoys and fraying ropes hung on every boat. Farther along River Road, where the river spread wider, were the gravel and mud flats where Dad brought us, spring after spring, to pick eulachons.

Mike slowed and pulled on to a jetty. Like a lot of the other jetties along the riverbank, it had a weather-beaten shack at the end of it, hanging precariously over the water. That one had probably been there for years, all greyed, its windows broken, and looking as though a man's weight alone could send it crashing into the river. Mike cut the engine and leaned back against the door. His black hair was nearly blue in the sun. I hung my arm out the side of the truck and felt the cool air off the river. When I looked over at Mike, he had a twitching smile on his face, his earlier teasing confidence gone, replaced by an excited nervousness that I had seen many times. Not in Mike, but in other boys, before they asked, or didn't ask, for what they wanted. I was irritated by my attraction to Mike and by that familiar wave that was taking me out to sea, my body once again making a pact, without me, with the gods of desire who danced around saying, Oh well, what does it matter?

All I wanted was to get out of the truck and walk, but we were miles from home. "So, Mike," I said, in an ugly tone, "What are you doing with Geordie, anyway?"

"What do you mean?" Mike asked. My words had smacked the tentative smile from his lips.

"You better not be touching him. Are you?" In the silence that followed I felt I'd disturbed some pristine place with my angry words.

Mike looked horrified. "What are you saying, Lulu? Do you think I am . . . Are you saying that I am . . . molesting Geordie?" He pronounced every syllable of *molesting* slowly.

"Geordie said . . ." I knew from the hurt in his eyes that my accusation was unfounded, but I couldn't stop. I shut my eyes and pounded my fists on my bare legs: "Geordie said . . ."

"Geordie said what? I was molesting him? I don't think so. What the hell, Lulu."

"Geordie said he was in love with you."

"Lulu, Geordie is a grown man but he's got the brain of a child."

"He's not a child." The irrational tide kept sweeping me along.

"No, he's not a child. I just said that." Mike spoke slowly. "He's a man that thinks like a child."

"He said he was in love with you, that you said you were 'special friends,'" I said snidely, making quotation marks with my fingers. "Tell me what you meant by that."

"Lulu." Mike suddenly seemed much older, and I felt myself regressing, a twelve-year-old, a four-year-old, a tantrum-throwing two-year-old. "Geordie was in love with Karla Cooper last Christmas. Santa's elf at the Cedardale mall? Remember that? And before that it was Heather-Lynn Gustaffson. How many crushes has he had in his life?"

I turned toward the river.

"How many, Lulu?"

"Lots," I said sullenly.

"Dozens. And have you accused anyone other than me of molesting him?"

"Well, you're the only guy he's had a crush on."

"Yeah, so I'm a pervert because Geordie has a crush on me?"

"I'm not calling you a pervert."

"Yes, you are. I would never touch Geordie."

I was silent. I had dug myself in about something that I hadn't ever really believed. "This seemed different," I said, finally, still angry. "He blushes when he talks about you."

"Lulu, my father might be a Bible-thumping tyrant, but I've heard him say one good thing. He said that we were put on earth to take care of each other. Now, that would make him a hypocrite because taking care of people, including his family, is the last thing he actually does, but if Geordie thinks he's in love with me, it's weird, but I'm not going to stop him from hanging out with me." He paused. "I'll tell him he can't be in love with a man."

"That's not what I meant." I shook my head. What did I mean?

I saw such hurt in Mike's eyes. I thought about the last time I saw his father preaching at the Reifel Road church. TJ's mother had bribed us—with the use of the car—to take an auntie and uncle from Kelowna to church. Mr. Tenpenny entered, dressed in his white minister's robes, a human tempest in the little church with its rock-hard pews. He'd looked around silently for a few minutes, as if counting and judging his flock. At the front sat Mike, Doris, and the pallid Mrs. Tenpenny, their heads bowed while Mr. Tenpenny began to rage on about the godless. Just when I'd thought my nerves were going to get up and walk me out the door—"Thank the Lord," Mr. Tenpenny was shouting—it was over. Mr. Tenpenny passed our pew, glaring as if he knew my sins, a God salesman with angry eyes. Not Mike's eyes.

The breeze was blowing in the window, water smells, not dirty but dank and brown. We were both quiet, listening to the river's swift flow beneath the jetty. The sun was warm. A motorboat loaded with people sputtered slowly by towing a small dinghy in which two young children sat, nets held high.

"Eulachons," Mike said.

"Yup."

"They say that the first spring eulachon has to be caught by a Native person. They have to cook it in a ceremonial way and thank it for coming to the river."

"Who told you that?"

"My grandfather. He said that people believed that if

humans didn't thank them the eulachons would be pissed off and wouldn't come back the next year."

"Sounds right," I said.

"Sounds crazy to me. I mean look how many of them there are. Can you imagine eulachons ever running out?"

It was true; I couldn't imagine it any other way, the oily fish flopping and covering the mud flats by the thousands, the sun glinting off their silvery backs in the river. My brothers and I had gathered eulachons on the river many times, bringing home buckets of them for Dad to dip in egg and flour and fry up in the big cast-iron pan.

"Let's bring Geordie back here tonight," I said.

"You sure? I mean, a pervert like myself . . ." His joke was feeble but his eyes shone with mournfulness and were a fishhook in my heart.

"I'm sorry." I touched Mike's knee.

As if it were an invitation, he leaned across the seat and kissed me. He slid his hands under my top and up my back, hesitated for a second, then took my breasts in his hands. His touch was feverish and I responded to the desperation of it; I opened my mouth and his tongue touched mine. He fiddled with the button on my cut offs and pulled them down. He half gasped, half sighed, and then uttered an animal-like moan. He pulled me to a lying position in a swift jerk, nearly bashing my head on the armrest, and unzipped those neatly pressed pants of his.

"May I?" he said, kicking the truck door open and lying on top of me.

"Looks like you already are," I said and laughed. Mike hesitated. He looked impossibly solemn as he hovered above me, shaking. It was a few seconds before I realized his polite question was real.

"Yes. You may." Memories of playing *Mother May I?* in the backyard rushed in. Mike's fists pressed into the seat on either side of me. He was looking down at my face with a sweet earnestness, a look of need and want I could neither fathom nor stand. I closed my eyes. *Mike, you may take two giant steps forward. Mother may I? No. Please don't.*

Mike came with a pause, a quiet sigh, and lay down on me. I stroked his hair absently, missing the soft burr of his brush cut that I'd touched so many times as a child. I could feel him softening in me and the spill of semen on the truck seat. He was crying.

"I've never done this," he said. Mike lifted his head to look at me and I pulled it back down. I wouldn't be a witness to his vulnerability.

We lay there, the wind rushing through the truck, bringing the smell of the Fraser and the cry of the gulls; the sun, reflected in the rearview mirror, found a spot on my cheek and burned.

●

We picked Geordie up at the end of his shift. The relief on his face was, as always, like the frantic mother's who'd just found her missing child in the next aisle of the supermarket.

"Smells funny in here," Geordie said as he pushed me over toward Mike. He sniffed like a gopher.

"Maybe it's you who smells, Geordie."

"I had a shower, Mike. I even washed my hair. Smell." He

pointed his head across me, at Mike. "I used Lulu's shampoo. What's it called, Lulu?"

"Herbal Essence." I laughed nervously, pushing him back.

"See. You two smell, not me" Geordie sat back and looked straight ahead.

"Well, we're going to get something really smelly now, Geordie. Want to come?"

"Depends," he said. Geordie could only remain mad for a short time. "What is it?"

●

Dad's favourite spot, where we had always gone eulachon gathering, was just upriver from the sawmill. We used to play in the huge sawdust hills when I was little, but something must have happened—some child buried or suffocated in the orange dust—because the hills were fenced and only reckless teenagers scaled the tall wire now. Upstream from the mill, at our eulachon spot, the riverbanks were firmer, the sand covering gravel; farther downstream it was all mud flats and lost boots in the suck of the sand. We were not the only ones who liked this spot. A dozen cars were parked at the river's edge. There were families of every kind bending and filling buckets and burlap sacks with the flopping fish that had spawned and then thrown themselves to the fate of being eaten.

Dad and Kat were lifting buckets out of the back of the pickup when Mike, Geordie, and I pulled up.

"It's just like Millet's *The Gleaners*, isn't it Lulu?" Kat said.

"What?"

"*The Gleaners*. The painting. Remember? I showed you."

Kat had a romantic notion of life that came from inside

that big art book of hers. The gluttonous gulls screaming and fighting needlessly over their easy supper didn't feel too romantic to me. Close to the road, old Velvet Williams had her wood fire burning. A few eulachons—she called them candlefish—sizzled and curled in a cast-iron frying pan on a grill held up by rocks. When Ambrose and Alan were younger, Mrs. Williams had taught them her eulachon-gutting technique. She showed them how to hold the fish's body in one hand, grab its head with the other, and, twisting it sharply, pull out the backbone and guts. *See, boys*, she would say, tossing the reeking bits to the screaming gulls, *one fell swoop*. Geordie wouldn't gut the fish, but the twins learned to do it almost as well as Mrs. Williams.

Dad and Kat, both in their rubber boots, had four buckets between them.

"Let's not get too many, eh? There's only so many eulachons you can eat," Dad said, despite the quantity of buckets.

Kat and Dad would gut and freeze a bunch, but no one liked them thawed as much as the fresh ones. A lot of them would end up as fishing bait or Dad would dig them into the already malodorous compost heap back between the plum trees at home. Kat was in a skirt and blouse, an unlikely eulachon-gathering outfit in my opinion, and her hair was tied up in a blue chiffon scarf. Dad was rolling up the cuffs of his jeans.

"Do you need a hand with that, Wally?" Kat asked. Her grin was flirtatious. Dad smiled conspiratorially back at her. I took a wobbly breath.

Though we could stand in one spot to gather our maximum quota of fish, the five of us dispersed along the riverbank, the way a beach will make even those intent on staying together wander aimlessly apart. Geordie was alone, ahead of us all, a red bucket in his hand, Kat and Dad together, and Mike and I following, unhurried, behind. We bent and picked, everyone choosing the fish that appealed most to them—size, colour, glint of green eye—as though it was not oily fish we were gathering but beautiful stones. I liked the mid-sized fish. I could taste the dry texture of the too-big fish just looking at them. Kat, I knew, liked the smallest ones, but I felt sorry for them. I always picked the little ones up and flung them into the river with a short invocation for a longer life: to the sea, little fish. Half the time they landed just a few yards closer to the river's edge and I had to guiltily turn my back on them and hope they'd survive.

I carried my bucket over to Mike and looked into his big galvanized pail. It was filled with fish of every size. I tried to convince myself that this was somehow more egalitarian. I bent, picked up a little eulachon, and dropped it in my bucket. I stood staring at it, its little green eye alternately pleading with me for a longer life and shouting imprecations against my firstborn. Finally I sighed, picked it up, and flung it, summoning more might than usual; it landed with a satisfying plop in the brown water. I imagined it like the fairy tale fish leaping out of the water in a golden glow, bowing to me for my kindness, reversing its curse—Your firstborn *will* survive you. You *will* live to a ripe old age. Your love life *will* be splendiferous!—before it disappeared into the rush hour of fish swarming to the Pacific.

I sighed again, picked up my bucket, and looked down the shore. Kat and Dad were working together, filling each other's buckets. Kat's ridiculous skirt was full and light. It floated up as she squatted and her hand reached out and hiked up the hem before it touched the wet sand. I watched as Kat finally stood, gathered the fabric of her skirt, and tied it in a knot at one side. I watched Dad watching. He stepped toward her and tucked a curl of hair behind her ear. Kat looked down at the sand and then back up at him. That tender look kicked a hard pain in my gut. I stood there, thinking of how her hair would smell of eulachons.

Geordie was way ahead now, a bit too far for my liking. The sun was lower in the west, over the sea. I heard Mike's boots squelch in the muck behind me and felt his hand on my waist. Making sure Kat and Dad weren't watching, he touched my face with his non-fishy hand and kissed me, very gently. I dropped my bucket and reflexively put my arms around him. He held me, one big arm pulling my head into his shoulder, the other wrapped around the small of my back. He leaned down, nuzzling my neck. Mike was sweet. No wonder Geordie thought he was in love.

The sound I heard next turned me to stone: Geordie was bellowing like a bull in pain. He had seen. His bucket had toppled and the eulachons were slithering out. Kat and Dad were standing upright, looking back at Mike and me, expecting to see something horrifying in the direction Geordie was looking. They were too late. When they looked back at Geordie again he was already running along the river, up into the underbrush behind the sawmill, and then he was gone. I screamed and the gulls seemed to reply. Mike was running too, shouting something to me, but I heard only the river roaring, the gulls screeching, and the strange tinkling of the silver eulachons, slithering on the beach for as far as the eye could see.

DORIS

Doris' shoes once knew all of the roads in Fraser Arm, but here's another brand new one—Dawson Crescent—branching west where Hemlock ends, at the bog. She is, the sign says, *Standing in Front of the Future Home of Esso. Working to Keep You Moving.* Doris feels angry. *Moving? Like a bowel movement perhaps?* Once Fraser Arm was forest and meadow, farm field and bog, foxes and weasels. Now it is house, house, store, store. Doris makes a noise of disgust at the Esso sign. *What good is a gas station to the bog voles?* Doris crosses the unmarked black asphalt of new Dawson Crescent and looks across the ditch into the bog. She identifies a patch of cloudberry by its small white flowers. They are covered in dust. The thought that they might pave the bog pinches a new ache in Doris.

Doris now owns a copy of *Silent Spring.* It is the first book she has ever owned. Actually, it is the second; she must own her Bible even though Father has not explicitly said it is hers.

Lewis Cray said he would renew *Silent Spring* endlessly at the library, even one hundred times, if she wanted. But Doris wanted a copy of her own. This meant pocketing five cents from the sale of every dozen eggs sold at the stand. Twenty dozen did it. One dollar. Doris has rationalized the theft; she needs this book. Doris hides it under her mattress, like the magazines that her brother William hid and Father found and called smut. She needn't worry. Father keeps no track of the egg money—it is she who tends the hens—nor does he ever enter Doris' room. In the end, Doris got her copy of *Silent Spring* for a mere five cents at the United Church bazaar. *Who would have given it away?* Father says the United Church is not a church, so it is just as well that it is many blocks away, because Doris has taken to attending their bazaars in hopes of finding other treasures. There is much that Father doesn't know, Doris thinks, looking at the dusty cloudberry flowers, and what he does not know is none of his business.

She did not put the ninety-five cents left over back in the egg-money pot. Doris thinks she would like to buy Masanobu Fukuoka's *One-Straw Revolution* next. Lewis Cray told her that it was not available at the high school library, so Raylene Dubé got it for her at the public library. One must read a book before one buys it, especially if one only has ninety-five cents. So far, Mr. Fukuoka's natural farming ideas are not so strange. Doris thinks Father and Mr. Fukuoka have more in common than not, though that might not please Father. Joan told Father that much of the farmland in Fraser Arm was confiscated during the war from families with names like Mr. Fukuoka. Father sniffed and said that could not possibly be true.

Doris turns her back on the Esso sign. She follows Dawson Crescent west. It curves along the edge of the bog.

Ahead, it looks as though it may hook up with one of the roads that run up and away from the ravine. When she was very young, Doris only walked to school and to church. But when she turned thirteen, her feet took her farther. If anyone wants to know, Doris can tell them when Forward Road was paved, when Hemlock Street went from dirt to tar and pebble, and when the first bottle was smashed on the Glassy Road—though she does not know who did it. They have paved new Dawson Crescent right over the animal path that ran along the edge of the bog. Doris keeps her eyes to the right, on the bog, remembering the soft earth feel of the path beneath her feet and the smell of humid peat.

There is something else new. Lewis Cray has invited her to walk with him. Doris thinks it is about time. She is not sure where they will walk. Perhaps in the Logging Trail. Doris buttons her sweater. It is not cold, but the sun is getting ready to go down and the heat of the day will go quickly with it. Better to be prepared. She realizes that Lewis might take her somewhere in his car. The vehicle approaching from the far end of Dawson Crescent is what makes her think of Lewis' car. Doris imagines herself in the passenger seat of Lewis' orange Datsun, going somewhere outside of Fraser Arm. She squints into the setting sun, thinking she would have worn a hat had she known she would be walking west along this new road at sunset. If Dawson Crescent, which is hardly a crescent, were not here she would be walking south on Hemlock instead. Doris stops walking for it is suddenly clear that the approaching car is not moving in a straight line. It is zigzagging from one side of Dawson Crescent to the other, as if the driver is confused by the lack of dotted line on the new asphalt. Most people would have jumped into the bog by now, but Doris is not most people. She does not imagine that she should jump until it is too late. Then, just before it is really too late the car swerves and misses her by six inches. Doris, who is frozen, has looked into the stunned eyes of Perry Gladish, Edwin Milton, and Pamela Mann.

A cold rush of adrenaline swoops down to her feet and Doris Tenpenny urinates in her dress.

LULU

"If he's gone in the river, Wally, he's a goner."

"He wouldn't *go* in the river, Verna. Geordie doesn't swim." Dad was calm.

Verna Barker was the kind of woman who had always been ignited by tragedy. She was practically panting. "All I'm saying, Wally, is that Geordie doesn't swim and if he's gone in the river . . . What set him off, anyways?"

"He hasn't gone in the river, Mrs. Barker, for Christ's sake," I said.

Ambrose's truck pulled into the driveway. He and Alan and Naomi jumped out.

"We don't know, Verna. Something upset him and he just suddenly ran off," Dad said, polite beyond my endurance. "Where would he go?"

I knew he was talking to me but I didn't reply.

"Did you follow him?" Verna put her hand on Dad's arm.

"Are you insane?" I muttered.

"Of course we followed him. Verna, maybe you could just leave this to us to worry about," Dad said.

"I'm just trying to help, Wally," Verna said, clearly offended.

I spun on her. "Help us, Mrs. Barker? Since when did you care for Geordie? All you ever did was try to convince everyone he belonged in Woodlands."

"Now, didn't you always have a mouth on you, Louise Josephine." We all stared. No one had called me by my real name since I was two. "If my son had've been retarded, I'd've put him there too," she said.

I lunged before the boys or Dad could stop me and pushed Verna Barker to the ground. My brothers hauled me back and Dad helped her up, apologizing over and over. She limped off along the path through the bushes that separated her house from ours and I shouted after her. "Don't you ever come into our yard again. Ever." Dad was white. Aunt Kat and a few neighbour women who had gathered in our house peered out the window. Jed barked desperately, the animal herald of something dreadfully wrong.

"We have to do something," I shouted at Dad.

Trevor asked me, "And what would you suggest, Cassius Clay?"

After a stunned moment Ambrose said, "It's Muhammad Ali, asshole."

"Stop," Dad said, his hands up. "Alan and Ambrose, can you check the SuperValu?"

"It's way too far from the river, Dad, and it's closed." Trevor was as scornful with Dad as he was with me. "Geordie wouldn't go there."

"Trevor's right," Ambrose said, though it must have killed

him to say so. "There's no way he'd go there. He's got to be lost somewhere in the woods. Raven Ravine, or the bog, or down in the Logging Trail."

"I hope to God he's not in the ravine," Dad said. "He's terrified of the ravine."

Dad looked west. I knew what he was doing—calculating the time before the sun would set. Darkness had snuck up on us. Trying not to imagine Geordie scared somewhere, wet and cold, only conjured him more clearly. I saw his jean jacket exactly where he'd left it, beside Mrs. Williams' campfire, hooked on the root ball of a tree that had swept down the river in the winter.

Mr. Jones' panel wagon pulled into the yard and seven Boy Scouts, three of them his own sons, flooded out. Mrs. Jones got out of the passenger side, saw the women in the parlour window, and headed straight for the house. The Scouts were pulsing. Caught in the purplish ultraviolet of our road's brand new streetlight and the glow of the yellow bug light at our front door, they looked ghoulish, bruised.

Mr. Jones had a box of flashlights. "From Beaver Lumber," he said. "My boss sent them."

In the end, Ambrose took charge: He and Alan would check the Logging Trail, walking south toward the bog. Mr. Jones would take the Scouts and start at the west entrance to the Logging Trail, following the path that curved south. Dad and Trevor would start at the north end of the bog. They would all meet up near where the railway tracks separated the bog from the forest.

"Mike and Lulu," Ambrose said, looking only at Mike, "can you check Raven Ravine?" I caught Alan and Dad exchanging a look and Ambrose reached out and touched my hand just for a second, as if to say don't worry, he won't be there.

"Should we call the police, Wally?" Mr. Jones wouldn't meet anyone's eye, and no one was convinced when Dad said that Geordie was probably just too scared to come home. Alan said he'd make the call.

If Geordie had been there, this would all have been a big adventure. He would have been laughing at so many boys pouring out of the Jones' station wagon. And I would be not-so-patiently waiting for him as he gathered the things he deemed necessary for the journey. He'd be bouncing into one of the cars, chattering away about the time we went to Whiterock with my kindergarten class and he tied his plastic bag full of seashells to the arm of his seat and forgot them. Or the time we went to Tofino and saw Lost Shoe Creek Number One and Lost Shoe Creek Number Two on the way. I felt sick to be setting out to search for him, without him.

●

Mike pulled into the parking lot at Fraser Arm Elementary, his headlights slashing through the principal's office windows. When I was at school, the principal had made the ravine that ran behind the school out of bounds, though only the tough boys hung out there anyway. We were warned of cougars and then of drifters after Mum and Mrs. McFee disappeared. As Mike and I entered the woods, I saw that another generation of kids was keeping the path to the old hanging tree clear. That was as far as I had ever gone alone, dared one summer by Nadine. Even with Mike beside me, the memory of standing alone beneath the sycamore pricked fear at the nape of my neck. I ran my hand over the thousands of initials carved into its scarred trunk and the beam of my flashlight caught the slow swing of the rope hanging from its reaching arm. Here the ravine was deepest; it dropped down steeply through ferns and moss-covered boulders to a small, trickling creek. Dark trees hung with sphagnum moss—deadwoman's tresses—lined its long narrow banks.

Only once did I see the cougar that lived in the ravine. From the window of my grade two classroom we all watched the big cat slip quietly from the trees, its tawny body low in the grass. We screamed as the animal snatched its distant relative, the school's tabby cat, and disappeared back into the ravine.

"Lulu. It's all right. We'll find him." Mike's voice was soft. And then he shouted Geordie's name to banish the shadowy hands reaching out from the twisted trees.

"Geordie?" The sound of my own voice was momentarily steadying. "Geordie." I tried to shout as loud as Mike, but the sound that came from my mouth was reedy and thin, the impotent scream of dreams. I forced myself to imagine Geordie at home, in Kat's parlour, on the burgundy couch, his big feet hanging over the armrest, spilling his tea and eyeing another chocolate-coated digestive biscuit. Safe and sound.

We reached the end of the ravine where the creek dwindled to a trickle and then disappeared into the ground and the path sloped gently up to a new housing subdivision. A dog barked and another dog replied. Mike shone his flashlight in my face.

"Jesus," I said angrily, closing my eyes and turning my head away.

"Sorry." He shone it up into the trees and my eyes followed

the beam up into the sky, through the twisting branches, to the stars.

Then he turned and started walking back, closer to the creek this time, bushwhacking. I followed, trying to keep up, while demons of my own making chased me in the dark. The light from Mike's flashlight beamed erratically through the bushes and down into the creek. He began climbing the steep slope at the foot of the hanging tree and I scrambled up after him grabbing roots and ferns to pull myself up. Halfway up I dropped my flashlight, but I didn't stop. At the top, I pushed my back up against the tree and looked down into the ravine. The flare of my flashlight shone up from beneath the black water of the creek. I grabbed the knot of the rope and stilled it.

"Geordie?" I called looking one last time into the darkness, and then I ran across the field into the glare of the pickup's headlights.

●

There were even more cars and trucks and a police cruiser in the yard. Kat was standing on the side steps. I shook my head and stepped stiffly into her arms.

"Lulu. What happened? Why did he run like that?"

She took my chin in her hand and held it, then lay the palm of her hand against my cheek. I avoided her eyes and pushed past her into the house. The kitchen was full of people. They all turned and looked as the screen door closed behind me. No one had to ask. I saw Aloysius McFee in the crowd and scowled at him. Mr. Chen. Lance Chen. Mr. and Mrs.

Jones and their boys, and a few others from the Scout pack were still there. The stock boys, Ross and Angus from the SuperValu were talking with Ambrose and Alan and Naomi. Mr. Balfour, and the chief of police, Mr. Smallwood, and another policeman in uniform were leaning up against the counter. Several neighbour women, including Mrs. Tanner and Mrs. Ogg, were washing coffee mugs.

"Chief Smallwood thinks we should call it a night, Lulu." Dad's eyes were red.

"We'll look again at first light," Mr. Smallwood said, and a mumble of disagreement rippled through the kitchen.

I pushed into Kat's parlour and slid down the wall. Cars kept pulling into the driveway. I could see their lights brightening the curtains as they turned onto the property. Doors slammed. People were parking on the road verge and talking outside in the yard. I could hear Mr. Smallwood trying to convince people to regroup tomorrow, his voice hesitating as the door continued to swing open and more people eased into the kitchen.

"It's two in the morning, gentlemen," he said, ignoring all the women present, "and there's not much we can do in the dark. Wally, no other ideas as to where Geordie might have run to?"

The room was silent as everyone waited for Dad's response. The door squawked open again.

"I've brought the percolator from the church," a woman said. "And some cookies." I recognized Verna Barker's voice. There was a general hubbub and the sound of more cups being pulled from the cupboard. Kat pushed through the parlour curtain and tripped over me. She crashed into her old china cabinet, setting everything inside it rattling.

"Jesus." She leaned her outstretched arms against the cabinet for a moment, steadying it or herself, then took a tray of her fancy teacups—they had no doubt run out of mugs in the kitchen—and stepped back into the kitchen after giving me a look of reproach. Gone was the tender inquiry of earlier.

"Screw you," I muttered, remembering Dad and Kat flirting on the beach.

I heard Mr. Jones volunteer to take the Scouts through Raven Ravine.

"We've been there," I said sourly from behind the curtain, but no one heard. I leaned out and shouted, "We've been there." But suddenly I wanted to go back again. We must have missed him. It was the only place he could be. I squeezed into the kitchen and followed Mr. Jones and the Boy Scouts out the door. The boys were a few years younger than me, in their early teens, and as excited as puppies. I slipped into the passenger seat beside Mr. Jones who glanced nervously at me as though the presence of a girl on his ship would bring bad luck. I shouted "Out!" at one of the Scouts who was trying to climb in beside me. He closed the door and scrambled into the back with the others.

At Fraser Arm Elementary we pulled into the same spot Mike had parked. The four in the back seat climbed out and Mr. Jones went around to the tailgate to let three more boys out of the station wagon. Equipped with flashlights they raced across the field and into the woods.

"Don't go ahead without me, boys," Mr. Jones called.

When we got to the hanging tree, one of the boys was swinging out over the ravine on the rope, another boy pushing him, all of them laughing. Mr. Jones grabbed the boy as he swung past and hauled him off. They were instantly solemn, remembering, as they saw me, why we were there. Then one of them let out a piercing shriek and I seized Mr. Jones' arm in fear. The boy pointed at a light glowing dimly down in the ravine.

I let go of Mr. Jones, my heart still bashing against my ribs. "It's my flashlight."

"Right," Mr. Jones said, catching his own breath. "We'll follow the creek bed, boys. Stick together. I don't want anyone going on ahead."

But the boys were off, a pack of young wolves, gamboling. Alone, not one of the boys would have ventured here in the middle of a moonless night, but together they were fearless. As they swung their lights side to side and walked through the woods, they shouted to each other, suppressing nervous laughter. I walked in front of Mr. Jones, glad only to have someone behind me. Everything else felt hopeless.

I froze in terror at the scream. The boys had gathered on our side of the creek bank, a septet of waving flashlight beams focused on the other side. They were calling "Mr. Jones" in deep, distorted voices. I stumbled down the bank and splashed through the creek and the cold water filled my running shoes.

Geordie was lying on the ground, his feet dangling in the water. His face was dark with mud and something else. A flashlight beamed across his face. There was blood, bright red and dried black. The boys came across the creek and held their flashlights on my brother. I kneeled down in the mud beside his inert body. Mr. Jones was beside me, feeling in the dark for a pulse.

"He's alive."

He pulled Geordie's bloody t-shirt aside and I saw the holes, two gaping slits below his ribs. I couldn't look away as he shone his light on the knife wounds. Mr. Jones took off his jacket and used it to press on the holes. "Run," he said to the boys. "Go. Wake someone up."

The boys were already running, a sobered pack through the woods.

I lay down in the mud beside Geordie and put my ear to his chest. In a prayer to no god I knew, I begged for his life. I held my breath and listened. There was the soft lilt of it—Geordie's beating heart, and the nearly imperceptible rise and fall of his chest.

DORIS

Doris sits up in bed. There was music. She is sure she heard it.

Father whistles in the truck, and the barn. And he now allows singing in the church, but he grumbles about it as though, even in praise of God, he would rather not. But music is never permitted in the house. Before she left, Joan asked Father whatever could be wrong with music. Father didn't answer. Later, after Father forbade even Mother to go to Joan's wedding, Doris asked Mother the same question. When Mother read the note, she sighed. She handed it back to Doris. She did not explain and Doris did not insist. Mother misses Joan.

Today is Doris' thirty-second birthday. Last night Mother brought a present to Doris' room. The socks are soft—hand knit in blue and pink wool left over from the blanket Mother secretly knit for Joan's baby that's coming. Doris remembers that she has the socks on and wiggles her toes under the blankets. She put them on to please Mother—they will not survive long inside Doris' rubber boots—but now their softness pleases Doris too. Perhaps she will wear them only to bed. She would like to safeguard the only birthday gift she will receive.

There it is again. The music stirs something in Doris. Excitement or fear, she does not know which. Doris puts her hand on her belly, below her navel, above her pubic bone, where the stirring is, and waits. What is inside cannot be felt on the outside. Her alarm clock says it is just a quarter past five. The sun rose nine minutes ago, according to the *Farmers' Almanac*.

Doris plants her sock feet on the floor. She smoothes her pyjamas along her knees, holding her breath to hear better. The music is at moments faint and then louder. The wind is playing with the notes, dragging them toward and away from Doris' window, which is open, as always, four inches. She stands and bends her ear to the window then rests her forehead on the sill. A fiddle. Doris' heart jumps and the thrumming in her belly deepens. She sees the music: night blue, dirt brown, eggplant purple, soot black. She leaves her cardigan where it is hanging and takes the back stairwell down to the kitchen. Before today it was of no concern to Doris that the creaking stairs might wake Father. Mother will not be up until the roosters have long since crowed, but Father rises shortly after the sun. Father waking and making the music end would be a tragedy.

The kitchen door is not locked. Doris goes out and pauses on the grass. The yard is still and quiet. An old pickup truck passes on Reifel Road with its fog lights on. The rising sun is casting eerie fog shadows across the shed and the barn.

The tractor is a prehistoric creature in the fog, its bucket jaw stopped in mid-swing. Small birds are throwing crow-sized shadows. Doris' slippers are wet already and now she feels wetness on her toes inside her slippers, inside her birthday socks. *Where has the music gone?* She holds her breath again. It is so silent that Doris begins to believe she imagined it. Then, there it is, by the chicken coop.

Doris is pierced by cerulean. Nothing in the world could be bluer. Even the roosters do not crow while this excruciatingly beautiful song is played. Exaltation—these sounds are the meaning of the word Doris has read but not felt. This morning, Doris touches exaltation.

When the song is over, Doris sees the shape of Lulu through the fog. Lulu sweeps her arm out and bows low to the ground before the chickens who have gathered by the fence to listen too. Then she disappears over the wooden fence between the Tenpennys' garden and the pear orchard. On her thirty-second birthday, Doris clutches Bramwell's fence, bereft.

LULU

I could not find my brother in his eyes.

He had been replaced. The infection and fever had gone, but the man in Geordie's wasted body stared back at me in wary confusion, a man who no longer remembered our immeasurable love. His eyes replied to mine not with accusations of betrayal—I would have preferred that—but with the mistrust of an animal that has been whipped, a child who has been broken by abuse. He would not smile. Would respond to neither wretched pleas nor gentle teasing. It was only when I looked at him in silence, unable to disguise my grief, that I saw a glimmer of Geordie, our pain matched, a pair of train tracks disappearing into the distance, six feet apart, and forever parallel.

Late one evening, about six weeks after we found Geordie in the ravine, I was walking along Cypress to Chen's for a pack of cigarettes when Aloysius pulled up. He waved me to his car.

I hadn't been to see him, not since the night he'd helped search for Geordie. Aloysius had been true to his word about stopping what we'd been doing. I was still drinking and doing drugs, just not with him. I kept walking. I didn't want to talk to anyone. He followed me slowly to Chen's, ignoring the cars honking and passing. When I came out of the store he was waiting for me, the engine idling. I got in. Aloysius reached out one hand and I fell into his arms, bawling. He hush-hushed me, holding my head tight to his chest and kissing my hair gently.

"Lulu, darling, it'll be all right. It'll be all right."

When I finally stopped crying he reached for my seatbelt and buckled me in, triggering a new wave of tears. We drove. That's all. Neither of us spoke. He took us down to River Road and then over the Pattullo Bridge, turning east and following the Fraser River past Woodlands and the Penitentiary and Essondale. We drove slowly through the old part of Coquitlam and back along the water past Burnaby Mountain and the university campus, then over the Second Narrows Bridge. I must have fallen asleep after Lynn Valley. When I woke up we were parked up a mountain, facing the lights of the city below. Aloysius brushed my hair out of my eyes.

"Where are we?"

"Grouse Mountain," Aloysius said. "Look."

It was near dawn. The sun was rising over the mountains and their jagged tops were on fire. He started the car and headed down toward the city. We crossed the Lions Gate Bridge as the sun reached it, turning its spans gold. We took the tunnel home. He stopped the car on Hemlock, on the Wesleyville side of Reifel Road. For old time's sake, I guess.

"I love you, Aloysius," I said.

Aloysius sang his final words to me. "I'll be seeing you

. . ." he began. Then he leaned over me to open the passenger door and indicated with his chin that I should get out. His tail lights blinked twice at the traffic light.

I never spoke with Aloysius McFee again.

●

That night, I played at an outdoor concert in Wesleyville to a bunch of happy stoners. The night was soft, with moonlight filtering through the trees in Cougar Creek Park, and a musician I'd just met—Louis-Joseph de La Vérendrye, all the way from Montreal—had his bare toes on mine. The audience had dispersed and I had put my fiddle in its case. His fingers were strumming a seductive tune on his guitar and he was singing gently in French. Louis-Joseph asked me to come play with him. Then he asked me to go away with him. He didn't know it had been fifty-seven days since my last period. He knew nothing yet of my dark bruise that wouldn't heal. Overhead, there were two crows, laughing.

NEARLY NOW

Together, finally together
Heart wings embroidered by doves.

LULU PARSONS, "Finally," *Lost Years*

LULU

There are still a few places in Fraser Arm where the world is wild. On my early morning, doctor-ordered walks I sought out these places. Places where the sidewalks were still made of dirt and grass. Where creeks refused to be buried, trickling doggedly along in dark gullies guarded by blackberry thorns and shadowed by cedars and old-growth ferns. The Logging Trail, where forty years earlier Nadine and I had shared our candy and imagined bogeymen at every turn, was as tangled and wild as ever. No one could build there, under the power pylons that ran from the Fraser River up through town, and by some miracle of town planning, most of it was never mowed. So we hobbled, my cane and I, along some of the same paths I had so long ago restlessly explored. In the Logging Trail, I felt as close to the untamed Fraser Arm of my childhood as I could ever hope to get. The deer paths still criss crossed through the salmonberry bushes, which were, by July, dotted with their watery orange and yellow fruit. In small clearings there were even the same littered fire circles with their smashed beer bottles and smoke butts that told me teenagers were still using the Logging Trail as we had.

But step out of that green swath and it was a concrete city. Thousands of people living in condos where our huckleberries once grew, shopping malls where we used to climb trees, banks and restaurants where cattle and goats grazed, and tall fences behind houses so that the wildness of the Trail wouldn't encroach on pristine lawns.

Snyder's Dun Roamin? trailer park backed on the Logging Trail, so most of my morning walks ended up at Raylene and Birdie's. Raylene would make me coffee, or some chicory substitute if Birdie was there. If it wasn't raining, Raylene and I would sit outside in folding deck chairs and sniff the air together and watch for unusual birds, or, just to be democratic, the usual ones. Raylene would tell me what she was reading. Old Irene Snyder was still kicking, though her husband Alf was long gone. Irene must have been a hundred-and-five because she was old when I was a teenager. Raylene still kept the old Airstream at *Dun Roamin?*, but she and Birdie lived in a new trailer home there, with all the amenities and a flower patch that would have been included in Royal garden tours had anyone but the trailerparkers known about it. *Dun Roamin?* was a little more crowded than it used to be, and the trailers were all permanent. Mrs. Snyder had refused to build a fence at the back of the trailer park. She thought of the whole tangled Logging Trail as her own backyard now. Birdie's influence.

Raylene had been retired from the library for a year and had taken to her time off like butter and honey to fresh-baked bread. She couldn't believe she received a pension for having encouraged people to read. Her old Airstream had become part personal library, part tool shop. On days it was too wet to garden or tend her bees, she went there, cranked up the heat, and read or tinkered with something that needed fixing. The trailer was parked so its main door faced out into the Logging Trail, and Raylene had let blackberry brambles grow up around it, making it look like something post-apocalyptic.

One morning in July, just as I arrived at the Airstream, Raylene came flying out the door with a Swede saw in her hand.

"Get in the truck, Lulu-Bird."

I followed her to the pickup and hauled myself gracelessly up onto the passenger seat. It still hurt like Hades to move too fast. "Where are we going?"

"Bee swarm," she said. Then she reached over and tried to help me with my seat belt.

I smacked her hand away. "There is nothing wrong with my hands."

"Okey-doke. Sorry." She put the truck in gear. "So, have you been coveting beer bottles in the Logging Trail again?"

"Raylene, I swear to God, I'm fifty years old but I still can hardly resist the urge to pick up those bottles and take them down to Wilkie's Wrecking."

"Too bad Wilkie's went the way of the dodo twenty-five years ago, Lulu. You could be making yourself a few bucks during your hiatus."

Hiatus. It was a nice word for the six weeks I'd spent in the hospital after the motorcycle crash. And it was an awfully nice word for the three months we'd been mourning Trevor.

If people were bees, the little group standing thirty feet from the apple tree would have been a very small swarm, but at least we knew where the bees were. When the Sikh temple had been built at the corner of Galiano and Walnut, twenty years back, the line of apple trees across the front of the Richardson's old farm property had been left standing. The trees no longer bore much fruit, but we'd pilfered so many apples from them when we were young I could still taste that hard, unripe but delicious first bite. In one of the trees, on a long, gnarled branch, a dark cluster of bees was moving like pepper being shaken from its cellar.

Alan or Ambrose—or was it Trevor?—stepped in a wasps' nest in the long grass once while looking for the ball during a neighbourhood game of scrub. We ran through the pasture, perfect banshees. Every one of us got stung, especially Geordie who ran awkwardly and too slowly, although there aren't many who can outrun a wasp. I remember Trevor hysterically swiping his hands around his head brushing real or imagined wasps from his hair, and me doing the same. Dad used to tell me to just sit still and the *dam-ned* things wouldn't hurt me. But the compulsion to thrash about in the presence of bees seems to me to be a universal instinct. I figure a bee could distract even an axe murderer from his victim. So, sting-phobic and barely off crutches, I wasn't the greatest candidate to be accompanying Raylene on a bee-rescue mission.

"How long have they been here?" Raylene asked the old man who presented himself as the one who had called the number on the *Raylene of Sunshine* honey jar.

"We saw them yesterday morning. But there were not even half this many," he said.

"Twenty-four hours. Good." Raylene nodded her cropped, grey head. She still looked like an eighteen-year-old boy. "They shouldn't be moved unless they've been here that long," she explained. "They don't go far when they swarm and sometimes they go back to their nest. But I guess these ones aren't."

The old man nodded serenely, his wringing hands belying that serenity. He was clearly in my camp in terms of bees. He translated for the rest of the old men and women in the group and they beamed encouraging smiles at both of us, as if I too was part of the solution. If they had offered even half an ounce more faith to Raylene she might have walked on water, but that was the wrong metaphor for this group, of course. I doubted that she needed that industrial-strength blessing to do what she had to do, but I wouldn't have budged without it.

She approached the tree with the caution and authority of someone attempting to disarm a desperate man of his gun. Crouching under the mess of bees she scrutinized the swarm from every angle. Then she raised her arm and, very slowly, began to saw through the branch. The bees began throbbing like a live heart skewered on a stake, a steady pulse in and out. The old folks and their grandkids and I moved back a few more feet. Finally, the branch sighed lower and Raylene stood and carried it and its hundreds of occupants toward us. We parted to let her through. Moving with a steadiness I'm sure we all appreciated, she walked to the passenger door of her pickup, opened it, rolled the window down, and with a clever bit of stick-handling, got in holding the branch and the bees out the window.

"Drive, Lulu. Back streets. To the hives, Bat Girl."

Droll Raylene. I imagined a thousand bees deciding they'd like to ride inside the pickup instead of taking the al fresco treatment.

"Now would be good," she said.

I hobbled obediently to the truck and stuck my cane behind the seats, wondering why Raylene's wish was still always my command.

"Gently," she warned as I jerked the pickup into gear and out onto Walnut Street. "Really slow now."

We weren't more than three blocks from the McFees' where Raylene kept her hives. I turned onto Forward Road doing three kilometres an hour. Looking in the rearview mirror, I saw we were the lead car in a cautious procession—grey-bearded men in bright turbans, tiny old women with scarves on their heads, skipping pre-schoolers, strollers tucked with sleeping babies, all following at a respectable distance. We drove past Dad's, and I glanced over, hoping he was in the yard. Dad was crazy about Raylene. And Birdie too. He would have loved the spectacle. I almost honked but had the wits to think better of it. Let dozing bees lie. I did wave at someone standing outside the Smallwoods' old house, though. No one I knew, but it was a queenly, royal wave, and Raylene started laughing. Halfway up Forward Road, Raylene and I became a pair of kids giggling uncontrollably at a funeral. She started it and I caught it. Up until then I'd been doing my job really well, but by God it felt good to laugh after months of crying.

"Stop. Stop. We do not want to shake a slew of bees off this branch in front of somebody's house."

"You started it."

"Get control of yourself, girl. There's a thousand lives at stake here," she said, and we lost it again.

We headed for the McFees' driveway, just past the busy intersection of Forward Road and Hemlock. Even with the stoplights, it required a tricky turn across traffic. I'd recently told Doris that I thought it was an awkward spot for a driveway. Doris looked at me as though I was ignorant and wrote on her notepad: *You mean it is an awkward spot for traffic lights.* She had a nasty habit of tapping her pencil on the paper, but she had a point: the McFees had been there first.

Our followers were dutifully crossing at the lights. I made my turns and stopped at the entrance to the driveway.

"Do not let this branch hit the trees," Raylene warned.

The driveway was just as tree-lined and narrow and rutted as it had been when I was a child. Even squeezing far to the left, we wouldn't be able to drive down it, not with a branch of bees hanging out the window.

"Get out," I said. "You'll have to walk."

Raylene got out and held the branch out in front of her and the whole lot of us followed her up the drive. She walked slowly across the grass, the morning light turning the bees into a burning torch. Raylene was strong, her arms tanned and muscular. As a child, I had thought of her as the goddess Artemis she'd told me about. Now she was the woman who said she would never be my mother but to whom, more than to anyone else, I came home. There, in the McFees' front yard, stood my own personal, sixty-six-year-old Artemis in sensible shoes and a short-sleeved polyester shirt. A feeling—maybe happiness, I didn't recognize it—reached in and plucked a string in my heart that I had not heard played for a long time. The smell of the cedars, the sound of them soughing in the wind, and the crows—black darts above it all—were all notes in the unfamiliar song in my chest. I felt a prickling in my eyes and neither my cane nor my feet could find solid ground. A very old woman looked up at me and offered me her hand. I took it.

Geordie and Doris came out on the porch and joined the crowd. Raylene led us along the south side of the house, past the vegetable garden, through the raspberry patch, around the hen house, and into the orchard. Raylene's beehives stood to the north of the orchard, beneath a bluff of old cedars. She laid the branch on the front step of one of the stacked hives and backed away.

"Will they go in with the other bees?" a woman asked her.

"That's an empty hive. Hopefully they'll make their way inside. Usually they swarm if they are overcrowded. This should be a lot better."

We watched the bees like spectators before a house on fire. Bees flew in and out of Raylene's other hives, their flight paths visible dark lines across the pasture. The swarming bees were climbing off the branch. They would survive or they wouldn't. They'd make a new home in the hive, or perhaps they would fly off together with their queen and maybe find a hole in an old apple tree. How perfect, I thought, a hole in an apple tree. Not here. Away somewhere. Gradually I felt as though I would suffocate if I didn't stop watching—the numbers of them, like too many jostling strangers at a bus station, shoulder to shoulder, inching to their destination.

Geordie broke the silence. "I don't like bees." I remembered the baking soda poultice Mum had dotted all over him.

Raylene laughed. "Yeah, well, you like honey," she said,

"so give thanks to those worker bees who put it on your toast every morning."

"They don't put it on my toast. I do."

She punched Geordie in the shoulder. The show was over. Raylene was just a woman. My song was gone. Our visitors, who had likely never been past the trees that surrounded the McFee property, seemed suddenly to be wondering what pied piper had brought them there. They drifted away like a crowd dispersing after a concert. Geordie waved goodbye, and then they were gone.

I sat down on the big porch swing, deflated. Geordie sat as close as humanly possible to me without being in my lap. I slung my arm around his neck and gave him a half-hearted knuckle rub on the top of his balding sixty-year-old head and he moved a millimetre farther away.

"Are you coming to live here now, Lulu?" Geordie always asked the same question and I always had the same answer: nope, I live in 'insert my latest address here' now. This time it was Nashville, Tennessee. Except, for the time being, while my body healed up, it was 221 Forward Road, with Dad and Kat. Normally, when I visited Fraser Arm, I stayed in a little Boler trailer that Raylene kept for me, tucked away at the back of *Dun Roamin?* There wasn't much to it—a bed and a table. It was my way of ensuring that I never stayed long. But when I got out of the hospital after the crash, the Boler wasn't an option. It made me cantankerous to admit it, but I needed help. At first, I had my seventy-one-year-old aunt/stepmother bathing me and my eighty-one-year-old father cooking my meals.

"I'm going to keep living at Dad's, Geordie. Just for now.

'Til I'm better." There was no point in adding "Then I'm going away again."

"You're better, Lulu. You drove the truck with the bees."

I pulled my head back so that I could focus on Geordie's too-close face. Doris and Raylene were looking at me too. I hate expectancy. The expression on Geordie's face was a mishmash of bewilderment and hope, with a heaping soup spoon of kitchen-table pleading. But the question was as plain as unbuttered toast: *Why* don't you come live with us? Raylene was always less readable but I think her face said something like this: I'm not saying anything, but I think you know what I think. And Doris. I never knew whether Doris was unwilling to show certain thoughts in her eyes or whether she was just really good at hiding them. What I did know, she had told me many, many times: there was a room upstairs for me at the McFees.

●

Doris and Geordie in the McFee house, a room upstairs for me—it's not such a long story. In fact, it was a fairly simple one, at least for Doris. The house wasn't the McFees' anymore. It was Doris'. Mine. It was ours. Aloysius McFee was twenty-five years gone; he'd died in 1982. Or, that's what we were told then, and it was apparently what the police believed. He went over the cliff just north of the China Bar tunnel on the old Fraser Canyon Highway. They recovered the car downstream in the river, a rusted-out Toyota Corolla he'd bought a week earlier.

The Toyota was my first clue that something was not

quite right with the story. Aloysius McFee was a convertible man, and the fresh-off-the-lot 1982 Mustang I'd seen him tootling around town in wasn't at the house. As far as I know it was never found. When I asked the police about the Mustang, they said there was no other car but the Toyota registered in his name.

"Poor bugger," the cop had said, "it was his birthday too." I didn't put it past Aloysius to have faked his death, the dodgy bastard. The Toyota was empty, of course, when they dredged it out of the Fraser River.

What did surprise me was his will. On the phone, the lawyer told me that Mr. McFee had left a suicide note on his kitchen table and a will. The coroner took this as ample evidence that he'd killed himself, despite the lack of body. Anyone who knew Aloysius well might have suspected something. I suppose there weren't many who did know him well, and I hoped there were none who had known him as well as I had. The disappearance of Alice McFee alone should have triggered a deeper dig. I knew he was not a suicide man, but nonetheless, Aloysius McFee was presumed dead, killed in the crash or drowned, then washed down the mighty Fraser River and out to sea. I'd have bet a million that Aloysius' body would never wash up on any beach. Only his dead body would have convinced me that he had not just cashed in his chips and was sipping single malt on some shore where honesty was not highly prized, a fine birthday present to himself.

However, dead or not dead, Aloysius Rufus McFee, of sound mind, etcetera, had left his house, twenty-two acres of prime Fraser Arm land, all chattels and such, and a few shekels, to Doris Tenpenny and me. An equal split. I was standing in a motel office in Butte, Montana, holding that black phone tightly. The motel manager brought me a plastic patio chair when it looked like I might be needing one.

I was twenty-five years old and nursing a fifteen-year-old wound. I was fighting a cocaine habit that left me more angry and confused than a hornet in a glass jar. And I was grieving a man who probably wasn't dead but who I'd never see again. Aloysius McFee had given me a life no child should have had. He'd made me a thief. The bastard had laid out my first line of coke. God knows what else he'd done with others, but with me he'd crossed boundaries that should have put him in jail for the rest of his life. Jail would have really been the end of Aloysius. Maybe that's what he finally feared—that I'd turn on him. But he had a safeguard and he knew it—he'd incriminated me. And he surely knew I was tired of losing people.

And here he'd given me another "gift," this great, big house and a weird co-owner—Doris. He left each of us a simple note too: I'm sorry. We didn't discuss what he meant.

A few days after that phone call in 1982 I'd come back to Fraser Arm and stood in the McFee yard. It was early morning. My body was in some other time zone. The shadow of the house was long and the grass still silver with dew. I watched a pheasant strut across the lawn, a king in his own yard, regal and cocksure. Aloysius loved that pheasant. "If I could be any animal I'd be that damn bird," he'd always said. He had the vanity to know he was already the human equivalent. I might have taken the pheasant as a sign from the other side, I suppose, if I'd ever laid eyes on his dead body. And if I believed in that kind of malarkey.

The shadow of the house slowly shortened as the sun rose and the objects on the big front porch—the huge swing, the wooden armchairs, the coffee table—became less obscure. I'd sat on that old porch, in those chairs, hundreds of times, playing cards with Aloysius, listening to his war stories, watching him sink into his gin. We'd sung together, me with my fiddle or guitar, him plucking away on his ukulele or drumming out a beat on his knees. I was about to step up onto the porch when I realized that Doris Tenpenny was breathing just behind me. She must have been almost forty back then. She was carrying a cardboard box. I think that box contained all Doris had in the world.

The next day, she and Mike Tenpenny were out back building a chicken coop. A couple days later there were a dozen hens and an admittedly gorgeous rooster named Heathcliff the Eighth pecking in the yard. Then Doris was covering the McFees' overgrown kitchen garden with newspapers and chicken shit and rotting leaves. She tore up an acre of sod out on the great back lawn where Aloysius and I used to play croquet, and she gave it the same treatment as the garden. When I asked what she was doing, she pointed to four grubby books on the kitchen table: Carson, Fukuoka, Steiner, Rodale. She wrote these four names at the top of the blackboard in the kitchen, and they stayed there.

About a week later, Doris sent Mike round to find me. I'd had enough of observing her bizarre transformation of the McFees' backyard and had retreated to my trailer. I didn't get many visitors at the Boler, so when I heard the knock I figured it could only be Raylene and I came to the door armed with a juvenile pout. There, instead, was Mike, looking as square as ever, his t-shirt tucked into his pants. The note from Doris was written on a sheet of first-rate writing paper with "Havelock & Hattie McFee" imprinted at the top, Aloysius' grandparents.

Dear Lulu Parsons. When will you be moving in? Sincerely,
Doris Tenpenny

I stared at Mike. The cat had his tongue too. I said thanks and shut the door. It was rude, but I had my reasons. I peered out from behind the curtain of the Boler's tiny window at his departing back, just like a few of my busybody landlords had done. He caught me looking and I was swept with shame.

Those days, Mike had found a role as Dad's surrogate Trevor. Through most of the late seventies and early eighties Trevor was alternately drifting around in the ethers of Vancouver's Downtown East Side sticking a needle in his arm or driving trucks back and forth across the country. Mike, on the other hand, was the living Boy Scout our father had dreamed his sons might be. Mike still had Geordie under his wing, which was a relief to Dad. On weekends Mike and Geordie would disappear in Mike's pickup truck to hunt around in old garbage middens. They brought home the trash of our ancestors, the kind of treasure Geordie adored—rusted license plates, roll-top cans, bits of china, doorknobs and skeleton keys, diaper pins and ivory combs, buckles and buttons, pipes, old coins, and medicine and liquor bottles from bygone times.

That summer in 1982, everyone expected me to move in to the McFees'. I had an infuriating, one-sided fight with Dad. "I can't share a house with Doris Tenpenny," I'd shouted. "What in Hell's name was McFee thinking?"

Dad, the king of gentleness, simply replied, "There, there, Lulu."

●

Now, there I was, another twenty-five years older, Raylene's bee drama over, sitting across from Doris in one of those same old porch chairs. Her hair was long and silver. At sixty-four, she was an oddly elegant creature with her high cheekbones, the flat planes of her face, her dark eyes, and the dirt tattooed into her hands. She shunned makeup, razors, and tweezers like a Baptist shuns dancing. Her approach to the garden was the same—only as much pruning or weeding as was absolutely necessary. Let nature be the caretaker was her motto. The McFee house and property; the animals that made up for Doris' silence with their snorts, grunts, and whinnies; the gardens; the fruit trees—they were all Doris', though officially, I still had half title. She'd made herself a reputation as the one person in Fraser Arm with a huge and valuable piece of land who refused to meet with real estate agents, so the city rose up around her. As she said, if she sold, one of the last bits of Fraser Arm's wildness would vanish. Raylene had told me about a time she'd seen Doris walk an unwelcome agent off the property, her hand just lightly holding the collar of her aggressive Billy goat, Boo.

"Yeah, well," I'd replied, "if she sold, we'd both be millionaires a few times over."

Doris had made the McFee house hers, but so had Geordie, and Mike, and Mike's wife Cidalia. Looking at them that afternoon, I felt an ache in my chest that reminded me that I had no place to call my own, no one's arms to crawl into, and a brother who would never come home.

"I don't know about you, but I'd sure like my morning coffee."

Doris pressed her lips together. I'd forgotten she didn't approve of coffee. Something to do with addiction, and why in God's name the whole world needed something to wake themselves up in the morning, as if God's beautiful morning itself weren't reason enough. I had often imagined Doris wearing a signboard and picketing the coffee shops down on Reifel Road. *Coffee Drinkers, Wake Up.* We squared off for a moment and I frankly had no idea what to do next.

Raylene came to the rescue. "I'm going to head home now, Lulu. I'll drop you off."

Geordie hugged Raylene and me, then turned apprehensively to Doris, even though neither of them was going anywhere. For years, Geordie had wanted a hug from Doris. It was never going to happen. Ever. Doris was parsimonious with touch. She gave animals more physical affection than most people give to their lovers—but people, at least physically, she could do without. I was still trying to figure out her relationship with Lewis Cray. Doris gave Geordie a noncommittal wave like she was brushing away a big bluebottle fly. She wrote on her pad and put it near my face: *Have a look at your room.* Then she gave her rubber boots a wipe on the mat and went in the front door, Geordie following her devotedly.

Raylene took me back to the Airstream where I paced around until she made me a strong latte. I sighed down into a big armchair.

"Why *don't* you move into the McFees'?" she asked.

Names take hold and they stick. When Doris moved in to the house twenty-five years earlier, she had listed the telephone under both our names and painted Tenpenny/ Parsons under McFee on the mailbox. Over time, our names had chipped away until they were unreadable flecks of black, while "McFee" persisted.

"If I haven't moved to the McFees' in all these years,

Raylene, it's not likely to happen now." It was a rare moment when I was miffed with Raylene. From childhood I had done everything I could to stay in her good books. "Why don't *you* move to the farm?" I said.

"I'm taking care of Irene. I'm not going to leave a ninety-four-year-old woman alone with this bunch of bickerers," she said. "Folks in this little trailer park would put its elderly on ice floes if I weren't around."

I highly doubted that. Irene Snyder ran a tight ship and the residents at *Snyder's Dun Roamin?* were, by and large, the miniature-poodle-and-kitchen-garden variety of trailer types who loved or feared Irene, or both. But I knew Raylene loved Irene the way I loved the dogs I'd had: unconditionally.

"I'm just asking you why," Raylene said. "I'm curious. It's a big place and you'd have plenty of room. It's a sight more comfortable than the Boler. And what about your dad?"

"You think Dad and Kat should move there too?" She had to be kidding.

"No. What about your poor old dad getting on in years?"

"I'll be out of his hair soon, Raylene. I'm promised to Tennessee in August."

"You're going to play already?" Raylene leaned back in her Lazy Boy armchair and wiggled her sensible shoe at my knee. "You sure you're ready?"

I wasn't sure I was ready. I wasn't even sure I knew why I'd agreed to play the bluegrass festival. It was a teaching and songwriting festival that attracted big talent, but I wasn't feeling much of that at the moment with my shoulder pro-testing every movement.

"I don't have a choice. Promises to keep, Raylene."

She looked at me as much to say, you're full of shit.

DORIS

One can never tell with chard. Sometimes it will take like dandelions do to the lawn. Other times it grows up like a poor cousin, runty and thin. Doris thinks of the Dashwood sisters—she is rereading *Sense and Sensibility*. Marianne and Elinor may have been thin, but they were surely not runty. Doris wonders if they ate chard. She is watching Geordie out in the chard, through the kitchen window, as she does the dishes. His big gumboots are tromping on the row behind him. He won't notice until he turns around, and then he'll tromp on some more. That's all right. They've grown a chard forest this year. Geordie stands up and turns around and notices the trampled chard, and Doris smiles when she sees him look right at the window. Geordie always checks to see if anyone has seen him make a mistake. No one here ever is mad at Geordie, but he acts as though they might be. He's got the biggest armful of chard anyone's ever seen, and it looks like he's going to cut more. The trampled ones. It will be the biggest armful of chard in Canada. Swiss chard, in Canada.

Doris is still pleased that Geordie came to live with her all those years ago. Leaving home was not something Doris ever imagined she would do. But everything about the experience of packing her box, saying goodbye to Father, and moving up the street is still peony pink after twenty-five years. It was not that Wally Parsons wanted Geordie gone. Doris just believed then, as she does now, that all children should leave home one day. Even the Dorises and the Geordies of Canada. Doris wanted Geordie to have the peony pink as well.

Father found out—Fraser Arm was still small—and he made it his business to tell Doris that she would rue the day. Father came and stood on the porch, on the outside of the door. "You will rue the day you let Geordie Parsons live with you," he said. *Rue. The. Day.* Doris did not ever let Father in the house and Doris has not once rued the day, even if Geordie does step on the chard and other vegetables. Even if Geordie eats more raspberries and blackberries and cherries and apricots than he puts in the bucket. Geordie is good with the animals. They like him.

Doris whistles a dishwashing tune. Father went to his grave having forgotten how to whistle. This strikes Doris as something that would make her very lonely. Lewis likes it when Doris whistles. Sometimes, when they are walking at night, he gives her hand a little squeeze and says, "Whistle for me Doris." Doris whistles the first song that comes to mind, even if it is not really an evening stroll song. When she was in high school, she thought that Lewis was old. But Lewis is only four years older than Doris.

Many years ago, Doris wrote to Lewis: I would like to talk.

Lewis, who was at the egg stand, said, "Okay, what about?"

Doris wrote: No, I would like to be able to talk. She tapped the word "able" several times with her pencil.

Lewis said, "I'd like to be able to sing."

Doris wrote: What?

Lewis said, "What, what? Or what would I like to sing?"

Doris wrote: To sing, what?

Lewis said, "I'd like to sing with Lulu Parsons."

Doris laughed. I'd like to sing with Lulu Parsons too, she wrote.

Lewis said, "I love you, Doris."

LULU

Trevor's girlfriend, Julia, let me into her apartment on
Harwood. There wasn't much of him in it. It was a girl's place
with floral curtains, pretty cushions, a nervous black-and-white
cat eyeing me from a corner. Julia was pretty too. I guessed that
she was in her late-thirties. I could still see the surprise in her
eyes. They said: I'm too young to have someone die on me.

"Would you like a coffee?"

I said, "Yes. Please." Then, "No. Sorry. I'm good." I didn't
have anything to say to Julia. I just wanted Trevor's things,
then I would go.

"I was so curious to meet you. Trev talked about you."

Trev. We never called him Trev. No one ever called him
Trev.

"That is, he talked about you all, but about you mostly."

"He did." I meant it as a question but I couldn't get the
right inflection.

"I shouldn't have said curious. I apologize. Curious to meet you sounds rude. I just, well, he always said he wanted me to meet you and I . . . I've heard your music." She pulled a tattered album from a shelf. My first. "There's a CD around here somewhere. I guess you should take his old record player as well. I sing too, sometimes. Well, not like you."

I suddenly felt cruel letting her talk on nervously while I just stood there taking in the room. I smiled at her and tried to make it genuine. Julia smiled back and held the album out to me. She had little hands and they looked soft and girlish. I imagined them touching Trevor and fought back a wave of raw grief and regret.

"Keep it. And the record player. Can't do much with albums and no record player, eh?"

"I went to the funeral." She laughed lightly and then her eyes filled with tears. "I had to introduce myself to everyone as his girlfriend."

"No one knew, Julia. I'm sorry." I wondered how long she'd known him.

Julia put her hand over her mouth. "I know. It's okay."

"I would've been there too," I said, "but they wouldn't let me out of the hospital. Our father didn't want to wait."

"Of course," she said.

The police told Dad. In the hospital, when I was conscious enough to hear the news myself, Alan told me how the police car had pulled into the driveway and sat there, as though the cops were working up their courage. When the two policemen finally got out of the car, Dad said, "Someone's dead." Of course, two sombre police officers at your front door can't mean much else. Thank God Alan was there. Dad didn't know either of the policemen, not like in the old days when the cops in Fraser Arm were his friends. Alan said Dad dropped to his knees right there on the front steps. I think he had the funeral right away so that I would live. If he delayed, it would mean he was waiting for me to die too, waiting to have a double funeral. He'd made that declaration by burying Trevor: Trevor is dead. I will not lose another child. Lulu will live.

I thought that if I was alive, Trevor must be too. But I thought wrong. Trevor died in the middle of the road.

The autopsy report said that his helmet was gone; he'd experienced severe head trauma, internal injuries, a broken neck, and countless other broken bones. The report gave details that Dad shouldn't have read and that he refused to let me see. That's all he would tell me. All eighty-one years of him hung onto me as if without me in the world the grass would no longer grow, roses wouldn't bloom, spring would never come again. Maybe I got better because he believed so hard. He wasn't religious, but he prayed to someone during those weeks I was hanging in the balance.

Coup contrecoup, they called it. A doctor still new enough to be willing to spend the time drew me a diagram: here was my brain hitting one side of my skull, here it was bouncing back to hit the other side. Here was where the bruising and bleeding happened. This is what the swelling looked like. Here was where the shunt went into my skull while I was still unconscious. This was why I was unconscious then semiconscious for so long. There was more bleeding and more swelling. Convulsions. Infection. There was my ruptured spleen, which they took out. They also jammed my dislocated shoulder back into place, set my broken ankle, and sewed up my ripped skin. You're lucky, they said. You'll likely play again. The torn ligaments in your shoulder might cause a condition known as chronic instability, but that's all, they said.

You're lucky. Lucky is relative.

"Here it is," Julia said, putting her hand on a suitcase. "He never unpacked it. He just said that if anything ever happened to him to give it to you."

"Can I sit down?" I asked. The suitcase was Mum's.

Julia brought a kitchen chair. I leaned my cane against the couch and it clattered to the floor. She picked it up and then stood above me, her hands fretting and smoothing down her shirt. I looked around the apartment, imagining Trevor here with her. Everything was dowdy, despite the efforts Julia had made with the pretty bits. The carpet was worn and dirty at the door, there were water stains on the floor near the windows. The kitchen cabinets were dark 1970s wood. But it was so 221 Forward Road I could imagine Trevor at home there. Julia was watching me explore the place with my eyes. She may have felt I was judging her, but nothing could have been less true. Julia had had something I wanted: she'd just loved Trevor. She'd told me that. It wasn't complicated; she wanted him back. I wanted that—to have been able to just love him, for it to have been that simple—just once. I wanted my brother back too.

When I took the suitcase from her she held on to the handle a little too long, as though in taking it I would be erasing Trevor's last warm trace in her life. She had to carry it to my car for me anyway. As we passed the bedroom door I caught a glimpse of a folded blanket hanging on the back of a chair. My mother and I had knit it together years and years earlier. It was an inexact thing, our couch blanket for years, knit by a nine-year-old in three shades of purple squares and crocheted together by my mother with black yarn. In Julia's bedroom, the July sun shone through it, illuminating its centre, making it beautiful.

"Do you mind if I keep it," Julia said and she began to cry. She kept patting her belly and smoothing her shirt down. I don't know why it took me so long to figure it out. She had been showing me with her hands. There it was in the curve of her belly.

"You're pregnant."

Julia cried harder.

"Christ."

"We wanted it."

All I could do was reach and put my arms around her.

●

I didn't want to be alone. Jericho Beach was noisy, a midsummer's Friday afternoon crowd. I found a parking spot facing the ocean and rested my forehead on the steering wheel. I could have slept, and might have. I don't remember. Trevor's suitcase sat on the passenger seat, a living thing beside me. I'd wanted to put a seat belt around it, open the passenger-side window to give it some air. Whatever was in there would have something important to say, but I couldn't open it. None of us knew much about Trevor's life. He was on the road most of the time, driving big rigs across the continent. Except for our short telephone conversation the day before we'd met up in Vancouver, I can't remember him ever having called me. Anything I knew about Trevor came from Dad, or occasionally, one of the twins. Even Dad's information was thin. Often no one would hear from Trevor for months. Sometimes he'd phone and leave a number and then, when Dad called a month later to say hello, he'd be gone, the number disconnected, or there'd be a woman with a disappointed voice on the line.

We weren't so dissimilar, Trevor and I. At first we'd both come home for important events—Dad's birthday, Ambrose's wedding. Then there were the years neither of us turned up for Christmas. He made excuses and so did I. One year he was in jail, though we didn't hear about that until after he'd been released. Other times he'd call from somewhere in the States, too many miles away to make it home. A year or two would pass before we would set eyes on one another. When we did, we didn't have much to say to each other. He'd have a new girlfriend or some get-rich plan. Often we argued. Jesus. It broke Dad's heart back then, and now it broke mine.

I carried the suitcase with me down to the beach and bought a hot dog for supper at the concession stand. I knew I'd regret it. I could see Birdie's horrified face as I took the first bite. There are worse regrets. For three months I'd been thinking *if only*. If only I'd never agreed to meet him. If only I'd said no to the motorcycle ride. If only we'd stayed on that log in English Bay and I'd picked up the wedding cake and gone home.

Trevor's suitcase and I sat on the crowded beach, anonymous and ignored, a middle-aged woman with no reason for being there. At suppertime the young families stopped building sandcastles. Parents gathered plastic buckets and shrieking children and went home. Then the sleek-bodied teenagers arrived, otters flirting with one another. Later there were the gay guys cruising with their cute butts and bulging bikinis. When the sun finally set, I left them all to their paramours, picked up what was left of Trevor, and went back to Fraser Arm.

I put the suitcase down in the kitchen. It would have elicited too many questions if Dad and Kat had seen it. Kat looked up when I came into the parlour, the hopeful face of a person waiting for news, nice news; the worst news had already been delivered. Dad was asleep sitting up on the couch next to her. He was smaller since Trevor's death. The television was flashing brightly but the sound was turned off. Sleep had loosened Dad's grip on Kat's hand, but as she began to gently remove it, his hand unconsciously tightened on hers. She left it there. As I'd grown older I'd learned to be grateful for Kat and the sweetness she brought Dad. He was a man who deserved some. They'd married, years ago, after Mum had been declared legally dead. They'd snuck away to Victoria for a weekend without telling us about it until it was all said and done.

Kat had done nothing more than put her finger to her lips but Dad woke, like a child sensing the babysitter tiptoeing from a room. Now there were two sweet old people gazing up at me. And I was a child again. They wanted something from me. I felt a prick of exasperation; they should have remembered that I'd never been a particularly dutiful child. Maybe parents never give up on their kids, except those parents who do so completely. Dad was so gentle. I'd eaten benign men alive for breakfast in my twenties. But benign's opposite was caustic and difficult, like the men I'd so often wrangled with—sexy, messed up bass players, nomadic saxophonists. I looked at my father's absurd comb-over and bent to kiss him. Leave the old man alone, Lulu.

"I think you should invite Julia to supper sometime," I said.

I kissed Kat too, picked up the suitcase in the kitchen, and went to my room. I sat on the end of the bed and stared at the two faded and dusty paint-by-numbers Mum had done when she first came to Canada. I remember her hammering them to my wall when I was about nine. I tried to imagine her sixteen-year-old self in Canada with a brand-new baby and husband, doing a paint-by-number. I ran my finger along the bookshelf. A few old familiars, but the rest were newer— bedtime stories for Ambrose's boys. Ambrose's late marriage to Resentful Roberta, as Trevor had uncharitably but accurately dubbed her, had produced three boys and ended in divorce. The boys' baby toys, now outgrown, were in a box at the foot of my bed beside a wicker dog basket. I tucked my toes under the ragged quilt that had been on one of our beds when we were young, wishing for one of Alan and Naomi's soft-bellied dogs to rub my feet on. There was always a room for me out at their place in Langley, Naomi said. If I wanted one. And a fat black lab to sleep with. Everyone, it seemed, was keeping a room for me.

I waited until I heard Dad and then Kat go to bed. If there were any more secrets in that suitcase like the one Trevor had told me at English Bay, I didn't want Dad to know. That secret had ruined Trevor. In the end, I thought, it had killed him.

I bent my nose to the suitcase's brown herringbone. It had smelled the same way forty years earlier, already with the mustiness of a thousand journeys, though it had really had only one. "Eau de long mildewy voyage," Trevor had once called it. Geordie and I'd lugged Mum's suitcase around, filled with tinkertoys or jars of bugs or junk mail and pretended to board ships bound for England. Sometimes we'd collect every shoe brush, hairbrush, and comb in the house, and pretend to be the Fuller Brush Man our father had been before he got his job driving the dry-cleaning delivery vans.

The locks on the suitcase were sticky but worked; they both clunked open. The satiny lining was intact though the elastic had gone on the top pocket and the gold-coloured fabric had bled white in spots as though someone had splattered it with bleach. It was tightly packed, and at first glance looked like the memorabilia of a life that had ended at fifteen. On top was a goofy caricature of Trevor and his first girlfriend, kissing. Under that there was a dog-eared LP—Otis Redding's *The Dock of the Bay*—that Trevor had played until we both knew every note by heart. Beneath it, still in cellophane, was a pristine copy of the Beatle's *White Album*. A pair of kid-sized cowboy boots was stuffed with track-and-field ribbons, a little soccer trophy, his Scout knife, and a paper bag containing his Scout sash, the one onto which I'd sewn his badges. I had forgotten how many merit badges Trevor had earned. He'd always seemed so unmeritorious.

There was a stack of Trevor's C to C+ report cards signed on the back by Dad or Mum and another stack of letters addressed to Trevor in the tidy handwriting of girls and women. I opened a letter with a fourteen-cent stamp on it. It was from a girl named Kathi who dotted her i's in daisies—a girl in love, poor thing. I shook a handful of undated photographs out of a manila envelope; Trevor with women I had only briefly met—his wives, a few early girlfriends—and many, most, I'd never set eyes on.

I pulled out a shoebox tied shut with kitchen string and undid the knot. Inside, wrapped in softened tissue paper, was a neatly folded wool sweater, the inner half of a sweater set, cream coloured, with a pearly button at the neck. I pressed it to my face. I was just imagining Mum's scent, I knew, but I instantly saw her leaning back against the kitchen counter in a pose in which she must have frequently stood because the memory was iconic: her arms crossed, both sets of fingers stroking the soft wool of this sweater at her elbows.

In the shoebox was a black-and-white photograph of Mum wearing it, but not in the pose I'd remembered. She looked like a teenager and was flanked by Dad on her right and a man I didn't recognize to her left. Both Mum and the man were wearing the stupid paper crowns of Christmas crackers. All three held cocktail glasses toward the photographer but Dad was looking to his right, slightly away from the camera and away from Mum, who was grinning like a drunkard. I studied the other man's face. He looked like a very young Aloysius McFee. I felt my arms grow numb. I turned the photograph over. Mum had written *Wally, Al and me. New Year's Eve 1955.*

Wally, Al, and me. The words stung. They couldn't have known Aloysius that well. Neighbours, hellos in the street, handshakes in the hardware store; we all knew the McFees. But New Year's drinks together? No. The boys would all have been born at the time the photo was taken, but not me. At New Year's in 1955, Mum would have been twenty-four. Aloysius had never mentioned knowing Mum or Dad well enough to have posed for a New Year's photograph with them, his fingers wrapped tight around my mother's waist.

There was something else in the shoebox—a postcard with an ornate, black-and-white illustration of a skeleton walking with a cane, and above it in gothic letters, the words

Memento mori. On the back, in his immature scrawl, Trevor had written *Fuck You.* And on the right side, *Mrs. Wally Parsons.* But no address.

At the bottom of the suitcase were a dozen or so tattered file folders. There were dates written on the outside of each folder and at first I thought they were just his trucking records. But when I opened them I felt I had climbed into a small boat at the shore's edge and someone had given it a violent shove. Every folder contained information about our mother. Out to sea I drifted, farther and farther away from the shore of knowledge, with nothing but my bare hands to paddle me home. Trevor couldn't have believed she was still living. He had decided that she was dead before Dad had. He'd erected the little cross in the yard for her. He'd been the one to insist Dad have the memorial, call the lawyer, and start the process of declaring her dead. But he'd been looking for her. I flipped quickly through all the folders, hoping to find something that told me why. Then I sat and, until dawn, read the contents of every folder.

There were copies of the early police files. I found letters from the RCMP and from Scotland Yard reporting no trace of a woman named Elisabeth Margaret Parsons, née Fenwick, born February 10, 1931. A letter signed by a police constable in Carbonear, Newfoundland, said that a Mrs. Parsons was not known in the area. One folder was filled with what must have been private detectives' reports: No tax returns had been submitted. No passport or driver's licenses issued. Trevor had even torn the Fenwick and Parsons pages from telephone books across Canada. Nothing in the files was dated past 1980, when it seemed his search had dribbled to an end.

I got up and went to Kat's parlour. It was finished now; the plywood and studs had finally been covered with gyproc and painted or wallpapered. Sometime in the late-eighties, after even Geordie had left home to live at the McFees' and there were no mouths to feed but their own, Kat had insisted on progress. Outside, too. It had taken a while, but Dad, Geordie, and Mike Tenpenny had put up fresh tarpaper and covered it with cedar siding. Since Dad had retired, a healthy patch of grass had replaced the mud ruts. Kat had insisted that the dry cleaning company tow away the dead delivery vans too.

Trevor's ashes were on a small table of their own in the parlour. Kat had cleared away a few knick-knacks out of respect for him. Her prize piece, a bosomy ceramic woman wearing a red bathing suit and reclining on a crocodile, was under the table for now, until we decided what to do with Trevor. I thought he would have liked to recline against the bathing beauty and her voluptuous breasts for some time, if not for all eternity, but Kat wouldn't hear of it. I picked up the cardboard box of ashes. The funeral director had made some fawning comment about us surely wanting to honour our dead with a fitting urn. That was the fatal trigger. Dad took a plastic bag and a box.

I took the box to the bathroom and stood on the scale with it. Then I put it on the counter and weighed myself. Trevor weighed five and a half pounds, give or take a few ounces. I opened the cardboard box and unrolled the top of the plastic bag. I put my fingers in and touched the ashes. I was surprised by how soft they were. Could this be all of Trevor? Tears welled up in my eyes. I rubbed my fingers together but the traces of ash wouldn't come off. It seemed wrong to wash the ashes down the drain or wipe them on the towel so I left them where they were. I wondered what part of Trevor those ashes on my fingers had been. Shoulder, cheek, toe?

"What were you looking for?" I said, crying.

I missed him. I was struck by how violent the pain felt. By how staggeringly brutal it was to lose a brother, and not just because it was before his time. That we had not been close added a dimension of suffering that ached through my bones like influenza. I'd behaved as though we had eternity to heal the wound that had separated us as brother and sister. Or maybe that was hindsight, and if I were honest, I'd admit I hadn't thought about it at all. Perhaps I hadn't cared until the fates had already sung, "It's too late, baby." *Memento mori*—a reminder of the inevitability of death. Maybe Trevor had understood. His calling me might have been the smallest opening of the smallest of gates.

Back in my room I fitted the box of ashes into the suitcase. I slid it under my bed, where it wouldn't be found, and slipped out the kitchen door. Dad had hung a load of laundry out the night before. The dew on the tea towels at the end of the line was sparkling in the sun's first rays. I'd never had Dad's faith. It wasn't just that I questioned whether the blue skies would turn to clouds and that it would rain overnight. I felt that I had never known whether the sun would rise again in the morning. But Dad was gutted now. Through his grief I had begun to understand that loss and death were not twins. With time, loss could be understood; however torturous the path through it, it would soften. But death—it was inexplicable. That there was not even a second between life and death was what I could not comprehend. Trevor alive, then dead. Forever.

It felt as though some guy named Regret had taken me to

the dance, we'd danced all night and I was exhausted, but he wasn't going to put me to bed. So I walked, caneless, out the driveway and onto the street. I turned instinctively toward the sun. Walking east up Forward Road toward the McFees' as the sky turned from pale grey to blue then pink in unhurried degrees.

I was thinking about another early morning when I'd been up all night. It was 1983, about a year after we'd heard about Aloysius' death. I was in Fraser Arm for two weeks, staying in the Boler. I'd been getting gigs all across the States, and, miraculously, was about to record my first album at the tender age of twenty-six. Someone believed in me even if I didn't. Geordie was still living with Dad and Kat. Alan and Trevor were gone and married, and Trevor was already divorced from the wife of his first short marriage and onto his second. Ambrose was logging in Haida Gwaii. One night during that visit, I'd gone drinking at the Fraser Arm Motel with some old boyfriend who no doubt hoped to get me into bed again. After the bar closed we went to someone else's place and drank some more. By the time we got back to his apartment he was so drunk he passed out before he could get his pants off. I remember feeling as though I'd been rescued by some angel. That cool spring night I walked all the way up Reifel Road and ended up at the McFees'. On the porch of the house that by then belonged to Doris and me, I'd curled up in a chair, clutching my sweater around my body, and waited for the alcohol to stop playing with my blood. When the sky grew lighter I got up and cupped my hands around my face to peer through the window on the front door. There were no lights on. Suddenly the door opened and Doris was standing there in a pair of men's pyjamas. There was a lamb behind her.

Doris' silence didn't make her uncommanding. Follow me, her gesture said, and I'd obeyed. The lamb followed her, and I followed the lamb into the kitchen where there were quite a few more lambs. Nine, in fact. Doris had acquired a dog, a sweet looking black-and-white mongrel, and it was disgustingly cleaning up the lambs' droppings. Doris was stirring a pot on the stove. She poured warmed milk into a line of baby bottles on the counter and shoved a big black rubber nipple onto each one, then handed me two bottles and pointed to the lambs. I did as I was told. Two fat lambs butted their heads against the nipples and sucked the bottles dry in seconds. I tried to keep track of which ones I'd fed. Doris knew. She wagged her finger at me when I went to feed an opportunistic one who'd already had his fill. They seemed only slightly different—one dark ear, a bit of black around an eye, a tail with a brown spot. The only one I was sure of was the fat fellow, a real bruiser, who'd pushed the others out of the way. The lambs, fed, seemed to know there wouldn't be more for a while and settled on floor rugs or in the dog's basket.

Too many twins, Doris wrote in a notebook. *Mother rejects one twin or both.*

"For how long?" I asked.

Until they can eat grass and hay.

"When is that?"

She wrote, *A few more weeks? Sometimes a mother takes them back. Or another mother takes them if hers dies. They'll go outside. Soon*, she wrote. Then: *Why are you here? Will you be living here? Would you like to see your room?*

I had no idea what in God's name Doris meant by "my room." And it was awkward having a conversation with someone who wrote while I talked. I felt that I should be writing too. I wondered if she would seem so blunt if her words came out of her mouth instead of out of her pencil. "No, I'm just here for another week. I'm recording an album next week in Nashville."

Yes, she wrote. What she meant by that wasn't clear either.

I stood to leave. One of the lambs had fallen asleep against my leg and it fell onto my feet. I picked it up and was shaken by how much like a baby it was, the girth and weight of it. It nuzzled its woolly head into my neck and I buried my face in its fleece. It fell asleep in my arms. I'd eaten my share of the little fellows with mint sauce. I wondered whether I would be able to do so again. I carried the lamb around the kitchen. Even after a year in the house, Doris had changed almost nothing. The furniture was the same, the curtains, the tea towels, the art on the walls. Doris hadn't even taken down the previous year's calendar. It was still on the month that Aloysius had "died." Beside the calendar, dozens of bits of paper were tacked to the wall. Doris nodded her head at them, expressionless. I went closer. They were notes, written on small pieces of paper, lined, unlined, torn from the edges of newspapers and envelopes: *Parsnips contain vitamin C and calcium. Mrs. Halfnight named her daughter Bonnie Rue. Elizabeth really cared for her dog most of all. Love at first sight is horse manure. God sees the little sparrow fall. The truth will set you free. A, I know. A*

I'd wondered that early morning, with some anxiety, whether Doris was even stranger than I'd thought. "Did you write these?"

I found them.

"Where?"

She pointed at the canisters that had been on the McFees'

kitchen counter for as long as I had known Aloysius, then she tapped the red lid of the flour canister. We had an identical set at home—Flour, Sugar, Coffee, Tea written in curlicued letters circled by red roses. I'd never had reason to touch the canisters in Aloysius' kitchen, except for when I made Aloysius his instant coffee with his half teaspoon of sugar. Keeping his figure, he always said.

"Who wrote them?" I asked.

Doris shrugged. She pulled out a thumbtack and handed me one of the notes, turning it over to show me the hand-written A on the back. She flipped up a few more. Each one was marked with the same A. Aloysius or Alice? What, I'd wondered, could anyone have meant by these?

Suddenly, the dog barked and the lambs leapt up and the herd of animals all ran to the back door. The door opened and Geordie came right in.

"Doris, I'm ready. And I fed the chickens and the pigs," he said. When he saw me he clapped his hand to his mouth. "Oops. Oh, no. Lulu." He looked nervously at Doris.

"What are you doing here, Geordie?" The door opened again and Mike Tenpenny came in. "Lulu," he said, looking surprised and uncomfortable. "Morning." He picked up a single key off a hook behind the door and rattled it. "I got the post-hole digger. We good to go, Doris?"

Doris nodded and Geordie and Mike went out as fast as they had come in. Doris stepped over the lambs' baby gate and followed them out to the back porch, and I followed her. Geordie climbed up into an old pickup truck and slid behind the steering wheel. Geordie loved to pretend to drive. I expected him to slide over, but he started the truck up and Mike hopped into the passenger seat.

"Whoa. Whoa. Geordie can't drive. What's he doing?" I started off the porch.

Doris touched my arm and removed her hand quickly, as if she'd been scalded. She pulled a pad and pen from the breast pocket of her pyjama top and waved it at me. The truck was already bumping off along the back driveway into the woods. I read Doris' note: *He stays on the farm. He's a very good driver.* Then she bent to snatch up the little bruiser of a lamb who was making a break for it. She cuddled him close and waggled and pulled each of his ears and rubbed her chin on his forehead. Then she looked him right in the eye and nodded and shook her head and squeezed him again as if they had just had a long conversation. She went in the house and closed the door, leaving me standing on the porch wondering whether those were Mr. McFee's pyjamas she was wearing.

It must have been eight o'clock by then. I stomped over to *Dun Roamin?* and stood outside the Airstream, wondering if it was too early to knock. Birdie came out the door with a basket of gardening tools and seed packages. Raylene followed her in rubber boots.

"Just going up to the McFees', Lulu," Birdie said. "Want to come? See our gardens?"

"Geordie's driving the truck," I said.

Raylene and Birdie exchanged a look. "Yeah," they both said at once and smiled.

"And Doris has lambs in the kitchen. The house can't be like that. It's a pig sty."

"She doesn't have the piglets in the kitchen too does she? That Doris." Birdie laughed.

Raylene knocked on Mrs. Snyder's trailer door and out she came, also dressed for gardening.

The realization that my family and friends were making a life at the McFees' swam through me like cold water. "I think I'm going to sell. I think we should sell the McFees'." I'd shouted it.

"It's hardly yours, Lulu," Raylene had said very calmly. She took Mrs. Snyder's arm and the three of them hiked out the driveway.

•

A quarter of a century later, there I was standing outside the McFees' at dawn, mourning my brother and wondering whether Doris had lambs in the kitchen again. A light came on. Doris would be up. I almost felt like going in for a cup of hot goats' milk. Almost.

DORIS

This is not the first time this summer that Doris has noticed Lulu Parsons standing in the driveway, but it is the first time she has seen her without crutches or cane. Lulu has every right to stand and stare. The house and farm are half hers. But why Lulu doesn't come live in the big room upstairs troubles Doris. Doris feels some impatience bordering on annoyance over Lulu's resistance. Twenty-five years is a very long time. Raylene says Doris will have to wait until Lulu runs out of excuses. This morning, however, there was something heartening: for the first time, Lulu's colour and the colour of Lulu standing in the driveway were the same: a deep turquoise green, like the ocean on the other side of the world.

Doris wonders whether she should break her rule. Perhaps Lulu would come to stay if Doris had some coffee in the house. It is not that Doris does not like the smell of coffee. God knows she cannot walk down Reifel Road—which she rarely does anymore, for more reasons than one—without smelling it in every second doorway. But the people spilling out of the coffee shops with their wasteful paper cups in hand—I can't start the day without my coffee, they say—make Doris sigh.

Doris does not believe in wishes like Geordie does. Geordie is wish mad. Geordie wishes when he blows out birthday candles. He wishes on the first star and when stars fall. He wishes when an eyelash falls out, when ladybugs land on him, and when he catches a dandelion fluff. Sometimes Geordie wishes on nothing at all. This seems a more commonsensical wish strategy to Doris. This morning, Doris wishes on nothing at all that Lulu will move in to the house. She makes a second wish . . . that her first wish will come true. Even Doris knows that's ironic.

Doris' pencil hovers over her pad. Chore lists come in handy now as she frequently forgets what she went downstairs for and has to go back upstairs to remember. Raylene and Birdie, who are two years older than Doris—sixty-six—assure her that this is normal for women their age. Father said that Raylene and Birdie were an abomination, but Doris knows this to be untrue. And, what's more, Father is dead.

It does not please Doris to think of Father's death, nor the manner of it. But it does not displease her that Father is gone. Father was eighty-eight, and that is a long enough life. At the burial, she had hoped he had not been disappointed when he met his maker. Father was disappointed by everything else, *God knows*. Mother had had Father's name carved in plain letters on a plain tombstone. She'd added another Tenpenny name: Baby Isaiah Mark, who was born and died before the rest of them. When everyone saw Baby Isaiah's name, Doris thought someone would take Mother's hand but no one did. Later, in Mother's kitchen with her sister and brothers, Joan began to laugh. And then she began to cry. They were middle-aged children, laughing and crying in their old mother's kitchen. And Mike took Mother's hand. Mother's colour has changed since then. She is more the outside of lemon peel now.

Doris' chore list has stuck to the kitchen table. Spilled milk again. What had she written?

Wild Things Café: beans, 6 dozen onions, zucchini, eggplant, baby turnips, peppers (red, orange), garlic, parsley and rosemary, arugula and coriander, kale (as much as can be spared)

Organic Grocer: will pick themselves at 12:30. Today.

Move chickens

There are eggs to gather and package up for the café and the health food store. Goats to milk. And the cow. Pigs to feed, raspberries to pick. There is always wood to chop and stack. Someone is coming from the restaurant to pick up the hens and quails. Birdie will be here soon. And Mother. Doris takes a knife and scrapes the gluey list from the table and puts it in the paper recycling. She doesn't need a list.

LULU

Aunt Kat and I used to play a game when I was little. Whenever we had to wait in the dentist or doctor's office we'd make up stories about our fellow waiting room prisoners: their name, what crime they'd committed, and how they were planning their escape. Just before I was released from the hospital I had asked if I could skip physiotherapy. My doctor looked at me horror-struck. She said: "Sure, if you never want to walk properly or play the fiddle again." So there I was, prisoner again, waiting my turn to be pushed into stretches that would have been beyond my ability before the accident and making up stories in my head about the sweet-looking redheaded woman across from me and the preppy kid with the toe-to-thigh cast. I was wiggling my foot, pretending to read one of the well-pawed trashy magazines, and trying to come up with some interesting crime for the preppy boy when I noticed the man kitty-corner from me staring unabashedly. I don't think I'd ever seen anyone with eyes quite like his—almond shaped and lightly slanted, dark as a crow's feathers, with lashes thicker and longer than a woman's.

"Lulu Parsons?" he asked.

"None other." Was I forgetting someone I'd gone to school with? Or—*God*—slept with? I wouldn't have forgotten those eyes.

"I knew it. I'm a huge fan." He smiled at me as though he'd just won first prize on track and field day. Happily, my physio came to the door and waved me in.

"Thanks," I said, gathering up my things.

I came out half an hour later feeling as though someone had worked me over with a rolling pin but with my physiotherapist's assurance that everything was getting better. Mr. Crow Eyes was just going out the door.

"How fortuitous," he said, holding the door for me.

"Fortuitous."

"What a goof, I am," he said, stealing my very thought. "I'm Robin Chaudhury."

"Lulu Parsons."

"Yes. I know. Lulu, ah . . . would you like to grab a coffee?"

I had a weird mix of followers, from the young alternative type to just plain old folksters, and not one had ever asked me more than when was I coming to their town. I wasn't used to Robin Chaudhury's level of enthusiasm.

"Sorry, I'm being really forward." His face flushed. "It's just I've been following your music for about thirty years and here you are right in front of me."

Trevor would have called him a goofus. But he was kind of a sweet goofus. I hadn't thought of my most recent ex, or any other man, for quite a while, not in the way I was now thinking about this dark-eyed person before me. I heard Aloysius McFee in my ear: Nothing ventured . . . .

Robin ordered something called an Ayurvedic soy latte and a spelt muffin. I had an Americano—black, the closest to plain old coffee I could get—and hoped he wasn't in Doris Tenpenny's camp. It was a funky little café and the young granola-type baristas seemed to know Robin, which made me nervous.

"I heard about your accident. I'm very sorry about your brother."

Where people read about me I don't know. I'm not that famous. My manager runs a little website and she also writes a blog for me, but she hadn't written about the accident there.

"Yeah, it was rotten," I said. "He was only halfway through his life. We're all just trying to move on."

Robin looked alarmed and apologetic at once. "Sorry, sorry."

"So, what are *you* doing physio for?" I said, changing the subject.

He held up an arm. "Wrist," he said. "I broke it."

"How?"

"A stupid accident. I was running and I fell. Did the old reflex thing—two hands out in front. It's lucky I didn't break both."

Lucky. Like me and my brain. Lucky just because it could have been worse.

Robin was tracing lines and creating patterns with the sugar I had spilled on the table. "Will you, uh, be able . . ." he asked.

"Will I play again? Yup. I've been warned that there's

a possibility I could end up with something called chronic instability, but I'm not going to put those words into my vocab for now." They already seemed to be overly fitting descriptors of my life so far, and the other condition the doctors had warned me about—permanent dislocation—didn't sound any better. "I'm booked at a bluegrass festival in Tennessee in August." I had no idea whether I was going to be able to perform well, but I was going anyway. I'd outstayed my own limits in Fraser Arm. It was only the physiotherapy that was keeping me in town now.

"Which festival?"

"Badger Hills. It's a fiddle and banjo teaching gig. Songwriting, too."

"I saw you in Nashville ten years ago," he said. He looked shy. "It must be amazing to be able to play an instrument and sing like you do. I wanted to be a country and western singer when I was a kid. I was totally into the Grand Ole Opry. Then I hit high school and our sadistic music teacher— Mr. Burge—suggested I just mouth the words during the Christmas concert."

"Mr. Burge. I know him."

"Really?"

Wow, what kind of an innocent, I thought, is Robin Chaudhury? "No, I mean, I know of his kind. All your dreams dashed by a music teacher. Not an uncommon experience."

"My mom went to school and took Burge to task. It didn't do any good, of course. My country and western career dreams were dashed. And I was mortified. She's a fiery thing my mother. Scottish. Everyone said she could shoot light-ning out of her black eyes."

"Which would explain you. Your eyes, I mean," I said,

wishing instantly that I hadn't let it slip that I'd been looking at him so closely.

"Partly. My father's from India. They met there when Mom was working with a Christian charity in the fifties."

"So did you grow up in India?"

"I was born there and we emigrated to Canada in 1965."

"So you don't remember much about it. You must have been just a baby in sixty-five."

"Oh no," Robin said. "I was eight. You and I are the same age. In fact, you're just a few days older than me." He was beaming again.

All of a sudden I felt uneasy. Was I sitting in a café with a fundamentalist Christian non-coffee drinking bluegrass fanatic who'd been stalking me for thirty years?

"I should go," I said.

Out on the street we shared an awkward handshake. Why is saying farewell to someone you wish to be quickly rid of so difficult? I had to go around him to get back to my car and his beaming tallness was blocking my route. Suddenly, and thankfully, a rain of acorns fell from the oak tree above us and scattered on the sidewalk. While we stood there looking up at the crow shaking the tree, another nut landed with a 'ponk' on my forehead, bounced off, and Robin's unwounded hand snapped out with perfect precision and caught it. He pocketed the nut.

"I'm not stalking you," he said.

"Okay."

So, what was he going to do with that nut?

DORIS

Doris has found Henry, the Crèvecœur rooster, dead by weasel. She finds expressions such as "in the prime of his life" trite and beside the point, but Henry was. She strokes his glossy black feathers and folds them over the wound on the back of his neck. Doris feels a trace of anger with God for creating an animal that will kill for sport. Henry is not the first chicken the weasels have killed for sport. Nor is this the first Henry the weasels have taken in the prime of his life. The weasels could not know, of course, that the Crèvecœur chickens are rare and their conservation status endangered. Doris knows her irritation with God is unfounded and illogical. She has read enough science. In fact, Doris reads science with the fervour of a born-again. Father would not be pleased, but though Doris cannot imagine preaching what one does not believe, she has begun to question the veracity of Father's belief in such improvable things. Father was not an illogical man.

Doris touches Henry's v-shaped comb and finds his tiny earlobes beneath the feathers. Could God not have stopped the weasel? Why *does* God just watch the little sparrow fall? She puts a stop to this unempirical thinking. Doris knows that human beings cannot blame or thank God for their own hellish or heavenly states. Henry cannot blame God for his weaselish demise. Crèvecœur. Broken heart. Nevertheless.

Doris pushes the brutality of the animal kingdom out of her mind as she buries Henry. The way the rising sun is turning the eastern sky pink makes her think of the conversation she had with Trevor Parsons a week before he died. Some might be frightened by the early morning arrival of a stranger in a black leather jacket on a noisy motorcycle, and in truth, Doris did feel a small jolt of alarm. She even picked up her hoe. How could she have known the man was Trevor Parsons? Trevor took off his helmet. Remember me? he said, with a very nice smile.

Doris did not expect Trevor to say yes when she offered him a cup of tea, but he took off his leather jacket and hung it on a raspberry post. Gladly, he said. He sat down on the old porch chair and stretched out his legs. Flustered, Doris wrote: *For whom are you looking? Neither Mike nor Geordie is home.* Trevor smiled a little at that. "Nobody in particular," he said. "I just wanted to see what you all were up to here." Then he said, "Forget the tea, Doris. Come sit beside me here and we'll have a chat, yeah?" Doris is not given to sitting in the morning, but sit she did.

Trevor tugged the notebook from her hands, plucked her pencil from her fingers with a grin, and wrote: *How's my big bro?*

Doris made a round-faced shape with her hands—Geordie?

"Yup," said Trevor. "Sounds like the big fella's really in love. You approve?"

It has never occurred to Doris that she might approve or disapprove: Geordie loves Pepsi—the woman, not the vile drink—and that is all that is important.

"I'm in love too," Trevor said. He smacked the arms of the porch chair and laughed, as if he were talking to himself rather than to Doris.

"It's for real this time too." Trevor had Doris' notebook and pencil, so she could not reply. She nodded at Trevor and looked pointedly at her notebook in his hand. "So, what else?" Trevor said. "When's Lulu coming home?"

Doris reached over and took the notebook from Trevor. He waggled the pencil at her and she took it. It was more of a snatch than she had intended, but Doris does not like to have her voice in someone else's hands. And she'd had enough of that one-sided conversation.

Trevor was surveying the garden. "I did something really terrible, Doris," he said. "You ever do something so bad you know you've got to atone for it? You know what atonement means, Doris?" Doris could not help the sharp look. "I guess you do," Trevor laughed. "Doris Tenpenny, you're freakin' fabulous," Trevor said as he stood up. "Give Mike and Geordie a hug for me. And Lulu. I'll see you at the wedding next weekend." He put his hands in his pockets and gazed around the yard again. He looked at once sad and happy. "I got some serious atoning to do," he said, and then he shook Doris' hand.

For a week after Trevor's visit, until they heard the dreadful news, Doris wondered what it would be like to ride on a motorcycle. And what terrible thing he might have done that would require some serious atoning.

Doris hauls a large stone from the wall onto Henry's grave. She must remember to tell Geordie not to collect the eggs where the Crèvecœur lay. If she lets the hens sit on the eggs, they shall have another Henry.

LULU

My father was alone at the kitchen table when I got up. The drab colour of grief had come in and touched everything—Dad, the walls and counters, the clock, Kat's knick-knacks. The teapot was cold and Dad's plate was empty. When I put my hand on his shoulder I felt the thinness of his bones through the worn terrycloth of his dressing gown. He reached up and took my hand and put it to his face. It was wet. His grief surged like a contraction through my body. Since April, he had been hovering over me, watching my recovery, hiding his sorrow from me. It wasn't until that morning that he gave me the first straight glimpse of his pain. It was unbearable.

"Where's Kat? Your tea's cold, Dad. Do you want me to heat it up for you?"

"It should have been me, Lulu."

"We don't have that choice in life, Dad."

"I should have done more for him."

I lied to Dad. I told him not to do what I had been doing for three months—blaming myself, regretting, enumerating the what-ifs. "Dad. What would you have done? We can't beat ourselves up about Trevor. He always did what he wanted to do. We can't change that."

"I could have told him I loved him."

We all could have done that, though some of us might not have known we loved him until he was dead. "You did tell him, Dad."

"Not often enough." I sat down on a chair beside him. He looked shrivelled and lost. "And I think I hit a cat this morning," he said.

"You've already been out this morning? What were you doing out so early?"

"I just went for a drive. I go down to River Road and watch the boats. The cat ran right out in front of me on Hemlock."

Dad began to cry so hopelessly that I panicked. Kat came in with a couple of bags of groceries. She flicked the light on, poured water in the kettle and plopped it on the burner, whisked Dad's plate and the cold teapot away, and snapped the kitchen radio on.

"Right," she said, "who's for scrambled eggs?"

I thanked God for Kat and for the fact that every morning I was one day closer to being able to pick up where I left off—miles from Fraser Arm, in the anonymity of my southern U.S. town. As far from everyone else's grief as I could be. I would figure out how to deal with my own in the privacy of my own kitchen.

Fleeing Dad's house, I found myself, as usual, at the McFees'. Doris was in the storeroom, emptying jars out of a cardboard box. It was rare that Doris showed much emotion on her face, and I had yet to find the roadmap to her expressions, but this one I read: distraught. She pushed the box into my hands and, snatching a tea towel off a hook in the kitchen, hurried out the door.

The crows had found the cat first. They took turns flying up into the trees or hopping to the sidewalk each time a car passed. The big orange tabby was still in the middle of the road, barely bloodied and relatively intact, thankfully, but clearly dead—a tom with a mangled ear and the scars to prove his street cred across his nose. There was a little blood on his mouth and his jaw hung crookedly. The crows had already been at his eyes.

Doris was making sharp snorting noises. It was clearly inconceivable to her that no one had stopped to move the cat's body off the road. She stopped traffic with an imperious gesture then indicated to me that it was my job to keep it that way. The cat was already stiff as Doris picked him up. She laid him gently in the box and covered him with the tea towel. A car honked.

"Yeah, squish a cat, asshole," I shouted in the guy's window. He gave me the finger. Incensed, I smacked the back of his fancy car as he went by. He jerked to a stop and leaned out the window, shouting some bull. For a second, I thought Doris was going to go after him, and I would have liked to have seen that, but he drove off. A couple of middle-aged women carrying a dead cat must have been too much for the creep.

In the backyard, next to what looked like another fresh grave, Doris shovelled furiously, digging, in five minutes, a hole deeper than I ever could have. She folded back the tea towel and took a last look at the old tom.

"Too bad about his eyes," I said.

Doris took her pad from her pocket and wrote: *Nature, red in tooth and claw. Tennyson.*

She placed the cat in the grave, without the box, folded the tea towel on top of him like she was tucking him in, and then, without ceremony, shovelled the dirt back into the hole and stomped on it with her rubber boots.

Doris pulled her pad out again. I wondered whether she used a notepad until it was filled or just picked them up here and there, like I did reading glasses. And did she keep them?

Would you like to say anything?

"Over the cat?" I shook my head. What was there to say over a dead cat? Christ. Did she expect me to have some sort of cat blessing in my repertoire? "Whose cat was it anyway?"

Doris shook her head. *Someone who will miss his cat tonight*, she wrote.

"Maybe," I said.

Most certainly, Doris wrote. *Who would hit a cat and not stop to take it off the road?*

I felt a spark of weary anger. Someone whose life was out of sequence, an old man worn out by life's capriciousness, that's who, Doris. I didn't say it out loud. "We might have compassion for the person if we knew him," I said. "We don't know what life has brought him. It's so easy to vilify people and shout at them from the safety of our cars." My eyes flooded with tears.

It is fortunate I cannot shout and do not drive, Doris wrote.

We stood over the cat's grave for another minute. I suspect we were both thinking the same thing: why doesn't she just go? Normally I would bow out gracefully, and Doris would just give her formal hand wave, a small chop in the air, and walk away. We stared at each other.

Finally she wrote: *Tea?*

I knew that even tea was a concession on Doris' part. And that it would not be caffeinated. In the kitchen, she poured water in a small pot and put it on the stove, then she sat down at the table. Aloysius McFee's kettle must have bitten the dust. I imagined Doris burying it out by the rock pile.

She gestured, *sit.*

Sure. Why don't you just get out the notepad and let's have us a little conversation, Doris, I thought cynically. But that was exactly what we did.

Do you believe the cat is happy now? she wrote.

I hardly thought a dead cat could be happy. "What do you mean by happy? He's dead."

That he's with God.

"I don't believe in God."

Do you not believe in the Afterlife? Doris tapped her pencil on the paper hard.

"No, I don't believe in Heaven, or in Hell, unless you create it yourself. Don't you think we have our fair share of Hell right here on Earth?"

If you don't believe in God, what do you believe? In.

When I was young and thought I had to have an answer, I used to call myself an Agnostic. It seemed the only sensible choice. But waiting for proof of God's existence—what would that possibly be? "Why do I have to believe anything?" I asked, wishing my question sounded more intelligent. Doris was much more articulate than me, even on paper.

Surely you believe something. A pause, then her tap-tap again, a little harder this time, on *Surely.*

I looked at her deadpan face. She was giving nothing away. She'd be good at poker. "I just don't believe in God," I said.

Doris got up walked out the kitchen door. I thought for a moment that the conversation was over. I'd offended her, perhaps. I stood up and peered out the window. She was crouching on the lawn pulling something up. She came back in a minute with a fistful of what looked like Creeping Charlie, the weed Kat spent half her life trying to eradicate from her patch of lawn. Doris tried several cupboards before she found Aloysius' favourite teapot. She rinsed the weed under the tap—all I could think of was dog pee—jammed it into the pot, and poured boiling water over it. Then she wrote: *Glechoma hederacea. Very high in Vitamin C.* She drew three lines, to indicate a pause, I suppose, and wrote: *That's not an answer.*

"Creeping Charlie." I paused, hoping she'd be impressed I knew what the weed was. "I don't think you have to believe something."

That's an evasion tactic. And ridiculous.

"Your judgment is baseless, Doris." I said, but I understood in that moment that she was right. No matter what I believed, I believed something, even if it was to believe there was no rhyme nor reason to all this. I thought for a minute about incomprehensible things—the universe, white flowers, Robert Johnson's guitar playing. "What do you believe, Doris?"

I believe in God.

Her manner changed, almost imperceptibly, and I understood that she'd been waiting for me to ask. I remembered the Tenpenny family walking down Reifel Road, silent and single-file, to the church on Sunday mornings, as if they were off to prison. I'd heard their father preach only three or four times. It would take a lot of guts to walk away from those kinds of beliefs. Mike had done it, and yet he'd lived with his parents for years after Doris moved out, until he married.

"What kind of God?"

A beneficent God.

Like the one who let your preacher father get run over and killed by his own car? I thought. "You mean a God who takes care of us? Well, then, he's doing a lousy job, all around the effing world."

Doris was silent. Of course she was silent, but her pencil was silent too. She lay it down and rolled it with her long fingers. Was the conversation over, I wondered again. Maybe it was the swearword.

"Your father and that cat, together in Heaven, I suppose." I tried and failed to not sound mocking. I couldn't help it. The concept was so ridiculous.

She nodded.

"Damn crowded up there, what with all those billions of cats."

Doris laughed. What joy. Laughter was the only sound I'd ever heard come out of Doris' mouth. I hadn't heard it very often and had certainly never been the one to provoke it. It changed her completely.

"Did your father like cats?"

This sent Doris off on another laughing fit. *No!* she wrote on her pad even though the answer was evident. She had tears in her eyes.

I might have been seeing, for the first time, what Geordie loved about Doris.

I believe that God loves us.

"I wish he loved us a little harder then. It's a mess down here."

It's not as simple as that.

"Why not?"

We are responsible for our own mess.

"Physical or spiritual mess?"

Both. She poked her pencil at her notebook so hard the paper tore. *The planet. Our life.*

I wasn't sure how much further I wanted to go on the God topic. Believers can be difficult to deal with. "I don't know Doris, I'm just as likely to believe that God is working through the dogs." I rubbed my bare foot on her hound dog Dante's smooth coat. He raised his contented chin from the spot in the sun on the floor and his long pink tongue curled out and licked my ankle before he clunked his head back down on the linoleum. "I have more respect for this beautiful beast than for the God-sees-the-little-sparrow-fall concept. For all I know, the dogs could be God."

If you were drowning you could see Him, Lulu.

It was the first time she'd called me by my name. "That's pure theft, Doris." What a surprise it was to know where Doris' mind had been.

Leonard Cohen wouldn't mind, she wrote. She stood up and then leaned over to add *Go see your room.*

In the twenty-five years that we had owned the McFee house I had never gone upstairs to see the room Doris hoped I would occupy. Early on I refused to go because the thought of sharing a house with Doris was ridiculous. Lately it was because I didn't want to give any of them, especially Geordie, even a whiff of hope. And it was Aloysius' room. I touched Doris' wrist. I don't know why I asked it. Or why I asked it then. "Doris," I said. "Did Aloysius touch you?"

She turned around sharply and glared at me, a person caught in shame. Finally she nodded. She pointed at me.

I nodded too.

I knew, she wrote. *About you. I am very sorry I didn't do anything to stop him.* She looked contrite. And upset.

"What could you have done for me, Doris? I'm not even sure how long it went on for," I said. "Maybe just the summer I was eleven. Or the next too. I don't remember."

Doris didn't believe me. *How could you not remember?*

It did seem impossible that I would not remember being molested by Aloysius, the extent of it, but it was true. God knows I had reason to submerge such memories. What I did remember was the shame that haunted me. "I don't. Not much, that is. It was always in the car, always while we were driving. Never at his house or anywhere else. Just a touch. It stopped."

Just a touch. There is no such thing.

Doris abruptly left me at the table with my untouched pot of Creeping Charlie tea. I poured all that Vitamin C down the drain, washed the teapot, and put it at the back of the cupboard. I felt shaky reviving the memory of Aloysius' hand in my underwear. In all the years we spent together we never acknowledged it or spoke of it. I wondered whether it had done him as much damage as it had done me.

I wandered around the house upset, not sure what to do with myself, poking at things with my cane. Apart from some newfangled, high-efficiency wood stove that Doris had had installed in the living room, and Dad's old Boy Scout semaphore flags that I found in a brass umbrella stand, the place was a museum to the McFees, or to Aloysius at least. In the living room there were still old *Life* magazines in the rack. His record player was exactly where it had always been. He'd always had a big record collection, but now it was overflowing. I checked a faded old Kleenex box under the stereo for drugs. Empty.

"Like her collection?" Mike Tenpenny was standing in the archway to the living room.

"Mike. Sorry, I didn't know you were home."

"No need to apologize, Lulu. It's your house too." Mike didn't move from the archway. "How are you doing?"

"I'm better, thanks." I wiggled my healing foot at him.

Mike was the same age as Trevor, fifty-five, but in much better shape than my brother had ever been. He and his wife, Cidalia, had moved into the McFees' after they married, about ten years back. Cidalia was a psychiatric nurse at the Children's Hospital, and from all reports, a saint—a very busy saint.

"Doris has been picking up old records at garage sales for the price of a smile."

I couldn't see that; Doris smiled by pressing her lips together and drawing her cheeks back, more a grimace than anything else, and rarer than her hens' teeth. But however she'd acquired the records, she had a collection that would break a vinyl junkie's heart. There were hundreds of LPs, a long shelf of forty-fives, and a couple of boxes full of old seventy-eights.

"If she could, I bet she'd sing like a bird," Mike said. "Have you heard her whistle?"

"She whistles?"

"Keep an ear peeled. I gotta go."

That would be keep an ear cocked, or an eye peeled, Mike, I thought, following him at a distance to the kitchen door with the semaphore flags in my non-cane hand. He was still kind of corny, still a bit of a misfit. But who on this farm wasn't? I watched him walk back to where Doris was picking raspberries. He plucked a berry from her tray, bowed slightly to her, and a couple minutes later I saw the dust of his truck kicking up along the laneway that led to the east end of the property and the gated exit on Birch Street.

I unfurled the old semaphore flags. The red-and-white cotton had yellowed with age and the fabric, though stained, was intact. The wooden handles were smooth from years of handling. My father had taught semaphore to the Scout packs, my brothers included. They complained about it, but I loved it. By the time I was ten, when they began to drift off into less earnest pastimes, I was fluent in semaphore. I used to love to stand on the back stoop and signal to the goats. I'd never found anyone else who could read the flags, but I fancied the goats understood. I started with my name, my formal name—Louise Josephine Parsons. "Lulu" also felt particularly nice to sign. L.U.L.U. The L was the opposite of the U, one up, one down; one down, one up. I loved the swing of the flags, the flapping sound they made, the sharp halt as they snapped into position. I sent the goats simple messages: *How do you do? Milking time is at two.* I experimented with signalling swear words and imagined the goats being scandalized by my foul language. Though Dad was supposed to be an expert in semaphore, he wasn't a terribly quick study either. He was a good sport, but he had to have the Boy Scout semaphore manual next to him while I signalled. Even the simplest message outlasted his patience, and mine.

Out in the raspberry patch, Doris looked oddly like a cigarette girl with a tray slung over her skinny shoulders in a sleeveless black dress and her long gray hair. I'd never seen her in anything but dresses, no matter the work she was doing. Other than her pyjamas. I took the flags up and signed her name, remembering the letters like a typist's fingers remember the keys. The flags snapped smartly: D O R I S.

She looked up and tilted her head at me. I signalled: I AM SORRY ABOUT ALOYSIUS.

Doris raised a finger at me—*wait*—then stepped out of the raspberries, pulled the strap over her head, and put her tray on the ground. She stood back up with two large rhubarb leaves in her hands and signalled back: D O G B L E S S Y O U R T O R T U R E D S O U L L U L U.

The inscrutable Doris Tenpenny knew semaphore! I was thrilled. And to top it off, she'd made a joke. I signalled: H O W ? but Doris turned her back on me, picked up her tray of berries, and went back to her work. I could tell by the movement of her shoulders that she was laughing.

DORIS

Where is everyone? Mother is on the porch with Louisa May Alcott; she does not like Virginia Woolf, it turns out. Geordie has not yet gotten out of bed, but he will soon, because Mike and Cidalia are making breakfast in the kitchen. Geordie is like a dog; his sense of smell is better than that of any human Doris knows. Dante and Ricky have gone squirrel hunting, or perhaps they are asleep on the couch. Wherever they are, they are doing dog things. They would not mind anyway. The dogs like the accordion. Doris opens the box and takes out the beautiful thing.

"There it is," Lewis said last Sunday afternoon.

The box has little brass buttons that must be slipped, the left to the left, the right to the right, so that the locks flip up. Lewis slipped them and they made a good clunking sound. Doris would like to keep sounds the way people keep photographs, in an album. Lewis reached out and tucked a lock of Doris' hair behind her left ear.

"Go on. Open it," he said.

Doris lifted the lid. She looked down on the accordion, all mother of pearly, like abalone, with silver cut into a pattern over top, and dark blue bellows. Doris has never owned a musical instrument. Lewis might have brought her a Buttercup chicken—she has always wanted a Buttercup— she is that pleased. It is not even her birthday.

"It's a little one. Start small, I thought," Lewis said.

With Lewis watching, Doris lifted the instrument from its case and put it on. The straps fit snugly around her back, like one of Lewis' hugs. She unsnapped the leather strap that constrains the bellows and it flowed out with a long low wail. Doris laughed. "And maybe take some lessons," Lewis said, grimacing.

She would have liked to have said, Father would hate this, but her hands were full. *Why does Father always come to mind?* She played the black and white keys and poked the small buttons and moved the bellows in and out all at once. It was a dreadful sound but the colour was magnificent, like oil on a puddle. Lewis' face was bright and expectant. "You'd look beautiful behind a big bass fiddle, but I can't afford one, and they're a little heavy anyway," he said. Lewis' smile is like a lamb's nuzzle.

Everyone likes to give relationship advice. Over the years, at the egg stand, Doris heard more relationship advice than she cares to think about. I told them . . . that's how they'd start. I told her he was no good. I told her to wait, he'd come round. One thing about relationship advice is true: everyone thinks they know best. In the past, no one offered Doris any, of course, but Doris held hands with Lewis at Trevor Parsons' funeral and now everyone is offering her advice. Raylene says get used to it. She says Doris has come out of the closet. They laughed about this, but it is true; it has been twenty-four years since Doris Tenpenny and Lewis Cray became sweethearts through a kiss on the mouth on the front porch. This secret was not hard to keep. Father had no expectations of Doris marrying; he told her so.

Doris pokes one of the buttons and for a very brief moment feels a quaver of panic as she wonders if Father knows, now that he is dead, as if he could look down from Heaven and see Doris in the same bed as Lewis Cray. *Don't be ridiculous, Doris.* Father would have wanted them to get married. But Doris does not want to marry Lewis. Lewis asked her. Doris said no. She doesn't want him around all the time. Doris likes the feel of Lewis next to her in bed, and the way his warmth changes even her colour, but after Lewis spends the night in her room, Doris needs to be alone. Now that she has come out, Doris does sometimes wonder why keeping it secret was so important. Secrets weigh.

Even Birdie gave Doris some relationship advice. Make sure he sees you for who you really are and not who he wants you to be, that's important, Birdie said. Birdie's relationship advice reminds her of how she herself turned Lewis into something else before he could be just Lewis. At first she couldn't stop it: Doris thought about Aloysius McFee when Lewis touched her. To stop it, Doris had to turn Lewis into an animal and not a man. Sometimes a cat and other times a goat or a lamb. Now that Lewis knows about Aloysius, Lewis is mostly just Lewis. Lewis and Aloysius McFee were such opposite secrets. Doris is glad she does not have to keep that secret anymore either.

Mother comes in from the front porch. "Wouldn't your father hate this?" Mother says, running her fingers over the blue velvet lining of the accordion box. "Lewis is a nice man, Doris. I think you should consider him."

Doris tucks her hair behind her left ear so she can remember Lewis' hand there.

LULU

Most people would not see owning a Mercedes as a crime, but I came by my class judgement honestly. My father, who religiously followed the adage that if you have nothing good to say don't say anything, only broke his own rule when it came to people who drove swanky cars. I don't suppose they teach working-class consciousness in high school, but Dad would have been a rabble-rousing teacher. I'm sure he drove his old junkers until they were rusting and unroadworthy just so he could be true to his word. It helped, of course, that he could monkey with a misbehaving engine, usually success-fully. But I'm sure the Parsons family, all of us, drove modest cars or trucks, regardless of what we could afford or wanted, just to not displease him. God forbid any one of us turned up in a Mercedes.

When I pulled up in the parking lot behind the physio-therapy office in Dad's pickup, a sleek chocolate-brown convertible pulled in beside me. Out of that swanky Mercedes stepped Robin Chaudhury. I could feel Dad's attitude jingling in my throat. Robin looked delighted to see me. He held the door to the truck open and stood way too close with his hand out to help me.

"I'm good," I said testily. He didn't get my warning so I waved him off.

He stood back a little but hovered like a man shouldn't, at least not any man I'd be interested in, as I got out of the truck. In the waiting room, he chattered on to me about a grand number of things until the receptionist said, "Dr. Chaudhury, were you going to see Kim or Petra today?"

"Kim I think, Sydney," he replied.

"I thought you were a patient," I said. A doctor and a Mercedes driver. Harumph, I heard Dad say.

"I am," he said. "I'm a patient, and a doctor."

"What kind of doctor?"

"I'm a surgeon."

"What kind of surgeon?" I said, trying desperately to lighten my tone.

"A neurosurgeon." He looked uneasy.

I snorted with laughter. "Don't be funny." Calm yourself, Lulu, I warned myself.

"I am not." He smiled. "Being funny."

I was staring. I'd become more than well acquainted with my share of neurosurgeons in the past few months, but they were doctors, professionals with scalpels and licensed access to my brain, not warm-blooded men sitting next to me in a waiting room with problems of their own. I wished my class-radar demons would shut up. They chanted, *Fancy car, fancy job, fancy pants*, and somewhere in the chorus, one of them was also singing, *Too good for you.*

"I specialize in pain research now mostly," Robin said, almost nervously. His black eyes were shining to match his seventy-percent dark-chocolate Mercedes.

●

We walked down Cambie Street and turned right onto Hastings. I hadn't been on Hastings for a long time, for good reason. Though I'd only been told the story years after it happened, I had a searing vision of Trevor, twenty, lying beside the girl who overdosed and never woke up.

"So, Robin, if you were so crazy about my music, why didn't you ever write or try to meet me? Well," I laughed, turning crimson. "That came out all wrong."

"Oh, I would never have been so bold. I just consider myself unbelievably lucky to have run into you at the clinic."

"Fate, then," I said.

"Sweet Fate," he said, smiling his head off.

●

When I left, Robin took my hand in his and kissed me goodbye, warmly, on the cheek.

"You smell like honey," he said.

Honey. I thought about an old friend, the newly divorced Francesca, who I'd had tea with earlier in the week. She'd taken a huge glob of honey, stirred it right into her pot of mint tea and said, "Which would you rather be doing—walking glumly down the street with someone you've been married to for thirty years, or sitting in a sunny café with your friend drinking tea with honey?" It didn't seem quite like a fair question, but just then, who cared.

●

I hated traffic almost as much as I hated thinking about revealing the details of my wretched love life to Robin. My walk with him meant that my drive back to Dad's landed me right in the middle of rush hour while he, I imagined, drove some short distance to a home near Kitsilano Beach with a heated garage for the Mercedes. He'd had, he told me, a long and relatively peaceful marriage to a woman who had succumbed to cancer three years earlier. Reverent might not be quite the right word to explain how he spoke about Mina, but it was damn close. His parents loved her as one of their own. His two grown daughters missed her dreadfully. He still visited her elderly parents regularly. A widower walks in a strange territory; the dearly departed's photo is still on his dresser, her name remains on everyone's lips, including his own, and there's a spot for him six feet under, right beside her. Was there, I wondered, a male equivalent of widow's weeds? How long should they be worn?

I'd been married too. Officially it was seven years, until new divorce laws made it easier to untie our knot and because dear Eddie Heller had finally met someone he really wanted to marry. Unofficially, it took us less than three months from our wedding day to determine that at twenty-five we were not destined to grow old together sharing the same mattress, kitchen, or car. In one of my less inspired moments, I'd suggested that we get the marriage annulled on the grounds that at least one spouse lacked the mental capacity to understand the basic meaning of marriage, but Eddie said he was sure that suggesting I lacked basic mental faculties wouldn't wash with any judge. Instead, we shook hands and promised to adore each other from a distance and to commit adultery when possible so that there'd be no arguing, come divorce time, as to who was most guilty.

I had friends who became lovers and lovers who became friends. And many I never saw or heard of again. In the eighties, I had twice as many boyfriends as I had apartments. I left them; but very occasionally, sensing my imminent departure, they saved their pride and left me. Leaving was as easy as turning over my keys to the landlord. Being on the road gave me an excuse to go, and being busy mostly took care of the loneliness. And when it didn't stop the blues from settling on my shoulders, there was always someone interested in a slightly aloof woman who could sing them to sleep.

I only reconsidered marriage twice. In my thirties I got desperate, I suppose. Everyone talks about a woman's maternal time-clock ticking at thirty. That wasn't it. I'd just looked ahead and seen a lonely bed in my future, that's all. Sean O'Kennedy—I always had a weakness for bass players— asked me to marry him after a gig at the National Folk Festival in Lowell, Massachusetts. When I took him home to meet Dukes, the four-year-old shepherd boxer cross I'd foolishly adopted in another moment of desperation, he made the fatal mistake of criticizing me for giving into those big, sad brown eyes and feeding the dog toast crusts at breakfast.

"How can you let a dog control you that way?" he asked.

"What, are you jealous?" I said. I didn't want to admit that Dukes was the only creature in the world that I would allow to have control over me. Sean's eyes looked a bit like Dukes' later that day—big and sad.

The last time I thought I'd marry I'd nearly gone through with it. Tristan Bartholomew had a fabulous name, a warm sinewy body, and the talent of a giant for cooking. I'd bought a black 1920s dress in a vintage shop and Tristan had found a couple of simple silver rings at a pawn shop and booked a restaurant for a party with his family and a few of my Nashville friends. I didn't exactly leave him at the altar. We were to marry in the Nashville Courthouse on a Tuesday. Monday night, Tristan very gently hinted that if I was going to be on the road, he didn't really want to be taking care of my dog, Cooper. Maybe I could give Coop up for adoption, he said. Find a nice home. A dog again. That night, I dreamed that someone knocked on my door and left a burning bag of dog shit on the sill. I never turned up at the courthouse. It was a shameful act of cowardice, I admit that now. But back then, I was sure I was doing the right thing for all three of us.

And I was. Of course I can't blame my lack of commitment on the dogs. I wasn't prepared to be in any kind of steady relationship, let alone a marriage. After that, I quit thinking about it. I was thirty-seven when I left Tristan. I stopped thinking about partners too, or good ones that is, in 1994. I did get my hopes up for the blasted theatre critic. But that was over now.

●

Robin hadn't asked me about my love life. I guess that might have been because he already knew most everything about me. I alternated between being grateful that he hadn't pried

and thinking him selfish for telling me all about his seemingly commendable love life and not asking me a thing about
mine. Anyway, I had told him goodbye. I was leaving for
Tennessee in a few days.

And I think I had the answer to my friend Francesca's
question: tea with honey, please.

•

Telling Robin I was leaving was a piece of cake. Telling
Geordie wasn't. I'd spent the morning steeling myself and
now we were sitting on the McFees' front porch, saying
our goodbyes. Geordie put his cheek to mine and wrapped
his big arms around my shoulders. That hug threatened to
swamp me. Everyone else understood that I had to go away
to work. Only once had Dad told me how much Geordie
pined for me every time I left, but I knew. Dad didn't need
to explain that it reminded Geordie of the time I left and
didn't come home for two years. If I'd known what misery
they were all living through, I would have returned. But I was
eighteen and ashamed and fleeing my own dark shadows. I
sent postcards—with no return address. At least they knew
I was alive. Dad called them NDIAD letters. Not Dead In
A Ditch. When I did come home, twenty years old and not
much wiser, Geordie's wounds had healed—the physical
ones—but he was still wary. Doris deserves the credit. She
was the one who found the path to his trust.

Now I shushed Geordie gently. His t-shirt had risen up
as he tightened his arms around me and I saw the old scars
from the knife wounds on his belly. I traced my fingertips
along the two lines of puckered skin.

"You went away, Lulu," Geordie sobbed.

"Yes, I did. I'm sorry, Geordie." The passage of thirty-two years hadn't done much to diminish a memory that Geordie had fused in his mind with my leaving, and with my kissing Mike.

"They were mean to me."

That was an understatement. They were brutal. They beat Geordie, and stabbed him, and left him for dead in the ravine. For nothing. For an empty wallet he refused to give them. For fun. They were a couple of monsters hepped up on speed, asserting their inferiority complexes by terrorizing someone more vulnerable than they were. Geordie: their perfect victim.

"I'm sorry, Geordie."

"You kissed Mike and I was mad and I ran away. And Edwin and Perry and the nice girl Pamela found me and picked me up in their car, right Lulu? Why'd you kiss Mike, Lulu?"

There was no use hoping that if I didn't give him any cues he wouldn't repeat the story of how Edwin Milton and Perry Gladish picked him up and took him for the opposite of a joy ride—all because I kissed Mike. I'd also have to restrain myself from telling him, again, that Pamela wasn't actually a nice girl. In Geordie's story, Pamela had become the archetypal avenging angel. The truth was Pam ratted them out after Perry dumped her. She handed Edwin and Perry to the police on a vengeful platter. Her testimony put both of them in jail—twelve years for attempted murder—and saved her scrawny ass. "Yes. The boys and Hell-hath-no-fury Pam," I sighed.

Geordie ignored me. "But I didn't want to give them my wallet and that made Perry mad. And Edwin was madder. Mum gave me that wallet."

"Yes, but it wasn't your fault, right?"

"Not my fault, no. Not Pamela's fault."

"Well . . ."

Mr. Jones and I had waited an eternity in the dark ravine for the ambulance to come. They took Geordie to Wesleyville Memorial Hospital—they were used to Saturday night knife wounds in Wesleyville. I can't remember how I got there, but I still have a picture in my head: all of us, and half of Fraser Arm too, standing under the ruthless lighting in the over-crowded emergency waiting room. Waiting for someone to tell us Geordie was dead.

Then we waited for Geordie to get better. It took a long time. More than a month. They sent him home forty pounds lighter, his body recovered, but his spirit unreachable. He was wary and wouldn't speak and there was fear in his eyes that had never been there before. Kat said that it was as though something had taken his soul. I had. It was me. I had taken it. I waited for Geordie to forgive me. When I had convinced myself he never would, I left. I fled off up the highway and didn't come back 'til I was twenty.

"You went away, Lulu," Geordie said.

Geordie leaned against me again and sighed. He stopped talking. Geordie never told the story of what happened after I left. I never managed to fool myself into thinking it was because he didn't remember. I was just hopeful that, if any of Geordie's filters worked well, it was that one. What that psychiatrist did to him was unforgiveable.

"Can I call Pepsi?" he asked.

With profound relief, I tiptoed into the living room and got Geordie the phone. Doris was asleep on the couch.

DORIS

Eavesdropping was not at all Doris' intention. But on a summer's day when the windows are open and the breeze is eastward, all porch conversations can be overheard from the couch in the living room. If you were someone who likes to overhear conversations, you might lie on the couch in wait of one. Everyone talks on the porch. But Doris is just having her two o'clock nap. She does not want to get up now, while Geordie is crying and Lulu is saying goodbye. It would be awkward. Awkward is the colour of school hallways: a hopeless unnatural green.

There are so many misquotations in the world. Everyone thinks it is "Hell hath no fury like a woman scorned," but it is not. Doris has read the original—William Congreve, *The Mourning Bride*, 1697. Even when police captain Smallwood—God rest his soul—stood at the egg stand after Perry's and Edwin's arrests and said, "Miss Tenpenny, Hell hath no fury like a woman scorned," Doris said nothing. Doris thought of writing the correct quotation on the brown paper bag in which she gave Captain Smallwood his eggs: Heav'n has no Rage like Love to Hatred turn'd, Nor Hell a Fury like a Woman scorn'd. But even now, she knows that Captain Smallwood would have said, "Same diff, Miss Tenpenny." Doris does not think it is the same diff, but she does think that Pamela Mann was, indeed, a Woman scorn'd.

Cidalia says that Geordie does not have certain filters. This is a very clever concept. Doris has been attempting to list and categorize the filters she herself does not possess, though this is proving difficult. Geordie's filterlessness means he tells his story to anyone who will listen, even strangers. Geordie tells it less often now, but only, Doris thinks, because Geordie's filing cabinet holds more stories now. Lulu's voice is pale blue. It is always pale blue when she says goodbye to Geordie.

What happened to Geordie after Lulu went away even Doris does not like to remember. But people do not forget such things. Doris thinks it is probable that Lulu still blames herself for what happened. When she came home, Lulu said: "This is all my fault." It was not. Not completely. Some people, such as Verna Barker—God rest her soul—agreed with Lulu and told her so, but Verna Barker was a stinky old rat. Doris feels slightly remorseful for thinking Verna Barker was a stinky old rat, but she was. Lulu should not have gone away without saying goodbye. But Lulu was young. She thought her brother no longer loved her. She fled before Geordie found his forgiveness, and her fleeing made everything worse. Wally Parsons' heart had already been ripped to pieces once. But teenagers, Doris has learned, have no notion of their parents' aches. Doris learned this from all the parents who leaked their sorrow, like cracked eggshells and spilt yolks, all over the old egg stand.

The sprung couch is poking her in the kidneys. Doris pulls a cushion to her chest. The doctor told Wally Parsons that Geordie was depressed. "It's going out of fashion, apparently," Wally Parsons told Mike, "but the doctor says electroconvulsive therapy is a cure-all for cases such as this." What did Wally Parsons know of shock therapy? If Geordie remembers it, he doesn't speak of it. Doris remembers Wally Parsons crying at the egg stand. That, she will never forget.

When Mike told Father, Father said: "God's will manifests itself in surprising ways. That boy should have been institutionalized the day he was born."

Mike's words were red, "So, Fraser Arm would be safer without Geordie Parsons?"

Father said, "Yes. Abnormal people should be in the care of people who know how to handle them."

Mike looked at Doris. Mother slunk away from the lunch table, like a small animal. Doris looked at the placemat. They had drugged Doris. Drugging Doris did not produce a voice in her. Nor did shocking her. Doris knew that drugging and shocking Geordie Parsons was not going to bring Geordie Parsons back.

Doris keeps her eyes closed as Lulu gets the phone. Then Doris sits up. A button on the cushion has left a round red indent on Doris' forearm and her kidney is surely bruised. Lulu is in the kitchen. Perhaps she would know what happened to Pamela Mann, the Woman scorn'd.

LULU

Do you know what happened to Pamela Mann? The Woman scorn'd.

How poetic Doris is. She came into the kitchen waving her little notebook at me, then she held it still in front of my face, too close. I took her skinny arm and moved it ten inches farther away so I could gaze down my nose to read the note. Reading glasses, another annoyance of middle age. Pamela Mann, the Woman scorn'd. It was a question I had rarely pondered. However, I could now picture Pammie sitting out in the high school parking lot on the back of someone's car, blond hair, uber-rouged cheekbones, big breasts in a tight blouse, high-waisted jeans—a classic Fraser Arm gal like the rest of us.

"I imagine that Pamela hightailed it out of Dodge before Perry Gladish and Edwin Milton were released from jail. She would not have wanted to be around when those two got out," I said.

Dodge? Doris wrote.

Doris was never one for pop culture references. "Guess you never saw *Gunsmoke*, eh, Doris? Get out of town, blow this popsicle stand, vamoose, beat it, skip town. Let's go."

Doris nodded. *Her family moved away after the trial.*

I'd heard that too. Pamela was in my grade at school. She was boy crazy from the start and her choice of boys was never too savoury, not that I was one to talk. Her mom worked at the beauty salon where everyone in high school got their hair cut. I never knew what her dad did. We called her Pammie back then. She was a small-time coke dealer. I'd even bought some from her.

"Well, I hope they went to Newfoundland and took her with them," I said. "Any closer wouldn't have been safe once Perry and Edwin got out."

She did a good thing. Doris poked her pencil on the paper for emphasis.

"Yeah. After the fact. She might have done something about it while they were knifing Geordie."

She had imbibed drugs, Doris wrote. *She was frightened.*

Oh, Pammie, you fine manipulator. I'd had this same conversation with Dad.

"Did you talk to her, Doris? I mean—"

Doris interrupted me with her hand. *No. I watched her on the witness stand. Testifying took great courage.*

I was learning that Doris was more complex than I had ever imagined. I never saw what Pammie did as anything but rat-like self-interest. She'd lived with Perry for a year after they left Geordie for dead in the ravine. It didn't weigh too heavily on her conscience then. She had told the cops that it was just Geordie's bad luck he was on Meares Road that day because the three of them, she and Perry and Edwin, were higher than kites. They all knew Geordie. That they knew him made it worse for me.

I'd been told the story so many times I could recount the details as if I'd been on Meares Road with Geordie myself. Kat, in particular, seemed to relish rehashing the fine points of the trial. On the witness stand, Pamela said that they were just teasing Geordie at first. They asked him what he was doing so far from home. They drove alongside him and Edwin leaned out the window and offered him a cigarette. Geordie told Edwin he shouldn't smoke and just kept walking, saying he had to get home. Edwin decided that it would be a riot to make Geordie smoke and told Perry to stop the car. Pamela said that was when everything went wrong. Edwin lit a cigarette and tried to get Geordie to smoke it. Geordie refused and pushed Edwin. Mum was always trying to quit and she'd drilled it into Geordie's head that he was never to put a cigarette to his lips. Then Perry told Edwin to leave him alone and he got out of the car and put his arm around Geordie. Perry asked Geordie for his wallet. Nicely at first. Apparently they'd siphoned gas from a pickup truck down on River Road earlier and Perry had gotten a mouthful of gas. Edwin had laughed at him and Pamela thought that this was what had put Perry in such a foul mood. They were stoned, hungry, and broke. Geordie, of course, was not going to give up the wallet. It had nothing to do with money. There was none in it. But Mum had given it to him, one of those beaded souvenir wallets they sell in Chinatown, and he carried it around like a lucky charm.

Pamela wasn't very clear on what happened after that except that Edwin went for the wallet and Geordie started running. If he hadn't run, she said, the rest might not have happened. "Dogs gotta chase squirrels," she said. Dogs gotta chase squirrels. Pamela ought to be a philosopher. According to Pamela, when Perry and Edwin came out of the ravine she asked them where Geordie was. Perry told her to shut her trap, and Edwin said, "Let's just say the stupid asshole won't be pulling that kind of trick again soon." Then Perry tossed the empty wallet into the bushes. There was one happy outcome of the trial: Mike went looking for the wallet and eventually found it, rotting but recognizable. Noble Mike.

Perry and Edwin swore that Pamela had been the brains behind the attack on Geordie. Edwin testified that Pammie said that Geordie'd be an easy mark. The jury was more inclined to believe a teary blond in a Peter Pan collar than a couple of scruffy punks in cheap suits and Old Spice aftershave.

"Pamela was an opportunist, Doris," I said.

Doris stood quietly for a while, thinking. Either her thought processes or how she expressed them were excruciatingly slow. I was getting used to her pauses, but I still found them frustrating. I had to stop myself from leaping in to fill the conversational void. That would have been the equivalent of interrupting, and I was learning to wait.

Doris wrote for a long time, scratching things out and scribbling more before showing me the paper: *They say that love is an addiction. They say that both being in love and using unlawful drugs alters a part of the brain, the reptilian brain, and that the rest of the brain is flooded with dopamine as a result.*

"Who's they?"

I read an article.

When Doris wasn't working she could usually be found sitting upright at the kitchen table with a book or magazine in her hands. She had subscriptions to a half a dozen hard-core science magazines, and the living room bookcase was stacked with books on the brain.

"And?" I gave in to the urge to hurry her along.

If Pamela were in love with Perry, when he severed the relationship she would have been craving dopamine, like an addict would his drug.

I nodded. I wanted nothing more than for Doris to have an audible voice. The pace of this conversation was killing me. I made a note to check out talking computers.

The severing of the relationship left her a Woman spurn'd.

"Exactly. She was a woman spurned, Doris, an addict without her drug, so she manufactured a story that would shine a favourable light on herself and incriminate Perry. And Edwin."

Perhaps you would believe that she was heartbroken if you could see it in scientific terms.

"Scientific. Poetic. Whatever. Heartbreak doesn't necessarily make you honest, Doris. Nor does it necessarily make you a victim. In Pamela's case, it was pure revenge, just like the line Hell hath no fury."

Doris rolled her eyes, something I'd never seen her do before. Then she uttered a soft sigh of what might have been exasperation. It was difficult to tell. She seemed to be experimenting with her expressions. I raised my eyebrows at her, and she turned away with the tiniest smile on her face. *Perhaps you are right,* she wrote.

"I'm not trying to make you change an opinion you formed three decades ago, Doris, but I guess you can tell you're not going to change mine. Being spurned ain't no excuse for malice."

Doris dismissed me on her little pad. *Goodbye, Lulu.*

"Goodbye, Doris," I said.

East Nashville had begun the inevitable crawl toward gentrification a few years back, but there were still apartments above shops to be had for relatively cheap. The streets in my neighbourhood were a songwriter's inspiration: jazz bar patrons spilling out into the night, recording studios taking the money of dreamy young musicians, newcomers hoping to turn East Nashville into something else, locals swimming against the tide, and late-night partiers who couldn't care less that the times they were a-changin'. Mixed in was your standard assortment of panhandlers, prostitutes of every gender, and buskers playing lonesome country songs. Beer was cheap at the corner store and, for twice a king's ransom, I could get a fantastic chocolate-raspberry cupcake at the trendy little food store at the foot of my street.

My friend, starving-artist-Cleo, as she liked to call herself, had been staying in the apartment while I was away, and it smelled of rosewater and linseed oil. The apartment wasn't particularly clean, and the bed wasn't made, but she'd stocked the fridge with the essentials—a bottle of white wine, a pint of cream, and a couple of blood oranges. I called her to say thanks, but I got her message service. I went through the mail—nothing important or exciting—and thought about doing a shop, but instead peeled an orange and cracked the bottle of wine. Not a great combination. The news was all about the weather. The taxi driver from the airport said they were breaking records all over Tennessee, with temperatures soaring into the hundreds for days. No wonder Cleo had left white wine. It was sweltering in the apartment and I had all the windows open, the fan going full blast, and the little air conditioner turned off. There was no point in busting its noisy guts for the feeble output it offered. I pulled a chair up to the window and leaned out, hoping for a breeze. The street was eerily quiet, not that there weren't people out there doing Thursday-night things. It was the heat tamping down the city's sounds, air molecules thick as tapioca, the voices of passersby rising up as if from under water.

I missed Dad. I poured more wine, noticing the dust on the foot of the glass. I'd never missed him before, not like this. His age and vulnerability were waving their arms at me, tenderly whispering: you might not have a lot of time. I missed Trevor too. I missed what I had missed of his life. I missed Geordie's balding head and Doris' inscrutable expressions and her damned accordion. And the dogs. The McFee household had gotten its fingers overtop the wall around my soul.

A cat yowled on the fire escape. I wiggled my fingers out the window and the cat leapt up to the sill, purred loudly for a few seconds, and, when I reached out to touch it, ran off into the night. The phone rang and I answered it quickly, hopeful. A ship's horn blared. I'd won another cruise.

●

I taught a couple workshops on Friday and Saturday at the bluegrass festival and had an evening performance on one of the side stages Sunday night. I noticed this skinny kid in the audience. A few couples were dancing at the front, but this kid was lost in the music, twisting and turning, burning up the grass in his bare feet, and looking more like someone who belonged at a rave than a folk festival. I recognized him from one of my workshops. It was still hot as Hades and he had his shirt off. He was skinny but had strong wiry shoulders and arms. His jeans hung off his bony hips, exposing his underwear. I had met this kind of kid before—their young hearts and groins on fire and filled with some sweet sense of gratitude, as if I were playing exclusively for them. He kept smiling at me, so I smiled back. I knew I was pushing my shoulder beyond its limit—I was in nearly unbearable pain and had popped a few serious pain killers before the performance—but my fiddle was hot in my hands, and I played my last song, tapping my mostly healed foot to the beat.

When it was over, the kid picked up his shirt and sandals and lingered near the stage. I packed up my fiddle and my guitar and was unplugging the amp when he was suddenly beside me on the stage.

"I can do that for you."

"Well, go ahead, then. Thanks." He bent over to unplug and coil the extension cords. He was dangerously pretty, just my type a thousand years ago. But he was giving me the hand I needed, and my aching body had never been so grateful. The kid finished with the cords and stood with his arms hanging by his sides.

"What are you grinning at?" I sat down on the edge of the stage and fanned my skirt over my knees to temper the heat.

"I don't know. You, I guess."

"You guess?" I patted the place beside me and he came and sat. "You play the fiddle too?" I could smell him, sweet, musty, sweaty. I remembered that smell. He told me his name. Elias. His parents were second-generation Greek Americans.

His dad had taught him to play the bouzouki when he was a kid, he said.

"When you were a kid? You're still a kid."

"I mean when I was really young. I'll be twenty-one tomorrow."

"Aha. I could be your grandmother, Elias."

"No way," he said.

He wasn't going to believe that. I tied up my hair and knocked off my shoes. I could feel the heat of his hand where it lay beside mine on the stage. His fingers were long and tanned. He touched the turquoise rock in the silver ring I wore on my bowing hand then put his hand down close enough for our baby fingers to touch. It could have been an innocent move, but when I looked over at him, the kid's hazel eyes had dilated. Nip this in the bud, Lulu, I thought.

"Shall we go for a walk, Elias?" I know. A walk wasn't exactly nipping it in the bud. He carried my guitar case as we walked through the long shadows of a row of poplars along the lane toward the musicians' trailers. The sun was setting. There was a picnic table outside my trailer, and, to my relief, no other musicians around.

"Let's sit here," I said. "You can tell me about your life."

Elias took my hand and led me up the trailer steps. Inside, he gently pushed me against the closed door, slid his warm hands up the back of my shirt, and skillfully undid my bra.

●

The smell woke me. Sweat, both his and mine—yeasty, salty.

Elias had one warm leg flung over mine and was leaning up on one elbow, watching me.

"Um, hello," I said, counting in my head the number of painkillers I'd taken the day before and wondering whether I'd had anything to drink. I was trying hard to beat back the feeling that I had just done something particularly sleazy.

Elias lay his head on my breast. I could feel his heart beating against my ribs. He sighed and reached for me under the sheet. I brought my hand down gently on top of his.

"Didn't we just turn out the light, youngblood?" I tried to sound cocky but my voice shook.

He turned his glowing face to me and smiled. I saw the look of a young man lost in the tenderness of skin on skin, heat on heat, wet on wet. I got out of bed and pulled on my robe. The guilt clenching my throat was preventing me from taking regular breaths. He lay there golden and beautiful, unselfconsciously aroused, an immortal being. Nearly irresistible were it not for the frank light of a new day and my suddenly awake conscience.

"You've got to go now, Elias."

"Lulu, I've never met anyone like you. You are totally cool."

I sat on the edge of the bed and smoothed his hair out of his eyes. He leaned and kissed me. His skin was so soft, almost whiskerless, it was like kissing a woman.

"Elias, don't get yourself all worked up. You're a beautiful young man and I am older than your mother." I wasn't sorry to introduce the thought of his mother to the room; it would be a good tactic to get him to leave, I thought. But Elias took my hand and held it against his heart. I kissed one of his fingers and stood up, passing him his boxers.

"You've really got to go, Elias."

Outside the trailer someone was singing some twanging tune about Lester Flatt and possum fat.

"Lulu? You in?" The trailer door creaked open and a grey-haired man proffering dandelions dropped heavily to one knee. Barrel-chested and sixtyish, he crooned, "Baby, marry me."

Elias and I froze. It was Donnie Coulter, a fellow musician I'd seen kicking around at the festival.

"You should knock, Donnie," I said.

I picked up Elias' jeans and shirt and handed them to him, as casually as I could. I took the dandelions from Donnie.

"Maybe you could wait outside, Donnie. Elias was just leaving."

Donnie closed the door quietly. I watched Elias dress and search under the bed for his other sandal. His copper bracelet was on the window ledge. He avoided my eyes as he scanned the room for it.

"You should've told me," he said, looking as miserable as a spurned person could.

The guilt clenched tighter. "What's to tell, Elias?" I handed him the bracelet. I took his chin in my hand and looked him in the eyes. I kissed him on each cheek.

"Happy birthday," I said, and opened the trailer door.

At least Donnie had the grace to look in the other direction as the poor man walked away as nonchalantly as possible on his newly twenty-one-year-old legs.

"Still up to your old tricks, huh, Lulu?" Donnie said. "Leastways you're a few thousand miles from home with no one to witness your illicit doings but for little ole me." He was smiling his fool head off—as he might have said—and leaning up against a big yellow poplar tree. What is it about Southerners that makes you want to talk like one?

"What do you know about my old tricks, Donnie? You haven't known me for more than, let's see . . . Friday, Saturday, Sunday . . . two and a half days." I waggled three fingers at him and sat down at the picnic table. Despite my bravado, I felt a little sick. I could feel a blush creeping up on me and I cursed my propensity to turn red. After fifty years of barefaced living you'd think I'd be too old for blushing like an ingénue.

"Oh, I heard about you," he said. "You're one hot topic on the circuit."

"What?" The blush—and my remorse—took full root.

"Jes kiddin', Lulu." He laughed and sat down in a weathered Adirondack chair plainly on its last legs. The chair creaked and slanted sideways with his weight, which was considerable, but Donnie was entirely unperturbed. He stretched his legs and gave his cowboy boots a careful once-over, like some women would their nails. "But, that one looked like he might be illegal in Tennessee at any rate. You know the age of consent in this state?"

"Jesus, Donnie. Cut it out."

He had a smoker's laugh. "Kiddin' again, Lulu. So, you earn a living doing this?" he said, waving his hand around in the air—a very unusual hand, if truth be told, because it had a thumb, four of the weirdest and shortest fingers I'd ever seen on a guitarman, and what looked like a toe where his baby finger ought to be.

"This," I laughed, waving my hand around too. "Yup. Royalties. And I give workshops here and there. Fiddle and guitar lessons too, songwriting. Adults mostly. Fills in the blanks between festivals, if you know what I mean."

"I've been on the road for more than forty years, playing this club or that. Festivals mostly, now. Bluegrass. Folk. Country music," Donnie said.

"I'm surprised we've never bumped into each other before."

"Oh, you're a lot famouser than me. I haven't ever done any recording of my own, 'cept as a backup man. I've got a few of your albums. One I like in particular."

"Which one?"

"What's it called? *Lulu's Lament*."

"That's an early one. I've changed a bit since then. Matured, as the critics say. Literally."

"Uh-huh. You from Vancouver up in Canada, right?"

"Thereabouts."

"I'm from Athens, Tennessee. You ever heard of it? Some great-great-granddaddy of mine moved to Mouse Creek about a hundred and fifty years ago and the Coulters been settled there ever since. My son and his wife and their girls moved up to Bellingham out in Washington, and they're always telling me I ought to visit and they'll take me up to Vancouver. Seems like they've fallen in love with it. You got kids?"

The words fell out of my mouth: "A couple."

"Where would they be at? They musical like their mama?" Donnie grinned and looked at me out of the corner of his eye. He was flirting with me now. *Men*. I'd just risen from a night with someone else, as Donnie was my witness, and he was hankering for some too, sniffing around like a dog. And there I was, I realized, in all my glory, barefoot and naked but for my robe, telling him about my sons. What the hell?

My heart was suddenly a bleeding pincushion. "I don't know where they're at," I said in a Tennessee drawl, acting far less emotional about it than in reality I was. "I gave them up for adoption. They were twins. Boys. It was thirty-one years ago."

We were both silent. Or at least I was. Donnie was humming a little tune I couldn't catch. I had no idea why I was telling some man I'd only just met something I tried hard not to think about most days, but there I was spilling my beans to a short-fingered guitar picker from Tennessee. If Donnie was surprised he didn't show it.

"Well, you must've had a reason for doing so," he said.

●

Louis-Joseph de La Vérendrye and I had travelled across Canada and back across the States in his little VW, earning pennies busking and playing music festivals—for free or for food half the time—until my belly was too big to fit behind the steering wheel no matter how much backseat rearranging we did. That made me feel that someone had robbed me of my independence, so somewhere into my eighth month, we made a rather crooked beeline for snowy Montreal where Louis-Joseph—in some kind of desperation, I think—took me to his mother.

Louis-Joseph knew from the start it wasn't his baby. I'd made that plain as day by all the puking I was already doing the day we drove off up the highway toward Hope, before we'd even slept together. But from one side of the country to the other and back again he kept looking at me with a hungry longing—more loving than carnal—saying we should keep it. I said no. He loved my belly and the kicking and punching going on inside it more than he loved me, but I didn't want to know where my baby was going and I didn't want it knowing anything about me. A girl I knew in high school had gotten pregnant in grade eleven and her parents sent her off to Alberta to a home for unwed mothers. Everybody knew. And if they didn't, the despair in her eyes when she came home gave the story away anyway. No one was going to know what had happened to me.

In Montreal, Louis-Joseph's mother dragged me to a doctor. Dad had always avoided doctors. We had to be delirious and burning fevers of a hundred and five for him to consider taking us to see the ancient man in Fraser Arm who Dad said was probably just masquerading as a doctor, so I wasn't much practiced at respecting the medical profession. For starters, I figured, I didn't need a doctor to tell me I was pregnant; the whole world could see that easily enough. But the day we went to the clinic somewhere down on Ste. Catherine's, I wasn't doing any kicking or screaming. Madame de La Vérendrye was a doctor herself; she'd taken one look at me and, in her French accent, said something like, "What do you think you're going to do when Goliath wants to come out?" I had found some meekness built of terror inside of me and let her buckle me into her big Cadillac and drive me and my belly downtown.

The doctor was furious with me for having missed out on all those months of prenatal care. He poked and prodded and called another doctor in. He did the same, and what I thought was just one unruly baby kicked back. The doctors were talking to me in French. I had no idea what they were saying; I just kept nodding, pretending I did. One of them must have caught on because finally he said, "You have two. Do you understand? You have twins." I thought I'd drop dead there on the table.

On January 21, three days later, I gave birth in Hôtel-Dieu hospital—God's Hotel always seemed ironic—under the care of a young intern who nervously told me he'd caught exactly ten babies up 'til then. The doctor from the clinic on Ste. Catherine hovered like the patriarch behind him and a team of sympathetic nurses held my hands, one of them whispering "good girl" at me 'til I understood they must have been the only English words she knew. At the point when I thought I wouldn't survive, the first baby came out, born with the caul. A boy. One of the nurses said, "Oh, a caulbearer. He is born to serve mankind. And he will never drown at sea." She smiled at me as though she was really offering me comforting words. The second baby came minutes later. He was smaller.

I named them, but I never held them. I only knew what weight they were later, when the discharge nurse gave me two little cards: Stevie Parsons, 6 lb 5 oz. Bruce Parsons, 5 lb 6 oz. I hadn't thought up any middle names. My breast milk came in with a vengeance a day later, the cruelest reminder.

●

Neither Donnie nor I spoke for a few minutes. I was defending, in my head again, my reasons for leaving my sons in Montreal. Madame de La Vérendrye had taken care of everything. I had just walked away, leaving Louis-Joseph as well.

Donnie said, "Don't mind me asking, Lulu, because I'm sure it's none of my business, but did you ever try to find them boys?"

"I've thought about looking for them," I lied. "I could

register now that the laws have changed and see if they've registered, too."

Donnie nodded. "I reckon people always want to know where they came from, and even if they was raised good elsewhere not much would keep them from wanting to know who their mother and their father was."

"I named them Stevie and Bruce."

"Nice names, I guess."

"After Stevie Wonder and Bruce Springsteen." I laughed. "It was 1976."

"I wasn't listening much to those boys in '76. In Tennessee it was pretty much Conway Twitty and Loretta Lynn."

"What if they're pissed off?" I asked.

"Your kids? Sort of like facing the music, ain't it? We was adopted out, my sisters and me." He pulled up his jean leg and scratched inside one of his cowboy boots with a twig. "My father died of cancer or something or other. My first mother was never too clear, last I saw of her. And she couldn't afford to keep us all. I was ten and my sisters was eight and seven. She kept the babies. They was just little. Two and four then. I guess she figured they needed her most."

"My God. What happened to you? Who would adopt three older kids?"

"No one, it turned out, least not together. We all got separated. I lost track of one of my sisters, Margie. Still ain't found her. And life didn't turn out so pretty for Darlene. She died, I heard, when she was still a girl in foster care. I met the little ones again when Mama died. My first mama."

"What about you? You seem to have made it through unscathed."

"Oh, I had my share of scathing, but I'm standing here before you on solid ground, I guess. Doesn't serve to dish up your sorrow too often."

I was silent again. Finally I said, "Can I use that line?"

"You songwriters. Go ahead, little magpie. But hey, Lulu, I'm not saying this to make you feel bad. Probably some nice family adopted your boys."

"Probably."

"Now your grandson there . . ." and he waggled his hand toward my trailer. I turned red again. "I'm jes' teasing, Lulu." He reached his hand out to me and flashed a mouth full of silver.

"Jesus, Donnie, this getting old business is hard."

"Eventually we all wear comfortable slippers, Lulu."

I laughed. Another good song line.

"My second mama, once she got a little less ornery, always said getting old ain't for the faint-hearted."

I sighed.

"Don't take it all so hard, Lulu. That's the trick."

"Yeah, well, some people have the gift for that and some people have too much baggage on the flight."

Donnie didn't say anything to that. He just looked off and whistled some tune. It might have been "Don't Worry, Be Happy." I followed his eyes up along the row of poplars planted years ago by someone with some foresight. Or anal retention. I looked over at Donnie and he caught me staring at his hand.

"Like my toe? Most people ask. Kind of Frankenstein-ish, no?"

"How?" I asked.

"Chop saw."

"You cut your fingers off with a chop saw? Forgive me, but that's almost impossible."

"Not if you're a forty-seven-year-old drunk with a sense of self-preservation as thin as a ten-cent piece. Least I didn't lose 'em all, and the toe's a help. Foot hurts sometimes though."

I winced. "Jesus, Donnie."

"Kind of turned me around, that moment. I was drunker than a Tennessee teenager on prom night and showing off to one of my wives who needed a shelf or some such thing put up. Ain't had a drink since."

Donnie and I were near strangers, and there we were telling each other a bunch of awful truths. I'd seen on-the-road relationships produce some kind of honesty before, but I'd never gone this far. Until then, not a soul knew that much about my life. And no one but Aloysius McFee knew about my sons. I'd written him after they were born; I had to tell somebody.

"I just want to be normal," I said. "I want all that to not have happened. Your hand. My kids. I want to play in a band with regular people. Sing 'Hark the Herald Angels' in a church choir."

"Those folks in the choir got as many sorrows and troubles as you, Lulu. You kidding?"

He looked really shocked, and I felt embarrassed.

"I wanted to take my wife dancing at the local on Saturday nights. Because I didn't don't make me abnormal," he said.

"Just a regular guy, eh?"

Donnie hoisted himself up out of his chair and wiped a tear off my cheek with his toe-finger. "I'm just a regular guy," he said. He waved his weird hand at me again and smiled his tinsel smile, showing me I was forgiven for being so inconceivably stupid. "I'm off. Give me a call when you think you'd like to play with someone your own age."

"Donnie!"

"Jes' kiddin'. Look for those boys of yours, Lulu. Promise me."

"Promise."

Donnie reached down, with some difficulty, and picked up a chestnut. He shined it on his chest. "Put this under your mattress tonight. You'll sleep like a baby. My old second ma taught me that. Some Polish trick."

DORIS

It is not such a long walk to *Dun Roamin?* through the
Logging Trail. Everything smells and looks different after a
storm. The grasses are flattened and the wind or the rain—
Doris does not know which—has plucked all the salmonberries from their white cone-shaped receptacles and splattered them in the mud. Doris is coming to tell Raylene about
the tree branch that fell on one of the beehives during the
storm last night. Her feet are soaked in her running shoes.
She should have worn her rubber boots. But her feet aren't
moving now anyway because the big word spray-painted on
the back of Raylene and Birdie's trailer home has stopped
them: DIKES.

   Doris rushes to the door, ready to knock, but it is early in
the morning and she is still unsure of what is too early; Birdie
says seven and Lulu says ten. She feels so short of breath
she knocks anyway. When no one answers, she imagines the

worst. She knocks again, hard, and rattles the door handle. Doris panics. She is pounding on the door, her heart beating violently. She is sweating. She rushes down off Raylene and Birdie's steps and runs to Irene Snyder's. She will wake the rest of *Dun Roamin?* Someone must call the police.

"Doris?" Raylene's head is sticking out the door. Her hair is askew. "What the hell is going on?" Doris can hear her blood rushing in her ears. She will be forced to sit down if her heart does not stop pounding. *What a racket.*

Raylene takes Doris' arm and leads her across the lane. Doris needed to show Raylene something but all of a sudden that something is gone. *What was it?* Birdie is on the steps in only a t-shirt. Doris remembers: the word. She pulls Raylene to the back of the trailer home.

Raylene laughs, "At least they could have spelled it right." Birdie looks at the thing and hoots. Doris had not expected laughter. She has been thinking lately that she is good at correctly analyzing situations and reacting or responding accordingly. But here are Raylene and Birdie, laughing about something that seems to be no laughing matter.

"It's got to be those guys from the Second Cup yesterday, eh, Doris? Too much of a coincidence to not be the same couple of jerks. They probably paid some kid to do it for them." Raylene touches the word to see if the paint is still wet.

Birdie says, "What happened at the coffee shop?"

"You want to tell, Doris?" Raylene asks. Doris shakes her head. Doris would just like to sit down.

Birdie says, "Doris looks like she could use a cup of tea."

Doris could *not* use a cup of tea. She does not drink tea. A glass of tap water will suffice.

"So," Raylene says, "Doris and I make a quick stop at that

Second Cup on Reifel on our delivery yesterday." Raylene taps Doris' arm, an apology for the coffee, Doris assumes. "And I get my coffee and one for Mike, and I'm following these two guys in fancy bicycling outfits out the door. You know, the kind of outfits that leave nothing to the imagination." Birdie nods and Doris does too, even though she does not know what in heaven's name Raylene is talking about. "Only they don't hold the door," she says. "They just let it slam in my face. You saw, right, Doris?"

Doris feels too weary to write. She sits on the steps and leaves her notebook and pencil in her pocket.

"So I say, 'Thank you, boys,' all polite and nice, because they're standing on the sidewalk, and Doris and I, we head to the truck. And one of them says, 'Hey, Lady. Hey, Raylene of Sunshine.' He's pointing at the logo on the truck and his buddy's splitting his sides. And I say, 'Yeah?' And he says, 'You're so busy teaching other people manners. Guess you don't have any children of your own.' And I say, 'Oh, none that I know of,' and I jerk my pelvis at them."

Birdie squawks with laughter until Doris thinks Birdie will fall off the porch. "Come on, Ray," Birdie says. "Let's go get some paint. This place needed a paint job anyway. What do you say to something in the chartreuse range?" Raylene loves Birdie enough to paint the trailer home chartreuse. "It'll go perfectly with the magenta roses," Birdie says.

Doris is halfway home, thinking about the paradox of love, before she remembers about the beehive.

LULU

I lasted exactly two weeks in Tennessee. If my shoulder hadn't been feeling like some brute had me in a permanent half nelson, I wouldn't have been sitting next to a long-winded drunk, flying in a giant silver shark toward Fraser Arm. I'd be behind the wheel of my car with the windows rolled down, deep breathing the hot Tennessee air.

I was thinking about how flight attendants have transformed over the years from the high-heeled uber-pretty young women who tottered down the aisles when I first started flying to a more down-home lot. They were intimidating back then with their perfectly arched eyebrows, their knack for walking in stilettos, and their ability to not slop coffee into our laps no matter how turbulent the skies. Or maybe I was just younger and more easily intimidated then. Molly, or so her name tag read, who'd been pouring my coffee on the flight back to Canada, was so beautifully plain—overbite, lopsided smile over crooked teeth, hands a little chapped, jaunty scarf completely askew, sweat crescents in her armpits—I had already started writing a song about her.

I was fantasizing, erroneously I knew, about the simplicity and steadiness of Molly's job, when my seatmate leaned out into the aisle, one hand holding onto the armrest between us for balance, and slurred, "Molly." Fantasy dashed: who but a saint would put up with the public the way flight attendants do? I wanted to elbow him in the solar plexus. Saint I wasn't. I'd hoped he'd get off in Calgary. I'd heard enough about his self-diagnosed near aortic aneurysm and his bitch of an ex-wife, but he was still there, his booze-induced loquaciousness mounting, as we flew toward the mountains. He was a rye-and-Coke man. Molly brought him another one and he fell asleep, or passed out, blessedly leaning away from me.

I pressed my forehead against the window. The earth from flying height is beautiful, no matter what human messes lie below. Oil spills, demolition yards, sixteen-lane highways, garden gnomes—they all become pristine and interesting from above. I watched the majestic Rockies pass beneath us. Just minutes later, it seemed, we were over the Coastal Range then we were casting a dragonfly shadow on the muddy Fraser River flowing out to the ocean below us. A train was snaking alongside the river, small as a toy.

•

The taxi pulled into the driveway on Forward Road. There was no hyperactive dog to greet me anymore. Dad had decided they were too old for dogs after the last one died. I could see the flicker of blue light through the parlour curtains as I paid the cabbie. My father and my aunt were curled up on the couch together watching a Got Talent show. I had to marvel at the depth of their affection for one another. Dad kissed Kat goodbye even if he was only going to the corner store for a box of crackers. They seemed to be engaged in an endless conversation that had started forty years earlier. I imagined that when Dad was gone, Kat would lie on her back on his grassy grave and just keep talking, staring up at the sky, calmly keeping him up to date on what was going on in the world. He'd lie down there beneath her, listening, each of them patiently waiting for her to come over to the other side so they could carry on the dialogue. Maybe they were just making up for the monstrous losses that had marked their lives, making sure that they lived out their days as though each was the proverbial last.

Kat looked at me as though she knew what I was thinking, and Dad put down his cup of tea and started to get up. Getting up wouldn't have been that much of an effort if they'd just replaced that damn old settee that was too close to the ground for anyone over fifty.

"I'm going to pop up to the McFees' for a bit and say hello to Geordie," I said, pulling him up with my good arm. "Don't wait up for me. I'll tell you all about the bluegrass festival tomorrow, okay?"

Kat kissed me and gave me a tight hug. It wasn't just Dad she loved. Her sweet smile said: I'm glad you're home.

"Night night, dear," they said in unison.

Dad put his arm around Kat's shoulders and they waved at me from the kitchen door. I would have given both hands to Lucifer to feel as content with someone as they were with each other.

—

I never knew whether to knock on the McFees' door or just walk in. I'd never knocked when Aloysius was alive, but it was late and dark inside. I tapped lightly then opened the door. I heard dogs barking and then Geordie laughing, so I flicked on the hall light. He and Doris were lugging a mattress down the stairs. The mattress had folded in half and pinned Doris against the wall. Geordie seemed oblivious to the fact that Doris was half his size and that they were both in their sixties. Not that size mattered much when it came to Doris. I'd seen her hauling timber as big as herself. Dante and the mongrel Ricky rushed over and gave me a waggling greeting.

"We're sleeping out on the deck," Geordie cried, rushing over for a hug, and abandoning Doris with the mattress. "Sleep over, Lulu. Have a sleepover with us."

I helped haul the mattress onto the back deck where a folding canvas army cot was already set up. A pillow and the fat roll of an ancient sleeping bag, surely reeking of the basement, lay beside it. I'd slept off a teenage hangover or two on this deck before, on that exact cot.

"That's Doris'. This's mine." Geordie thumped down on the mattress.

Doris disappeared and came back with another cot. I had already learned that when Doris made up her mind you might as well just take off your hat. I should have said a polite nighty-night, and left, but instead I found myself stretching a hunting scene–lined sleeping bag out on the cot.

"Dad'll worry," I said, in a feeble attempt at getting out of the sleepover. Doris put a hand up to her ear and pointed to the kitchen.

Geordie translated: "Call Dad."

"I don't have pyjamas or my toothbrush. Or my teddy bear," I laughed.

Doris disappeared again and returned with a new toothbrush still in its packaging—it looked like it'd been manufactured in the 1970s—and a pair of men's pyjamas. If they weren't Aloysius McFee's I'd eat that hat I'd already taken off. The jammies smelled of cedar. They were ironed and clean and as soft as well-worn cotton can be.

Do you need a bear? Doris wrote on her pad, as earnest as they come.

"I can do without one tonight, Doris. Thanks."

On the back porch at the McFees' we were protected from the streetlights, but there was still too much ambient light to see the stars the way we used to when we were little and the town's night skies were ebony. Geordie pointed to the three bright stars of Orion's Belt. While we were searching for the North Star and the Big Dipper, Mike and Cidalia came out onto the porch. I sat up in Aloysius' pyjamas, glad for the darkness. Cidalia gave me a hug, then sat on the end of Geordie's mattress. She pulled one of his feet out from under the covers and gave it a massage.

"Cidalia's nice," Geordie purred. Exactly what I was thinking.

I looked up at Mike. My promise to Donnie Coulter to find my sons sat like a grizzly bear on my chest. My sons. Mike's sons.

"Tell them about the outhouse, Mike. We're going to dig up the outhouse, Lulu. Tell Lulu, Mike," Geordie said.

"Yup. There's always been a midden out behind the outhouse. Which probably means there's stuff in the outhouse pit, too. A lot of people are digging in them now. I don't think ours has been used since they got running water in the house, which was a long time ago."

"Like a hundred years," said Geordie.

Geordie and Mike's treasures had accumulated over the years. The barn was a museum to their old license plates and bottles. The more precious items, like the pennies from the nineteenth century and an intact shaving mug, had found spots on shelves inside the house.

"They find really cool stuff, right Mike?"

"You guys are weird" I leaned over and poked Geordie.

"There isn't any *poo* in it anymore, Lulu." Geordie giggled and we all hooted.

"On that bright note, I'll say goodnight," Cidalia said, giving my toes a squeeze too.

●

The three of us lay in silence, staring up at the heavens.

"Doris knows the stars and the universe too, you know," Geordie said, his voice sleepy.

"Is that so?" I tried to imagine Doris explaining the universe to a man who couldn't read.

Geordie was silent for a long time. I couldn't tell whether his eyes were open or closed. Suddenly, as if I'd asked or had made some kind of declaration he had to deny, Geordie said: "The universe doesn't end, Lulu. It goes on forever and ever." Then he was snoring gently.

"Yeah, but what is beyond forever?" I whispered.

I listened for Doris' breathing but heard none. She may have been asleep on the other side of Geordie, or maybe the pair of us were awake, suspended in time on our army cots, staring up into the dark night waiting for a shooting star to wish upon. I wondered if this was what Aloysius had imagined for us.

●

Doris' bed was empty when I woke, or rather, Doris was gone and little Ricky was curled up in her sleeping bag. Geordie was still asleep, his arms flung wide and dangling off the narrow mattress. Dante was fast asleep too, sprawled open like Geordie, his chin on the mattress, catching a patch of morning sun.

I was lured to the kitchen by my body's morning chant for caffeine. I groggily eyed the coffee canister. More of a chance there'd be lima beans in there than the dark roasted ones I was craving. I shook the other canisters. All empty. I peered around the kitchen. The strange notes that Doris had found in the flour canister were still tacked to the wall, curled and yellowed, some words faded to traces. One by one I pried the thumbtacks out and peeled the notes from the wall. I put the notes and the grimy tacks in the tea canister then tucked all the containers, like Russian dolls, into the flour canister and pushed it to the back of the cupboard under the sink. I stared dispiritedly at the spirographic rust circles the canisters had left behind on the stained turquoise arborite. This house needed a facelift, badly. Outside, the McFee property had been completely transformed, but inside, no one had touched much of anything—no new paint, no new furniture, the same old drapes in every window. Doris, Geordie, Mike, and Cidalia had just added their own meagre collection of possessions to what had been there in the seventies.

I scrubbed at the counter with some kind of useless organic cleansing liquid. No Ajax in this house. Using baking soda, I reduced the rust circles to muted orange stains before I gave up. None of this scrubbing had reduced my need for coffee, of course. The café at the corner brewed a good cup but that would mean getting dressed, and whosever pyjamas these were, they were too comfy to take off. I opened the cupboards above the stove and poked around amongst the bizarre collection of old jars and bottles for something remotely coffee-like. Gleaming like a beacon in a storm was an ancient bottle of Postum. I gave praise for Doris' lack of house-tidying until I opened the bottle. Along with the dregs of the weird matter normally found in a Postum bottle I found a dainty ring—a small diamond with two tiny rubies set on either side of it. It was the first ring I stole for Aloysius, from the house in New Westminster.

Doris came into the kitchen with a basket full of eggs. She looked at the Postum bottle and the ring in my hand and looked quickly away. I'd swear I saw a little flicker of embarrassment.

"Have you seen this Doris?" I asked.

She nodded.

"How long has it been here?"

She shrugged.

"Like, twenty-five years? Like, it was here when you moved in?"

Doris nodded again.

"Doris, that is weird."

Doris shrugged. She looked at the empty wall where the notes had been. I tried the ring on. It fit my ring finger so perfectly I took it off and put it in my pocket. I rinsed out the jar in the sink and held it up over the glass-recycling container. Doris nodded. If she thought it was odd that I was taking the ring there was nothing in her face that told me so. It was on my lips to ask her whether she felt it was a bit strange to have never changed a thing—there was still an old black dialer telephone on the wall, for God's sake, and I was sure I'd find a pack of petrified dates and crumbling, rancid walnuts in the Postum cupboard if I looked. Clearly she did not think it weird, or she would have done something about it.

She held an egg up to me, eyebrows raised.

I nodded and sat down at the kitchen table. Geordie stumbled in, tousle-headed. Doris was slicing a loaf of her homemade bread and I got up to put it in the toaster.

Go look at your room. After breakfast, Doris wrote.

"Why?"

Are you coming to stay?

"No. I can't Doris." I wasn't coming to stay. She had to know that.

Doris placed a plate with two beautiful sunny-side-up eggs in front of me. The fat round yolks were school-bus orange. She stacked four slices of toast on a plate—the McFees' good china that she used every day—and put another four slices in the ancient toaster. Aloysius had repaired the cloth cord on that toaster with electrician's tape—surely it couldn't still be alive. While I buttered the toast I made a mental note to abscond with that fire-waiting-to-happen. In the meantime, I couldn't wait for some of Doris' blackberry jelly.

After breakfast Doris and Geordie went off with the compost bucket to feed some beast or other and left me alone in the kitchen. While I washed the dishes I pondered the latest note Doris had left on the kitchen blackboard. *Why don't we drink pig milk?* Jesus. I hoped she'd been under Geordie's influence when she wrote that. I dried and put away the dishes and wandered into the front hall. The house was huge and silent. I remembered Aloysius sitting at the telephone table in the dark hall, his long, long legs crossed awkwardly, an adult in a child's desk.

"Aloysius?" I called, waiting for the echo. "Alice? Yoohoo, Alice." I was Jackie Gleason in *The Honeymooners*: "Straight to the moon, Alice. Pow!" I felt Aloysius and Alice McFee inviting me upstairs. The door to the room—their bedroom—was closed. I had been in Aloysius' room only once as a teenager. I'd snuck in looking for cigarettes one afternoon when Aloysius was out. Otherwise I'd prudently avoided it. The room was huge, running the full length of the south side of the house. On the west side, a single door led to a small, wrought-iron balcony overlooking the front yard. I wandered from window to window, feeling the warmth of the sun streaming in. The linen drapes might have preceded Alice McFee's time. Each one gave onto some green scene— the garden, the side windbreak, the treed front yard. The heavy old dressers—oak and cherry possibly—were dusted and polished. There was a huge roll-top desk opposite the bed and a round table between two armchairs by the balcony door. The desk was full of Aloysius' papers, but the dressers and cupboards were empty and there was nothing but clean towels and a new bar of soap in the en-suite bathroom. I sat on the bed. Then I lay on the bed. Then I pulled the quilt over me and closed my eyes. Clever Doris to offer me both a room of my own and a room with a view.

●

Later that day I drove into New Westminster and cruised the streets behind the hospital looking for the house. I remembered sparkly grey stucco and a large front door, but not much else. The little diamond ring had jerked me back to that day. I saw my eleven-year-old self, standing in that plush bedroom. I could feel the red leather of the jewellery box and hear the silence of the cream-coloured carpet. It took me half an hour to realize how pointless my search was. Was I going to knock on the door and return the ring to the original owner? And what story would I have told as I handed it over? What about the rest of the stuff, the charm bracelet, and the emerald, and the other things I took that day that were still packed in a box at the back of my closet at Dad's house? The woman who'd bought the cookies from Aloysius and me had been old. She'd be dead now or languishing in a seniors' home, her wicked, disappointing grandkids my age.

I gave up and drove down Columbia and handed the ring to a squeegee kid after she washed my windshield.

"It's real," I said.

"Yeah?" she said without enthusiasm.

Ingrate, I wanted to say. When did indifference become fashionable? I felt instantly guilty for my thoughts. If she was on the street she probably didn't have a home worth going back to. Why should she trust *me*? I took Marine Drive into

Vancouver for my physio appointment, Aloysius' route, for old times' sake. I guess I shouldn't have been surprised when the brown Mercedes purred into one of the spots reserved for physio clients. I was back in my usual time slot, and Robin Chaudhury had probably not been so stupid as to give his up and leave the country, imagining he was all healed up.

"Lulu, hey. What are you doing in town?"

What I was doing just then was squatting by a chain-link fence, nose to nose with a large dirty dog. "This is terrible," I said.

Robin came across the narrow lane behind the parking lot and squatted down beside me. The dog whined and began pacing back and forth behind the fence on an excrement-strewn cement pad. She was skinny and filthy and there was nothing in the two bowls in her enclosure but murky water.

"Look at the crap. She's living in total squalor."

"That's disgusting." Robin waggled his fingers through the fence.

"We should phone animal rescue," I said.

"Better yet," Robin said, getting down on his knees, "we should set her free."

He hauled on the bottom of the fence until I thought he'd break his wrist again. In a minute he'd pulled the wire up about a foot. He called the dog and patted the ground and she got down on her belly and shimmied out of her prison. She skulked back and forth between us like a contrite ex-con on parole.

"What do we do now?"

"Let's get her out of here." He whistled and the dog followed him and leapt into the immaculate Mercedes. He stood there, holding the door open for me. "Coming?"

Robin's house wasn't his wife's or his daughters'. It was a small condo he'd moved into a year after his wife died. It *was* in Kitsilano, but not quite on the beach. On one of the side streets, closer to 7th Avenue than the ocean. There were no photos of his wife anywhere, unless there was one in the bedroom, which I didn't explore. The dog raced around the condo, poking her blond-bearded chin into everything until Robin caught her and we took her to the bathroom and washed her in the tub. We were both soaked and filthy by the time we finished.

"What shall we call her?"

"You name her. You're keeping her," Robin said. "Well, I can't keep her here," he said when I looked at him, shocked. "And that's false shockery, Lulu."

False shockery. I laughed. "You're right. Okay. I'll call her Betsey."

It was Robin's turn to look shocked.

"What?"

"You'd name your dog after your mother?"

"Jesus, Robin, do you know everything about me?"

"Not everything." He looked at me sweetly. "At least not everything I'd like to know."

"It was Bette, like B.E.T.T.E., not Betsey."

"Close enough."

"Not close enough at all, actually."

I looked out the front window. A line of birds quivered on the telephone wire as if waiting for the bang of the starter pistol. Suddenly they flew up. I wondered which one had made the first move. Robin's girls, young women now, smiled at me from a framed photo on the windowsill, their bright youthfulness like a glass of fresh water. "They're beautiful."

"They've got Mina's good looks," Robin said. "We wanted another child. We might have had more if Mina hadn't gotten sick. She was first diagnosed when Chloe was three. She was sick for a long time and then she was better for a long time. We really thought she'd beaten it. But it came back to bite her."

"You must miss her."

Robin said, "I'll miss her 'til the end of my days." He looked directly at me, his eyes tender. "But the day you die, the roses still grow."

"They do." I said.

"You've got exactly what I always wanted, Lulu. A big family. Siblings. Being an only child sucked."

Why dash his fantasy. The grass is always greener, even in someone else's wrecking yard.

"Can I call you next week? I'm going to Chicago for the weekend to visit my daughter, but I'd like to see you again."

I looked him in the eye. "I'm not your kind of material, Robin. I'm way too . . ."

"What? What do you think you're way too . . . ?" He put his warm hand on my shoulder.

Cautious? Angry? Wounded? Unmarriageable? "Busy," I said.

He didn't look disappointed. He just smiled.

"Well, if ever you change your mind," he said, and he gave me a card. It was printed in chocolate brown ink on thick cream-coloured paper, just his name, Robin Chaudhury, and a telephone number. A bloody calling card like Mr. Darcy might have carried.

"You have nice taste," I said begrudgingly.

"No," Robin said, "just money."

●

The next morning, Saturday, I took Betsey to the vet and then up to the McFees'. I tied her to a chair on the front porch. "I promise you your freedom will not be short-lived, Betsey," I said, scratching her behind the ears. "Just 'til I see if Doris won't mind having you around for a bit."

Dad had already made it clear that, so long as he was alive, I was not going to be living in the Boler with an unruly dog. So the options were for me to keep her at Dad's—and I'd already decided that he and Kat were too old to take her on—or to see if Doris would keep her for a while. I left Betsey whining and straining against her binder twine lead while I went around the back. I figured I'd introduce Betsey to Doris first, and Doris could introduce Betsey to the other dogs. As I came in, however, Doris, Dante, Ricky—and Betsey—were already prancing into the kitchen from the front hall like four old friends.

What's her name? Doris wrote.

"Betsey," I said.

Doris gave me a look. So maybe it was a bit odd.

Like most dogs, within a few hours of her arrival, Betsey had been claimed by the farm. She took up her role as beta dog to Doris' alpha. Geordie and Betsey greeted each other like souls who'd been twins in their last life. The same fate had befallen other creatures that had wandered onto the property, humans included. I had a sense that the current inhabitants—or even the gods—had cooked up a clever plot to claim me too; everyone wanted me to be another dog in Doris' pack. Who said "Resistance is futile"?

●

Tuesday morning brought a light rain and a serious case of cabin fever. I headed over to the McFees' to check on Betsey. It was early and no one was around. I stood restlessly under the verandah on the back porch, smelling the rain on the cedars and the wet earth and wondering what had changed in that familiar landscape. The outhouse. The sturdy old building was now standing ten feet to the left of its usual spot. There had always been wasps' nests under its eaves, which made the fat blackberries that grew around it unpickable, and therefore even more desirable. I heard Mike and Geordie and the dogs before I saw them. They were coming around from the side of the house, shovels and a ladder in hand. I slipped in the back door. I wasn't ready for humans.

There was something new written on the blackboard: *Does Her Majesty Queen Elizabeth II ever wear trousers?* Trousers. Her Majesty. Doris. What a mind. It wasn't something I'd ever pondered, but the question having been posed, it was now imperative that I know. Ah, the joys of being forcibly aimless. I was betting on the trouser answer being yes as I poked through the enormous collection of books in the living room, looking for a book on the Queen. Her Majesty seemed a trousers type; she had dogs, after all.

As I searched I became conscious of a sound drifting in the air, like a radio left on upstairs. Doris played music all the time and the eclectic nature of her record collection meant that we might hear Sinatra, the Stones, and Pink in the same half hour. But this was something different. I stood at the foot of the stairs and listened. The sound was deep dark honey, and so hauntingly beautiful I shivered. When I realized what it was, I climbed to the top of the stairs and sat down. Behind a closed door, Doris was whistling a song that always cracked me open, and even more so now. It was Otis Redding. Trevor's song. My song: "The Dock of the Bay."

Her door opened. If she was surprised to see me sitting at the top of the stairs Doris didn't allow it to register on her face for more than a nanosecond, but she must have seen the expression on mine. She stopped whistling and sat down, in her pyjamas, beside me.

"Have you heard of the Oregon Whistlers Jamboree?"

She shook her head.

"It's a whistling competition. In Portland. People come from all over the world. I think you should go. We should go."

Doris didn't have her pad and pencil. It was the first time I'd seen her voiceless.

"Do you have any other songs? You'd probably need three for the competition."

Doris nodded. She went to her room and returned with a pad and a pencil and sat back down beside me, a little closer this time.

The Saints.

"Go marching in?"

Doris nodded. I shook my head. "Too conventional. I've been to the jamboree. They want something difficult. Everyone can whistle 'The Saints.' Even my dad."

Your Cheatin' Heart?

"Perfect." And bizarre, for Doris, I thought. "Anything else? Your favourite. Your best."

Suzanne, she wrote. *Cohen.*

Leonard Cohen. I remembered our cat burial conversation.

"Would you like to go, Doris? It's at the end of September. I can arrange everything."

I caught a flicker of pleasure in her eyes. Doris rose and made fork-to-mouth motions with her hand then wrote something on the pad and held it in front of my face, at exactly the right focal distance. *Thank you.*

A giddy ounce of glee was already flowing in my veins. And Doris was about to make me another couple of sunny-side-ups.

As we entered the kitchen Doris stopped suddenly in front of me and I felt her tighten, instinctively, an animal caught in the crosshairs. She might even have uttered a sound. Mike was standing at the open back door, his face ashen, his eyes hollow. He kept wiping his feet on the mat, staring at Doris, unspeaking.

Mike broke his gaze with his sister and looked past her to me. He opened his mouth: "We found a body. There's a body in the outhouse. A skeleton."

My legs went liquid.

"Where's Geordie?" I said.

DORIS

What colour is this? Mike is calling the police. Mike is not grey. Mike is dark brown. He repeats the address. The first sirens arrive. The hall ceiling turns red and blue. No one has needed to call the police from this house. Not since Alice. Now Alice has been found; Doris knows it in her bones. This is Alice McFee. How would Doris dial 9-1-1 if Mike were not home? Where has Lulu gone?

Doris opens the front door. There is a fire truck nose at the end of the driveway. *Too late. Mrs. McFee is dead.* The fire truck can't pass. Who is that gesturing there? Hamish Wheatley. He will send the fire truck to the back driveway. Doris counts the policemen in the yard. There are seventeen, but they are not individuals: seventeen policemen become a force, just as seventeen cows become a herd and seventeen trees an orchard. This must be the intention of large numbers of uniformed people. How many fewer of them would make them men again?

The force comes up the front steps, noisy like a drum. Doris steps aside. Black boots thump on the kitchen linoleum. Radios shout static. The dogs pant around legs. Ricky howls, objecting to a frequency the humans cannot hear. His mouth is a grey-whiskered circle. The room is a balloon inflated to near bursting. Mike opens the door and the air flies out. He leads them through the garden. The troop is careful not to trample the plants. "Keep the dogs inside," one of the force says. Doris ignores him.

Curiosity—that is what turns them back into individuals. They surround the hole at the back of the garden and peer into the hole. They are two-deep on its edges, transformed into curious people. Doris' own curiosity is itching. She wants to see as well, but seeing means that Doris must touch a policeman in the bodywall around the hole. She uses her elbow and one of the police officers turns. The eyes that look at her are anxious blue. A woman. Doris leans past her to look at what remains of Alice McFee but there is Lulu, crouching in the outhouse hole. Her hands are scrabbling at the dirt.

Extracting Lulu from the pit will not be easy especially since it is clear to Doris that Lulu does not want to be extracted. It is not deep—perhaps just a few inches over Lulu's head, if she were to stand up—and the wooden ladder is in the hole, but Lulu is not listening. Red Rover, Red Rover, the police call the firemen over. Doris has never seen a fireman up close. The firemen are Clydesdales, much bigger than the police, who are Quarter horses. The Clydesdales want to lift Lulu as if she is a naughty cat, by the armpits, but this, Doris can see, will be impossible. The geometry is wrong. "Ma'am, I will need you to exit the hole," a policeman says. Exit the hole. Lulu does not answer. *Curiosity might have killed this cat.*

A fireman holds the ladder and the blue-eyed police-woman descends. Lulu is forced to stand up. Now there's Alice McFee, Lulu Parsons, and a blue-eyed policewoman in the outhouse pit. The policewoman makes Lulu rise up the rungs and Doris wants to reach out her hand. Lulu's eyes are wild. She is a horse—it doesn't matter what kind—trapped in a barn on fire.

The police look into the pit. Doris looks too. Someone shines a light. Even Doris makes a sound. *Huff.* Wedged by the wall at the bottom is a creamy white skull, an eye socket, half a jaw. But there is more, the cause of Doris' public *huff.* To the right and just below the other is a second gleaming skull.

What for a second was silence becomes noise again. Someone barks. It is not a dog. Doris is not sure what her feet are for. She observes herself from a short distance away. How skinny her shins are. For a very short time it is some-one's job to have his hand on Doris' elbow. There is a button missing on the hand's sleeve. Doris hears purple. Lulu's voice is pale. Where is Geordie?

Inside the barn it is very warm. In her house slippers and pyjamas Doris climbs the bales to where Geordie is. She sits beside him. She will let the goats out later. Geordie leans his head on Doris' shoulder and Doris puts her arm around him. "That's not Mum," Geordie says.

Doris isn't listening. She could go across the street to the Wheatleys in an emergency. Hamish and Trixie Wheatley are almost always home, and despite her name, Trixie has always been very reliable. They would call 9-1-1.

LULU

We were standing in the kale. The man was saying, "I could kick myself," and looking at me familiarly. I had no idea who he was. He had crossed his arms and was standing too close to me, surveying the scene before us like it was the Grand Canyon, the white cuffs of his shirt showing dully out of the sleeves of his black suit.

"We searched the property with a fine-toothed comb. Captain Smallwood was sure it was McFee. We knew it wasn't your dad. But we couldn't pin anything on McFee. No evidence. Nothing. Anywhere. And there they were, in the bleeding outhouse. Right under our noses. Shit." He snorted a laugh. The man's voice had a strange inflection to it, rapid paced and pinched. He reeked of aftershave.

"They interrogated the bastard for hours. They didn't want to let him go, but McFee kept his story straight. And he had a semi-credible alibi. There was no sign of a fight. No body. I saw him coming out of the station when they let him go. You should've seen his face. Smirking. It made my blood boil." He paused and took a pack of cigarettes from his jacket pocket. "You smoke?"

I shook my head. I'd quit years ago. Usually, the click of the lighter still set my salivary glands to watering, but my mouth was bone dry.

He inhaled deeply and blew smoke out through his nose. "No one wanted to go near that outhouse. There were two huge wasps' nests on it. I remember it clear as a bell. A big sucker above the door, a smaller one on the side, and the bloody thing was surrounded by blackberry canes. It was like a fortress. Boarded up too. We figured McFee couldn't have gotten in there so why should we? No one wanted to admit they were afraid of a bunch of wasps, not even the top dogs." He smoked that cigarette, sucking hard, like it was going to be his last. "We figured he'd done the wife in, but we weren't counting on your mom. Smallwood figured she'd just run off."

"Who are you?"

"Sorry. I thought you knew me." He smiled and stuck out his hand. It was raw-knuckled and cigarette stained. I didn't take it. "Martin Currie. Remember me?"

I couldn't see a trace of the young Martin I remembered from Dad's Scout pack, the boy who'd come to the house the night Mum disappeared. The card he handed me said Detective but there was a little spot of dirt or something on it that made it read Defective. His face was haggard, with sallow bags under his eyes, like he'd survived a war, but barely. Martin had become the enemy when I started doing drugs. I don't think I'd seen him since I was eighteen.

"That's my mother?" I don't know why I made it a question. I already knew it was.

"Shouldn't say anything before Forensics does their job, but it's pretty coincidental, right? Two females disappear the same day, and two bodies found in the crapper?"

I looked over at the outhouse. Females. I hated the term. The place was crawling. Someone was stringing up yellow tape between the trees. The fire truck was still there and there were two ambulances now. There were cop cars everywhere. I wondered why they never turned off their flashing lights. Didn't the endless flashing just add to the panic? It was adding to mine.

"Women," I said. "Not females."

"Yeah?" Martin looked confused.

He dropped his cigarette and stubbed it out in the dirt. I stared down at it. Doris wouldn't like that. She had a war waged against cigarette butt litter in Fraser Arm. No one ever smoked on the farm. Martin's butt lay under the kale like a note sung flat.

"Pick that up," I said.

Martin hesitated a minute, a crooked grin on his face. When he saw I was serious he bent down and picked it up. He held it in the air for a second then slipped the butt into his pocket.

"Yes, ma'am," he said.

"Fuck you, Martin Currie, Defective," I said. I gave him back his card.

●

Sirens do that. They turn people into shameless gawkers and intruders; strangers made bold by emergency vehicles. They'd done it when Mum disappeared. The whole neighbourhood turned out for that event. Now they were doing it again—like it was her fortieth anniversary party. People who never knew her, people who'd never set foot up the drive, were standing around in the garden chatting as if the circus had come to the McFees' backyard and we were selling tickets. The circus tent, though—couldn't they see?—was collapsing. The choreographer was on drugs. "Just stay outside the yellow lines, folks," a policeman droned. I wanted them off the property and away from my mother's grave. Get out, I shouted, but no sound passed my lips. I moved my feet to get out of the kale, to chase away the voyeurs, but didn't get any closer to them. I seemed to have been assigned a fireman. He was following me. Slowly. He was handsome like a movie star—a wrangler without a horse. Would he help me turn this chaos into order? I think he nodded yes.

●

"The murderer among us," Kat said.

She said it to no one in particular, but she reached over with her blue-veined hand and gave mine a squeeze. We'd been sitting around the dining room table as morning turned to day, for the most part in stunned silence. Everyone was there—Dad and Kat, Alan, Naomi, Ambrose, Mike and Cidalia, Raylene and Birdie, Doris, even Lewis Cray—we and the dogs, banished from our own backyard. The police regulars had been replaced by a forensics crew. A white tent had been set up around the outhouse pit and silhouetted figures were moving about inside it like ghosts. Another crew was rigging up spotlights on poles. They'd be there all night, they told us.

"The murderer among us. How so, Kat dear?" Dad asked. Nothing anyone said would have made sense to him.

"The person you talk to every day. You shake hands with him. You ask after his health. You think you're talking with a nice neighbour. You have no idea you're shaking the hand of a murderer, a rapist, a child molestor." We stared blankly at Kat, dull with the awful discovery. "Mr. McFee always seemed so lovely and warm. We liked him, didn't we, Wally? But he murdered Bette."

"I never trusted the bastard," Ambrose said.

Alan nodded. "How the hell did they miss two bodies in the outhouse?"

"There were wasps' nests. They didn't look," I said. "Martin Currie told me."

"Martin Currie. Jesus effin' Christ. Is he here? How could they not have known McFee offed Mum and Mrs. McFee?" Ambrose said.

"Language, Alan," Dad said.

"Why?" I asked my brothers. "Why didn't you trust him?" How would my brothers have known him well enough not to trust him? I didn't trust him, but I knew him. They didn't.

"McFee? He was creepy. Don't you remember him, always cruising around in his convertibles? And that mysterious death of his. It was doubly creepy that he left you this house." Ambrose looked at me like he'd finally caught me lying. "Did you ever figure that out?"

I shook my head. We were back in 1982 again, Aloysius gone, his will read, and the same question hanging over my head. Ambrose asked it then too. And the police wanted to know why as well. No one knew anything about him and me. I'd kept that secret from everyone. It wasn't hard in those days. I could have drowned in a well in the morning and no one would wonder where I was until I didn't turn up for supper.

"He was always coming into Beaver Lumber and asking me if we'd heard anything about Mum. I remember the bastard. He'd sidle up with this toadyish look on his face and say, 'Any word, Ambrose?' Every bloody time. 'Any word?' As if I'd tell *him*. And the way he looked at the girls who worked there. I could puke."

"They suspected him, you know. They just couldn't pin it on him. Currie told me years ago," Alan said.

"They suspected me as well," Dad said. "It's often the spouse who . . ."

Kat leaned her head against Dad's shoulder and he stopped speaking.

"Oh, Dad." I stood up. I was going to vomit. How could they have suspected him? And Aloysius? Aloysius was a liar and a thief, but no one had ever told me he was a suspect. Now I could remember him keeping me away from the outhouse with an urgency that was excessive. Most people would get rid of wasps' nests so close to the garden, but he let those wasps' nests be. The perfect defence. I'd sat on the back porch and played my fiddle with Aloysius McFee while my mother's body mouldered in the backyard, fifty feet away.

"It might not have been McFee, I suppose," Cidalia said. "Someone else might have killed them and put them . . . in there." She shivered.

My brothers guffawed and even Mike protested. "Not likely, Cid. You had to know Aloysius McFee. He was something special. You wouldn't be saying that if you'd met him."

Doris wrote something on her pad and held it up. *It was him,* Mike read aloud. She rose from the table and signalled for me to come with her.

●

The police had moved the outhouse even farther away from its former spot, and its door, which had been nailed shut with a crisscross of weathered two-by-fours for as long as I could remember, hung open on rusted hinges. Doris and I peered inside. Long nails poked out of a couple of two-by-tens that were leaning up against the back wall.

"Don't touch anything, ladies." I hadn't seen the detective coming. He leaned a heavy hand up against the outhouse and it rocked slightly. Removing his hand he said, "It's evidence."

Doris pointed at the nails in the two-by-tens. They were antique, square instead of round, the kind that no one had used for more than a century.

"Those boards were nailed across the seat," he said. "McFee must have used old nails to make it look like no one had touched it since the turn of the century. If anyone had looked. A farm like this, there's usually a pile of old nails like that somewhere. You never seen any in the barn or the sheds? Tobacco can full of nails?"

Doris nodded. Yes. Then she pointed at the seat hole and looked at the detective.

"Looks like it was premeditated. Like he prepped the outhouse beforehand. Either that or he killed them first then tried to figure out what to do with the bodies. He had to cut the hole bigger. Jigsaw, I'd say." He spoke with a blunt detachedness, as if he wasn't speaking to us, as if, even for himself, he could make the bodies in the outhouse a story instead of real.

The hole was irregular, with a roughly cut jagged edge; it was a child's nightmare, too big to sit on without falling through. The detective's shoulders wouldn't have fit through that hole, but my mother's . . . and Alice McFee's . . . I closed my eyes. It didn't help. Who went in first? Were they already dead? How could he have spent all those years with me, done what he did to me, after killing my mother? My nausea swept up into my throat. Doris circled my wrist with her fingers. Her skin was rough but her touch was so light. She led me back into the house.

●

Thursday it poured. It was cold, a late August warning of the coming fall. Doris had succumbed to my arm flapping and had let me light the wood stove in the living room. She was baking bread in the kitchen, something I was learning she did when life's rug was rumpled. The police had thrown a big blue tarp over the outhouse. It looked like a modern version of itself, a Johnny-on-the-Spot, all tied up in red reflector tape. They'd strung another tarp up over the excavation site, securing the tent already there. I could hear the steady heartbeat of a hydraulic pump under the tarp. No one but a security cop was out there, and he was sitting in a lone cruiser parked beside the outhouse, the rain sheeting off the windshield, the engine running. Doris had already been out there twice in her yellow rain slicker to mention the idling law, but the officer had told her he had to leave the car running "for security reasons." Mike and Geordie had given up blackberry picking when the rain came. They'd gone to visit Pepsi. Cidalia was at work. As for the rest of the clan, I was glad they'd stayed away. The endless conjecturing was useless. And painful. Until the police analyzed the evidence there was nothing to do and nothing to decide.

I dropped into an armchair in front of the wood stove and pulled a blanket up over me. I tried to build barricades against the visions my mind was live streaming, but alone in the living room I felt Mum's hand reaching out for me from that dark hole. The vision of Aloysius forcing my mother's head and shoulders through the hole in the outhouse repeated like the floods of dreams—then there was water pouring out from under a locked bathroom door, darkly staining the carpet and flowing down the stairs. "Mop it up, Lulu, mop it up," my mother shouted. But the towels were locked in the bathroom. I rattled the bathroom door. My feet were soaked blood red. It wouldn't stop.

My own cry woke me. I'd been picking the loose stuffing from the worn upholstery of the old armchair I was curled up in. I stared at the wad of dirty old cotton batting, disgusted. Aloysius McFee was everywhere in the house. I threw off the blanket, remembering Aloysius stretched out on the couch under it, sleeping off another gin or coke binge.

"Doris," I shouted. "Doris!"

She appeared in the doorway. I held the ball of batting out toward her.

"This has got to go. All of it. Look at this. This is a fifty-year-old couch. This armchair. It's filthy. It stinks of Aloysius." I grabbed the blanket and shook it at her. "How old is this?" I put the blanket to my face. I swear I could smell him. I could smell his dirty cigarettes and his clean summer sweat in his short-sleeved shirts, the chemical of his dry cleaned suit, his mints, his gin, his aftershave, his hair cream. I fell to my knees, clutching the blanket, sobs guttering from my throat. I had laughed with him. I had danced with him. I'd made music with him. I had loved Aloysius McFee. I had loved the man who had abused me and killed my mother.

Gently, Doris pulled the blanket from my clenched hands. She folded it and opened the wood stove and shoved it in. She slammed the door shut, but the smell of burning wool was instant and disgusting. I retched and lay down on the floor, crying so hard I was only barely conscious of the flickering light of the blanket burning through the glass front of the stove. Doris stood above me for a few seconds then disappeared. I saw her feet and felt her lift my head. She pushed a soft clean-smelling pillow under my wet face. Then she laid a blanket over me and tucked me in like a child, circling me like she would one of her lambs. I cried harder. It may have been the first time in my life that I'd cried in front of someone. I didn't care anymore.

At some point I became aware of the hardness of the floor. I could smell Doris' bread baking. The rain was still pounding on the porch roof. It hadn't stopped. I'd slept. The blanket I was wrapped in was the quilt from the bed upstairs, new and clean. Doris was reading on the couch. She got up when she saw I was awake and brought me two pieces of warm bread, buttered and slathered in blackberry jam. I sat up and ate them. Doris put another log in the wood stove.

"Why, Doris? Why did he kill them?"

I do not know. Something must have happened, she wrote.

"There's a picture of them," I said. I described the photograph I'd found in Trevor's suitcase. Mum, Dad, and Aloysius, the drinks in their hands, Mum at twenty-four with Aloysius' hand around her waist. "It said New Year's Eve, 1955, on the back. Did they know each other well, Doris? Do you remember?"

I was twelve in 1955, Doris wrote. *I do not remember them ever being friends.* She hesitated, then she added: *Mother might know.*

I couldn't imagine Ann Tenpenny knowing anything about my parents or Aloysius. Another time, later maybe, I'd ask Dad. "If they weren't friends why would my mother have kept that photo? Where was Alice that night? If they were all friends, what happened? Dad has never talked about the McFees. I can't imagine Dad and Aloysius spending a minute together." Dad was a pet rabbit to Aloysius' wild fox. I stretched the stiffness from my legs and sat beside Doris on the couch.

Your mother was different. She had— Doris' pencil rested above the paper for a moment.

"Had what?"

Longings.

"Did you know Mum, Doris? Did she talk to you?" I wanted desperately for her to have had a conversation with my mother, to know something that I didn't. "What did she long for?"

Doris stared at her paper voice. *No. I did not know her well. But I do not think she was happy.*

"Could they have had an affair?"

Doris waggled her pencil back and forth and I understood it as a shrug.

"Or he touched her. He molested us. He could have touched her too. Oh, God, Doris. He was sick."

Doris nodded. *Perhaps there had been a falling out between them.*

"A falling out? Big enough to kill over?" Mum held a grudge like a Scottish clansman; it was an enduring family legend. "Maybe she'd tried to get back at him somehow and it failed. Maybe he killed her, and Alice saw. Then he'd have had to kill Alice too."

But the photograph was taken at the end of 1955. Your mother and Alice died twelve years later. That is a long time for your mother to wait to wreak revenge.

Doris was right. "Do you remember Mrs. McFee? What was she like?"

Mrs. McFee was unusual for Fraser Arm, Doris wrote.

"How so?"

She was artistic. She liked to read. She was not from here.

"People here read," I said, thinking of Raylene. "Where was she from?"

Montreal.

"She told you this?"

Yes. People used to tell me many things when I had the egg stand. I do not know where she was born but she told me she was studying art in Montreal when she met Mr. McFee. She said she hated her parents so she married him and came to Fraser Arm.

"What was Aloysius doing in Montreal?"

I do not know. Perhaps a road trip?

"Poor Alice. What kind of life could she have had? She runs away from parents she hates with a child molester who eventually murders her."

She did seem happy most of the time. She made excellent blackberry jam.

I couldn't remember Mrs. McFee, not even what she looked like. "They never had kids."

Perhaps it is a good thing, Doris wrote.

Good for the children they didn't have, but not for me. "Do you know why they didn't?"

Doris shook her head.

"Sorry Doris, sometimes it seems like you know everything."

She hesitated again. *She told me they tried. I do not know the whys of it. But at least we know that he did not kill her because she could not have children. She was past her childbearing years when she died. It may well have been his fault.* Doris crossed out *fault* and changed it to *problem.* Then she scratched that out too.

I'd never dared ask Aloysius why they had no kids. It wasn't my business, but I'd been curious. Once, drunk, Aloysius had called me the daughter he'd never had. Even then I knew it wasn't a role I'd like to play.

The police would bring nothing of all this—Alice's childlessness, her happiness, her hateful parents, her time in Montreal, her blackberry jam—out of her backyard grave. Just her skeleton. I thought of the strange notes in the kitchen.

"You know the notes that were on the wall, Doris?"

Doris nodded her head slowly. *They are gone*, she wrote.

"They're under the kitchen sink. Should we give them to the police?"

Why?

"Evidence?"

No. They are meaningless. We do not know who wrote them. The McFees are both dead.

"Do you really think they both are, Doris?"

What difference does it make? Mrs. McFee is a skeleton and Mr. McFee is presumed dead. If he is not dead, then he has committed murder scot-free.

I stared at *scot-free* wondering about the origin of the

word and if she'd spelled it right. Why should I doubt? Doris spelled impeccably. "But that's the point, Doris. He got away with murder." For the first time I knew of, Doris had said something that was not rational. "Maybe the police would reopen the case. Look into his death again."

He has been gone twenty-five years. If he were alive, would they not have found him?

If he was alive somewhere, scamming, molesting, murdering other girls and women, no, they'd never find him. Not if they weren't looking. He'd be eighty-four. An old man with a new identity, a new wife, or a new gullible fool like myself. Aloysius was capable of anything, and he'd be good at anything, too.

"Poor Alice," I said. "I keep thinking about their last conversation. What did they talk about? What happened? Do you think she knew about his secret life?"

What secret life?

"Oh, Doris. You know what I mean."

I do not.

Doris did not write anything more for some time. She looked at the wood stove, out the window, at my plate on the floor. One day we would exchange stories, but it was not going to be now.

I wish he were dead, she wrote finally.

"Me too."

You brought your fiddle here, she wrote. *Why?*

Doris had changed the subject. She knew her limits even if I didn't know mine. I *had* brought my fiddle. My favourite, the only one I'd named—Darlene. Darlene was not the most expensive of my fiddles, nor the best, but I loved her. My intention that morning was to restring her and give her a polish, just to keep my nattering mind occupied while we waited for news.

Would you play a song?

I picked up Darlene and drew my bow across her strings, letting her fill the room with a long, melancholic moan. "What would you like to hear, Doris?"

Perhaps something sad would be fitting.

Doris settled herself upright on the couch, her knees together, her hands folded in the lap of her skirt, not looking at me, ready. My heart sighed. How odd and sweet these two Tenpenny siblings were, Doris and Mike. I stood in the middle of the threadbare carpet, my fiddle and bow hanging, and gazed around the room. The walls were of an indeterminate grayish-green colour, marked with the smudgy prints of age alone, for no child other than me, and Aloysius himself, had played in this room. No child that I knew of. That someone might have been my successor in Aloysius' sordid life made me unable to think.

I'd written my share of sad songs in my fifty years, but the only one that came to mind was not my own. It was a traditional song Aloysius had taught me when I was twelve or thirteen—"MacPherson's Lament." I fell in love with it the first time Aloysius sang the song to me, and the romantic tale I asked him to tell me, again and again, of Jamie MacPherson's real life—a Scottish Robin Hood—had doubly endeared it to my adolescent heart. I raised my bow and tucked Pauline under my chin. I played to the rain that slanted across the front porch, to the young Lulu who'd been in Aloysius McFee's thrall, to the silent woman on the couch, to the skeletons of my mother and Alice McFee.

I could barely sing the last line. "Ach, little did my mother think, when first she cradled me, that I would turn a roving boy, and die on the gallows tree."

Doris had her head bowed. She was stroking the brow of old Ricky, who had come and settled his head in her lap while I played. She didn't look up. A knot of anger constricted my throat. I wanted to smash the fiddle to pieces. How satisfying it would be to give it all up—my aching shoulder, my sorrowful heart. I sat down in the batting-leaking armchair opposite Doris and pulled the quilt up off the floor. Through closed eyes I could see the fire flickering. It felt like the end of the road.

Finally, I felt her finger on my knee. Doris, her eyes softer than I'd ever seen, was holding her pad out for me to read.

You have played me this song before, she had written. *Or you played it to my chickens. One morning before you left. When you were but a girl.*

But a girl. I remembered that morning. It was foggy. I was pregnant, ready to run away from a weariness of life that no person should have at eighteen. "You were there?"

You woke me with your song. It was my birthday.

"Not a very good birthday present," I said. "A little sad, no?"

Until Mr. McFee gave me this farm it was the best present I had ever had.

Ricky moved from Doris to my feet, resting his grey muzzle on my knee. I stroked his warty forehead and he made a soft grunting sound of pleasure each time I lifted my hand and pressed his snout up against my hand for more. There was no doubt the farm had completely changed Doris' life. She had a home, one that she must never have imagined for herself.

"What should we do next Doris?"

Do you mean immediately or in the long-term?

I thought about it. What did I mean? That morning the police had told me that it would take at least a week to gather all the remains from the backyard and, in the meantime, we should look for some of Alice's and Mum's genetic material. My heart had sunk when the forensics detective told me it could take weeks for the results. What would we do in the meantime? We'd already had a memorial for Mum. "We'll bury her bones somewhere nice," Dad said. And Alice McFee would have a proper burial, he'd said, as if she too was his responsibility. There was no one left to mourn Alice McFee. It was the least we could do, Dad said.

Wrapped in my quilt, I shrugged at Doris. Ricky made a motion of wanting up, and I pulled the old dog onto my lap where he struggled to turn then collapsed awkwardly across my knees and closed his eyes, seemingly satisfied. If everything were only so easy.

Doris held up her notepad: *We wait.*

DORIS

The rosehip jelly is refusing to set. Doris used nineteen cups of rosehips and fifteen cups of apples. Surely the apples would have provided enough pectin. And fifteen cups of sugar should have been enough. Doris has been accused of scrimping on the sugar in her jellies, but no one needs that much sugar. No, it is something else that is causing the problem and the something else annoys her. Doris has noticed that sometimes jellies do not set if her attention is elsewhere. This morning, in the kitchen, Doris' thoughts were on Lulu.

A water bubble burps to the surface and rattles the boiling jars. She is even less prone to giving up on jelly than she is to believing inattention could ruin a set, but Doris is an experienced jelly maker and she knows a failure when she sees one. Doris sets her mother's egg-timer for three minutes. At the three-minute mark she will fill the sterilized jars with the jelly, no matter the set. It is a pity this batch will not be sold, but God knows—and so does Doris—Geordie and Mike will not care. Doris leans over the pot to smell the jelly. Her glasses fog up and she stares around the kitchen semi-blind. *How curious*. As the fog clears in circles from the centre of her lenses, Doris remembers what else she was thinking about: Aloysius McFee's Secret Life.

The timer pings and Doris uses the long-handled tongs to lift a jar from the sterilizer pot. Rosehip jelly is neither red nor orange nor pink, but all three at once, like the sunrise. The colour makes Doris feel reverent and grateful. There are other things for which Doris is grateful. Chanterelles, for one. Other people pick chanterelle mushrooms throughout August, and other people wait until the first frost to make rosehip jelly. Let other people be other people; for Doris, the end of summer is always the same—rosehip jelly in the last week of August, chanterelles on September first. *Eight days to go*. The chanterelles in the woods are crowned creatures, water goblets filled with rain. In the mossy place, the forest floor is beautifully orange with them, as orange as a poem. On September first Doris will eat the first chanterelles she finds. She will bring home three or four big ones. She will sauté them in butter, grind pepper and a small amount of salt, and eat a plate of them. Doris, alone in the kitchen, before anyone else is up.

Doris ladles the rosehip jelly into the jars and Aloysius McFee surfaces again. She has wrestled with this demon for twenty-five years and now it has been confirmed—she owes a murderer a debt of gratitude. *Shoo, Aloysius McFee*. Doris must gather her wits. She has things to do. Where are her boots? She pads in her slippers to the front door but the boots are not there. She peers into the dim living room. Betsey is asleep on the couch. *What is that under Betsey's snout?* Doris squints. It is the dirty matted clump of batting that Lulu picked from the armchair. Doris sniffs the grey air. Lulu is right. Aloysius McFee's horrid presence stinks. She will ask Mike and Geordie to remove the couch and the chair. The dogs will have to find a new place for their naps, as will she herself. She rubs her back where her kidney is and harumphs, thinking of the wastefulness of furniture in the dump. Betsey raises her head and harumphs back. Another noise for Doris' sound album.

His Secret Life. She spies her boots under the telephone table, but she cannot make herself move. Doris is stabbed with the knife of guilt. *Dear God, what did he do to Lulu?* Doris knew, but she did nothing. She didn't tell the police. She didn't tell anyone. She feels a thickness in her throat and an electric vibration behind her eyes. She takes a breath, and another, bigger one. She must think of owls, goldfinches, scapes.

She rushes back to the kitchen and stops before the blackboard. Someone has altered her Rachel Carson quote. It is surely Lulu who has erased everything but *to the very marrow of our bones.* Above it, Lulu has added two words: *It hurts.* Doris turns away. She peers at the new calendar that Lulu has tacked to the wall. She has trouble reading what someone—a child from the looks of it—has written in the September first square: Wesleyville Agricultural Fair. Doris will not be eating chanterelles on Saturday. She will be going to the Fair. Doris takes out her handkerchief and wipes away the wetness from her glasses, but somehow there is no end to the water on her face.

LULU

Waiting is sad. While we waited for the official confirmation
that those were Mum and Alice McFee's bones, every scrap of
my grief over Trevor resurfaced. I wasn't used to sharing my
sorrow, except in song, but crying in front of Doris had broken
something open in me. I'd become heartache sung in public.

Ten days after the outhouse discovery, they were gone—
the diggers, the photographer, the police cruisers, the bones.
They'd catalogued each human piece they brought up—femur,
fibula, clavicle, scapula, mandible, pelvic girdle, skull—laying
them out on canvas sheets inside the tent. Would they eventually test each bone for its genetic owner? Separate them—the
skeletons, the dead women—like the pieces of two mixed-up
jigsaw puzzles, the right hipbone connected to the right thigh
bone? Was it Mum or Alice whose skull was cracked? And the
gold wedding band they found, still on a skeletal finger, that
didn't belong to Mum—where would that ring go in the end?

After the discovery in the outhouse, people prattled on to us about closure. I couldn't blame them. We tried to reassure one another with the word as well. Alan alone thought that knowing she had died in the pit of an outhouse, a violent death, was better than not knowing. Or better than holding out hope that she was alive somewhere. I knew that those were her bones being treated so delicately out there in the backyard. But I still prayed they weren't.

Geordie spent much of the ten days the forensics team was there, sitting on the back porch watching, rocking gently and talking to himself. I often sat with him. When they told us they'd brought the second skull up Geordie shook his own sombre head.

The police asked again for anything that could be used for DNA testing. As missing persons, their dental records were supposed to be registered somewhere, but no one seemed too clear about where. Mum's dentist was long gone, and if Alice had had one he was probably six feet under too. Forty years is a long time. Finally, from the basement, Doris produced a hairbrush that must have been Alice McFee's. It was in a small box of bathroom things Doris had decided to clear out of the master bedroom twenty-five years earlier. That hairbrush stirred some old memory of Dad's and he came to the McFees' with a yellowed envelope. Nestled in it was a curl of dark hair tied with a soft red ribbon.

"Oh, Dad, whose is it? Mum's?"

"Your mother's and Geordie's," he said and fell against me, crying. His old hands took the curl and with trembling fingers he showed me there were two colours—one dark and another just a shade darker. "Geordie's first haircut. He was so small. She snipped off one of her curls, too, to show him it wasn't so bad. She tied them both together and told him she'd keep them forever. My God, Lulu, she was just a child herself."

Geordie was beside himself watching Dad cry. He stepped from foot to foot and waved his hands until I asked him if he'd like to see the curls. He cupped his hands together and held the lock of hair as though it were a live bird. We sat for a long time watching the chickadees at the feeder. Geordie held Dad's hand. Later, when I gave the curls to the detective he spurned our precious thing, saying, "Not much use without the roots, but we'll see."

"I want this back when Forensics is done," I said.

"We'll see," he said.

●

Thank God for the Wesleyville Agricultural Fair.

My presence was required at the crack of dawn on the Saturday of Labour Day weekend. When I arrived, Doris was in the pantry, rattling her jars of jams, jellies, and preserves into cardboard boxes. Mike had already packed her pumpkins and squashes into the back of the pickup, all of them wrapped in blankets like babies the night before. I'd offered help of any kind, but I was elected just to drive Geordie, Doris, and Ambrose's son, McKenzie. And Ann Tenpenny, who'd taken to spending her afternoons on the porch at the McFees', reading through Doris' book collection like someone starved.

Doris was in an interesting yellow dress with a fitted bodice, a lightly flared skirt, and a cherry pattern all over it, something from the fifties. I couldn't imagine anyone in the Tenpenny family ever being allowed to purchase something so joyful. I was staring. She waved gruffly toward the kitchen, indicating I might want to sit and eat, then she smacked her hands together. *Quick, quick,* I understood. *And don't look at my dress.* I laughed, and she grimaced at me. She pulled on her old grey cardigan and put on a pair of very clean rubber boots, wrote something on a pad, handed it to me, and took herself and her preserves out the door. I had a quick look at her note: *Birdie made me buy it.*

Geordie was already at the table, eating porridge with blackberries and creamy milk fresh from the cow that morning. I hoped there'd be some earnest organic coffee roaster at the fair because, even during this crisis, Doris hadn't broken.

"Hurry, Lulu," Geordie said.

"We've got half an hour before we have to go, Mr. G.," I said. "And we have to wait for Ann." I sat down beside him and picked a fat blackberry from his bowl and popped it into my mouth. "Isn't Pepsi coming?"

Geordie shook his head. "She's working."

"Do you really love Pepsi, Geordie? I mean, do you love her a lot?"

"Yes. I really love her a lot, Lulu." Geordie pushed his curly head into the crook of my neck and I put my arms around him. Even at sixty, Geordie might have been the only person I knew who loved unreservedly. How he'd managed to live through everything and still do that was a miracle.

"Tell me about Pepsi. Why do you love her?"

"She smells good."

"What's she smell like?"

"Hmmm. Like chocolate and rabbits and toffee. And Pepsi-Cola."

I laughed. "I think those are all things *you* love, Geordie.

Does Pepsi really smell like a rabbit?" He snuggled deeper into my arms.

"She does!"

Geordie had met Pepsi at the grocery store, where he was a produce assistant. She worked in the bakery. Pepsi also had another part-time job at a Wesleyville courier company that hired people who'd been in psychiatric institutions or who had an intellectual disability, or in Pepsi's case, both. Geordie wanted a job there too, but he couldn't read well enough.

"Who do *you* love, Lulu?" Geordie peered at me.

Someone famous, I can't remember who, asked why people are afraid of honesty and not afraid of deception. Geordie's honesty had always made people squirm, me included.

"I love *you*, Geordie."

"Yes, but who do you *love*?" He was annoyed.

"The chickens?" I said, laughing. He didn't laugh.

"No, Lulu. Not the chickens."

I knew what he was getting at. He wanted to know who my Pepsi was.

"I don't know who right now, Geordie. Someday I hope I will."

"Do you love Mum?"

"I did love Mum, Geordie. But I think we know now that Mum is dead, right?"

"Why?"

"Because she's been away for too long. No mother would stay away from her children for forty years unless something had happened to her. And because we've found her bones, Geordie. You saw that, right? When we get her bones back we'll bury her."

"Mum might be under a spell."

"Mum's not under a spell, Geordie."

Geordie tapped his forehead onto my shoulder. "No," he said. "No."

"Do you want to come to Portland with us to hear Doris whistle?"

"Yeah, and Pepsi too."

"Pepsi can't come."

"Why not?"

"Because I can't afford to take Pepsi with us. You'll have to tell her about it later."

"Is Betsey coming?" I recognized Geordie's sly tactic.

"Betsey might come."

"Why can Betsey come and Pepsi can't?"

"Because dogs are free, Geordie. Betsey can sleep on the floor."

"Pepsi can sleep on the floor too."

"No she can't. Pepsi needs a bed."

"Well, we'll see," he said. Geordie, king of the last word.

●

Two of Ambrose's three sons were showing animals at the fair. At sixteen, Maddox had sworn off the 4-H Club—for girls but hopefully not for drugs and cigarettes—but Shaver and McKenzie at fourteen and twelve were still keeners. The 4-H Club motto seemed smart, if rather earnest: Head, heart, hands, and health. Doris took it seriously, and Shaver and McKenzie were willing disciples. Shaver had raised a piglet at the McFees' and was going to the fair in the pickup with his father and the striped pig, appropriately—I learned from

Kat—named Rothko. McKenzie was showing a chicken. Ambrose was going to stick with Shaver and the pig. Doris and I were in charge of the chicken boy.

In the van, Doris, Ann Tenpenny, McKenzie, and even Geordie, competed for who could be most silent. If it weren't for the chicken in its carrying cage in the very back seat I might have thought I'd gone deaf. On the other hand, the sound levels in the chicken building at the fair would have sent even the best soundman running. It was deafening. Rows of long wooden tables, set up as if we were there for a boarding-school banquet, ran the length of the building. Wire cages sat cheek by jowl on the tables, each containing a creature more magnificent than the previous one, and not necessarily something I'd identify as a chicken.

"What's she?" I asked McKenzie, pointing at the brute of a bird he had heaved up onto a table. It had the glossiest black-blue feathers and thighs that belonged on a speed skater. The *rooster*, he told me, was a Dark Cornish, also aptly named Gorgon. It looked like the rugby player of the chicken breed and reminded me of Donnie Coulter. It could have taken on a miniature poodle any day.

I was as shy of McKenzie as he was of me. It was only a slight exaggeration to say that I'd seen more of Ambrose's sons in the ten days since the outhouse discovery than I had in their entire lives. It was an unfortunate way for them to spend their summer vacation, watching their murdered grandmother being unearthed, but they weren't complaining. They liked their Uncle Geordie—and they loved the McFee place, despite its being the only internet-free zone in Fraser Arm. I couldn't, or, more accurately, wouldn't, identify the feeling I had when I first realized how much they liked

Doris, but by the time we went to the fair I knew it for what it was—the green-eyed monster, jealousy.

Gorgon's group was up first. Doris stood at the table beside McKenzie and wrote something on her pad. McKenzie nodded his head and took Gorgon out and tucked him carefully under his arm trying not to ruffle his feathers. Doris chucked Gorgon under his chin, looked him right in the eye, and nodded. Gorgon looked like he'd just agreed to a secret football play. McKenzie looked up at Doris. He was still a little boy, his face a summer peach, unlike his mustachioed brothers who'd hit their teenaged growth spurts.

Behind Doris' back I whispered to her, "I thought you weren't supposed to name animals you're going to eat?" thinking more about the pig than the chickens.

Doris' look singed my eyebrows.

"Sorry," I said. But really, I thought, what were these boys going to do when their pets had to go? Wouldn't Rothko soon be a giant animal that Doris would want for bacon?

●

Mike was sitting with Maddox in the bleachers at the chicken ring, one grown-up farm boy, one wannabe hipster. The place was packed. Who knew a poultry show would draw such a crowd. Peach-faced McKenzie joined a lineup of about twenty kids and adults, each with a struggling Gorgon look-alike in their arms. Doris, Geordie, and I picked our way to the top of the bleachers opposite Mike and Maddox. I watched their dark heads nodding, splitting their guts laughing over something. Maddox noticed us and waved. I knew Mike's big grin was meant for Geordie and Doris, but it was the first time since 1975 I'd seen that unreserved smile pointed my way. I could think of nothing but that I'd kept secret from him the most important thing in his life: he was a father. At eighteen, I'd convinced myself that he'd have wanted to keep silent about it too. I'd imagined his father pointing out that special place in Hell reserved for fornicators. He'd be spared that misery, and I'd be the only one to suffer. But watching Mike with Maddox in the stands, I knew what I'd done was unforgiveable. I'd robbed him.

I got up and picked my way down the stairs, stepping on a few hands. Something was screaming in another part of the building. I walked through the crowd toward the sound, sick with the smell of caramel corn and cotton candy. It was the pigs that were squealing. In the ring, Shaver's pig was down on his elbows and had dug his nose under the sawdust in the ring. I wanted to do the same.

When all the judging for our gang was done, Geordie and Maddox found me with my forehead pressed up against the refrigerated glass surrounding the prize butter sculpture. It was, appropriately enough, a troupe of flying pigs. Geordie took my hand and I watched out of the corner of my eye as he reached out and took Maddox's hand too. I thought big tall sixteen-year-old Maddox would drop it like a hot-cake, but he didn't. He held it, and the three of us, and my thankful heart, skip-to-my-Lou'd through the fairgrounds. I sniffed the air. This was a dog's paradise—the sweet, acrid pong of barnyard animals mixed with the sautéed onions and bratwurst sausages the firemen were serving up. I got Maddox and Geordie each a sausage and myself a cone of french fries. Who could resist the olfactory lure of the deep-fried potato?

Agricultural fairs, I realized, are not so different from folk festivals. All the creatures, two-legged or four, have their moment in the spotlight then move on to make room for the next act. On the main stage you always found the blue-ribbon bull drawing the biggest crowd, a ring in his nose and his great, pendulous balls everyone but the children pretended not to look at. We lesser beasts—the goats, the sheep, the pigs, the chickens—were his opening acts, or the sideshows, a miscellany of mediocre to great-but-overlooked musicians. There were some tricksters—the guinea pigs that looked like bits of matted wool, for example—who were so weird and underwhelming they left everyone wondering who they'd slept with to get put on the bill. Some musicians got too drunk or high to perform, like the pig in Shaver's group that came unglued and bashed through the barrier to run amok through the crowd. The chicken barn was the costume room at the Grand Ole Opry—a whole lot of primping and preening with feathers, fancy footwear, and flopping wattles and crowns, and some mighty fine squawking going on. And then there were the animals that were the real stunners, the ones that blew everyone's socks off but who always played second fiddle. The whisper rippled through the crowd: go see the gorgeous small-breed Holsteins over on Stage B. And finally, the audience—we were the same, enthusiastic, motley crew everywhere.

"Aunt Lulu," Maddox said.

I nearly looked around for the person Maddox was addressing. I felt my stupid heart thump.

"Do you think we could play guitar together some time? Dad got me one for my birthday."

I waited to reply until I was sure my voice wouldn't shake. "Sure, Maddox. I'd love that."

From our perch on top of a round bale of hay I watched Cidalia, Dad, and Kat in the sausage lineup. No sign of Mike, Doris, Ambrose, and the boys. Birdie and Raylene had come and gone after the chicken judging. Geordie said Alan and Naomi were there too, but I hadn't seen them yet. It occurred to me that all this togetherness might not be just because we'd found our mother. For all I knew the whole lot of them were regulars at country fairs, and in my many years' absence they had taken to having family suppers together every Sunday night.

Shaver and McKenzie caught sight of us and raced each other to the bale. Shaver had the advantage of leg length. He made it up on the round bale with us in one nimble, bum-first leap, but McKenzie had to be pulled up by his brothers. We sat in a circle, our backs to one another like muskoxen— three boys who would soon be young men and one man who, unlike my nephews, would never lose his boyness. My record label had been after me for ages to walk into this unknown territory and do what every folk singer is obliged to do—a children's album. "I don't know kids," I told them. But there was Maddox holding Geordie's hand, Shaver with his Rothko pig, McKenzie and his Donnie Coulter look-alike. Three songs at least. These boys, more than halfway to adulthood, were too old for a children's album. But I could write about what they, and my sons, had missed from me. What I had missed.

DORIS

Towhee, sparrow, bunting, finch. Oriole, warbler, mead-
owlark, thrush. Doris and Dante are on the back porch,
watching the birds at the feeders. Doris takes off her boots.
Doris has a dilemma. The police have taken everything away:
all the bones, all the walkie-talkie buzzing sounds that Doris
would *not* like to put in her sound album, all the yellow tape.
The only thing left is the evidence that they were there—
trampled grass, stake holes, tire tracks, and the outhouse. The
outhouse looks like a barber pole in its blue tarp with the red
reflector tape wound round it. If the police still think of the
outhouse as evidence they should know that the blackberries
will have covered it before the end of September.

That is not Doris' dilemma, however. It is the berries.
Doris has inspected the blackberries around the outhouse
now that the police and the wasps have gone and, oh, the jelly
they would make. But in the past forty years only the birds

have picked the outhouse blackberries. It is not that Doris is overly reverent when it comes to graves; she has picked graveyard nettles for spanakopita, for Pete's sake. But when Doris ate one of the outhouse berries this morning she saw Aloysius McFee shoving Alice McFee, his own wife, through the hole.

Doris realizes this vision might go away if she stopped staring at the outhouse, so she and Dante go inside to make lunch. Since it is Tuesday, she will have a fried egg sandwich, and today is her goat milk day. Mike teases Doris about her sandwich schedule: egg sandwiches on Tuesdays, Wednesdays, and Fridays. Peanut butter and cucumber on Mondays and Thursdays. Leftovers on the weekends. Cidalia has warned her about cholesterol. *Pooh, pooh.* One day they'll find out that cholesterol is not to be feared. Doris slices the bread and sets the butter to melt in the pan. Doris is sure that Mike and Lulu will agree; the outhouse must go. The outside boards will make good pantry or shed shelves. The others can be split and stacked for kindling. Waste not, want not.

She washes her lunch plate and glass and everyone else's breakfast dishes. Mike wants a dishwasher. It is true: an extraordinary number of dishes have had to be washed in the past twenty-one days, but Doris is still resistant. How can a dishwasher be more environmentally correct than four human hands with a rag and a tea towel? They do not even use electricity. Besides, Doris likes the feel of the water on her hands. Someone has removed the curtains on the window above the sink and washed the window as well. Doris turns her back on the view.

If the taste of a blackberry conjures Aloysius McFee it would not be wise to build pantry shelves with the outhouse boards. Doris remembers the furniture maker who came asking for old barn boards. She had none to give away then, but perhaps the woman would take the outhouse. Doris packs eight cartons of eggs and the vegetables she picked this morning into her cloth bags to drop off at the food bank. On the way back she'll stop for blackberries in the Logging Trail. She'll look for the furniture maker's card later.

LULU

I wasn't moving to the McFees' by degrees, though others hoped I was. I wasn't sleeping at the house. I wasn't eating there either, unless Doris happened to offer me breakfast or the whole family had gathered for supper. But I'd found myself walking in the McFees' front door every morning since the discovery. My physio had threatened to report me to my doctor if I didn't take it easy, so I'd cancelled two gigs—another folk fest in Tennessee and a songwriting workshop I was supposed to lead—and was writing and singing instead of picking and fiddling. I took refuge upstairs. There was something about the big room that drew me, though sometimes I was chased from it by the fresh waves of revulsion that surfaced when I imagined Aloysius tying his half-Windsor knot in front of the mirror or flossing his teeth in the bathroom.

The birds were on the roof again. They'd been there all week, getting ready to fly south. I could hear them, a team of small football players scrabbling in cleats from one end of the field to another. Starlings. Stupid starlings, I suppose, because all of a sudden I could hear one flapping around in the chimney. I imagined the flock flying in unison off the roof, dark angels making their undulating murmuration in the sky. One of them says, "Hey, where's Jim?" "I dunno, he was right behind you." "Right behind me? Shit. He's gone down the chimney. Just like his dad. We gotta go back." "Forget it, Jake. It's Chinatown. He's a goner."

Geordie, Mike, and Doris were showing pumpkins or squashes again at a fair out in the Valley. Cidalia was at work. So it was me and the bird. I went down and checked the cleanout in the basement, but the bird was inside the chimney, somewhere between downstairs and up, probably trying to get his footing on some small brick overhang. I thumped the wall and prayed he would drop down to the cleanout before he went the way of all things.

If I couldn't get him out, I decided, I could at least fix the problem with the chimney. I'm not sure what made me think I could even carry a three-storey extension ladder. After a brave three-minute struggle trying to get the damned thing off the hooks on the side of the house, I settled on the one-storey wooden one that had been in Mum's grave. I hauled it up the inside stairs through Aloysius' room to the balcony. In the basement I found a small roll of chicken wire, a pair of snips, and some plyers. I tossed them all into one of Doris' cloth bags.

Getting up was easy. My ankle was a little stiff, but I'd climbed my share of ladders and the slope of the roof above the balcony wasn't particularly steep. I climbed over the eaves-trough and crawled up to the chimney. Someone had already wrapped chicken wire around the open part between the cap and the brick where the birds could get in, but a bit of the wire had sproinged back, leaving a perfect bird-sized door. Jim the starling was either an adventurous little fellow or as dumb as a gunnysack. I folded the chicken wire back over the entrance and crimped the edges hard with the plyers. Then I inched my way up to the peak of the roof to get a Yertle the Turtle's–eye view of the kingdom of Fraser Arm.

The windbreak out front was miles taller than the house. When I was little, old rumours of a dead woman in the well had kept us off the property. But after Mum disappeared I spent a lot of time in those trees. Trevor and I used to choose a tree and race each other to its top. It's a wonder we didn't kill ourselves, the speed we went up. He always beat me, and by the time I got close to matching his speed he got too old to want to race his little sister. So, alone, I'd climb as high as I could until the sway took me out on a boat in a storm, Jacques Cousteau on the high seas. Up there, it was private and secret and I was at once all powerful and small and safe, cradled in the great bough arms of a Douglas fir.

From my perch on the roof, I picked out all the old neighbourhood houses—though their big properties had been carved up for subdivisions—and Fraser Arm's original streets, running amongst the new ones. The Tenpennys' house, the barn, and a quarter of their garden were still there, although Ann had sold most of the property when Mister died. I was Lulu Parsons, age ten, up a tree again, revisiting my childhood haunts—the peat bog and the Logging Trail, *Dun Roamin?* and Raylene's Airstream, Chen's. The wind was warm. The deciduous trees were just beginning to turn. A glossy crow was being chased by a flock of small birds.

I turned around and lay on my belly, hooked my armpits over the crest of the roof, and looked out over the back acreage. Doris' garden was inspired. There was row upon gorgeous row of vegetables she was still harvesting. Cabbages and dusty purple broccoli. Swiss chard with red and yellow stems. A sea of carrot tops waving their lacy tendrils in the wind. Kale, beets, what was left of the green and yellow beans, even corn. Three long rows of raspberries. And, at the back of the garden, sweet peas flowering so thickly you'd never know there was a chicken wire fence beneath them. Birdie's garden was beautiful too. She and Raylene had their own little vegetable patch in a corner of Doris', but Birdie's triumph was her flowers. She sold her roses and zinnias, dahlias and brown-eyed Susans on the organic market, to that breed of people who wouldn't buy flowers from Argentina or China and were willing to pay the hefty price for locally grown. She supplied florists from Chilliwack to West Vancouver. From way up there I saw the pattern Birdie had created—a huge, psychedelic peace symbol of flowers. I'd have to tell her how beautiful it was. It had taken me a long time to get over my aversion to Birdie. That wasn't her fault. Turned out Birdie Feathers was her real name, too.

Doris' bizarre collection of hens and roosters was pecking free in the yard and in the garden. Sometimes she just let them out. She liked the chickens to get the potato bugs for her. I don't know why they didn't destroy everything, but Doris knew best. This year she was experimenting with growing spelt in a field beyond the garden. Past that was the orchard. Near the gnarly fruit trees someone had planted decades ago, she'd put in pears, apricots, cherries, and a few varieties of heirloom apples. Raylene's beehives were over to the left of the orchard, by another, younger cedar hedge.

I counted thirteen hives beneath the trees. My eyes roved over the greenhouse, the barn, and the big pond Doris had had dug for the ducks. Down in the paddock, I could see the mongrel Ricky hanging out with Loretta, the old blind donkey. Ricky'd apparently been trying to wedge himself, successfully it seemed, into the long friendship that existed between Loretta and an old goat named Blanche, who were inseparable. Everything looked beautiful, even the pile of rusting farm equipment and the remains of a Ford truck and a DeSoto car that were there before Aloysius learned to drive. The blackberries and wild Oregon-grape had long ago reclaimed the old vehicles.

In the middle of all that beauty was the crime scene—the outhouse in its blue shroud. Mourning Mum twice was peculiar. There were moments when it wasn't the same fresh, deep wound it had originally been, with all that bright red blood. More like picking a scab or maybe nicking open an old scar. Other times I was washed with the horror of how she'd died and then I would lapse again into unbearable sorrow. I also burned with anger imagining Aloysius on some beautiful island, a young Lulu-dupe by his side. It was time to bury them all. I was ready.

I turned around to climb down from the peak and froze. It was twenty impossible feet to the ladder. My limbs were as uncooperative as balloons filled with water, leaden and incapable of movement. I lay down on my belly again, dizzy, and hooked my arms over the peak. Those fucking starlings.

I don't know how long I'd been hanging there, my forehead pressed to the shingles, when I heard the car come into the driveway. I lifted my head. A chocolate Mercedes. Robin. Never in the history of humankind had someone so unwanted been so welcome. I saw Betsey run into the yard to greet him. Robin was down on his knees and holding her face in his hands, scratching her under the chin. I imagined him saying, "Where's Lulu, Betsey? Where's Lulu?"

"On the roof," I whispered. "Here I am."

He walked up onto the front porch and disappeared from my view. I pictured him standing at the door, nervous, manufacturing some pleasant excuse about being in the neighbourhood. Whatever it was, I most sincerely couldn't wait to hear it. What in Hell's name was taking him so long? My neck was killing me and I was going to pee my pants if I had to wait much longer. I began to laugh, and tears welled up in my eyes. What was he doing, writing a note, for God's sake? A long-winded explanatory note. Or, God forbid, sitting on the front porch waiting for someone to come home.

Finally he appeared. He turned around once and shooed Betsey back on the porch. He had on a white shirt and a pair of brown corduroy trousers—an unbearably handsome man.

"Robin."

He looked around.

"Robin. Up here."

He looked up and I felt my heart surge with a joy I am sure no one in the world had ever experienced. This nice man, this very nice man, was standing on my front lawn.

"What in the world are you doing up there?"

I started to cry. I just shook my head.

"Just a second."

In a minute his head popped up over the eavestrough like a groundhog. I was blubbering by then. Then he climbed gingerly the twenty feet to where I was beached and lay down beside me.

"Nice view," he said.

This crying in public business wasn't getting easier, but there was no stopping it.

"Oh, Lulu," he said, "you are even better than I imagined." He didn't look at me or touch me. "Let's wait until you're a little calmer to get you down, shall we?"

I nodded. We were a pair of tawny lions taking in the sun, two recovering fifty-year-olds hanging out on a roof. The most natural thing ever. Right.

"What's that?" he asked.

"Somebody's grave." I had to say it aloud. "My mother's."

Robin looked serious. "Will you tell me?" he asked.

Where do you start? For forty years I had believed that my mother had run off. In reality she was dead. A vile man with whom I'd spent my formative years stealing, drinking, doing drugs, and singing merrily in the car had actually murdered my mother. And his own wife. He'd stuffed them in a revolting grave, yards from the porch on which he and I later played cards, and he'd sealed their coffin with two-by-tens.

"I hated her for it. I have hated her for forty years for leaving us. My mother gave us inconsolable lives, all of us. Trevor's dead because of it. But she's dead too. She was all along. God, Robin, what have I done?"

He didn't reply. I felt the sun's warm hands on my shoulders and I let go a little. I wouldn't slide. I knew that now. I could get off the roof by myself, even if Robin wasn't there. We inched on our bums toward the edge of the roof. Then he turned and stepped a few rungs down the ladder and held his hand out for me. I stepped over the edge backwards and we went down the ladder together, me a few rungs above him until we reached the balcony.

"We have two things to do, Robin. First, I've got to pee." I stopped. "That's not one of the two things," I said, laughing.

He followed me to the basement. I opened all the windows and then unscrewed the bolts on the chimney cleanout door again. The starling flew out in a flutter of ashes and soot. He bashed into the wall, then, as though he instinctively knew that the place where the colours green and blue met was the direction to go, he flew up to the windowsill, stood and shook for a second, and flew off out the window. From panic to peace in two seconds.

"Goodbye, Jim," I said.

The handle of every tool in Doris' garden shed was painted with bright yellow paint. She wasn't planning on losing another one in the woods. I gave a shovel to Robin and took one myself and led him out the driveway, across Hemlock, and down Forward Road. Dad had held out a long time before selling the goat pasture, but he said he'd go to his grave before he sold the land on either side of the house. The tree fort had been in the woods to the east. It had rotted away and a new neighbour with property values in mind had asked Dad if he minded if he cleaned up the derelict remains. So the fort was gone, but the two Douglas firs between which Dad had built it were still there.

"We're looking for a glass jam jar," I told Robin. I stood between the firs trying to remember where I'd buried it. The roots had grown and heaved the ground, their gnarly veins stretching upward then down deep and wide into the earth. I looked up and saw the petrified remnants of the wooden ladder rungs we'd hammered into its bark forty years ago or more. I used to shimmy up a rope to the first rung, ten feet from the ground, to reach them. Since then, the tree's bark had slowly wrapped around the rungs. Now they were part of the tree and forty feet closer to the heavens.

I had a vision of myself at ten, trying in vain to dig a hole close to one of the firs, then deciding to bury the note in the less reluctant earth, right between the two trees.

"Here," I said, drawing an X on the ground with my toe.

Robin watched without a word while I tried to break the soil. In a minute he picked up his shovel and began to dig in earnest.

"How deep?" he asked.

As deep as a grieving ten-year-old could dig. Forty years of secrets deep.

He dug half a dozen holes. I let him get sweaty and dirty in his clean white shirt. That jar contained my childhood confusion and rage. I needed to hold it in my hands and unseal it. After twenty minutes we'd unearthed nothing more than a few broken bits of a white dinner plate. Robin looked up, waiting for my next suggestion. I indicated with my toe, farther east than we'd tried, and finally the shovel hit something with a dull clank. I got down on my hands and knees and dug in the loosened soil until I unearthed the jar. I could scarcely breathe.

The tin rim was mostly rusted away and the glass lid was stuck to the jar. I smashed it open with a rock. But the jar didn't hold my note. I took out, instead, a small cast-iron cannon on spoked wheels. It had been Trevor's. A rusted antique toy he'd found in a midden in our woods years ago. I had coveted that cannon. I remembered with a vividness that was painful how much I'd wanted to have found it first. Robin held his hands out to me and I gave it to him.

"More?" he asked.

"No." I was exhausted. And maybe it seemed a fair trade—Trevor's cannon for my note. But it was odd. Both our treasures buried under the tree fort.

We walked home and sat on the front porch swing for a while. Robin gently pulled me toward him and I lay in his comforting arms. We were silent while the swing squawked something unintelligible. After a while I took Robin's hand and led him into the house and upstairs. I set the cannon on top of the song I was writing. Two clumps of earth fell out of it onto the paper. Then Robin and I lay down on the bed together.

"Oh, Lulu," he said.

●

Afterward, still lying in a loose embrace, I drew back a little, bringing my eyes to reading focus on Robin. He had closed his eyes. I missed them. They were so dark brown they were black, like the centres of black-eyed Susans, opaque almost and without flecks. Coffee and carbon. They gave me pause, the way white flowers do.

The afternoon sun was low and leaned in the window like a touchable thing. Robin was golden in the pale mote-filled light, and asleep. I examined his still face. Crow's feet grew from the corners of each eye. I touched the stubble on his jaw. He had a slight underbite that was more noticeable when he was sleeping. His beard if he grew one would be grey now. Or white. His forehead had deep worry lines running up from his eyebrows. His salt-and-pepper hair was slightly curly, longish to the nape of his neck, and pulled back from his forehead. There were black hairs in his ears, which seemed ridiculously dear. He stirred as I traced a circle around his face, along his jaw, and, in a muscular undulation, he moved from his right side to his left, presenting me his warm back. I felt his skin; it was soft, almost honey coloured, moveable and freckled with a constellation of small moles. At the small of his back, a little patch of downy silver hairs glinted in the sun, a small indentation like a footprint in the moss. His hands were tucked together, as if in prayer, between his legs. My throat ached and my eyes flooded at his unconscious vulnerability.

I pressed my breasts against his back, spooned him, wrapped my arm around his chest, face to nape of his neck, hips to his buttocks, knees to his crooks, and his arm swung slowly back across me and drew me closer. Maybe, I thought, Birdie is right. God is in bloody everything.

DORIS

The detectives are on the front porch in their shiny black shoes. Martin Currie smiles. "Do you want to hear the good news first?" he says. It does not take the expression on Lulu's face for Doris to know that Martin Currie's method of delivery is unsuited for whatever news might be delivered.

Lulu's face is made of stone. "Is this a game show, Martin?" she says. Her voice is slate grey. Martin Currie smells of cigarettes.

"So," he says, "the evidence is in. Alice McFee was killed by a blow to the skull with a blunt instrument, possibly a large stone or a brick. The DNA sample proves her identity, as does the circumstantial evidence. There was a gold wedding band with *A and A Sept 3rd 1947* inscribed inside. We checked. That was their wedding day." Martin Currie looks so proud of himself.

This cannot be the good news. Lulu's face has not changed. *What is the good news?* Doris writes. The other detective who has not introduced himself speaks to Lulu.

"The other body is not your mother's," he says. "I'm sorry, Ms. Parsons."

The good news is unsettling news. The second body, which is not Bette Parsons', is male. A man. He was reported missing in Vancouver in 1962, five years before Alice McFee disappeared. "A bit of a small-time hustler," the other detective says. "Known to police."

What is his name? Doris holds out her notepad.

"We can't tell you. Privacy issues," Martin Currie says in an authoritative tone, as if the newspapers will not be carrying this news and the man's identity by tomorrow. Doris has been working around this dead man's grave for twenty-five years. She wants to know his name. She glowers at Martin Currie.

"It was a cold case," the other detective says.

Martin Currie says, "His family has already been told. What's left of them. They have some closure now," he says. Lulu does not say anything but leans toward the wall.

How did this man die? Doris writes.

"Inconclusive," says Martin Currie. "No sign of trauma. It's possible he went into the pit alive." Martin Currie's eyes are curiously bright. "McFee probably nailed down those boards with him in there alive," he says.

How do you know it was Mr. McFee?

"Who else could it be?" Martin Currie says.

Lulu shuts the door on the detectives. From the other side of the door Doris hears the other detective say, "I'm sorry," again. Doris wonders how the man's family could have closure knowing these facts. Sorry would not help Doris. Doris looks at Lulu: what is the opposite of closure?

●

It seems ironic to Doris that earlier, before the policemen came, she was having trouble deciding which of the two things that took place today pleased her more: that the young people from the Arms Around Fraser Arm Gleaning Society came in the early morning for a canning lesson or that in the early afternoon Lulu Parsons arrived in Wally Parsons' old Honda Accord hatchback with a suitcase and a cardboard box. That suitcase is still in the hallway because the detectives knocked on the door one minute after Lulu arrived. Doris does not want this news to make Lulu take her suitcase and box away again.

Lulu has gone to tell Wally Parsons. Doris sits at the telephone table in the hallway. Without lifting the receiver, she dials 0 several times. She likes the sound of the dial returning to its place. Cidalia has told Doris of a telephone system that speaks what someone types. Everyone is always suggesting ways in which Doris might use modern technology to speak. Doris is not sure what is wrong with her own method of communicating. Except that she cannot make phone calls. But who might she call other than Lewis? Mike and Cidalia are camping with Geordie on Vancouver Island, in the rain. They do not need to hear this news right now.

Doris puts an album on the record player: Erik Satie, Gymnopédie No. 1 and goes to the kitchen. There are forty-eight jars of blackberry jam on the table, made by the gleaners this morning. She likes the young people who founded the Gleaning Society. She likes seeing all the gleaners riding around Fraser Arm on their bicycles with their trailers filled with apples and pears and blackberries. They asked Doris if they could park their bicycles in her barn, so on weekends, in the late afternoon, there are sometimes eight or nine young people in the barn telling Doris what they have gleaned. This morning, one of the young gleaners called Doris a pioneer. Doris laughed at that. These young people grow heirloom tomatoes in their window boxes and conceal chicken coops and beehives in their backyards, and share everything with the food bank.

Purposelessness. That is the blue word Doris sees. She puts on her rubber boots, finds an umbrella, and whistles for the dogs. Only Betsey will need a leash. Ricky is too old for a long walk, and Dante is a leash-free boy. Doris should be practising for the Oregon Whistlers Jamboree, but today no longer feels like a whistling day.

LULU

It was pouring. Ricky was sitting on the kitchen floor, his back to me, staring at the couch that Doris had moved there from the living room just for him and the other four-legged animals. The tyranny of old dogs. You can have just settled down in a comfortable chair with a coffee and the newspaper and they will fix you with their baleful eyes demanding that you put it all down and do them a favour—lift them onto the couch, get that ball from under the bed, feed them, pay them some attention. Old Ricky did just that. A quick turn of the head to make sure I'd noticed he was there, then back to facing the couch. He couldn't jump up anymore, too much arthritis or rheumatism in his hindquarters. I put Trevor's suitcase down, picked Ricky up, and put him on the couch. He turned around a few times and lay down with his back to me.

"You stink, Ricky," I said.

He deigned to raise his head, give me a look over his shoulder as impassive as Doris', and lick his chops as if to say, yes indeedy, I do smell bad.

I would have given almost anything to curl up on the couch with stinky Ricky and go to sleep, possibly forever. Instead I stood aimlessly in the kitchen, counting the jars of blackberry jam lined up neatly on the kitchen table. Forty-seven. Today's blackboard message was another question: *How do they clean the inside of a milk truck?*

"What do you think, Ricky? Do you think they have a great big bottle brush that goes inside and swishes it out?" Ricky didn't answer or even turn around, so I took the suitcase and went upstairs.

Dad and Kat didn't believe me. "It can't be," Dad kept saying. I had to tell them three times about the man whose body had shared Alice McFee's outhouse grave for forty years. I didn't repeat Martin Currie's words about how he might have died. No one needed to hear that. We sat quietly for a while. "Who was he?" Dad finally asked. I understood his wanting to know. Doris had asked too. We'd find out in time. Dad called Alan and Ambrose and they each asked to speak with me. I had nothing more to say to them than I'd said to Dad. We hadn't really wanted it to be Mum, though we all believed it was. As dreadful as being murdered by Aloysius McFee would have been, thinking that we'd found her had allowed us to start tidying it all up in our hearts and minds. Now, with this news, we'd all been tossed, with fresh vigour, back into the appalling territory of not knowing. *Dis-closure*, Doris had written.

There was a light knock on the door, and Betsey came in followed by Doris with my box in her arms. She looked sad.

We both sat down on the end of the bed. Doris pulled out her notepad.

Bastard, she wrote.

"Bastard indeed," I said.

Shall we sell the farm?

"What? No. Doris." I put my hand on her shoulder. I had a horrifying vision of condos covering the farm. "This is your place. Absolutely not."

I couldn't tell whether Doris was relieved, but I believed her question had been genuine. She would have been willing to sell it.

"But let's do one thing," I said. "Let's stop calling it the McFees'."

I do not, Doris wrote. She raised her eyebrows at me.

I thought about it. She was right. I'd never seen her refer to it as the McFees'. It was me. I'd been hanging on to that name.

Doris pulled my tattered old rooster pillow out of the box she'd brought up.

I made this.

"How? When?" I'd had that pillow as long as I could remember. It was my teddy bear equivalent.

Before you were born. Your mother believed she was having another boy. I did not think so. I wanted to make something for her. A hen for a girl. But I made a rooster. Silly.

"Oh, Doris. It's the thing I loved most in the world. They never told me it was from you."

She shrugged and nodded at the suitcase and the box. Doris probably thought I was moving in. I wasn't. I'd brought Trevor's suitcase, and a few things of mine, as inspiration for a song that was sitting somewhere I couldn't quite reach. Doris sat while I emptied the box onto the top of one of the dressers. I didn't have much more in my life than what was in the box anyway. Doris and I were kin that way. I tucked the suitcase in the closet to avoid any more questions and closed the door.

"What should we do with this stuff?" I said. The top of Aloysius' desk made a minor squawk and then rolled up smoothly. His papers were neatly stacked in the slots and cubbies and the small drawers were filled with desk miscellanea: erasers, paper clips, pen nibs, sharpeners, a collection of flag pins from around the world. Fountain pens and sharpened pencils lay in grooves meant for such things. Two dried-up bottles of black India ink sat in crusty inkwells. I pulled out a small sheaf of the elegant *Havelock & Hattie McFee* writing paper that Doris had once sent me a note on. Doris held her hands out for it.

Scrap paper.

I put my finger on the spine of a leather-bound journal that stood in one of the slots alongside a couple of passports, then thought better of taking it out in front of Doris. I remembered Aloysius sitting on the couch with the journal in his lap. I could almost hear his fountain pen scratching away. He wrote in that journal with such focused concentration that I knew never to interrupt him. After about fifteen or twenty minutes he'd go up to his room with it and return empty-handed. At the moment I didn't want to know what it contained. And I certainly didn't want to end up sitting on the bed, reading it with Doris peering over my shoulder.

In one of the small drawers I found a carved wooden box filled with what looked like about ten diamond rings. On a small label in the box Aloysius had written *paste.*

"Fakes," I said. "Geordie will like them."

Doris cocked her head at me. I shrugged. I didn't know if she was asking how I knew they were fake but this was not the moment to tell her about my criminal past.

Doris took the box from me and put a ring on every finger. She twinkled them at me. We both laughed. Doris looked like the cat that ate the canary, which made me laugh harder.

"Okay. You and Geordie will like them."

Aloysius had taught me how to tell the difference between a fake and a real diamond when I was about twelve. Why he had this big collection was a mystery. Maybe they were his own early mistakes. Finding the journal and the rings made me nervous about what else we might find in the desk. I was ready to close it but Doris reached past me to one of the cubbies and pulled out a small bundle of old photographs, tied with a faded pink ribbon. She went through them like she was a very slow card dealer, examining the back for notations and placing them one on top of the other with a slight snap. There was Aloysius as a baby in the lap of a sweet-looking woman who must have been his mother. He and Alice on their wedding day, September 3, 1947. I thought of Alice's ring and wondered what the police did with dead people's things. There was a photo of Aloysius and Alice posing hand-in-hand with the Second Narrows Bridge in the back-· ground. The photo of a very young Aloysius in a military uniform stirred a nanosecond of guilt in me; so he hadn't lied about being in the Seaforth Highlanders. Doris went through a few photos of people neither of us recognized and whose names weren't familiar either. Then she held up the New Year's Eve photo of Dad, Mum, and Aloysius that I'd found in Trevor's suitcase. The handwriting on the back was Mum's, and it read exactly as Trevor's photograph had: *Wally,*

Al and me. New Year's Eve 1955. Doris slid her glasses down her nose so she could see over the top of them and examine the photograph carefully.

She picked up one of Aloysius' pencils and wrote on a piece of writing paper. *The one you told me about.*

"Yes, but this must be a duplicate. That's Mum's hand-writing, though. She must have given it to him."

Doris put the photo down carefully in the pile and we both looked at the next one. Cold swept through my veins as I looked at the colour photograph of myself as a child. I was wearing jeans that hung on my hips and a striped t-shirt. I was leaning up against a canary yellow convertible I didn't recognize. I wasn't smiling. I looked defiant and fierce. I read Aloysius' handwriting on the back and felt another chill pass through me: *Sweet Lulu. 4.*

Did you know him then?

"Not that I know of."

He had a car like this. It is a Ford Thunderbird.

"Jesus, Doris. What is going on?"

Should you ask your father?

"I'm not sure I want to."

I understand.

"Do you, Doris? Do you understand? Aloysius was my friend. I . . ." I wanted to tell her that I'd learned more from Aloysius McFee than from anyone else in the world, and that despite everything, I'd loved him.

A man like that does not have friends.

I wasn't sure she was right. Aloysius had loved me too. He didn't have men friends he went to the bar with. No one he played cards with. He did that with me. "I was his friend," I said.

Lulu, you left Fraser Arm when you were 18. You could not have known him for more than 8 years. You were a child. Doris smacked the paper with the back of her hand. She was angry.

I shook my head. I mumbled something stupid about them being my formative years. Doris made a sharp horsey snort that involved blowing air out her nose.

"You've been around the animals too much, Doris." I snapped at her.

Doris snatched the photograph from my hand and flung it like a Frisbee across the room. She scribbled in her notebook and held it up in front of my face. *Lulu Parsons,* she'd written, *if, like the animals, you spoke less and listened more you might learn something.* Doris ripped the notebook away again and bent over the desk, writing for a long time. Waiting for Doris' written reply made me feel like I was being berated in slow motion. I'd have preferred a quick smack across the face.

Listen to me. Aloysius McFee was not your friend. He was a murderer. He killed his wife. He molested us both. He trapped a man alive in an outhouse. He orchestrated his own false death. He is probably molesting other girls elsewhere. He was not your friend. He was NOT your friend.

The furious look on her face unnerved me. "He was. He—"

"No!" The word came out of Doris' mouth with hurricane force and shocked us both. Her eyes were wild. We were silent, just breathing, until the doorbell rang and I heard Raylene's "Doris? Lulu?" in the front hall.

Doris stood and picked up her notepad. *Burn his journal,* she wrote. *After you read it.* She closed the door quietly as she went.

DORIS

No. It is a simple word, and yet it will not be replicated. Doris is in the very back seat of the van, mouthing the word soundlessly out the window into the wind, like a dog. Like Betsey, with whom Doris is sharing the back seat. No. NO. Nooooo. Pepsi and Geordie are asleep, her head on his shoulder in the middle row. Mike and Lulu have been talking since they left Seattle and they are already past Bellingham. Before they ate the fish and chips at the chip wagon in Seattle, Lulu and Mike had been talking all the way from Portland. Lulu has the music on with the speakers playing in the back, which makes Doris slightly disoriented—she is used to music coming from in front of her—and prevents her from hearing what they are talking about. Not that she is attempting to overhear; Doris is just a little lonely at the back. And she would admit, if asked: curious. Lulu and Mike never have long conversations. On the way down, everyone took turns in the front seat. Betsey is not the best of seatmates. Doris can't have a conversation with her. And Betsey farts. Doris makes a note to adjust Betsey's diet. Farting is not an inevitability.

Doris laughs, about the farting and about Pepsi's hair, which is blowing in the wind and tickling Geordie's ear. Geordie keeps flicking it away in his sleep. Lulu said Pepsi couldn't come to the Oregon Whistlers Jamboree, but she came anyway. Doris had never been to the United States before, and she had most certainly never stayed in a hotel. How strangely beautiful the world looked from the eleventh floor of the hotel, room 1111, with all of Portland rushing along on its grid of streets. They hid Betsey in the bathroom while the young man brought Lulu's cot in. *Is this like a pyjama party?* Doris wrote on Saturday night. Lulu called Doris sweet—*hardly a valid descriptor.* Lulu said she'd met too many bed bugs and fleas to be excited by hotels anymore. Geordie and Pepsi ate the expensive chocolate bars from the tiny refrigerator while Lulu was out buying cheaper chocolate bars and chips at a store. Geordie said Mike told them they could. Lulu told Mike he owed her *big time.* After they finished the chips, Lulu sent the men to their room next door. Number 1113. Mike and Geordie had never stayed in a hotel either.

Doris reaches out and strokes Betsey's haunch and Betsey climbs into Doris' lap and puts her head out Doris' window. Doris doesn't mind that she didn't win a prize at the Oregon Whistlers Jamboree. Three-hundred and fifty people clapping at her rendition of "Suzanne" and "Your Cheatin' Heart" was prize enough. Doris saw Mike and Lulu and Geordie and Pepsi in the audience and their faces were like beacons. The winners were better than Doris by a mile and a half.

Doris smiles into Betsey's blond shoulders. Everything and everyone is a different colour.

There is not much of a lineup at the Peace Arch. Lulu turns off the music as they roll up to the checkpoint. Betsey pokes her head out Doris' window and the Canadian border guard holds his hand out for Betsey to sniff, then scratches her behind the ear. He looks in the windows of the car. "Well, who have we got here?" he asks.

"My family." Doris hears Lulu say.

My family.

LULU

I told Mike. It was time.

I'd seen them from across the street, waiting for me on the sidewalk. They all looked so peculiar and beautiful. Geordie and Pepsi holding hands like there might not be a tomorrow. Doris, so surprisingly filled with that taste of the pleasure of performing. My dognapee, Betsey, looking from person to person, her mouth in a grin and the two dark spots above her eyes rising and falling as though she was following the conversation as gaily as everyone else was. Mike, he was waving his hands around telling them a joke, probably, and they all cracked up.

When I told Mike, the look of anger that swept across his face swamped me with guilt and agonizing shame. Then he bent over on the park bench where we were sitting and sobbed into his knees until I thought I'd have to get Doris. When he finally raised his head he continued weeping silently as I told him where our sons were born, what I'd named them, where I'd left them. I took off my sweatshirt and gave it to him and he let his tears flood into its sleeve.

"I'm so sorry, Mike," I said finally.

"Let's get them. We'll get them," he said.

I pictured him imagining the boys as babies, wee things in car seats we could pack up and change history by bringing home. Sitting on that bench with Mike, I think I saw them that way too. But I made myself remember. "They're thirty-one now, Mike."

"I know," he shouted angrily. "Let's get them."

"We will," I said. We would.

We talked quietly all the way home in the car. Mike wanted to know everything I could remember. What was the birth like? he asked. What did the babies look like? Did they have hair? What colour? How much? What exactly is a caul? What was the weather like? Who took me home? Did the doctors and nurses speak French? He was reconstructing a thirty-one-year-old experience. He wanted to have been there.

My memories of the birth were vivid. I tried to recreate them for him: I remembered the blue cotton blankets on the bed, the shiny steel railings up the sides, the powerful contraction that Stevie's first cry provoked in me. His head of black hair and his long skinny legs. I remembered the other-worldly blue-white of his umbilical cord, holding us together until they cut it and took him away. Bruce came flying out like an otter and the doctor and nurses made the kind of noises one makes when the quarterback has nearly fumbled the ball. Bruce didn't cry and I'd sat up in panic, imagining him dead. But they wrapped them both in flannelette sheets with pink-and-blue striped edges and two nurses stood by the bed for a few seconds with my sons, living and breathing, in their arms. What I remembered most, I couldn't reconstruct for Mike—the stab of that knife as the nurses went out the door without my having touched them.

As we came into Fraser Arm, Mike, in a gesture that acknowledged the link we would have forever, put his hand on the back of my neck and asked if he could tell everyone about his sons. I wanted to pull over and get out of the car but I kept my wet eyes on the road and drove home. It was both our news now.

At home, Mike took Cidalia into the garden with him. She came back into the kitchen ten minutes later and put her compassionate arms around me. She held my face in her hands.

"Thank you, Lulu."

"My God, Cidalia, what for?" I asked. "There's nothing to thank me for."

"There is," she said. "For having the courage to tell him."

I thought of how uncourageous I'd been. How for years I'd run just two inches ahead of the memory of those dark-haired babies in their flannelette sheets. Eventually, I'd found a way to widen the gap—making music, sleeping with men who'd have made lousy fathers, keeping friends with the childless, avoiding my own nephews. The alternative was insanity. "A very late announcement, I'm afraid. I'm so sorry, Cidalia. You might have known them when they were younger too, if I'd been braver."

Cidalia slid her hands down my arms and held my hands. Then she wiped a tear from my cheek. Doris waved her hands at the three of us in an impatient gesture. Cidalia looked at me and I nodded.

"Mike's a father, Doris," Cidalia said. "And Lulu's a mother."

Doris' expression was one I'd seen on her face at the birth of the barn cat's kittens earlier that week. It would take some explaining for Geordie to understand the whens and where-fores, but no one, including Geordie, seemed to care just then.

"What? Call Dad," Geordie shouted. "Where's the babies, Lulu?"

●

We called Dad, and Alan and Ambrose, and Raylene and Birdie, and Ann Tenpenny, and Geordie insisted we call Julia. Mike wanted to tell everyone. Everyone came, and around midnight, everyone went. They were all shocked and I was wracked with guilt despite the excitement. I kept catching the look on Mike's face—alternately shock, elation, and some kind of well-sublimated rage. Dad and Kat both cried, hopeful tears this time. Naomi held my hand most of the night. Geordie eventually understood that there wouldn't be any babies coming home to the Tenpenny–Parsons house, but that he had two new nephews—grown men—who we would start looking for tomorrow. He asked me a dozen times how they got lost. There would never be a comprehensible answer for that. Raylene was for calling every de La Vérendrye in the Montreal phone book right then and there to see what they knew. Thankfully Julia took some of the attention away from our news with her seven-and-a-half months pregnant belly in which there was a real baby. Trevor and Julia's baby, who'd be joining us before too long. I had a vision of Donnie Coulter proffering dandelions and thought of the promise I'd made him. I said a grateful thank you to him.

•

For a couple of days I hid in my Boler at *Dun Roamin?* I couldn't bear everyone else's excitement or Mike's pain-filled eyes. Robin came over and I told him about Stevie and Bruce. At least that was something he hadn't already known about me. He listened and kissed me so sweetly afterward. I told him how it turned out that looking for the children one has given up for adoption wasn't quite the leaping-through-fiery-hoops I had imagined. There were a few tidy doors we would likely be able to step neatly through, and then all there'd be left was the waiting. If the boys had already registered, or ever did, the agency in Montreal would let us know.

When Robin left I climbed quickly back into the warm place he'd made in the bed—a good spot for a satisfied song-writer on a rainy Wednesday morning. I shivered and pulled the duvet up around my neck. In the few seconds I'd stood at the door to wave him goodbye, I'd noticed the change in the smell of the air. Winter was coming. Trevor had been gone for six months, a full half rotation of the earth around the sun. The fall temperatures were about the same now as they were in the spring, half a year earlier, but the season that would follow this one wouldn't be bringing flowers. We were entering the period of decay and dormancy. Trevor died just when Persephone, that queen of the underworld Kat had long ago told me about, was returning to earth for her six months of spring and summer. Everything about dying in April was inside out and back to front. No one should die just as the sweet peas start to wind their delicate tendrils around anything that will hold them up. Just as Persephone's mom Demeter gets her daughter back.

I thought about what Robin had asked me. Was I going to write a song about Trevor? "What are you, my manager now?" I'd replied, and rolled him over onto his back, pinning his lovely arms.

"Just asking," he said. "You've done pretty well without me 'til now." I leaned down to kiss him.

"I'm not sure about that," I whispered to his mouth.

No one other than Robin had said anything out loud, but the expectations were as tangible as stone. By then I could think of Trevor without always feeling the hard, hot slide of our bodies across the pavement. It was just regret that I was walking with now. And the "what if" kind, that had diminished. I was regretting that we hadn't known one another. That we hadn't been able to face our terrible loss together or find ways to console one another. None of us had. Since I first left home, I'd seen Trevor no more than thirty times. I wrote *Thirty Times Zero Is Zero* in my notebook. A good title for a song. This one would come easily.

I dressed and went up to Doris' and hauled Trevor's suitcase out of the closet. I felt my heart open with that familiar clunk of the latches. There lay Trevor's life, all that he had finally judged important, and everything I would ever know of him. Item by item I reconstructed him on the bed. His head was the box of ashes, lying on the pillow. A photograph was his neck. Mum's sweater and the albums his chest, file folders his legs, track and field ribbons down the centre of Mum's sweater, like a tie. I stood back and looked down at my creation. His Scout sash was going to be a bit much, but

I put it on him anyway. The little cowboy boots were his feet, his baseball glove a single hand, the left. I took the pile of love letters and lay it where his heart would have been. The pile of photographs of the women, I placed at his crotch. I put the photograph of Mum and Dad and Aloysius on his forehead, on top of the box of ashes.

"How're you doing, big brother? Us? Not too bad. Not sure we'll ever get over your fucking death, though." I pulled one of the armchairs over and sat at the end of the bed and put my bare feet against his, remembering a game he and I played when we were kids. We'd position ourselves at either end of the couch, the soles of our feet together. The winner was whoever could straighten their legs first. We eventually broke the couch and Mum forbade us to play it anymore. I pushed against Trevor's cowboy-boot feet but they didn't push back. "Come on. I'll let you win," I said, wishing for his live feet against my soles. I drew my feet back. Trevor always won, and I had always resented it. I couldn't sugarcoat the truth; it was a stretch to say there was much sweetness in my life with Trevor, but I was grateful for the few tender memories that were surfacing. Thirty times zero is zero. But thirty times one is thirty.

I pulled the empty suitcase into my lap and closed my eyes, feeling again in all the elasticized pockets on the sides and in the lid, running my fingers around the lining. On my second time around I noticed a thickness at the rim of the suitcase lining, just inside of the handle. My eyes jerked open. The lining there was stained and thicker along the edge than anywhere else. It looked as though it had been re-glued, and the fabric had discoloured and hardened. I could feel something behind the lining. I pulled at the cloth and when it didn't give I got the letter opener from Aloysius' desk and tried to pry the cloth away from the edge. Finally I stabbed a hole through the lining and ripped it open. Trevor had hidden two things in there: a glassine envelope stamped with a red skull and crossbones and the words "dead dog" upside down beneath the bones. A bloody packet of heroin. The other thing hidden behind the lining stopped my heart—it was a letter addressed to Dad in my mother's hand.

Seeing my mother's handwriting brought tears to my eyes. There was a five-cent postage stamp in the corner, a blue-toned Christmas stamp with an Inuit carving of Mary, Joseph, and Jesus, presumably. The cancellation was clear: Carbonear, Newfoundland, Dec. 27, 1967. On the back my mother had written Poste Restante, Carbonear, NFLD. I carried the letter to the armchair by the balcony window and sat for some time, turning it over and over again in my hands. I didn't want to open it. I didn't want to think about how different our lives might have been had this letter ever reached Dad, whatever its contents, because surely it hadn't. I held it to my forehead and to my mouth. I smelled it. There was no special odour of Mum, just the old smell of the suitcase. When I finally found the courage to open the envelope and pull her letter out another small folded piece of paper fell into my lap. My poor, lost mother had written just a few simple lines.

Christmas 1967

Dearest Wally,

I have been foolish and self-centred. I have hurt you and the children. I ran away from my responsibilities. Could you ever forgive me if I came home? I want to come home. Please reply.

Your foolish Bette

I thought I had run out of tears. My mother was alive. Or she had been, six weeks after that Tuesday night in November. I had a vision of Trevor collecting the mail the day her letter arrived: there he was taking it and reading it. And keeping it.

I read her letter a dozen more times, then I picked up the folded paper that had fallen in my lap. I already knew what it was. I'd memorized the shape of it forty years earlier. My ten-year-old hands had smoothed its edges until it was soft and worn. On the outside of that milk-stained note she'd left for Dad there was something that had not been there before: a small drawing of a cannon and the letter "T." Trevor. He must have seen me burying her note beneath the tree fort or found it later by accident. I could see him burying the toy cannon and keeping the note—an exchange, his treasure for mine; a message to me that he knew what I knew. Shaking, I put the note and the letter carefully back in the envelope. Then I rushed at the bed and I threw Trevor on the floor.

I flung the photographs and letters across the room. I ripped as many badges as I could off his Scout sash and scattered all the file folders and track ribbons. I smashed the soccer trophy against the wall and then threw it and his baseball mitt off the balcony. I screamed as I tore the White Album from its pristine cellophane and gouged both disks with the letter opener. Then I opened his cardboard box of ashes and used his penknife to stab the plastic bag inside. I spun in a circle with the bag, shaking Trevor's ashes all over the floor. I heard and ignored a knock on the door. I stood panting over the mess. On the bed, Otis Redding lay crookedly cradled in the arms of Mum's sweater. Hope, so unexpected, hammered through my rage. She wasn't dead. My mother wasn't dead.

The knock on the door was firmer. I opened it and stepped past Doris. In the hallway closet I found the vacuum cleaner. Doris stood, worried and quiet, in the doorway until every trace of Trevor's grey ashes, every bit of bone and tooth, spleen and damaged liver, had been sucked up and was gone.

"Didn't we have a wedding planned, Doris?" I shouted. "Let's have the damned wedding."

Doris picked up two file folders from the floor and signalled O.K. in semaphore.

"Doris Tenpenny, you are freakin' fabulous." If I'd felt more ecstatic she'd have needed to grab hold of my ankle to keep me from floating away.

DORIS

The sun is not yet up. Doris has been forced to turn on a small desk lamp to see the confounded typewriter. She pokes away at the round keys, but nothing will change the fact that she is a very poor typist. There is no reason why she ought to be better at this contemptible task. She did not take typing in high school. Father said she would never work anywhere but on the farm so Doris took home economics instead. What white cupcakes with orange cream centres have to do with home economics remains a mystery to Doris, but they made up for the teacher's redundant egg lessons; the cupcakes were delicious. Even Father said so.

Doris rips out one paper and puts in another. Today there are more important things to think about than Father and cupcakes. Doris has a wedding menu to type. Lulu said she wanted wild food for the wedding. This seems appropriate because Lulu looks as though she might be found growing wild in the forest herself. *Why should she not be; she has two sons and a mother to find.* Apart from wild mushrooms, which are sometimes tricky to identify and occasionally poisonous, Doris thinks wild people are quite similar to wild food—likeable and interesting. Doris knows wild food, but she is not inclined to fancy cooking. Anne and Bonny from Wild Things Café will take care of that. What can be foraged and gleaned in October is different from what they might have found for the wedding lunch had it taken place when it was supposed to, last spring. But the Gleaning Society people have brought plenty home from the forest and fields and backyards. Everything is ready for tomorrow and Doris has nothing to do but to type the menu.

She begins again on the fresh piece of paper, growling and greatly displeased with her contribution to the waste in the world. She makes a mistake in the first word in this new attempt—appetizers with only one "p"—and she snorts in frustration. A handwritten menu will do. Even Anne and Bonny's rough notes, which she rereads, would suffice at this point. They will have appetizers of home-smoked wild sockeye salmon, Doris' wild pear chutney with her goat cheese, and Beeton's Bog dried cranberry crackers, which she baked this morning. There will be a salad of wild greens and chickweed with Mike and Cidalia's salmonberry wine vinaigrette. The cream of chanterelle soup with roasted cloves, nutmeg, and mace will satisfy the vegetarians. For the carnivores there will be roast venison with huckleberry jam. The provenance of the venison is ridiculous: one of the Ogg daughters' husbands says he witnessed two rutting stags blunder off a cliff, or so his story goes. He offered one of them to Doris for the wedding. Doris cannot decide whether that makes this venison tame or wild. It was gleaned, at least, though potentially not legally. *Pooh, pooh.*

Roasted root vegetables from the garden are not so wild—parsnips, beets, sweet potatoes, onions, garlic, and fennel—but they are simple, which is what Doris likes. The Wild Things chefs will make two kinds of mushrooms—cauliflower and lobster—sautéed in venison drippings, and with no drippings for the vegetarians. Dessert will be wedding cake—this time Ambrose has promised to pick it up at the baker's in Vancouver—and rosehip ice cream with blackberries and blackberry coulis. The cake itself is a wild-apple hazelnut layer-cake filled with Oregon grape compote—Geordie's dream. Why they call jam compote is beyond Doris.

Doris feels a small amount of guilt at her relief that no vegans will be at the wedding supper. Vegans are so difficult, and yet she'll give them this: they are potentially right on a number of counts. Birdie and Raylene are the only vegetarians, thank goodness, and most of the rest of the guests are omnivores although Lulu is not sure about Ambrose's new friend Marietta. Some of the gleaners are vegans, but they are not invited. Not because they are vegans, of course, but there had to be a cut-off point. One of the young vegan gleaners asked Doris the other day whether she believed animals were beings or things. *Beings, of course*, Doris wrote. "So why do you continue to eat them?" the boy asked. Doris did not have an easy answer. Doris does not eat much fish anymore; if anything is unsustainable it is the fishery. But Doris eats the animals she raises—the pigs, the chickens, the sheep, and the goats.

"Would you eat your dog, this *being* for example?" the boy asked, while he scratched Dante under his chin.

If I were starving? Yes, Doris told him.

"If you weren't starving?" he asked.

Dante looked up at Doris just then with his sorrowful

eyes and she laughed. *No,* she wrote. *Tell Dante I would never eat him.*

"Would you eat a *human* being?" the boy wanted to know.

Doris thought about eating Mike or Geordie. *Probably not.* The boy gave Doris a small smirk as a sign of her hypocrisy.

What about you? Would you eat meat if you were starving? Doris asked.

"I'd rather die," he said.

Doris makes a decision: there will be no menu. Photocopying fifty menus so that people know what they are eating is nothing short of shameful. *If they want to know what they are eating they can ask.* Doris knows someone might accuse her of coming up with an environmental excuse just to avoid typing a wedding lunch menu—she has been accused of such things before—but both Lulu Parsons and Trevor Parsons called Doris freakin' fabulous. Doris feels plainly satisfied about that. She types *The quick brown fox jumps over the lazy dog* three times. Nine words a minute. Perfectly satisfactory. Now, where are her boots? The sun will be rising soon.

●

Doris climbs the fence into the back pasture. She sniffs the air. Crisp. Nearly winter. Grey, white, rust. She is not sure what was ever sown in these acres. Something, once, because they are meadows, not forest. She has left them that way for the barn owls. The tussock grasses here are home to the mice, moles, and voles—the owls' supper. The nesting box she and Geordie built for them sits in the rafters of the old shack that tilts in the meadow. In the dark, in her coat and hat and thick socks and rubber boots, Doris sits on a stump and waits for the owl. But soon the sun is rising red and the pasture is rosy in its light. The grasses are otherworldly, rimed with shimmering pink frost. This morning, pink *is* pink. She'll see no owl today.

Doris reaches into her coat pocket. The ring is small and of a pale gold. She thinks of Alice McFee's hands on a carton of eggs, wearing this ring, her fingers stained purple, picking fat blackberries for jelly, striped gooseberries for jam. Holding a book. Hanging laundry on the line. Doris pushes her glasses down her nose and looks again at the engraving inside the ring. *A and A Sept 3rd 1947*. Once, Aloysius slipped this ring onto Alice's very alive finger. Doris is careful not to let it slip onto one of hers. She pockets the ring and scans the sky, a last tail of hope.

She shifts on the stump, then stands up and stretches. Everything is glinting and gleaming in the meadow, but Doris' feet and hands are cold. She heads toward the orchard, her coat hem dusting the frosted dew off the tall grasses. An apple tree, one of the old ones with its gnarly bits and holes, is where she'll put the ring. She thought of giving it to someone—one of the gleaners, perhaps—but its provenance is poor; *no one should wear Aloysius McFee's ring.*

Doris leans her breast against the old apple tree, reaches up, and lets the ring drop into the hollow. She presses her ear against the tree, imagining the sound of the bit of gold dropping to where it will soon be enveloped by nature. Nothing. It is impossible to know how deep the hole is and what creature might be living there. The ring won't bother a red squirrel or a possum. Holding the tree in her arms, she looks up into its branches.

The owl is peering down at her, its clown face tilting. It lifts, and on great white wings, soars with Doris' heart.

LULU

The night before Geordie's wedding I collected a couple dozen glossy chestnuts from the sidewalk and slipped one under the mattress of everyone in the house including the dogs. I made stealth visits to Dad and Kat's, to Raylene and Birdie's, even Mrs. Snyder got a chestnut under her mattress. The rain pounded all night, but early in the morning, it let up and I went out. I walked through the Logging Trail, down to Beeton's Bog in the dark, wet silence, smelling the cold that had descended with October. As the sun rose, a western red-tailed hawk flew over, low, hunting, and I imagined Doris' endangered bog vole, safe from the hawk in some warm peaty spot beneath the bog's shimmering surface. What would I find in one square foot there, Aloysius? Nature, red in tooth and claw?

Old Ricky joined me in Doris and Geordie's driveway. Past the mailbox, I saw something glittering beneath the trees. I knelt and reached under the sodden boughs of those ancient firs and cedars. I stood, triumphant and smiling—at Ricky, at no one, at the quiet damp dawn—with an old Orange Crush bottle in my hand. Circa 1967. I must have missed that one.

Inside, there was my sweet prince, Geordie, at the breakfast table with Doris and Mike, complaining that he hadn't slept well because of something lumpy under his mattress. Everyone else, including me, had slept like a baby.

●

Geordie was in a grey tuxedo with tails, a white shirt, and a pale-yellow vest rented from a shop in the Wesleyville mall. He insisted on a blue and orange paisley tie that belonged to Mike. Who was I to argue?

"You look GQ handsome, Geordie," I said.

"You do too, Lulu." He was rocking from foot to foot not looking at me.

"Stand still for a minute," I said. I tied his tie and pressed my ear against his chest listening to his bountiful heart. "Ready, Geordie?"

"Ready, Lulu."

Geordie wanted everyone in the family to walk him down the aisle. I started to tell him that normally it's just the bride who walks down the aisle while the groom waits for her at the altar, but I bit my stupid tongue. Dad, Kat, Ambrose, Alan, Naomi, Mike, Cidalia, Doris, Raylene, Birdie, Julia, and I joined hands and formed a big chain around Geordie and he walked in the centre of our circle down the aisle of the Royal Canadian Legion Hall #273. The crying started pretty much at that point and I wasn't alone. We left Geordie at the front with his best man, Mike, and went back to get the bride. Pepsi was waiting at the front door with her friend from work, Mary. Pepsi wore a pretty white dress, knee length, with a funky little pillbox hat and a tiny veil that just covered her eyes. And a smile to make your heart explode. The bouquet Birdie had made for her, entirely of yellow flowers, was only slightly less radiant than the bride. Pepsi and Mary walked hand-in-hand down the aisle to the "Wedding March" and we followed, not a dry eye in the hall.

How many of us had told Geordie he couldn't get married? We had always, gently or not so gently, discouraged his dreams of romance. When he'd sweetly pondered who he would marry one day, we'd teased him. You've been watching too much TV, we said. You can't get married, you funny boy. It was sweet but out of the question. We had a dozen unreasoned excuses when he asked why not. But when Geordie told Dad he and Pepsi were getting engaged, Mike said, "Why not?" I wasn't the best candidate for answering that question. I could only imagine another bad ending and heartbreak for my brother. I asked Mike, "What if Pepsi dies? What if it doesn't work out?"

Mike had laughed at me. "Yeah," he said, "I've never heard any better reasons to call off a wedding."

After the I dos and I wills and their happy kiss, I played my love song, *Finally*. Dad sang it with me. I couldn't take my eyes off of Geordie and Pepsi. A finer, more beautiful wedding couple there had never been. My big brother, our resilient, brilliant man, was married. Hand-in-hand he and Pepsi led the celebrants to the big folding tables set up in the Legion hall. Everyone Geordie loved and who loved him back tucked into Doris' wild lunch together. I thought of Trevor, and for a brief moment understood him. For a second, I forgave him. I took a big spoonful of chanterelle soup. It was like heaven.

PART TWO

Mothers

1967, 1968

*I'd give my food and drink
to see my home again
to see my mother's hand
against her apron edge.*

HEY ROSETTA! "Carry Me Home," *A Cup of Kindness Yet*

How far away can one get?

She catches the bus on Reifel Road into New Westminster and another into Vancouver. At the bus station in Vancouver she scans the departure schedules. A bus is loading for Calgary. She buys a ticket. The bus stops at Chilliwack, Hope, Kamloops, a dozen other B.C. towns. She doesn't sleep. At Salmon Arm a man with a hopeful smile takes the seat beside her. She gets up and moves to the row behind the driver. She is awake when they cross through the Rockies in the middle of the night. It is snowing and the bus grinds uphill, a slow beast along the dark highway. At every curve, the road disappears and the headlights shine out over the abyss. Snow slams onto the windshield, dizzying. She moves again, with her small rucksack, to the back of the bus. It is snowing in Calgary. She continues east, buying another ticket and another. It is snowing in Medicine Hat, Regina, Winnipeg, and Thunder Bay. In Sudbury, she stops. A man waiting in the station for someone else on another bus takes one look at her and offers her a waitressing job at the Nickel Range Hotel. She buys a black skirt and a white shirt and a pair of shoes at the Salvation Army thrift store and disappoints the man by leaving within a month.

When the bus unloads in North Sydney, Nova Scotia, she is the last off. The bus driver has found her asleep across the back seats.

"Wakey wakey, lady. You're not going any farther, at least not on this bus," he says.

She sits on a bench in the bus depot for half an hour until hunger and the cigarette smoke bluing the air drive her out onto the street. The wind slaps her coat open and snags her breath. Clutching her lapels, she heads toward the only traffic light she can see. There is a coffee shop on the corner. The restaurant is busy, the counter filled with men. They sit in a familiar row of plaid shirts, toques, and coveralls on the stools, their broad backs toward her. Men in white shirt-sleeves and a few women in dresses occupy the booths. The waitress, in a uniform, bustles back and forth with pots of coffee and platters of food.

She stands outside gasping deep breaths until the waitress inside pounds her hand against the windowpane and gestures at her with a quizzical look: Are you stupid? Come in.

The wind shoves her inside and the waitress slaps an empty stool at the counter. Another instruction: sit. She takes a seat on the cracked orange vinyl. The waitress pours her a cup of coffee without asking, slides a pot of milk toward her, and points at the menu with her chin. It's warm inside.

"Whattya say, boys?" the waitress says to the men at the counter. "We gonna get more snow before Christmas?"

"Not likely, Jo. Just more of this damned fog. But if you're going home you'd better be prepared for some."

"You think so, Barney? Snow in Newfoundland at Christmas?" Jo the waitress winks at her.

"Does a bear shit in the woods?" the man says.

"Mind your language, Barney. There's a lady present." She winks again. "These boys'll be gone in two minutes. Lunch hour's over. Isn't it, boys?"

The blue-collar men zip up their overcoats and tug their toques down over their ears, and the white-collar men push their brimmed hats down so the wind won't take them. They all disappear at once. The waitress waves an imaginary magic wand after them.

"Poof," she says, smiling. "Best moment in my day."

She clears their plates and cups, pockets the nickels and dimes the men have left, and wipes the counter clean.

"Now that the hordes have departed, what would you like to eat?" she asks.

The words on the menu are jumping like ping-pong balls and won't stay still.

"I recommend the egg salad. Russell's specialty," the waitress says. And when she receives no answer she shouts to the cook in the back, "Russell, egg salad on white. Make it thick. I think we've got a starver here." She heaps a ladleful of chowder into a bowl. She pulls a paper napkin from beneath the counter, places it neatly beside the bowl and puts a spoon straight down the middle of the napkin, then straightens it, just a smidgen. When her customer doesn't move, Jo picks the spoon up and puts it in the woman's hand.

"What's your name, dear?"

"Bette."

"Bette, from the looks of you I'm guessing you might not want me asking where you've come from. Safe maybe to ask where you're heading?"

"To England," Bette says. She looks at the waitress. Jo's hair is straight and dark and the front is cut into short bangs. Her eyes are frank behind her glasses. Bette is being called dear by someone who can't be older than twenty-five.

"On a plane?"

"No." Bette hesitates. "On a boat."

"A boat?"

Bette nods. At nights, in Sudbury, when the numbness of her flight from her family turned to the terror of being found, she'd pictured herself on a boat. She would find a ship and sign on as a cook, or a cleaner. She'd go back to England. No questions asked.

"You've landed yourself in the wrong town anyways, Bette. Montreal is where you'd find those kind of boats. Or maybe Halifax, but not North Sydney."

Bette can't remember where she saw the map of Canada, what bus station. North Sydney was nearly the end of Canada. "Surely there would be a ship here . . ."

The wind slams so hard against the window it bows.

"No," the waitress says.

•

Jo Pretty is going home to Halley's Cove, Newfoundland, for Christmas and, as she tells Bette, she isn't leaving her on a foggy wharf two days before Christmas looking for a boat ride to England. They sleep in Jo's bedsit apartment above the restaurant, and in the morning, while it is still dark, Bette is squeezed into the back seat of a car jammed with Jo's Newfoundland-bound friends. Just as Bette is becoming sure that Hell would be no worse than sitting on the lap of a stranger in a car meant for five, they pull into an airport parking lot and everyone tumbles out.

Jo insists on buying Bette a standby ticket. "You've got nowhere else to be, right, Bette? Ma paid for my ticket. She complains how I'm never home. So I'm paying for yours. It's the milk run anyway, so you'll find out soon enough I'm not really doing you a favour, but you can owe me one day," Jo says. "What's your last name, anyways?"

"Tallis," Bette says. It is her mother's maiden name. If she

397

thought she had control over even one tiny aspect of her life, she was wrong: she hasn't.

When the ticket agent calls Bette Tallis, Jo hoots, jumps up, and takes Bette's hand. She holds it as if one walked around every day holding another woman's hand. But Jo's grip is fierce, as though she knows Bette will flee the first chance she has. The airplane jerks out of the fog and this time Bette clutches Jo's hand. Jo opens and holds a vomit bag for Bette. As the airplane skids to its third stop, Bette finds brutal solace in believing that this is some vengeful god's punishment being meted out—and she deserves it.

From St. John's, an Uncle Carl to one of Jo's friends drives them along dark roads. There are occasional glittering pockets of light, small houses in which, Bette imagines, people are celebrating Christmas Eve. They're wrapping presents. Having drinks. Getting the Christmas stockings ready for the children. She is stabbed by the memory of Lulu and Geordie opening theirs. Wally fills the stockings with odd things—homemade fishing lures, small paper bags of licorice babies, blood pudding, jars of pickled herring or gherkins, impossible-to-shell Brazil nuts—Christmastime-only treats, chocolate coins, and a Japanese orange in the toe. She turns to watch the mesmerizing snow in the headlights. She would cry, but there is no liquid left in her body to produce another tear.

"Slow down, Carl. Ma should be here," Jo says after an eternity, and sure enough, a car waiting in the street flicks its lights at them. The young fellow's Uncle Carl pulls up alongside and, despite the blizzard, windows are rolled down and unintelligible greetings are shouted. Jo pulls her bag and Bette's knapsack out of the trunk.

"Hurry, hurry in," the woman in the car shouts, "before you freeze."

"Merry Christmas, Ma." Jo leans across and kisses the woman as Bette climbs into the back seat. "This is Bette Tallis. Bette, this is my ma, Florence Pretty."

"You'll be home soon, Miss Tallis," Mrs. Pretty says.

They bump for some time along an unploughed road. Mrs. Pretty drives in the two tracks in the middle of the road and seems unperturbed by the possibility of meeting another car coming in the opposite direction—at least her speed shows no indication of such a worry—or of breaking down in her old beater of a car in what must be the middle of nowhere. But they pass no other car, no houses, just rocks and stunted trees briefly illuminated by the car's headlights. Mrs. Pretty slows when they come to a sharp turn in the road and the car pulses as she pumps the brakes. They seem to be gliding down a steep hill straight toward the black ocean. Out of instinct, Bette puts her own brakes on, but Mrs. Pretty turns the car neatly into a driveway beside a wharf where a number of fishing boats are tied. Bette can make out a dozen or so house shapes, their windows dark.

"Welcome to Halley's Cove," Jo says.

They walk single-file along a narrow path dug through the snow to the front steps. There is no porch light on at the house, but a yellow light flickers from within. Inside, it's a kerosene lamp that is casting the light, burning on a small kitchen table set for two. Mrs. Pretty pulls another placemat from a drawer and a mug and plate from the cupboard and sets them, with Jo's same tidy precision, on the table. She has not removed her great coat, nor has she asked for Bette's. She holds a plate of dark brown buttered bread toward Bette then draws it back.

"Silly me. Sit please, Miss Tallis," she says.

Mrs. Pretty pours them each a cup of tea. In the lamplight, her arms cast long, strange shadows across the table.

"I did my baking this morning, thank God. Molasses?" she asks, passing Bette a jug. "For the bread." She makes a swirling motion over Bette's plate and nods.

Jo nods. Bette nods too.

"Ma's porridge bread is the best in Halley's Cove."

Florence laughs. "That is not a high achievement, Jo, given there's not three women in the village who bake porridge bread anymore."

"Pshaw. Yours is the best in all of Newfoundland. How long's the power been out?"

"'Bout six hours now. Went off before it got dark. Looks like the problem's from somewhere down the shore because Monty came by to say there's nothing wrong with our lines."

"Not a surprise it's out. We got quite the blow on the plane. I thought they'd send us back for a while there. Touch and go."

"No. No." Florence takes a little breath after each word. "Not a surprise."

It comes as a surprise to Bette that the power is out. Sometimes, in the early days before sleep was a precious commodity, she and Wally used to light a kerosene lamp on weekend nights, just because it was pretty. Half the time it had puffed black smoke, but they didn't care. Later, when it stopped feeling romantic to have to trim the smoking wick, the lamp disappeared into a closet. Bette looks from Jo to Mrs. Pretty. Their faces look flat and yellow in the flickering light, making her think of black-eyed Susans. She wonders what conversation this mother and daughter would be having were she not here. She picks up a dark slice of bread. A drip of molasses rolls down her finger and she licks the bitter taste off, glad for the shadows in the room.

"Well, I'm going to throw another log on the fire and then I think we should all go to bed."

"I'll do it, Ma." Jo rises and disappears into a room off the kitchen. The cold sweeps in as she opens the door.

"Everyone's been telling me to get rid of this old wood stove, but on nights like these . . ." Mrs. Pretty says to Bette, leaving the sentence hanging.

"Thank you for the bread, Mrs. Pretty," Bette says.

"Everybody here calls me Flo."

Bette nods. She knows she should say that Flo should call her Bette, but she cannot fathom whatever possessed her to spend Christmas at a stranger's. She would rather be a body sinking in the frozen sea.

"Well," Flo says.

Jo's back. She drags a ragged blanket loaded with firewood into the kitchen then pushes the door to the back room shut. Flo helps her daughter with the load, stacking the wood against the wall. She lifts one of the lids on the wood stove with a cast-iron prod and Jo pops a log in.

"Good thing I came home, Ma," Jo says with a tone of mild recrimination. "How come you didn't have any wood in the kitchen?"

"Good thing you came home, Jo," Flo says, casting a conspiratorial grin at Bette.

●

Flo has led Bette up a narrow stairwell to a small bedroom with a tilting floor. She put the candle on the dresser, drew the curtains, plumped the pillow, and folded down the blankets on the bed before saying goodnight. She has gone now. Bette hears her careful steps on each squeaking stair. Still in her coat, Bette sits on a single hardback chair in the room. The candle splutters and the noise startles her. She blows it out and finds herself in pitch darkness. She feels her way across the narrow room and, taking off only her coat, climbs into the sagging bed and pulls the many blankets up to her chin. This is Jo's room. Jo will sleep downstairs on a daybed in the parlour, to keep watch on the fire, she said.

"I know bald-faced misery when I see it," Bette hears Flo tell her daughter, downstairs. "You and I have had our share. But your Miss Tallis looks like she might die of hers."

●

Bette wakes some hours later, surprised to have slept. A pale light fills the room. It must be near dawn. She is warm under the blankets and she was dreaming—something plain and quiet, not the waking nightmares of the past few weeks. She tries to bring it back but feels it slipping away like a turtle off a sunny perch. It was Wally and May Ogg. They were shopping together and the Ogg girls were in the SuperValu with them, walking dogs. It made no sense. The Oggs don't have dogs and they wouldn't have been allowed in the SuperValu. Bette curls up and faces the window. As she has done every morning, every day, every night for weeks, she replays what happened before she left Fraser Arm. They'd had a fight, she and Wally, the night before she left. An argument really, if you could even call it that when Wally was involved. A one-sided quarrel. It had started at breakfast. Wally, in his infuriatingly docile manner was, as usual, ignoring the most important issue, in Bette's mind, and that was that it was, in fact, probably illegal to do what Lulu had told them the teacher had done.

"It ain't illegal, Bette," Wally had said.

Isn't. "Well it ought to be. Admit that, at least. How teachers think they can get away with things like that, I will never know," she'd said.

"You've said that twelve dozen times in the last fifteen years, Bette, my sweet. Why don't you get back on the phone to the principal?"

"Thank you for your support, Wally." Bette had glanced over at Lulu's pointed little face. Try as she might, she had never been able to read her daughter well. It was as if Lulu resisted revealing herself and had since Bette had first looked down at her ten years earlier, those dark newborn eyes looking back at her. Their girl, sombre, intelligent, and somehow fierce.

Lulu would no doubt have been wishing she'd never mentioned what her teacher had forced Kevin Bates to do in the classroom. Bette knew, at least, that Lulu thought there was something wrong with it, though she had started with, "Something funny happened yesterday." Mrs. Hudson had made Kevin get down on his hands and knees and push one of those blue and pink erasers, with his nose, from the front of the classroom to the cloakroom and back ten times while the rest of the class studied the times table, up to ten. Trevor and Alan and Ambrose thought this was hilarious and set off on a recounting of their own tales of peculiar punishments handed out by teachers. They seemed to think such atrociousness was acceptable.

"Kevin's an asshole," Trevor had said, testing a fifteen-year-old's mettle and eyeing Wally for a reaction he didn't get. "That was nothing," he said. When he was in grade five, Mrs. Hudson made some stupid kid erase the blackboard holding the chalk brush with his forehead."

Alan and Ambrose said Mr. Taft made anyone caught chewing gum wear it on the end of their nose for the rest of the day. There was more hilarity over this, Geordie clowning and trying to make a piece of soggy puffed wheat stick to the end of his own squat nose. Bette had hesitated between amusement—they so rarely all got along—and annoyance, until Lulu snorted milk out her nose, and she angrily told them it was a despicable thing to make a child do and sent them all off to school or work or wherever it was they were supposed to be on a Monday morning. All but Geordie. He looked up at her expectantly and she absentmindedly picked a dried piece of cereal from his cheek. Once, someone had said that Geordie was God's punishment for having sex before she was married. May Ogg said that if that was God, to hell with him.

"It's not really funny, Geordie, what happened to Kevin," she'd said. Geordie put his serious face on, and Bette licked her finger and stroked clean his stubbled cheek. What had happened to Geordie in his first attempt at school wasn't funny either.

They were still at it in the evening. She and Wally were at the kitchen sink, she washing, he drying the supper dishes, and Trevor—it was always Trevor who picked at scabs—said, "That would be easier than a regular Pink Pearl eraser."

"What's your point?" Ambrose growled.

Bette turned back to the greasy, lukewarm dishwater, exhausted. Ambrose hated Trevor and Trevor hated Ambrose. It was something Bette guiltily understood; she hated them both, now and again, mostly when they snarled up against one another, a couple of mismatched cats in the ring, one large but the other wily. The boys were all so different. When the twins were born, Ambrose came out first. He was big and red and madder than a hornet. Alan, full of grace, followed five minutes later. Ambrose spent his babyhood competing with his charming twin whom everyone plainly preferred—the so-easy-to-love Alan—but when they were two and Trevor was born, Ambrose simply stopped trying. Bette watched first shock and then what must have been resignation cross Ambrose's face as he stared down at the new baby. By the time Lulu was born, Ambrose, though only seven, had retreated to his own little world into which no one but Alan was particularly welcome.

About the erasers, Alan, always to the rescue, said, "They're bigger, the Pink Pearls. You could roll 'em over and over. The blue-and-pink ones are hard and half the size."

Trevor let out his usual air-from-a-tire sound and got up to leave the table. "Yeah, but they're slipperier." As he stood he grabbed one of Bette's homemade cookies from the plate Wally was just putting on the table. Ambrose's hand snagged out and grabbed Trevor's wrist, squeezing it hard and twisting until Trevor dropped the cookie.

"That's mine." Ambrose said.

"Asshole, Amber," Trevor whispered loudly in Ambrose's ear and skipped quickly back to avoid Ambrose's shooting fist.

"Get out!" Bette screamed at Trevor. In her fury, she

reached out to smack him but didn't connect as he slid out the door. She turned to the table glowering and at a complete loss. That morning they'd all been united in laughter, even at her, playfully mocking her English accent, repeating *despicable is it mutha?* Laughing hyenas. Even she had laughed. Now they were dogs on the hunt, bringing out the very worst in each other—mean, arrogant, disrespectful.

"Bette, dear," Wally said.

Bettedear. Bettedear. "What?" She grabbed to take away the plate of cookies, impotently resorting to something that had long ago ceased to work on these boys who would soon be men, but the cookies slid off the plate onto the table. Besides, the boy she most wanted to punish had left the room. Geordie picked the disputed cookie up and offered it to Bette.

"It is entirely absurd," she'd said, trying to slow her heartbeat and ignoring the tears she saw rising in Geordie's eyes, "that you would argue over whether Kevin should use a Pink Pearl eraser or a blue-and-pink one next time Mrs. Hudson decides to humiliate him." She could hear Trevor snorting in the next room and was swept with a familiar rage that felt like only smacking him silent would subdue. "It is a wonder that these delinquents don't grow up to kill their teachers. And what," she said, grimly looking over at Wally, the limp tea towel flung over his shoulder, "is this fixation with noses?"

"Well, at least Lulu's class got their times tables down," Wally said.

Bette remembers staring at him, disbelieving.

"Bette, I'm just joking, dear," he'd said and his hands flew up in comic supplication. She watched the smile playing on his mouth. His eyes flicked from her to the table and back. His trousers were tight around his belly and a dark dishwater stain had spread horizontally across the front of his blue work shirt where he'd pressed up against the sink. Why he hadn't changed out of his uniform was incomprehensible. It would just mean more laundry and ironing. He looked foolish and nervous. She'd wondered whether he'd been nervous back then too, when she, just sixteen, had thought him so marvellous. Wally Parsons—her ticket to anywhere other than St. Helens—in his Canadian soldier's uniform. Was he a foolish man back then and it had just taken her twenty-one years to finally see it?

Wally's hands were fiddling with the tea towel, twisting it and getting ready to flick her with it. She remembered the first time he'd touched her with those hands: everyone was out—another post-war ceremony in Liverpool that all of St. Helens was at—and she hadn't known that Wally, the Canadian boarder she'd been flirting with at breakfast and supper for a few months, had stayed home too. They'd bumped into each other in the second-floor hallway outside the bathroom and after a minute or two of inane chit-chat he'd leaned shyly to kiss her. How they later ended up on his narrow bed upstairs on top of her grandmother's tufted bedspread, his square fingers lying across her naked white belly, she still cannot quite remember. But it happened again and again and then she was pregnant with Geordie, and they were married and she was sailing alone across the Atlantic to meet up with her new husband.

After the cookie farce, the kitchen was quiet. Wally had turned back to the sink, indecision obviously getting the better of him, and Lulu and Geordie were the only ones left at the table, side by side in some impenetrable conversation as always, their ten-year age gap marked mostly by physical size. The cupboard doors hung open, mouths waiting for their plates and glasses. Alan came in from outside, bringing with him an armload of wood for the old cookstove and a cold breeze that spoke of snow. She watched the sparks that flew up as he pushed a log and then another in through the hole. Bette had looked down at her hand. She still held the cookie Geordie had given her. The chocolate chips were melting. She ate the cookie and licked her fingers. When she looked up everyone had melted from the room as well. She heard their voices in the living room, setting up the nightly checkers board, the television emitting the familiar murmur of a hockey game.

Just carry on, she'd thought. "A cup of tea, Wally?" Bette had finally called out, the words cardboard in her mouth, knowing the predictable answer.

"You bet, Bette, ha ha," Wally shouted from the living room. *You bet, Bette. Bet. Bette. Ha ha.* His daily joke made her want to fling things.

"Kettle's on the stove, Wally," Bette said, "Listen for it, please." She went down the three stairs in to what they had begun to call the laundry room, an alcove between the kitchen and the back door where Wally had only recently knocked gyproc up over the studs. Bette kicked three big pairs of boots out of the way and carried a basket of the boys' jeans and t-shirts back up to the kitchen. She went back down and turned the wringer washer on, shoving in a load of greyed sheets and grubby towels and watching the frothy water gush into the tub. Then, as she always did, she flicked the switch that set the rollers turning, just to watch. She thought with fascination, for the umpteenth time, how she might look, her body pulled through the wringers arms first, flattened like those cartoon characters run over by a steamroller. If she held her hands just a pinch away from the rollers she could feel the tugging pull of them on her fingertips. She turned around, calmer and thinking about the words wring and wrung, ring and rung, and leaned against the old round machine, listening to the soothing hum of the rollers spinning one against the other, and the water falling. Upstairs, she knew, Wally would be losing badly at checkers to Geordie, on purpose at first, and then for real.

The second she heard the shouts and the checkers spill on the floor Bette knew what she had done. They all reached the kitchen at the same time. Flames had engulfed the laundry basket quickly and orange and yellow was licking up toward the ceiling.

"Jesus," Geordie screamed, panic flapping his arms.

"Jesus isn't going to help us now, Geordie. Hurry, Lulu," Wally said, "bring me the hallway rug."

The kettle sat on the kitchen counter beside the sink, where she'd left it, heavy and cold with condensation. She sloshed the water onto the flames and Trevor held a small box of baking soda out from behind the shelter of the fridge door. Wally threw the rug over the burning basket. The cookstove groaned and belched black smoke that made them all cough.

"That laundry was clean," Bette had said. It sounded like an accusation. She wasn't sure why it came out that way.

"Bette, my pet, you put the basket on the burning stove. What in the world were you thinking, girl?"

Such a sourness had flickered through her when Wally had looked at her with nothing more complicated than wonder in his sweet brown eyes.

They'd fought again that night, in the living room, and too late she'd realized that Lulu was in her spot behind the couch. Her heart constricts thinking about what she'd said. She hadn't meant it about Geordie and Woodlands. The school, the doctors, people in Fraser Arm, they had all wanted to see Geordie put in an institution. It'd be for the best, everyone said. No one keeps a *retarded* child, they said. It was as if everyone except she and Wally was ashamed of him. So they'd gone there—to Woodlands—when Geordie was five. Just an interview, they'd agreed. Maybe a school like that would be good for him. Even Wally was shaken by how the doctor had looked at Geordie. Even if she and Wally wanted to keep him at home, the doctor assured them, Woodlands should take him anyway. "It's in the best interest of the child to have proper care," he said. Proper. For months they'd lived in fear that someone from Woodlands or Children's Aid would come for him. Wally knew that she would have never let Geordie go. He must know that she didn't mean what she said the night of the fire. There was no other way to tell him how, unless something changed, she felt she'd go mad.

Maybe she had gone mad. She'd certainly become as sour as the pocketfuls of green apples the kids brought home from the Richardsons' farm in the spring. But weren't there a thousand reasons to be sour? The boys' uncertain futures, Lulu's hateful teacher, the nonstop shopping and cooking, Geordie's endless needs. Even the peeling linoleum and the boot closet, that impossibility of a cupboard filled with two decades of unmatched shoes and boots and roller skates. It had all begun to make Bette feel as though a teenaged biker gang lived in the house and she was a meal-making captive within it. There was not a stitch of order to anything. And worst of all, there was Aloysius McFee and his calls and pleading notes: "Don't tell me you don't love me. Don't tell me you don't want me." The guilt of her infidelity, the fear of being found out, and everything else uncertain and unfix-able had slowly plated together over the years, like armadillo armour sewn into her clothing. The weight of it—that is why she is here. The world tilted and her leaden suit slid out the door, with her a passive passenger inside it, all the way to the other side of this country. To bloody Halley's Cove.

●

Winter in Newfoundland sounds like a battering ram. Bette sits up and swings her legs to the floor. Another surge of regret attacks her as she sees she is still in yesterday's clothes. She lifts an edge of the curtain. It is still snowing and the sky is an odd pink, like blood seeping into a damp white towel. Though she knows they are only a few yards from the water, she can see neither the wharf nor the boats that were tied there last night. But she can hear the ocean. It sounds furious.

She draws her fingers through her hair and looks around for a mirror. She's never seen a room so spare. She opens the bedroom door and on the sill finds a pair of red-and-turquoise knitted slippers tied with a green ribbon. Christmas. Unbidden, unwanted, comes the image of the children in the living room in Fraser Arm, Christmas morning, but not as they are now. That she cannot, or refuses to, imagine. She sees them as they were when Lulu was a baby, the young boys taking turns holding her, shaking her rattle, each of them opening their single present one after the other. Trevor's only five. He adores Lulu and wants to hold her the most. The twins are seven. Wally's hair is mostly brown still, and he's slimmer and in high spirits. He's got the box of chocolates from the store in Vancouver, their annual gift to each other, and he's handing it to her with that look of love that has never diminished. He was never done with Bette, even when she felt done with him. Even when he should have been able to guess that she had strayed.

She undoes the bow and puts the slippers on. They fit.

"Still have to use the bucket of water to flush." Flo is standing at the bottom of the stairs in a floor-length flannel nightgown, a padded hunting vest, and slippers much like the pair Bette has on. "I'm sorry you won't be able to run water to wash. No power yet," she says. "But tea's on."

Jo appears beside her mother, dressed in striped flannel pyjamas and a woolly cardigan. The two of them are beaming up the stairs as if Bette were their sister, long lost and now returned to them. Flo is taller than her daughter, by an inch or two, but they're peas in a pod with the same haircut, similar glasses, and toothy smiles.

"Merry Christmas, Miss Tallis," Flo says.

"It's Bette. Please call me Bette."

The window in the bathroom is small and the curtain is thick. She fumbles with a pack of matches left on top of the toilet tank and manages to light the candle there. Another image of her family rises now, the memory another dagger: Lulu helping Geordie light the Christmas candles. Bette sits. Wally would have found her note. Wouldn't he know from her words that she'd just had too much? That she couldn't go on? He'd be angry, and sad. He wouldn't understand. But he'd know that she'd left him. Left them.

She reaches up and pulls back the curtain. The colour of the sky has changed. It's less pink, more grey, brighter. It might have stopped snowing. It's hard to tell. A lone gull flies low over the house, its wings doing a slow flap as if the sky were a cream soup. The Fraser River gulls are smaller. Suddenly she misses the children like someone has punched a hole through her skin, spread her ribs, and dragged everything out, including her heart. This is new, missing them. Until now, she has felt only the torture of guilt, her own blunt weapon thumping bruises all over her body. She wants to go home. She blows out the candle and steps onto the landing. Bette can hear the soft voices of Flo and Jo talking, a mother and her daughter, as it should be.

In the kitchen, Jo is stirring a pot of porridge. She points the gloppy wooden spoon at Bette's slippers, then at the ones on her mother's feet.

"They were Grandma's creations. She went a bit off in her later years, wouldn't you say, Ma? But she could still knit. There must be fifty pairs. It's not much, but Merry Christmas."

Suddenly the kitchen is lit and the radio comes on. Jo lets out a whoop.

"Hurrah. Power. Now we can have something other than mush for breakfast."

"Shhh. Shhh." Flo is tapping her ear with her index finger. "Her Majesty."

Even with that introduction it takes Bette half a minute to understand. It's the Queen.

When Her Majesty's annual Christmas address to the people is over, Flo looks like a woman whose pie won first prize at the fair. Pie, jam, *and* lemon pound cake. She's got a bowl of eggs out of the fridge and is putting one of them to her face. She touches Jo's face with the egg too.

"Still cool. We're safe," Jo says. "'Sides, eggs don't really go off, Ma."

Flo looks like she might like to touch Bette's face with the egg too. "You're from England, Bette," she says. "Did you ever see the Queen?"

Bette's mother and father used to ride home on their bicycles from the Pilkington Glass factory in St. Helens, often delivering the latest Socialist paper on their way. Before she was five, Bette's vocabulary included the words union and capitalist, socialism and hegemony. On weekends, her parents' supper guests were likely to include fellow workers from Pilkington Glass, union reps, disgruntled members of the Communist Party, as well as the boy down the street whose father had first told him to get a job then given him a black eye to drive home his point. Sometimes they had paying guests, such as Wally. But mostly the Fenwicks took in human strays. Royalists they were not.

"No," Bette says. "I never met her." She has drifted, thinking about her mother and father and the house on Ridout Street in St. Helens. They'd liked Wally. Her father once said he had "a socialist mind," his kindest compliment. Wally had gone with her, hand in hand, to tell them she was pregnant. Bette shivers. What a trail of broken hearts she has left.

"Flo, would you have some paper?" she asks.

Flo pauses her furious whipping of the eggs. "The writing type or the wrapping type?"

"The writing type, please. And an envelope, if possible. I want to write a letter."

Bette sees Wally opening the mailbox the way he does at the end of his shift. She always has a look first, especially since Aloysius' letters started coming, but she leaves the mail for him. It pleases him to bring it in, even if it's almost always bills. Tears fill her eyes imagining his relief at finding her letter there. She'll ask for his forgiveness. She'll wait for his reply, then she'll go home. This terrible mistake will be over.

"Nearest post office is Carbonear, but there's plenty who go that way every day. 'Course not today, being Christmas, or tomorrow. Maybe not 'til Wednesday." Flo's looking concerned. "You could put it in our boxes at the top of the hill here, but I like to take my mail right into Mrs. Best. She's the postmistress at Carbonear. Wednesday would be the earliest we could go. Would that be satisfactory?"

"It would be. Thank you."

For the first time in forty-five days Bette feels a ladybug's wing's fluttering of hope. The fluttering takes Bette halfway to a smile. Jo and Flo, both motionless and with their eyes fixed on her, take one another's hand. The room is so quiet they all hear the long, high, animal squeak of a burning log releasing moisture in the wood stove. Something flits across Bette's consciousness and punctures the silence: Trevor, bending to kiss her, his hand cradling the back of her head.

●

"It's like a place we went to in Scotland up there in the woods," Bette says. She takes off the rubber boots she's been borrowing from Flo through the winter and spring and hangs her coat on a hook by the door. She strips off a pair of thick grey socks that had belonged to Mr. Pretty.

"I can't imagine that, dear." Flo shakes her head. She nudges a plate of margarined porridge bread toward her. Butter is only for special occasions. "Sit."

Bette forces a smile at the plate. If Flo can't find a way to make Bette happy she'll at least fatten her up.

"It is. It's the stream. I found it. It reminds me of a time when we were little, in Scotland."

They'd been in Scotland on a summer holiday with their father and mother, just before the war. Bette was seven and Kat barely two. That Bette might remember much about the ten days they'd spent in a caravan near a sheepfold—on some distant cousin's country property not quite near enough to the coast to walk—would be questionable, but there was a photograph her mother loved. She had framed it and hung it on a nail by the kitchen light switch so that she could see it every time she said goodnight. Bette was quite right in her remembrance of a stocky gentleman in shirtsleeves and suspenders, a bushy black mustache lifting and falling as he bent over his camera, directing them *there* and *not there* in a Scottish accent. And the lecture he'd given her after the click of the shutter. In the photograph Bette's father wore a white shirt and a suit vest and no smile, though his feet were bare and his trousers rolled up. Her mother looked happy. The tow-headed baby already nicknamed Kat, sat on her lap in a plain dress, her head thrown back in a baby laugh. Bette, barefoot too, wore what looked like boys' dungarees and a sleeveless blouse. Her short dark hair was caught in a blurred swing that obscured most of her face as she turned to look at her father just as the camera clicked, the curve of her brown shoulder to the photographer. Behind them, the caravan, hardly big enough for the four of them, was tucked against a stone wall, and a little table sat blurred in the foreground. "Can we go again?" Bette had been turning to ask her father. She meant the cold stream that ran parallel to the stone wall in the meadow behind the caravan. They'd waded barefoot there, earlier, she and her father.

"Who's we?" Flo asks. "You said 'when we were little.'"

"My sister and me."

"You hadn't said you'd a sister, Bette."

"I do. I did, I mean."

"She's passed away then?"

Bette looks at the floor to avoid Flo's pitying eyes. She was racking up a tome of lies she'd have to remember she'd told. An orphan. No children. No husband, not anymore. And now a dead sister. "Yes. She's dead."

"How awful. She must have been young."

"She was." There is no point in making up some cause of death. She'd just have to remember that falsehood too.

"What was her name, dear?"

"Kat." Bette chokes. "Katherine." That, at least, was a truth that could be told.

It is late April now, and the snow is gone, even in the

puny trees up the hill across the highway and behind Halley's Cove. Bette found the stream that Jo Pretty had promised was there. It was barely a stream, a creek then a rivulet really, still bound on both sides by bits of glistening ice, and winding through the sparse trees to get lost in the rocks and lichen. She hadn't dared to take off her boots to feel the icy water, but she remembered the headache the stream in Scotland had given her and her father. She remembered too the feel of her father's hand holding hers as they waded until neither of them could stand the cold a moment longer.

Flo clicks her spoon a few times on the side of Bette's mug. "Eat."

Bette takes a piece of the bread and Flo passes the sticky molasses jug. This bread is their staple, and a holdout, since they might much more easily buy bread at the supermarket. Flo brings two bowls of tomato soup to the table and sits across from Bette.

"I'm sorry, Flo," Bette says for the twentieth time this week.

There is some relief in being able to say sorry now. After the letter from Wally came, sorrow sewed shut Bette's lips and she went to bed. She could neither thank Flo nor apologize for her silence. All of February and most of March, Flo had fed her. She changed her bedding every two weeks, tucking the sheets in tight like a hospital nurse would while Bette sat in a hardback chair beside the bed. She brought her a clean nightgown every Sunday and opened the curtains every morning to let the light in. Bette watched the ocean when it was visible and listened to it when it was not. She learned its mood from the tempo changes of its voice.

She knew that people came and went, staying for tea or, sometimes, supper. Once a week there'd be the clamour of a dozen or so women's voices, Flo's rug hooking group, laughing, clinking spoons in coffee mugs or tea cups, serving cake, then the sound of the door closing and Flo in conversation with one other woman, doing the dishes. Afterward, Flo would sit on the chair beside Bette's bed and tell her about the women: Harriet Moores' son had gone to work in the Alberta oil fields, and Flora Duff's cat gave birth to thirteen kittens. Jenny Marshall's son Samuel would be finished university soon. Sally Pike was in remission from cancer; she'd made her husband promise not to take her boys so far out to sea. Jean. Doris. Rose. Nell. Annie. Bette memorized the names.

Sometimes Flo went out and left Bette on her own in the house. Bette only knew she'd been listening for Flo's return when she heard, with relief, the click of the door latch. Jo telephoned once or twice but wouldn't come again until the summer, she said. A doctor came. Flo had called him. Her depression would come to an end, he said. It always does. Do you know the circumstances of her sorrow? he asked. Flo did not.

"Don't be silly, Bette. You don't need to thank me again. You know that I'm pleased to have you here and that you're welcome in our home as long as needs be."

As long as needs be has turned into forever. Bette looks at Flo across the table and wonders how anyone could be so generous. A perfect stranger, that's what Flo is. Two weeks. Twenty days. That's how long Bette imagined it would take for her letter to get to the other side of the country, and for Wally's letter to come back.

"If I could be so presumptuous," she'd said to Flo. "If I could stay for two weeks or twenty days, I'll cook and I'll clean."

"We'll each do our share," Flo'd said.

For twenty days, believing that she'd soon be on another long journey back to the West, Bette had taken off her armour and hauled wood, learned to bake porridge bread, shovelled snow, and washed dishes. The women of Halley's Cove brought their curiosity to the door, but Flo politely kept them from crossing the threshold when Bette was downstairs. When twenty days had passed, Bette again apologized for her presumptuousness. But Flo said something about desperation and presumption being strange bedfellows and that it was good to have someone else in the house since Jo was gone. "Stay until the winter's over," she'd said. "It'll be good for us both."

On January 26, a full thirty days after Bette mailed her letter, there came a reply. She wept with relief. Bette ripped the envelope open in the Carbonear post office while Flo waited in the car. But the words typed on the sheet of paper were for another kind of weeping. Above Wally's signature— as always his W—were the bitter words: *No. You've made your bed, now lie in it.*

Bette shakes salt into the soup until Flo gently touches her hand.

"It's canned," Flo says. "It's salty enough."

The soup warms her throat but she cannot taste it. Bette has tried to turn away from her own heartache to imagine only the grief of everyone she has hurt, but she might as well try separating the salt from a cake batter.

"What am I going to do, Flo?"

Bette knows Flo is somewhat at a disadvantage. She has not told Flo the "circumstances of her sorrow" but Flo has seen the silver wedding band she still wears. She might presume that Bette's husband was a man who beat her and left her no choice but to flee. No one, not even the most cynical of women, would imagine abandoning five children and a husband who was a prince.

"When my husband Cecil went to sea and never came back, I thought I would die." Flo says. "But I guess sorrow doesn't kill you. For a while I wished it did. One foot in front of the other, Bette. That's how it's done."

They finish their soup in silence. The angle of the sun has changed since Bette's first days in Halley's Cove. Now, at lunchtime, it slants across the table making the cutlery shine. Flo picks her knife up and plays with the reflection until it shines in Bette's eyes.

Bette laughs despite herself.

"We'll find you something to do, Mrs. Tallis."

Sally and Moses Pike's oldest boys had been there in Flo's kitchen with the rest of them a minute ago; now they're out on the porch. Harold and Boyd had lit up cigarettes in the kitchen and their father sent them outside.

"Think of your mother, for God's sake," Moses said.

But he doesn't tell them to butt the cigarettes out, Bette notices.

Bette has already cut Aiden, Boyd, and Harold's hair. They're like all the boys in 1968, wanting to grow their hair long, but their father Moses won't have it. He'd have them all in brush cuts if it were up to him, but the boys are fourteen, sixteen, and eighteen. Nearly too old to boss around.

Sally pulls on one of the curls at the nape of her husband's neck. "This is worryingly long, Mo," she teases. "Bette, the scissors. Quick."

Sally doesn't look so well. She's over her cancer, but she's wan. And she hasn't asked for a haircut or taken off her toque even though it's August.

"Up we go, Jimmy." Sally lifts their baby up and puts him into the highchair Flo has hauled out of a shed and cleaned up for Bette's Beauty Parlour, as Flo calls it. The wooden chair is as old as Jo, if the peeling decals are any indication. Bette gave her own boys their first haircuts at Jimmy's age, but Jimmy isn't keen on any of this and he's bucking the way only a two-year-old will.

"Let's put him down and try another way," Bette says. She touches Jimmy's curly hair and an ache flows through her.

"No. He'll manage. Jimmy, sit still," Moses says. "Our little mistake gets away with everything."

"Mo, let him be." Sally picks Jimmy up and kisses him, then she pushes Moses down on another kitchen chair. "He's all yours, Bette. Shave it off it you want to." Sally carries Jimmy out on the porch and they hear her shouting at Aiden, the fourteen-year-old, to "put that damn cigarette out."

"Where you from, Bette?" Moses asks. He's looking at her with interest, the way a man appraises a woman.

Bette's hands are trembling as she wraps the white sheet she's using as a hairdressing cape around Moses' shoulders. She clips the cape closed with a clothes peg.

"I'm from England."

"What part?"

Bette should have her story down pat by now. She has met nearly everyone in Halley's Cove and some of the essential folk of Harbour Grace and Carbonear—the postmistress, the man who sells fish at the wharf, the owners of the dry goods store, the pharmacist, the undertaker, and a few others. She's already met Sally Pike—she comes rug hooking—but not Moses or her boys, until today. Everyone has heard Bette's story: She's from London. She's a hairdresser. No, she has no family there. And none here. Why Newfoundland? She always gives a shrug: it was closest.

"London," Bette says.

"Big city girl, then." Moses is twisting around to look at her that way again. "Can't imagine why you'd come to a place like this."

Bette straightens his shoulders and snips a lock of hair close to his ear. Shut up, she thinks.

"London was too big for me, I guess. I like the smallness of Halley's Cove. It suits me now."

"Give me the chance and I'd be out of here in a minute." Moses' tone has changed.

Bette is not sure what it is about having someone with a sharp instrument near one's ears that makes people want to reveal their deepest feelings, but she's heard slightly more than she'd like to know from many of the residents of Halley's Cove.

"I hate fishing. I do it because my dad did it. I want my boys to leave here. Harold's finished school, but he doesn't have the guts to go somewhere else. Wants to fish like his dad, he says. I told him that's because it's all he knows."

Normally, Bette knows when to keep quiet. "Maybe he feels at home here. Maybe if you took them—"

Moses interrupts. "I took them all to Town a couple of times. Didn't make any impression on them. And Boyd's gonna follow in his brother's footsteps. Boyd doesn't even want to finish school. What Harry does, Boyd does. Told him he's going to graduate if I have to take him to school myself. Aiden's my real hope. Aiden and the little mistake, Jimmy. Those two are not going to sea." He says it like Bette's insisting they will.

"I can imagine how you worry about the boys."

Moses grunts as if to say, no, you cannot imagine. Bette pushes the hair at the back of his neck up. His hairline is low. She'll have to buy some clippers if she's going to continue cutting hair. She keeps her scissors away from Moses' head while he's agitated. When he settles, slumping a little in the chair, she puts her hand on his shoulder. It's her signal—sit still—but he's still brewing under the sheet cape.

"Sally, get Jimmy in here," he shouts, suddenly standing up.

Bette jumps back with the scissors and Sally comes in with the little boy in her arms.

"He's gettin' his hair cut now. School next week."

"Aye, aye, Captain Bligh."

Moses is not smiling. "He's not a baby anymore, Sal. You'll turn him into a little sissy."

"Did you leave your funny bone at the laundry mat, Mo? Jimmy's not starting school. You'd remember he's only two if you got out your calendar. Now sit down and let Bette finish your haircut unless you like being lopsided."

"You should get a mirror, Bette." Moses sits back down.

"She doesn't need a mirror. She's starting at the Hall next week taking care of the kids now that Martha's run off with the Sally Ann man. Aren't you, Bette?"

Bette nods. Martha is the thirty-year-old daughter of the neighbours, Levi and Pearl Walsh. Martha announced two weeks earlier that she'd be marrying Major Roger Whelan of the Salvation Army and would be moving to North Sydney, Nova Scotia. This came as a shock to everyone not only because Martha had, for fifteen years, since she was fifteen herself, taken care of the children of Halley's Cove, but also because the Walshs were Pentacostals. Someone said Martha probably liked the idea of being a Major too. Except for a few women and old men in the village, everyone made their living by the sea: the men on it and the women at the plant down the shore, processing and canning whatever was in season. And that left a handful of children needing to be taken care of before they were old enough to attend school and a bunch who still needed a few hours of care between the time the yellow school bus came down the hill at three and their mothers got home from the plant.

"Looking forward to that, Bette?" Moses asks. "You know you'll likely get paid in cod's tongues and crab. You'll be lucky if you get some cans of Klik. Those folks haven't got a red cent to rub between their fingers."

"Those folks? You're not counting yourself among those folks, then?" Sally asks. "She'll be taking care of Jimmy too, you know. Hope you plan on paying her with more than an ugly old fish."

1977

Your daddy's a sailor who never comes home.

RON HYNES, "Sonny's Dream," *Face to the Gale*

Bette pushes hard on the pharmacy door. It has always been annoyingly sticky. This is her last errand and she's rushing. Flo is waiting at the snack bar. She just needs some aspirin for a tooth that's bothering her and then she and Flo can have their Saturday afternoon coffees and shared piece of pie. Mrs. Peddle is her slowpoke self, bagging the aspirin packet and handing Bette her change so slowly Bette can't help but wonder how the Peddles survive.

Flo's got the window table. She gives a wave, as if Bette might otherwise have walked on by. Bette laughs. The big piece of apple pie has been cut in two, patiently awaiting Bette's arrival.

"Been waiting long?" Bette asks. Her coffee, already on the table, is lukewarm.

"Just a few minutes. Moses Pike was just here," Flo says. "Said he's got a salmon for us. He'll bring it by later." Flo forks a piece of pie into in her mouth. "Heesh never ooked quite the shame shince she died, has he?"

"What?"

"Moshes." Flo swallows. "He's never looked the same since Sally died."

"True enough."

Flo nudges Bette's share of the pie over toward her with her fork. Neither of them bakes much anymore, so this coffee break on their weekly grocery shop in Carbonear is Flo's excuse for something sweet.

Flo looks past Bette as the bell above the door clangs. "Never seen him before," she says.

"You don't know everybody, Florence Pretty."

"Used to," Flo says. "He's chatting up the girl. Definitely not a local. Look."

"You're just trying to get my pie, aren't you?" Bette smiles at Flo and steals a look over her shoulder at the man leaning on the counter by the cash register. She can only see the back of him, but Flo's right, he is definitely not from around here. He's wearing dirty patched jeans and a black leather jacket and has put his motorcycle helmet on the counter. His hair is held back in a loose ponytail. He taps the helmet with a long index finger. Then he turns to smile at the other young waitress and Bette sees him in profile. She turns quickly, shivering. "The shadow of an owl flying over my grave," her mother used to say. It was the smile. It was as familiar as her own.

"From the look on that girl's face you'd think she was gazing into the eyes of Paul Newman." Flo gives a play by play. "Buying cigarettes, now. Export Plain looks like. Another tap tap on the helmet. Asking her to go for a ride probably." Flo picks up the last bite of the pie. "You don't want this?"

Bette shakes her head.

"Later, gator," she hears the man say and the bell on the door clangs again. In a second he's passing the window, his back to Bette. His motorcycle is across the road, half a block down. He leans against it, crossing his ankles, lights a cigarette, and gazes one way, then the other, along the street. He doesn't look like he's in any hurry.

"Let's go home, Flo."

Flo licks her untroubled fingers and rattles her car keys. "Your wish is my command."

●

Bette and Flo will be having salmon for supper and they'll have it for supper tomorrow too. Moses Pike dropped off the huge silvery creature half an hour ago and now Bette and Flo are out back and Flo's scaling and gutting the fish on the plank she's laid across two sawhorses. The shimmering scales fly up as Flo draws the kitchen knife against the grain. Bette feels, as she always does, an animal twinge in her own abdomen as Flo slits the fish from stern to stem. Flo pulls out the bits and pieces of dark red gut. Bette has never forgotten her first lesson in fish cleaning and anatomy; it left her nauseated. Flo, oblivious to Bette's queasiness, had pulled the guts out onto a newspaper, poking at each with the tip of her knife—liver, gall bladder, swim bladder, milt sac, digestive system, kidney. "Just one kidney," Flo'd said. "Heart. Just one of those too," she'd laughed. Bette has never told Flo how it makes her feel to hear the soft fish entrails hitting the galvanized bucket, nor how tipping the guts out of the pail off the wharf into the ocean makes her want to vomit. Bette wonders why she's not used to this yet, after ten years in Halley's Cove.

"Poor Moses. You've got to know, he and Sally have been sweethearts since they were fifteen," Flo says, as if Sally were still walking among the living. "I could never grasp why she tolerates, tolerated, his grouchiness, but Sally was your common duck. She just let it all slide off. Quite a handy habit, when you think of it." She is weighing what might be the salmon's liver in her hand. "Look at that, will you? I've never seen one so big." She tosses the organ into the bucket. "Besides, he's not got so much of that old sternness these days. Death changes you."

Bette looks away. At Sally Pike's funeral last year at the United Church, everyone stood to say something about her. It seemed there wasn't a soul in Halley's Cove who hadn't been babysat by her, rubbed elbows with her at the fish plant, stolen a dance with her on New Year's Eve, hooked mats beside her, sung with her at church, or wished he'd married her. When Moses stood to speak he called her his light. He looked grey, like a man who loved and relied on his wife does when his light has gone out. In the year since, he hasn't taken on much more colour.

"He's a lobsterman," says Bette. "What's he doing with a salmon?"

"Oh, if he's bringing home a salmon he's got a license. He's no lawbreaker, Moses. His dad used to take him salmon fishing up on Bonavista once a year. Fly fishing. God knows where he caught this one."

"You'd think they'd have enough of fishing."

"You would." Flo cuts four thick orange filets and holds them out to Bette who has a dinner plate in her hands. That's the extent of her role in the fish cleaning, that and tipping the guts. "But it isn't the same thing, fly fishing in a river and being on the sea."

"Fish is fish, no?"

"No. Fish is not fish." Flo hesitates, looking into the distance, letting her gory knife float in small circles in the air. "Same as babies is not babies. Each one's different. How we get them, the fish I mean, not the babies. But babies too, I guess. Ha. That's what makes the difference. Some people don't have to try very hard to taste the difference between one caught for the joy of it and, well, the other. I think it's in the experience, Bette. You know what I mean?"

Bette nods even though her memories of tasting joy are like the traces of chalk on an erased blackboard. There's more of the flat than the jagged in her life now—time, and being with Flo has given her that—but joy, no. When Flo watches TV she laughs like a jackal, wiping tears from her face, and sometimes clutching her chest as if she might have a heart attack if it gets any funnier, but Bette can't see the comedy in it. In fact, she finds it difficult to believe that anyone in the village or anywhere in Newfoundland, for that matter, can be happy. Life is too hard. The men are always setting off in any kind of weather in their own boats, or on the company trawlers, vulnerable dots on the massive, dark, unpredictable ocean. She's watched, season after season, as the lobster boats, overloaded with their wooden traps, churn out, the need to put bread on the table making captains and crew heedless of the weather. There are some who go out in dories too, the life jackets, if any, lying like debris on the floor of the boats. They've all lost someone. The women at the plant still have to process the fish each boat brings in, even if one comes back minus a husband, a son, a brother, a father.

"I don't think I'd be able to taste the difference," Bette says to the plate of fish.

"Oh, you would." Flo hands her the pail then ties a piece of turquoise rope to the handle using a professional-looking knot, the kind Wally would have tied. "If it was you doing it. The fishing, I mean." She rests the non-fishy back of her wrist on Bette's shoulder for a second and scrutinizes her face. "Bring back a bucket of water, will you, and I'll clean up this mess. You all right?"

Bette stares down at the rope and the guts. A memory of Wally in his Scout uniform shimmers weakly. She can't remember when she gave up for good. If Wally had replied to her second letter, she would have gone, shame-faced, but gone. But it came back with "Unknown at this address" marked on it. A third letter was never returned. And then a year had passed, then three, and seven. And now it has been ten. During her first years in Halley's Cove, Bette allowed the lions of despair to tear her to pieces, a searing gash for each thought: Lulu becoming a teenager, Geordie missing his mother, the boys old enough to leave home. Birthdays. But she has mastered the art of dissociation now, and sharp memories are quickly dulled. Not even in the unconscious realm does she dream anymore of a family that has forgiven her, of children who would still know or long for her, of parents who would understand. She long ago decided she would live out the rest of her years on this hand of land reaching out into the Atlantic.

Though the sturdy wharf has weathered forty winters or more, she has never trusted the way it slopes and how some of the thick timbers teeter-totter lightly when she walks on them. She smells the wharf's coat of creosote and the sea-weed rotting where the spring storms have tossed it high on the rocks along the shore. The shrilling gulls arrive, as always, before she gets to the end of the wharf. She'd rather just put the bucket down and let the gulls dive in for the bits they find so tasty—she's done that before, and is about to, but with a start she sees that Tuck and Bryan Snow are tinkering on the *Jenny Rose*.

Tuck's like a lot of the kids she cared for at the Hall. The day he turned ten, his father, Bryan, told Bette that Tuck was old enough to stay home on his own and take care of his little brother, Conrad. Flo said it was because they didn't have enough money to pay for babysitting. So what was Bette to do about it? She takes good care of the children at the Hall. Cuts, scrapes, tumbles, and fisticuffs, these are sufficiently

administered to. Their personal lives, their parents' woes—
she has made it clear that none of that is her business. They
must like her well enough; in ten years no one has tried to
take her job. And they keep having children and bringing her
new ones. But Bette's never offered any more affection to the
children than strictly necessary. Except for Jimmy Pike.

Jimmy took to Bette when he was still a baby, toddling
around the Hall sucking his thumb and never letting her out
of his sight. Sally didn't like to leave him with their older boys
when Moses took her to St. John's for her chemo appoint-
ments, so Jimmy stayed with Flo and Bette. No matter where
they'd put him at night, he'd climb out of his bed and Bette
would wake to find him standing silently beside hers, waiting
for her to take him in her arms and rock him to sleep, his
thumb in his mouth and the other hand curled in her hair.
Inch by inch he claimed her, seeking and finding her, as if at
the age of three he knew her past and their future.

Bette stands at the end of the wharf with her bucket,
wavering. The gulls are screaming above her, diving close
enough for her to feel the draft of their wings. She can feel
their warmth and smell their wet feathers. Then the bucket is
being taken out of her hands. Tuck stands too perilously close
to the edge of the wharf and with a long, graceful swing tosses
the bucket's contents into the air. While the fish guts are still
flying out over the water, the gulls catch them, mid-air.

"Thank you, Tuck."

"Uh huh." Holding the turquoise rope, he lets the bucket
splash down into the water then draws it up again full of
cold, briny water and a swatch of seaweed. Tuck picks the
seaweed out and tosses it. A gull swoops for that too, but lets
it drop, instantly aware that it isn't food. The bucket's too full

for Bette to carry, but she doesn't want to pour any out in front of Tuck. She picks it up with two hands on the handle and lurches stiffly back up the wharf, dragging the rope and sloshing water in her shoes and on her pants as she goes. Eventually, enough slops out that she can carry it without looking like the Tin Man.

Flo is standing out in the backyard and Moses Pike has returned. He's sitting on the porch railing, looking for all the world like a nervous teenaged boy.

"Good Lord, Bette. Get inside and change out of those wet clothes," Flo laughs when she sees her, then raises her eyebrows and swivels her eyes to impart some private message.

Moses slips quickly off the railing and takes the bucket from Bette's hands then Flo takes it from his. Flo's not much bigger than Bette, but she's got the strength of an ox. She folds up the fishy newspaper then sloshes the water on the makeshift cleaning table. Bette knows she has already cut up the rest of the salmon, packed it in plastic bags, and popped it in the big chest freezer for more suppers down the road.

"I'll just be a minute," Bette says.

She slips off her wet shoes and socks at the door and goes up to her room to get a dry pair of pants. The saltwater on her jeans needs a washing out or it will leave a stiff white mark. And so do her legs, which are rimed with salt. From the bathroom window she can see Moses and Flo still chatting out back. She runs a little water in the bathtub and steps in. She sloshes the water up over her shins and calves. She can't remember the last time she shaved her legs, nor the last time she thought about shaving them. Standing in her underpants in the tub, she leans to tuck the curtain back to get a better view of Moses and Flo. It's not clear to Bette why he is still here. Or even why he came in the first place. Moses has only ever come over to drop Jimmy off or to get his or the boys' hair cut. There's always lobster, in season, but this is the first salmon he's dropped by. She steps out of the tub and while she is bending to dry her legs she realizes with a flood of fear that that's what Flo is swiveling her eyes about: Moses is here for her. She snaps the curtain back into place. She lets the warm water fill the sink and mechanically rinses out the bottom half of her pant legs. She scrubs and scrubs until they could not be cleaner. She pulls the curtain back just enough to peek outside. Flo's disappeared but Moses is still there, splitting kindling, as if Jimmy hadn't already split enough for them, and it's June, for heaven's sake.

"Jesus," she says aloud. "It can't be."

A whisper from the doorway, "Bette? Are you coming down?"

Bette jumps. Flo's at the open bathroom door and Bette's still in her underpants. Bette knows Flo doesn't care—the Prettys wander around in their underwear without a care in the world—but with Moses downstairs and the way Flo has just whispered her question, as if he could hear, Bette might as well be as naked as a jaybird.

"I'm making tea. I'll be out in a minute with it." Flo's still whispering.

"Tea?"

Flo nods and Bette's panic swells. Tea in Flo's backyard is unheard of. It isn't done.

"Go down. Go down," Flo says, and flutters her hand at Bette. "He's waiting for you."

By the time Bette steps outside she has already started

to mentally pack her bags. Moses leans the axe up against the wall. He dusts off his hands, and, never looking at Bette, picks up the kindling he's chopped and places it in the box at the end of the cord. Bette's decided she's not going to say anything until he does. She's seething: men and their wants and needs. His wife's still fresh in her grave at the top of the hill, the boys are still mourning, Jimmy's getting himself into all sorts of trouble at school, and here's Moses already rooting around for a new nipple. Bette sits on the chopping block, heedless of the splinters and sawdust.

It's quiet until Moses says, "I was down at the post office today." Bette stares. What could be so important about being at the post office that he'd make it an announcement? "I just mention it," he says, "because there was a young man there asking after a Bette Parsons."

The gulls stop in mid-flight and Moses' words come from inside a drum, hollow and not synced with the movement of his lips.

"One of those hippie types, in a leather jacket and a stupid ponytail. 'Lots of Parsons around here,' Mrs. Best says, 'but the only Bette I know isn't one.' The young fella says something like 'Well, what's the name of the Bette you do know?' and Mrs. Best says, 'No name you would know.' 'Kind of an unusual name though, Bette, isn't it?' says the fella, with a smile at me, mind you. 'Not really,' she says, then she gives him one of her looks and asks him if he has any post office business. He says no so she says, 'Next in line,' which was me. Said to me afterward that she wasn't going to tell anyone looking like that about any of her customers."

Bette sits perfectly still.

"I saw him later too. Loading his motorcycle up a ramp into his eighteen-wheeler, up on the main road. I gave him a hand."

"Did you?" she manages.

"Yeah. I told him I knew someone named Bette a long time ago, but she's gone. Said I didn't know where." He pauses and looks at Bette with an intensity that frightens her. "Was that the right thing to do?"

From inside Flo calls, "Door?"

Moses beats Bette to it, and Flo comes out with a tray of tea and her famous lemon pound cake. Moses takes the tray and looks for a place to put it, his eyes roaming from the fishy sawhorses to a bottomed-out deck chair. Bette rises, and though Moses places the tray carefully on the tilted chopping block, the teapot pours itself onto the plate of pound cake.

"Dammit," he says.

There's a lot of fussing as Bette rescues the cake, Moses levels the tray, and Flo slips a piece of kindling underneath it until everything's smooth again.

Flo's surveying the damage to the cake but Moses says, "I'd eat your lemon pound cake even if it was drenched in saltwater, Flo," and he slides a soggy slice onto a plate and eats it with his rough fisherman fingers.

Bette is out of her body, watching from a few feet above as Flo struggles to make all the conversation. Something seems to have eaten Moses' usually cocky and long-winded tongue.

"How're the boys doing?" Flo asks.

"Fine."

"Aiden's leg's better?"

"Yup. Walking again."

"Bad break, that."

"Bad break."

"How's the catch?"

"Not too bad. Good enough."

"He's out on the lobster boat with you now."

"Yup. Town wasn't for him, I guess."

"Jimmy's been saying he wants to fish with you too."

That animates Moses. "Jimmy? Never. Jimmy's gonna do something different if I have to drag him to it and stake him down myself. Doctor, mechanic, circus dog trainer—it doesn't matter. Jimmy's never going to sea. I promised."

Bette remembers Moses saying that Aiden would never go to sea. He'd promised Sally that too. While Flo and Moses move on to the weather, Bette catalogues her possessions. She has accumulated a few things in the past ten years, but nothing she couldn't do without. She won't take much. Some clothes. A coat. Boots.

"Gale force winds tomorrow, I hear," Flo is saying.

Moses grunts, much more like his usual self. "The weatherman doesn't know his arse from his elbow," he says, and he grins at Bette.

●

The wind, which came suddenly and violently and brought with it rain, finally drove Moses home. Flo and Bette have slammed all the windows shut and filled the bathtub with water in case the power goes out. The candles and matches are on the counter, ready. This wild June rain is slashing against the windows and the house is shaking and whistling the way it only does when the wind is this fierce. Though it was warm enough to eat lemon pound cake outside a few hours ago, the temperature has dropped and the wood stove has been lit.

Flo has fried the salmon and stirred the boiled potatoes into the same pan after the fish is out, to give them the glossy coating she loves. Frozen peas too. She hands a plate to Bette. There's a single fish scale stuck to the side of Flo's cheek. Bette wonders why Flo hasn't noticed it and longs to peel it off. It is distracting her.

"Some would say it's too soon, of course." Flo says. "Harriet says he hasn't yet emptied the cupboard of her clothes."

Flo goes on. Bette has heard all this before, from more than one source: Harriet's granddaughter, Misty, had been helping out up at the Pike house before Sally died. Last month, Moses let her go. He can't really afford Misty. His housekeeping standards are lower than Sally's were, anyway. That's what Moses told Misty, who told Harriet, who told Flo.

"That's the part that's hard. I remember the day I gave Cecil's things away. I called up the Salvation Army. They take pretty much everything, you know. I started packing as soon as Jo was off to school in the morning. I was folding everything up tidy. I got through the pants and shirts and undershirts. That was all right. But it's the little things that wrench you. The tie he wore to our wedding. His eyeglasses. His wallet. What in heaven's name do you do with those?"

Bette is trying to remember where she put the rucksack she arrived with. In a drawer somewhere, in her room. Or the cupboard.

"The worst was his eyeglasses." Flo takes Bette's plate. Bette's still holding her fork. Flo plucks it from her hand. "The thought of his eyes looking through them every day." She pauses and Bette looks up and watches, expressionless, as Flo collects herself. "Anyways, maybe it's a bit too soon for someone new for Moses?"

Bette flushes. The way Flo tends to her—like a plant that if watered will eventually bloom. She knows she'll disappoint her. She has nothing more to offer. Only May Ogg was as devoted to Bette, but even May Ogg would have long ago left Bette for dead.

"Forever is too soon for me," Bette says.

"Bette." Flo drags out the word with more pity than Bette can bear, as if any amount of pity isn't too much. "You've been on your own for too long. You're only forty-six. It's time to think about a little happiness for yourself."

"You should talk," Bette snaps, "the old spinster."

Flo turns to the sink taking her shock with her. She rinses the dishes then washes them, and even takes up the tea towel to dry them before she turns back to look at Bette. She has a smile on her face, as if smiling will erase Bette's insult.

"Will you never give up on me, Flo? Will you never just say you've had bloody enough and tell me to go? For God's sake, you're ruining your life waiting for me to be happy. And ruining mine too with your hopes. I wouldn't get involved with Moses Pike if my life depended on it. You're just sitting around here waiting for something good to happen. As if. You even think Jo's going to get married. Can't you see? She's never going to, Flo. She's—"

"Don't say it, Bette." Flo's tone is low and angry.

Bette stops herself but she's as angry as Flo. She feels a cheerless shimmer of satisfaction at seeing the eternally positive Flo riled.

"I am not going to be happy the way you want me to, Flo. Ever. Do you hear? Stop expecting it. Stop hoping. I am sick and tired of feeling that I will always be a disappointment to you."

"And I am sick and tired of watching you brood around here like some character from *Wuthering Heights*. Don't arch your eyebrows at me. I've read it. I don't know what the hell happened to you, Bette, but there are other people in this world who have suffered too. Stop thinking of yourself as so special."

"Special? That is the last thing I would call myself."

"Well, then open your frozen heart to the rest of the suffering world. God knows, maybe you'll discover you're not alone. You act as if this is the permanent winter of your life. Ten years is long enough." Flo says this with a cold, even calm that makes Bette feel like she's been hit.

Flo finishes drying the dishes and puts them away. Bette doesn't move. Finally Flo looks at her with her unwavering grey eyes and says, "There isn't any dessert."

It could not be a more bleak dismissal. Bette gets up from the table and mounts the stairs to her bedroom. She finds her small rucksack on the top shelf in the closet where it has been for ten years. She slams underwear, sweaters, blouses, pants, socks, a nightie into it. The money she has saved is in an old tobacco can under the bed. She pushes the can into the bag without counting the money. She knows how much she has: enough. Tomorrow she'll ask someone to take her into town where she can catch a bus. She'll go early, before Flo wakes. She'll wait on the road for someone to pass. Ernie and Flora Duff, or the Marshalls on their way to church. They'll take her away from this godforsaken place.

Bette drops onto the bed. The energy of her anger has left

her. She looks down at her bedside mat, feeling its soft nap with her bare feet. Flo hooked it for her. A birthday present years ago. Bette traces the map of Newfoundland on it with her big toe. The land is green and the ocean is blue. There's a brown moose in one corner, and a jumping fish in another. She is afraid; that is the only reason for her unkindness. Bette lies down and draws the quilt Flo made up and bites it with her wretched mouth. The young man in the post office and the snack bar. She knows who he is. She knew when she saw him. The memory of his smile seizes Bette's heart. It was Trevor.

●

She wakes and looks at the clock. It is only eleven p.m. There is a light on downstairs. Bette stands at the top of the stairs for a minute or two, and then goes down. Flo is sitting in the parlour, a single lamp lit in the corner. Bette has never seen Flo with nothing in her hands. Flo knits, and hooks, and crochets, and reads, but now she is sitting in the chair with empty hands, examining them as if checking for new signs of aging. When she looks up there's a sorrow in Flo's eyes that breaks Bette's heart. Bette goes to her and takes her hand and Flo's hand curls warmly around hers. She kneels in front of Flo and rests her forehead on Flo's knees.

"I am so sorry, Flo."

Flo squeezes her hand gently. "I know," she says.

"I don't know what makes me so cruel." Bette begins to cry.

"Shhh." Flo strokes her hair. "Shhh. It's over now. I'm sorry too."

Bette eventually calms and in the silence she knows that the wind has come up again, and the fierce rain that slammed against the windows before suppertime is back.

"I know about Jo," Flo says.

Bette stays very still beneath Flo's hands.

"I guess I have always known, since she was a teenager. She never liked boys. She always said she had to get out of the Cove. I was so angry when she left. The fish plant had done for me all my life, I told her. What was a single girl leaving home for? God, when I think what I said. I thought it had to do with her growing up fatherless. I hadn't been a good enough mother. I hadn't set a good example. In my bones I knew why she hardly ever came home, Bette, but I couldn't accept it. She needed me to just love her as she is, and I didn't."

Bette lifts her head. "Jo knows you love her."

"I do. I do. It's not natural, what Jo is, but I love her."

Bette lies awake in the dark room, listening to the howling wind. It is over. She will leave in the morning. All her secrets have been confessed. She has told her dismal story. Flo was silent while Bette spoke. She said she understood. But when she stood to say goodnight, she looked wary, as though the person she'd lived with for ten years had just admitted to a crime worse than infanticide. "What's your real name," Flo had asked, coolly. Bette's body aches with her reawakened shame. She checks the clock again. It is only two a.m.

A flash of headlights glides across the curtains. Bette sits up quickly. It's a strange time for a car to pass. Surely no one would be going down to the wharf in this weather. There's a quiet knock on her door and Flo comes in carrying a candle.

"Something's wrong," Flo says and puts her hand on Bette's shoulder. "I'm going out. Will you come with me, Bette Parsons? I don't want to be alone."

Bette follows Flo down the stairs in the flickering candle-light. Outside, the wind whips their slickers open and yanks at their hair. They are soaked in seconds. The beams of their flashlights illuminate the rain bouncing violently off the pavement. They hold on to each other as they make their way toward the wharf where half a dozen cars are parked, headlights shining out to sea. In front of the cars Bette can make out a crowd of people huddled together. She checks to see that the boats are all in.

"Please," she says aloud, counting the boats. They're in. It can't be that. But it is. The *Sally Once* is gone.

"It's Pike," Bryan Snow shouts into the wind at Bette and Flo. "He went out."

"Not with the boys?" Flo cries.

"With every goddamn one of them. There was that lull around eight last night and the damn fool went out. He said the worst was over. Said they'd just secure the traps while the wind was down. He called Ernie Duff to come along. Duff told him he was an idiot, so he said he'd take the boys and they'd be done quick. And then it came up again, the wind."

"Not the little one? Not Jimmy too?"

"Far as I know, yes."

"We called Rescue. They haven't heard a word from Pike."

"They'd have survival suits at least." Bette has to shout over the wind. She catches sight of Harold's wife and Boyd's girlfriend, clinging to each other.

Ernie Duff puts his wet hand on Bette's shoulder and she understands. They are gone.

There is nothing to do until dawn comes and the rain and wind abates. When it does, three boats untie and head out in the chop on the cove with all the men onboard. They don't have to go far. The women, who wait by Bryan Snow's boat, hear the news over *Jenny Rose*'s radio. They've found the *Sally Once* capsized half a nautical mile from the wharf. "She's on her side. No sign of Moses or the boys." As the day grows brighter, the women on shore can see the three boats with their bare eyes from the wharf. *Sally Once*'s pretty yellow hull is tossing in the waves between them like a sea bauble. Bette imagines Moses and the boys deep under the grey sea, their bodies dancing a ballet in the currents, eyes open, their hair waving like pickleweed. Breathing water. She prays they are together.

The Pike house overlooks Halley's Cove. The sky to the west, behind it, has broken into pinks and blues with long striated clouds in whites and greys. Dawn. If Moses had waited for dawn he and his boys would be alive. Bette starts running up the hill toward the Pikes' house. Rocks, caught in the torrents gushing down either side of the road are smashing against one another making hollow knocking sounds. Breathless, Bette's fury at Moses carries her to the top of the hill.

She pushes the front door open but stops in the hall. The house is silent and the hall hollow. She feels for a light switch and finds one, but the power is still out. The bedrooms are upstairs. The narrow wooden stairs creak as she climbs them holding the railing with one hand and sliding the other along the wall in the dim light. The bed in the room at the top of the stairs is unmade and there are jeans and shirts and socks scattered everywhere. Bette inhales the familiar boy scent. The next room must be Moses'. Folded up on one of the pillows is the pink sweater with lime green cuffs that Sally used to wear. Bette rushes to the last room in the hallway and stops.

Jimmy, dear gorgeous Jimmy, is lying there like an angel dropped from Heaven in blue hockey pyjamas and grey woolen socks, his blankets drifting drunkenly off the bed.

NEARLY NOW, TOO

I won't let go of your beating breast
'Til the world decides that it's time I rest.

OH SUSANNA, "The One," *Oh Susanna*

She had been feeling peevish. It was the only word for it. Later, even before she knew the worst had happened, she was angry again, at herself, for having felt that way when he might never hear her apology. She'd been standing in the barn doorway, arms crossed, her fingers kneading her biceps as she had a habit of doing. She was watching Jimmy's strong hands as he milked Sweetie, his head dark against the goat's tan haunch. The only blessing was that Jimmy seemed not to have heard her. He'd turned to her, smiled, and said, "Mum, come in, come in."

What she had said had been quite simple: "Why can't you ever remember to bring the compost bucket in when you're done with it?" Her tone was as snarly as she was peevish and she had repeated it twice, as if this minor sin of his could actually be the ruin of her day. But that's what he'd said: "Mum, come in, come in," and he'd smiled—the same beautiful, toothy smile he'd had as a boy—and then Bette thought he was going to stand because his body moved up a little from the stool, against the tethered goat who bleated in annoyance and shifted out of his way as best she could because Jimmy was falling into the straw beneath her.

●

Bette had knelt down by Jimmy in the barn, cradling his dearly loved head. His face was odd, his mouth drooping sideways. "Jimmy," she'd cried, and the goats nuzzled her shoulders and gathered round like sisters, looking down on him. She could think of nothing but that she must get to the telephone, that all she had to say into the receiver was "Jimmy Pike" and the volunteer firemen and first responders would know where to come. But she wouldn't leave Jimmy alone in the straw. His face had suddenly paled, and then she had screamed. The neighbour girl, young Ruby Clarke, out gathering wildflowers, heard.

They drove Jimmy over the potholed roads to the hospital in Carbonear, his unseeing eyes blinking open with every bump. Then they sent him in another ambulance to St. John's, while time's grains of sand stalled in the hourglass. There he lay, the nurses coming in every hour or so to check his bags of saline or plasma or God knows what, as devoid of sentiment and worry as they would be were Jimmy just a loaf of bread dough they had put in a warm spot to rise. What these casual people didn't understand was that he was Bette's loaf. Bette's crusty brown loaf, her whole wheat, her leavening agent, her soda, her sugar. Her salt.

"Are you his mother?" someone asked.

"I am," Bette said.

Jimmy's cousin Brody came and went, sitting in a hard metal chair, his big hand holding his cousin's. Brody's daughter Juliette brought flowers and a crocheted blanket, which she tucked up to his chin talking all the while as if he could hear her.

"You'll be fine, Jimmy. You'll be right as rain in no time. Your mom here needs you, you know," she said.

Flo came. "Jessie Smith's milking and tending the goats, Bette. And she'll keep the shop open, so you needn't worry about that. Everyone says hello and says for Jimmy to get well soon. And I've got the dogs," she said, "but they're pining for you both. And Bette, you should see, a spider has built the most beautiful web across the top of your compost bucket."

Bette told Jimmy everything. It had taken days. Jimmy didn't respond, though she prayed he might, that he might open his eyes and say, "Mum, it's all right." Or squeeze her hand, forgiving her. She told him quietly. She whispered. She wept silent tears for how long she had kept her secret, for the shame of it. She paced the perimeter of his bed on soft-soled shoes. Sometimes she slept lightly in the big chair they put out for her, the white curtains drawn around the bed, her body suddenly feeling its seventy-six years.

She'd begun formally: "Jimmy, my sweet boy, I have something to tell you."

He didn't take a deeper breath when she said, "I have . . . I had, five children." He didn't open one eye to scrutinize her when she said, "I left them." He didn't sigh when she told him their names—"Geordie, Ambrose, Alan, Trevor, Louise." He didn't laugh when she said they called Louise Lulu, almost from birth, or raise an eyebrow when she said, "My husband's name was Wally." But how she wanted him to. If only he would sigh, cry, scowl, do anything but breathe steadily and flicker blind brown eyes behind his half-open lids. If only he could have asked the question that had tormented her days and nights until it became some precious frayed cloth put away in a drawer, a shore scraped smooth by a savage ocean: *Why?* Or worse: *How?*

"November was miserable," she'd told Jimmy's still body. She crumpled and smoothed the edges of Jimmy's blanket, wondering, for the first time, if anything would have been different had it happened in sunny August, as if she might blame a month for her misery. It had been bleak and cold and raining without cease, the skies grey, never blue, and no other colour anywhere. The flowers were gone—none on the roadsides or in the pastures. The fields had been turned under, showing only their drab brown. Everything was pale and sodden. Even the evergreens wore dark dowager coats.

She'd been just thirty-six and so tired. Not just in her arms and legs, not just in the body that shopped and cleaned and cooked and lay beneath her husband when desire took him. It was a hopeless, given-up tiredness. She dreamed of the peace of the graveyard.

"I was only sixteen when Geordie was conceived," she'd told Jimmy. Her parents were shocked. Wally had deeply disappointed them, her father said. They'd asked him to leave, they had to, but they hadn't insisted Wally marry her, nor had they chastised her for being so careless. They'd done the opposite, as if they had always been prepared for the inevitability of a teenaged pregnancy; one would simply live with it. Or do something about it. Her mother had taken her into the kitchen and pushed a cup of tea in front of her. A single tear slid down her face as she said, "Bette, my Elisabeth, you do not have to go through with this, not any of this."

Wally's absence made her want and love him more. "Don't mistake the thrill of sex for love"; it was the only angry thing her father said. She pictured the little baby growing inside her and saw a pretty life ahead with a handsome man who loved her and a wee one in their arms some place ten thousand miles from St. Helens. So they left. How sorrowful her mother's face had been. How grim her father's. And Kat, just eleven, not to be consoled. As they stood waving after her bus, she knew how much they ached. Then she put their grief in an envelope, and sealed it; she knew it would poison her if she did not.

Ten thousand miles away they went, to Canada, to never

see her parents or sister again, to give birth to the little boy who the doctors, not at first, but soon, matter-of-factly, coldly even, said was "retarded" and would not live long. As though Geordie were not her flesh and blood. And then she bore four more children before she was twenty-six, all unplanned but for the pregnancy that produced the twins. The neighbour women, her same age, were just marrying and beginning their families and she was already an old hand at it; they said that—she was an old hand. And she was a saint—or a foolish martyr some of them said behind her back, some baldly to her face—for keeping Geordie at home.

Fool she might have been, but not a saint. Not an old hand. She didn't know what to do with the children. Their mouths and diapers—that was easy enough, if exhausting. It was their souls she knew nothing of and feared she would ruin—who they were, who they would become. When the boys became teenagers it was worse. She could offer them no pre-paved way, having so willingly given up her own teen-aged years.

Geordie would never grow up and leave home. He had surprised the doctor and been capable of learning much more than predicted, but he had constant and endless needs. As he became a man, she had begun to push him away. There was no helping hand, no one to tell them what to do, no one but the other children to take on Geordie's care when they were old enough or, and this thought filled her with both guilt and dismay, when she wanted to be free and done with children. There never had been any help; only the frightening institutions which, in her quiet desperation, she had begun to consider again. Then how her selfish heartlessness had frightened her and made her loathe herself.

Ambrose had always avoided her, and with good reason. After Trevor was born, she'd left Ambrose alone with his own guarded unhappiness and in doing so had no doubt been the cause of more of it. She'd spanked him the most, but she'd spanked them all, even Geordie. Even Lulu. Out of anger and frustration, and just out of habit.

She stared out the hospital window and thought of Alan, clear-eyed, sweet Alan. A bitter memory surfaced and filled her with remorse. She made herself tell Jimmy. The twins must have been eight, Ambrose, as ever, struggling with his spelling and Alan, the words easily, perfectly, not even memorized, just known, playing with the Tinkertoys under the kitchen table. She gave Ambrose a few words to spell. After a few minutes she snatched the paper from beneath his pencil and held it up—scrawled letters, backwards e's and s's, words erased or crossed out until the paper was thin or torn. She couldn't remember the last word she had asked him to spell. Perhaps it was paint, or ocean, or bright. But he could not. "Alan can spell it," she'd said. "Why can't you? Spell it for us, Alan." Alan had stood up and looked at Ambrose, Ambrose looking back, their green eyes the same. "I don't know how to spell it either, Mum," Alan had said.

She had risen from the table then, silent and shamed to the white of her bones, and left the house. She left the baby Lulu napping and six-year-old Trevor somewhere in the yard. She'd walked for an hour, through the Logging Trail, along the ravine, past the Jones' shack, thankful only that not a soul had called out some hello or to ask her jokingly what she'd done with all her children. What *had* she done with her children? When she returned, before Wally got home, the boys were playing with the train set on the living room floor and

Lulu—changed and with a warmed bottle of milk—was in Trevor's lap watching the boys. Lulu and Trevor had looked up, and then only fleetingly, Trevor said, "Hi, Mum," as only an occupied six-year-old could.

"Can you imagine, Jimmy, what it was like to be so young and have five children?" she asked. But how stupid a question. Jimmy shouldn't pardon her for being young and ignorant. Women younger than herself had been raising children since the dawn of time and not destroying their perfect souls. Not abandoning them. She pulled one of Jimmy's fingers out of its curl, felt its unconscious resistance. She wanted him to judge her for all her appalling sins. He would not, though, even if he could; she knew what Jimmy would say. "Mum," he'd smile, "you think too much."

It had struck her suddenly that Jimmy's mind might be in a state of agonized wretchedness, hearing but unable to reply to her words. She'd heard of this. She leaned over his face and peered into his eyes, but there was nothing there. The wretch was her. She tucked her fingers into the curve of Jimmy's hand. It was warm, but unfamiliar in its stillness. For thirty years she'd watched these hands pull weeds, milk goats, do dishes, shine shoes, button his coat—everyday things. His eleven-year-old hand had held hers at the funeral of his father and brothers. Then, through the years, she had held his at the funerals of others without his ever understanding the unfathomable courage that he had given her to live on. Having Jimmy kept Bette's ache in a realm just beyond the shores of their life together.

He'd never left her, never married. When he became a man she'd told him he must. He'd sat across from her at the kitchen table. "Too much to lose," he'd said. "I can't risk it.

I've lost too many already." He'd sworn never to set foot in a boat again, too, and he never ate fish or lobster. His rules, his way of keeping his own ache at bay. He made a living. Odd jobs at first and then they began to make and sell their goat cheeses. Their tiny shop in Carbonear, squeezed between the rug hooking studio and the new café on the main street, had been open for three years. Jimmy tended the garden and the goats and whistled about the house, and he called her Mum. He was happy. He made Bette happy. Now, without him, violent waves had breached her dune, and saltwater had spilled into the freshwater pond.

She sat by Jimmy's bed, wishing for a photo of the children to show him. Not having one didn't prevent her from summoning up Lulu's face.

"You'd think a baby would want her mother." Lulu had never been a daughter like the Ogg girls were, talking and laughing, arguing and crying in their mother's arms. But the long understood truth of it was tucked away tidily at the back of Bette's mind: she had never been the mother May Ogg had been. When Bette's period was late for the fourth time she'd stood cold and panic-stricken in the doctor's office. In every way she could think of that did not involve using the word, she had asked the doctor for an abortion. She'd read pity in his face and her heart had momentarily surged with hope. Then he'd lit a cigarette for himself, offered her one, and said, "You know I can't help you with that, Mrs. Parsons."

That night, already feeling the swell of hormones taking her body from her, Bette lay next to Wally and wept. He had an erection, pressed against her thigh with a mindless cheerfulness of its own. "Here, here," he said, patting her back. As if the responsibility of another mouth to feed, another baby to diaper and bend over while it learned to walk, another child to defend from dreadful teachers and neighbourhood bullies and untethered dogs, another living being to understand, meant nothing. "Just think, perhaps we'll have a girl," he'd said.

From babyhood, Lulu had favoured her father, held her arms out to him when he came home, her dark little face brightening, singing Dada in response to Wally's tickled greeting. At first Bette accepted Lulu's preference for Wally as an inevitable daddy phase, but as time passed her expectations of some special connection with her daughter diminished, replaced by a jealousy that embarrassed her. Finally, a resignation drifted in and she told herself it was a relief not to have another child clinging to her, though not one of them had ever clung to her for long.

"I left them, Jimmy. I loved them, but I left them." She didn't plan it, she didn't dream of it. It simply happened; one day the dull monster of despair tipped the scales and she simply slid off. She'd been at the supermarket. She'd driven up to the front of the house with another endless load of groceries and there it sat, her own personal tarpaper shack huddled on the mud. A box unfinished despite twenty years of promises. For twenty years she'd been throwing the bills into the air and paying the ones that landed face up on the floor or the table, if there was money to spare. She'd been caring for Geordie, watching the other children surpass him, for twenty years. Twenty years of washing, worrying, wiping up—vomit, spilled milk, crumbs, boot dirt, dog shit. Wally always said, "It'll be all right, Bette dear." "When?" she'd begun to ask. She'd sat in the car staring at the house, the exposed foundation, the curtain in Lulu's bedroom flittering out the window and made grey by the rain, thinking *When?* until the cartons of milk might have curdled and the meat might have spoiled if that November hadn't been so cold.

Even then, the timing of the letter in the mailbox seemed preposterously dangerous. She was so grateful she'd checked the mail. It was addressed—in Aloysius' loose scrawl—to Mrs. Walter Parsons. There was no stamp. It had been hand delivered. Bette laughed aloud when she saw it; it struck her as equally absurd both that she would be addressed that way by him and that she was, indeed, Mrs. Walter Parsons. It was not signed but she knew his hand. Thirteen simple words on the creamy paper: *Alice is gone. I'm free. Come to me, come to me, dear Bette.* What was he imagining? That she would leave Wally—Fraser Arm's scoutmaster, for God's sake—and live with him, in this tiny town where everyone knew everyone else's business? She sat at the kitchen table fingering the creamy envelope, the dozen brown paper grocery bags, stalwart witnesses to her infidelity, accusing her from the counter.

Before they all came home—before Wally came in with a kiss for her ear, before Lulu dropped her lunch box in a clatter by the sink, before Ambrose and Trevor began the ridiculous eraser argument again—she put Aloysius' letter on the coals in the cookstove and burned it. It was beautiful the way the heat first drew a perfect, slow-moving black circle on the paper, making room for a fiery tongue to plunge through the centre, a mad thing licking. The whole thing floated upwards for a second or two, completely black, and was gone. What she'd done with Aloysius McFee had been madness. One night's drunken mistake that then went on for months. Bette had to force herself to speak this truth to Jimmy. She told him how often she had scanned Lulu's face for traces of Aloysius. They shared freckles, but he was blond, and she so nearly black-haired. But there was that little tintype photograph of his grandmother as a child—another stern little Lulu. Aloysius showed it to her when Lulu was four or five, long after it was over, waving it in her face saying, "She's mine, isn't she?" The only thing Bette was sure of was that she wasn't sure. She'd so wanted to get rid of that last baby, their Lulu, so that she would never have to wonder.

After she'd burned the letter and its envelope, she put the groceries away and peeled carrots and potatoes for a kidney stew.

"I set the laundry on fire that night," she said, laying her forehead on Jimmy's arm. That fire was spectacular, the flames leaping through the weave of the wicker basket, all lacey. After the argument with Wally, after discovering Lulu behind the couch, after they'd all gone to bed, Bette made herself a pot of coffee and sat in the quiet kitchen with the lights out. In the wee hours, she opened the cookstove and looked inside for the thirteen words. She made herself another pot of coffee. At six in the morning, Trevor found her sitting upright in her chair, fully dressed, and wide awake. Trevor—her most complicated, most wily, most interesting child, and oddly, the one she might have loved the most—sat down opposite her without saying a word. Then he stood, came over to her, curved his hand gently around the back of her head, and when she looked up at him he bent and kissed her, his tongue pressing between her surprised lips. She let him. Felt her hand sliding up the back of his head, pressing his face into hers, kissing him back.

"Trevor went out the door to do his paper route with a look of confusion on his face that terrified me. I felt I'd gone mad. I was so ashamed I threw up in the sink. All I could think was how could I ever face him again."

"Very unusual, this kind of stroke, for someone only forty-one," the nurse said.

Bette sat up suddenly. She watched the woman place her hand tenderly on Jimmy's cheek and keep it there while she looked up at the monitor, checking the blinking numbers. Another nurse, the young one, had explained all the machinery to her after the first night, pointless since only the heartbeat monitor mattered at all to Bette.

"Did you say you feel sick? You've been here all day again. Go get a coffee," the nurse said.

Bette didn't want a coffee. The fluorescent lights in the cafeteria were an assault; the scrape of chairs, the clatter of spoons in coffee cups, food scraps congealing on abandoned plates, the hubbub of too many people, patients tugging intravenous towers behind them, loved ones waiting, like her. It was a world to which she refused to belong. People behaved as though *this* were normal. The scrubby apple tree in fruit behind the house. Sweetie's iridescent yellow eyes. The dogs sleeping on the forbidden-to-them couch. These were normal. Not this.

"We'll watch him," the nurse said. And then again, a little sternly: "We'll watch him."

Bette went. She followed the wide corridors until they let her out onto a parking lot where people were smoking, the hauled-out intravenous machines ticking beside them, their arms crossed, their sweaters and coats pulled closed in the new chill of the end of summer. A young man sat on a bench near the door, wearing only a flimsy hospital gown—two, in fact; one forwards and one backwards—and a pair of unlaced running shoes. He couldn't have been eighteen.

"Cigarette, old lady?" he said, holding a pack out to Bette.

"I've quit," Bette said, angry and confused at being called old lady. "A long time ago."

"Me too. Fifty times. If it's got you, it's got you." He shook the pack at her.

"Do you want me to tie your shoes for you?" Bette blushed. What could possibly have overcome her to ask such a strange question? The young man looked at her, uncertain, but then he grinned.

"I can do it myself, you know. I'm not that sick."

"I'm certain you can," she said, more brusquely than she'd intended.

"Go ahead then." And he slid one leg up on the bench and Bette sat, her eyes avoiding his lack of underwear, and tied first one shoe and then the other.

"That's probably enough time," she said giving the young man's foot an awkward pat and standing. Probably enough time away from Jimmy. Probably enough time to pretend to have consumed a coffee and a doughnut. The young man reached up and caught her wrist in his hand. "Thanks," he said, not letting go.

It began to rain, a sudden wild rain that drove against the windows and pavement, scattering the smokers who flicked away their cigarettes and scurried in through the glass doors. The young man didn't move. He held out his arms pocked with scabs and needle marks, while the rain soaked him. He turned and looked at Bette and said, "It isn't pretty, is it?"

She hurried inside and nearly ran down the corridor. She was confused by its turns and exit signs. Others were rushing along with her. She heard them, breathing behind her, their feet marking her frantic old woman's pace.

The young intern with the Greek name was removing a

paper gown. He looked at the floor when he saw Bette and she instantly knew him for what he was—a man too inexperienced yet to graciously impart the saddest news.

"No," Bette shouted. "No." He stood uncertainly before her, his bedside manner stalled. The nurse took Bette's hand and pressed it against her shoulder. Bette looked at the clock above what had been, what was, Jimmy's bed, for he lay there, still. Its digital letters said 5:37. But this would not be the time that Jimmy had ceased to belong to Bette. She needed to know when he had died, the exact time. Without knowing, she thought, she would not be able to go on.

"When?"

"Just after you left. It often happens that way. They wait to be alone."

"Alone? No. He wouldn't have wanted to die alone."

"People do. Want to. We see it," the nurse said.

"When exactly?" When exactly does one die? Surely not when the baby-faced doctor says so. "Did he say anything?" she asked. The nurse shook her head. "What do I do now?" Bette asked. She might have meant, who do I call about our arrangements. Or she could have meant, how will I go on without him. But the thought that most brutally assailed her, since she knew it to be impossible, was how she would turn her back on Jimmy and leave him here in this bed. It was that thought, finally, that split her in two, separating her body from her mind. Pain, that primitive beast, climbed onto Bette's chest and began squeezing. Her breath wasn't coming. She bent forward slightly. A vicious jackknife slid up from her gut into her throat and she heard a keening sound spill from her mouth. She felt a primal urge to climb into his body, unzip his belly, and lie within him. Then she did. She watched her flayed self lie on his breast, hold his face, saw herself rocking and moaning, urged on by the clamouring voices of the millions before her who had had to leave their beloved dead.

Then she was standing by Jimmy's bed, her arms at her side, silent. She heard the nurse asking, "Where is your family?" Bette thought she was speaking of Wally and her children, her sister, her parents, who were all suddenly, vividly present, witnessing her annihilation. Lulu, still ten, pressed against her side; the boys, sombre and tall, teenagers, watched her from the other side of Jimmy. Geordie, where was Geordie? Behind her, his chin on her shoulder, like he used to do. Her sister, her mother, her father, all there. And Wally, as always, gentle and nodding. Go ahead, he seemed to be saying. Let him go.

"Do you want to shut his eyes for him?" the nurse said.

"Why?" Bette asked, but the answer was in the woman's deep brown eyes—the living cannot bear to gaze inside and not find themselves reflected there. She touched first one eyelid then the other, pressing gently, but Jimmy's eyes wouldn't stay shut. The nurse put two fingers over Bette's and held them in place for a moment, closing forever Bette's windows to her son.

"There," the nurse said.

"There," Bette repeated.

●

Tomorrow they would bury him. They'd had their wake. The hearse had come back to the house and taken Jimmy and his pine coffin away, back to wherever it was they were keeping him, as if he were, just for today, a library book on short-term loan. He belonged now to something else—the earth. Bette had watched Brody raise his glass one last time to the cousin he'd loved, and his friends had poured him drunk, drunk, drunk into the passenger seat of his ex-wife's car and they had all gone home. The alcohol had been drunk, the potluck food consumed, and Flo and Jo had washed and put away the last dish. The goats had been fed and their heads scratched. The compost emptied. It was time for bed.

Flo sat Bette on a chair in her bedroom and took off her shoes.

"Lift," Flo said, and Bette lifted her arms like an obedient child. Flo pulled off Bette's dress, undid her bra, and let her soft breasts fall. She rummaged through the dresser for a clean, warm nightie and Bette lay down on her bed.

"Sleep," Flo said, sitting beside her and running her cool, gnarled fingers across Bette's brow.

"We are two old women, alone," Bette said, holding tight to Flo's hand.

"We're not alone, Bette. Listen." At first she could hear nothing, but as Flo sat beside her on the bed, the night sounds came. There was a bird—just the song sparrow. Then a village dog; one of the goats, Leandra probably, their night owl, bleating. The wind was there too, making the bushes rustle, and at some distance, the ocean's steadfast noise.

"Will you be all right if I go home now?" Flo asked.

Bette nodded and Flo called the dogs. They heard them leaping off Jimmy's bed, then the clack of their claws down the hall. They hesitated in Bette's doorway.

"They've always slept with Jimmy," Bette said.

"Well, they'll sleep with you now." She patted the bed and Pelé and Pete leapt onto it, circling and finding their new spots, little Pelé warm against the small of Bette's back, and big Pete by her feet. Flo left and the dogs fell into their animal dreams, but sleep sat stiff in the hard chair in the corner, staring at Bette, unwilling to come to her. Bette lay listening and remembering.

●

The clock read 4:30. She may have slept; the clamour of bird-song had intensified and there was a wisp of a dream floating away. Bette rose and the dogs followed her out into the dark, cool night, running off on their swift feet after scents only dogs could follow. She looked down the hill to the shore and saw that Flo's light was on. During the wake someone had moved Bette's garden chair. She dragged it back to her spot and sat looking out over the ocean in the dark until night gave way to day and the sun rose again and warmed her slowly.

She hadn't finished the story for Jimmy. He'd left her before she could. There wasn't much more to tell. Wally had come into the kitchen next. "You're up early," he'd said. "I didn't even hear you come to bed." As always, he had forgiven her comments about Geordie and Woodlands. Forgiven her or chosen to forget. He kissed her on the ear, as always, and she was sure that in that touch he would know that her spirit had abandoned her somewhere along this exhausting road and that she could walk along no more. The twins were next, then Lulu. They bustled around the kitchen, ate their puffed wheat, their spoonfuls of sugar, white and Demerara, burnt or buttered their toast. Wally made coffee and Alan and Ambrose had a cup too. Too young to drink coffee, Bette thought, but she said nothing. Lulu reached out to taste Alan's cup and made a face. "Where's Geordie?" Lulu asked. And Wally laughed. "That lazy buster, go get him, Lulu." And Lulu came back with Geordie, his eyes still all puffy with sleep and with a hug for Bette and for Wally. If Bette didn't speak, no one would speak to her, no one would notice her. Trevor came in and threw the newspaper on the table and Wally picked it up and opened it to the sports section. Trevor looked at Bette shyly for the first time in his life, and Bette thought she might throw up again. Geordie knocked the milk jug and it sloshed a little on the table but it didn't fall over. A miracle. And then they were gone. Ambrose and Alan would head up the road together, Trevor would be following fifteen paces behind, and Lulu with Nadine Ogg would go down the road to the elementary school. Wally took Geordie in the delivery van, and they were gone. Bette hadn't moved and no one had noticed.

She washed the dishes. She wrote a note on a piece of paper she tore from Lulu's scribbler. She put it on the table, under the milk jug. She hadn't known what to say. In the end, because May Ogg would be there as usual at 9:30 for coffee and she had to be gone before then, she simply wrote: *Wally, I will not live in a tarpaper shack for the rest of my life. Love, Bette.* It wasn't the truth. She could live in this tarpaper shack. What she couldn't live with was the overwhelming mess of needs inside it, including her own. She took the grocery money in her purse and the little bit of money she had secreted away for Christmas presents. Wally wouldn't have known about that. There was one hundred dollars in the emergency money envelope. They hadn't touched it for years and Wally probably wouldn't remember where she kept it. She took that too. Nothing more. Not a photograph, not a token of her children or her husband, nothing but his ring. She put a change of clothes and a pair of pyjamas in an old canvas rucksack of the boys' along with three peanut butter and lettuce sandwiches and some apples. She wore her boots and her overcoat and pants and a sweater. She walked through the pasture, unlocked the goat gate, and caught the bus that came up Reifel Road from White Rock every morning. Standing, and surrounded by strangers, she could think of nothing but that milk in the jug growing lukewarm on the kitchen table. That's the last thing she would have told Jimmy. She would have told him about that waste of milk.

●

The day is beautiful and blue, so rare here this time of the year. It is almost warm. Bette takes her sweater off and keeps it off despite the breeze, just to feel the sun on her shoulders. Walking up the well-trod hill path to the lookout bench, she stops halfway up to catch her breath. Jimmy would have loved this day. "Mum," he would have said, "let's go up to the bench," and he would have pulled her up the hill, and at the top he would have waved his arms wide and said, "Just look at that will ya?"

Everything sparkles—the ocean, the air, even the village, as if it had just put on a fresh coat of paint. She gazes back at their house. The goats are reaching through the fence for the greener grass, the three youngest playing King of the Castle on top of a barrel. When the wind blows in the right direction, she can hear the bells on their collars. The chickens scratch in the yard, unfenced and unhurried. She has left the greenhouse doors open to the breezes—though gated against the chickens—thinking how well the vegetables would like it. A small movement catches Bette's eye and she looks up. Hovering not six feet above her is a hummingbird, its pink head and grey-green body shimmering. Bette knows hummingbirds; Wally taught her their names—Rufous, red throated, Anna's, calliope. This one looks like an Anna's, but how it could be here is inexplicable.

Old Maud Best is coming down the path and she peers up to see what Bette is staring at.

"My God, Bette, that's a rare sighting."

"Anna's?"

"Yes, m'dear. Blown way off course. That one belongs on the west coast. You'll have to tell Royal Newhook about this one. Get your name in the birding column."

"You tell him, Maud. I don't mind."

"I'll tell him we both saw it. The old coot doesn't believe my sightings anymore."

The two women stand, faces skyward, while the bird hovers, seemingly as curious as they are. It makes a few more blurred triangles in the cloudless blue and is gone.

"Mind the path," Maud says with an exaggerated wink. "You're no spring chicken."

Bette laughs. For a few years Maud has been claiming she is one hundred and two. Ninety is more like it.

"You mind the path," Bette says. Bette watches for a few minutes while Maud pokes her way down toward her best friend Royal Newhook's house, then she turns back up the path. The wooden lookout bench needs to be shored up again—someone other than Jimmy will do it this year—but it will still hold a thin old woman. She shakes off her boots and then peels off her socks. She rubs her bare feet across the scratchy lichen. There are hundreds of dandelions around the bench, all facing the ocean, as if they too are scanning for icebergs and for whales and for sailboats on the sea. There are none. Just two magnificent shades of blue meeting across an endless, curving horizon. In the past few centuries, Bette thinks, surely nothing has changed here. She stretches her arms out along the back of the bench fingering with her left hand the indentations made by her son so long ago and now smoothed by thirty years of weather—JIMMY 1977. Then, batting away a self-consciousness that makes her look first to see if she is truly alone, she raises her arms heavenward.

"Just look at that, will ya?" Bette shouts.

●

When she comes down from the top of the hill she walks past her—and Jimmy's—house and calls on Flo. Flo makes her some lunch and when they finish eating, she takes Bette's hand. "I love you, old friend," Flo says. Then she leans her forehead against Bette's. They both know: Many years ago Bette buried her heart in Halley's Cove, population one hundred and seventy-three. She will have to dig it up now. She will have to go to the place that was once home. To the people who were once her family.

●

Flo drives Bette into town and drops her at the library. The young man patiently shows her how to use the computer to find the telephone directory, pointing with his long fingers at what he calls fields, and *you are ells*, and links. He waits while she pokes at the keys to enter Walter Parsons, then he leaves her on her own. Wally is still listed on Forward Road, still at the telephone number she can recite as easily as her name. She tries the boys: there are no Ambrose Parsons, twenty-five Alan Parsons, and too many A. Parsons to count across the lower mainland. Three Trevor Parsons are listed in Vancouver and dozens and dozens of T. Parsons. Of course, they all could have moved away, even from the province. She has to call the librarian back when the screen goes black. He shows her how to move the mouse to keep the computer from sleeping. A computer sleeping. She tries to make a joke about it, but the boy looks at her, deadpan. She sits for some time after that, scrutinizing the strange ads, avoiding looking for the last name on her list. If Lulu had married she would probably have changed her name. She might have children. Bette could be a grandmother. The boys could have had children as well. The thought makes her feel unsteady in front of the contraption. Finally she types her daughter's name. There are too many L. Parsons to count, and no Louise. When she tries Lulu instead, the Fraser Arm address that comes up stops her breath. She knows it well. It is the McFees' address on Hemlock.

Bette is pacing on the sidewalk outside the library, waiting for Flo to pick her up. Every worst-case scenario imaginable is pulsing through her mind. For a moment she is vaguely aware of the irony of her panic; for four decades she has pushed the thought of her children out of her mind and now, here she is, behaving as though she has the right to rescue them. She shoves that thought aside. By the time Flo's big old Buick pulls up, Bette is frantic.

"I can only think the worst, Flo," she says. "Aloysius has done something to get his hands on Lulu."

"She couldn't have married him?"

"What? He's thirty-five years her senior. He can't have."

"Stranger things have happened."

"Don't even say it. He might be her father. I've just got to go."

Flo nods. "You should take an airplane."

"I can't fly. I don't even exist. I don't have any identification, or none that I could use. They're not going to accept a driver's license from 1967. I'm probably a dead person."

"Well, you'll have to report yourself as alive then. Taking the bus would kill you. I don't even know if there is a bus."

"Flo, Flo. I can't wait for the government to realize I'm Lazarus. I've got to go back now."

"Call them."

"No." The suggestion feels like an electric shock. "I couldn't."

"I'll drive you then," Flo smacks her old hands on the steering wheel. "We'll drive together to B.C. We can call on Jo and Isabelle in Montreal on the way."

Bette looks into her friend's bright eyes. "You're eighty-four, Flo." She laughs despite her anxiety.

"Oh," Flo laughs. "I forgot. Damn. 'Tis not every day that Morris kills a cow, though."

"What in Hell's name does that mean?"

"This kind of promising opportunity comes but seldom. Do you drive, at least? We could take turns."

"I haven't driven for forty years, as you well know. But I did drive. I do drive."

"Could you do it again? It's like a bicycle, or so they say."

"Flo, you have never ridden a bicycle in your life."

"Not true. Cecil gave me a two-wheeler as a wedding present."

"And where, pray tell, did you ride a bicycle in Halley's Cove in, what was it? 1933?"

"I was ten in 1933, dear. We got married in 1941. Cecil wasn't from Halley's Cove, remember? He brought it over with him from New Harbour."

"And there was a nice smooth road along the shore here for riding a bicycle along?"

"I'll admit, it wasn't smooth, but it was paved. It was the

novelty of the thing anyways, Bette. We all had a turn, then Moses Pike's dad, Arthur, rode it off the end of the wharf one summer and it rusted away there." Flo is serious now. "But this has nothing to do with getting you home."

The word home strikes Bette like an arrow in the throat. "This is home now, Flo."

Flo nods, her eyes filling with tears again.

"I've got some music to face. But I'll come home here when it's done."

●

The taxi driver does not want to leave her there. Insistent, he asks her: "But what address do you want? I am not the kind of man who will leave an old lady in the middle of nowhere." She is seventy-six. Old to the young. Today she feels ancient, in her bones and in her soul. Despite Flo's insistence, she took the bus and then the train across the country; it did nearly kill her. Now, she reassures the taxi driver, calmly, so that he will go, "This is not the middle of nowhere *to me*." But it is. Nothing but the treed hedge is familiar. Where the taxi driver leaves her, finally, the wall of cedar and Douglas fir runs a country block in either direction, stretching exactly as it had the last time she saw it, but now it is four decades taller. The driveway is as long and treed as she remembers. Looking over to the other side of the street, Bette knows she has not come home. What was the hazelnut orchard is now shops and brightly lit signs. The Wheatley's barn and paddock are no longer, the house dwarfed by a glassy high-rise. They have built sidewalks over the ditches, hung traffic lights, paved the pastures for a car dealership—L I Q U I D A T I O N in huge orange letters is painted on the windscreens of the dozen cars. There used to be a church with wooden steps just there, down from Hemlock on Forward Road, and acres of impenetrable blackberry canes where the children lost ladders and buckets and sometimes had to be rescued.

It is after five, Saturday, and if she were capable of reasoned thinking, she would be grateful that no one was walking on the sidewalk to witness her confusion. An alarm is ringing in the place she has used so often to calm herself. It is as though she has taken the wrong bus, gotten off on the wrong corner, and cannot correctly remember the street she should be on. How ridiculous she is. She had imagined the familiarity of an old sweater.

She turns and faces the trees, the driveway that snakes to the house through dark boughs, the ditch. The McFees' ditch is still deep and green, filled with moss and lady fern and yellow buttercups and what looks like rows and rows of onions. Once, nearly sixty years ago, she lay with Wally in a field filled with ferns and buttercups. That day changed her. Geordie was a baby, asleep between them on a blanket amidst the grasses and fall wildflowers. Like a comforting hand, the breeze had been warm. For the first time in her new Canadian home, Bette had felt a stirring, the smallest tap on her shoulder, of happiness.

It had not been simple. There had been the sleepless, seasick journey from Liverpool with the other war brides. She was only sixteen, but some of those offering pitying or hostile looks when they saw she was pregnant were barely eighteen themselves. At the end of the voyage there Wally was, waiting for her in Halifax. They had their paperwork. Unlike others, the immigration officer did not comment on her age or her burgeoning belly. Then there was the train trip across Canada, the country so vast Bette did not believe Wally when he said there were still six, five, four more days to go, each day and each mile, each clack of the wheels taking her farther from her family. She was sure, even then, that she would not see them again. The men on the train, decommissioned officers some, and soldiers and sailors heading west for jobs in towns with strange names—Moose Jaw, Medicine Hat, Bragg Creek, Chilliwack—stood in the corridors and smoked and drank and played cards. Their Canadian accents were oddities in her ears and she wrapped a kerchief around her head to drown out the sound.

They had to take a bus from the train station to the bus station. Then they took another bus from Vancouver to New Westminster, and another to Fraser Arm. It was May and drizzling, not so unlike England, but the countryside was wide and unfamiliar, the trees too tall, the distances too far, the mountains higher than any she'd seen. Wally was jovial and said, think of Mary and Joseph on a donkey. In the face of Wally's cheerfulness, Bette was ashamed of her sour teen-aged feelings. She wanted to ask forgiveness of her parents for having been a troublesome child, for getting pregnant, for leaving, but they were so far away. A phone call to England cost more than they had in Wally's wallet, so it wasn't made. And for years they had no phone anyway.

The baby was a whale inside her, moving in deep hard turns. And when it was time for him to come out, there was no midwife, no Wally, only a belittling doctor annoyed at being woken so late, or so early, whichever it was. The doctor used forceps to pull Geordie from her unconscious body and the nurses kept her baby from her for the rest of the day while her breasts swelled, and as, between her legs, she ached and bled.

The tiny house that was the Parsons', so gladly vacated by Wally's aunts who moved to a dry apartment in Vancouver, was damp and ugly. Wally added to it as the years went by and as the family grew, but in those early years Wally chopped wood and Bette boiled water on the cookstove and washed diapers by hand, hanging them to dry on racks above the stove. Every week Wally promised her a washing machine, then left her alone all day while he did odd jobs or looked for work. Sometimes she took the baby out in the pram and collected pop and beer bottles in the ditches, to buy a chocolate bar. This she never told her husband. That winter she sat and watched the rain with placid Geordie on her knees and longed to be a child again herself.

But spring. Spring came with the delicate fiddleheads at the edges of the woods, and pussy willows, and daffodils in the ditches. And Geordie became just as fat and beautiful as she thought a baby should be, and they found a spot that became their favourite in the Logging Trail, to which they would go again and again. Geordie lay between them in the moss. She had to pee and Wally said, "Go ahead."

"Here?" she asked, astonished.

"Yes. Mark your territory," he said. So she did. They picked wildflowers, a bunch too big to fit in any jar they had for a vase, and that afternoon they tied strings to sticks and hung them with hooks and wriggling worms off a wharf on River Road. Bette caught a fish and they ate it that night with nothing else. "No vegetables or potatoes, Bette?" Wally had asked. And they went to bed tired and happy and made love and Bette forgot about the winter and the rain.

That spring, the Oggs moved in next door and May Ogg became her friend. May was twenty-one and pregnant with her third daughter. She was the only woman Bette met who had also had her first at sixteen. While their husbands were out, they drank pots of coffee and planted beans and peas, and that summer they made blackberry jelly, the cheesecloth bag strung between the legs of a chair placed upside down on the kitchen table, dripping dark juice into a bowl. And May Ogg couldn't have cared less that there was something different about Geordie; she loved him too.

Now, in front of the McFees', on Hemlock Street, Bette aches to return to that spring when, at seventeen, she felt she knew enough and that was all that was needed. The driveway is grassy, a tunnel between the trees. The wheels of her borrowed suitcase catch on the tufts of grass, and she stops. She should have called. Or gone to Wally's instead. What was her plan—walk up to the door unannounced, knock and say, "Hello, I was your mother. Remember me, dear"? What if Aloysius is there? Dear God. She hadn't thought of that. The foolishness of her decision to arrive unannounced, like some protective knight, fills her veins with lead. Even her ears seem stoppered with it for she can no longer hear the racket of crows and starlings in the trees.

She leans her suitcase against a thick fir and reaches out to steady herself against it, getting a little sticky pitch on her hand as she does so. The pitch is somehow comforting in its inevitability. She puts her hand to her nose. The smell of the forest comes to her from eons ago, and she finds a trace of numb courage in it. She walks forward, absently rubbing the pitch to black on her hands. Her feet tell her: slowly, Bette. Just before the driveway opens into the clearing she stops. There are people on the big front porch. She is close enough to be seen by them—it is still not quite dusk—but their focus is inward. "Play us a tune," one of them says, and Bette smothers the cry that rushes to her mouth. A woman puts a fiddle to her shoulder. She is laughing as she nestles her chin on the rest, raising the bow. She tucks a strand of hair behind her ear and gives her hat, a men's brown fedora, a push farther down onto her head. "Ahem," someone says. The people on the porch go silent and the woman starts to play.

The sorrowful note from the first slow draw of the bow stabs Bette's heart. She does nothing to wipe the tears that stream warm on her face, touching the corners of her mouth where time has drawn new and deeper lines surely just so she can taste the salt. Then the woman—it is Lulu, Bette can tell by the point of her nose and chin—begins to sing. Her voice is strong, rousing, part of the wind and the softening light in the trees, and the song is not sorrowful at all. It must be funny, though Bette cannot make out many of the words, for the whole group laughs and sings the chorus, their voices a mix of tuneful and not: beware the Aeolian winds, they have loosed the Aeolian winds. The music fills the hollow in Bette's chest. Her confusion furls and unfurls, a tattered flag in a windstorm. Her impulse to laugh and to cry is the same. She has a powerful urge to shout hello. She says it aloud in the woods. "Hello," she says, as loud as she dares.

They all clap and there's a wolf whistle. "Another," someone demands. Lulu lifts her fiddle and plays a jig. Bette peers toward the porch. She cannot tell if these men are Alan or Ambrose or Trevor, but they are hers. The teenaged boys she left behind have the thickened bodies and grey hair of middle-aged men. An old man sits on the porch swing with a young boy beside him. She is sure of this one: it is Wally. A woman has her arm around his shoulder but her back to Bette. She searches among the rest of them, people she doesn't recognize, looking for Geordie. When Lulu finishes the group claps again and someone says, "Doris, let's have a tune." Tall, grey-haired Doris Tenpenny steps forward. She clasps her hands in front of her chest and begins to whistle Leonard Cohen's "Suzanne."

Bette hears the words so clearly someone may as well be singing them aloud, and she no longer remembers what she was thinking when she asked the taxi driver to leave her here. She might have thought that she would be able to find the words to ask forgiveness. Now, she is just an old woman standing in the fading light of day watching a family that used to be hers. She has no claim to them. The clamour of her heart is deafening; the music is being filtered through layers and layers of felted wool. She must go. She is about to turn away when the porch screen door bursts open and a big, barrel-chested, balding man in a tuxedo comes through the door. Bette stumbles and reaches for a tree. Geordie is staring right at her. She stands up straight and he does too. There is a moment's hesitation on his part and he frowns, the way he always did, squinting his eyes at the figure standing where the grass meets the trees.

If a bull could fly, it would be Geordie. He soars off the porch toward Bette. He is shouting. "I told you so, Lulu! I told you so!"

A MUSICAL PLAYLIST TO LISTEN TO WHILE READING
The Very Marrow of Our Bones

"Mercy Now," Mary Gauthier

"Dandelion," Antje Duvekot

"Going to the Barn Dance Tonight," performed by Don Messer

"Till We Meet Again," performed by Don Messer

"Carolina in the Morning," performed by Judy Garland

"The Bare Necessities," performed by Phil Harris and Bruce Reitherman
    on *The Jungle Book* soundtrack

"Jimmy Mack," performed by Martha and the Vandellas

"Georgy Girl," The Seekers

"Soul Man," performed by Sam and Dave

"To Sir with Love," performed by LuLu

"Fool's Gold," Lhasa de Sela

The opera buffa, *The Barber of Seville*

"People Get Ready," performed by Sonny Terry
    and Brownie McGhee

"Somebody to Love," Jefferson Airplane

"Love Is All You Need," The Beatles

"Love Me Do," The Beatles

"Love to Love You Baby," Donna Summer

"When the Saints Go Marching In," performed by Louis Armstrong

"I'll Be Seeing You," performed by Vera Lynn

"The Dock of the Bay," Otis Redding and Steve Cropper

The Beatles' White Album

"Pearl, Pearl, Pearl," Lester Flatt and Earl Scruggs

"Don't Worry, Be Happy," Bobby McFerrin

"Your Cheatin' Heart," Hank Williams

"MacPherson's Lament," Traditional

"Carry Me Home," written by Tim Baker, performed by Hey Rosetta!

"Sonny's Dream," Ron Hynes

"The One," Oh Susanna

"Suzanne," Leonard Cohen

ACKNOWLEDGEMENTS

To the extraordinarily inspiring musicians . . .

Much gratitude for permission to quote your words: Mary Gauthier, "Mercy Now" from her album *Mercy Now.* Antje Duvekot, "Dandelion," from her album *Boys, Flowers, Miles.* The late Lhasa de Sela, "Fool's Gold," from her album *Lhasa.* An excerpt from "Carry Me Home," written by Tim Baker and performed by Hey Rosetta! on their album *A Cup of Kindness Yet* through Sonic Entertainment Group, Halifax. The late Ron Hynes, "Sonny's Dream," on his album *Face to the Gale.* Oh Susanna, "The One," on her album *Oh Susanna.*

Without whom . . .

Barbara Kyle and Marnie Woodrow who both pushed me off the figurative cliff and made me take this wonderful plunge. My agent, Hilary McMahon, at Westwood Creative Artists, for her brilliant dedication. Michael Holmes at ECW, for loving this story and for offering such wise edits. And

Edyepat Best, my True Newfoundlander, there is nothing to say but Thank Dog. Who would have known there are no crickets in Newfoundland?

Cathy Cappon, Joss Maclennan, and Lorin Medley for their endless encouragement and brilliant friendship.

The fabulous team at ECW . . .

Jessica Albert, Susannah Ames, Tania Blokhuis, Crissy Calhoun, Laura Pastore, Amy Smith, and Stephanie Strain. Gil Adamson, for the incredibly astute eye she cast upon my words in her copy edit. David A. Gee for this outstanding cover.

And my encouragers, readers, teachers, offerors of wisdom . . .

My family. Deb Rizun, Wendy Waring, Ken Higdon, Patrick Peachey Higdon, Ben Peachey Higdon, Bob Buckley, Cindy Sutherland, Liz Guppy, Amy Klein, Bruce Walsh, Heather Birchall. My Sunday morning walkers. My Nova Scotians. Maureen's West End Book Club women and Lieve's French class. The folks at the Creative Writing program at U. of T., including Lee Gowan and Kathryn Kuitenbrouwer. Mary McKeogh and Kathleen Holzermayr, for driving me around Essondale and Woodlands. Kimberley Noble, for NDIAD. Karen Sanderson and Sheelah Finlayson, for a couple of important lines. Deb Wise Harris, for our times at Jimmy's. Linda Ann Fear—Anne Bonny the fearless— for the wild lunch. Francesca Rose, dear faithful beast. And Tracy Westell, who believed, thank you.

And to my mother, June Higdon, who might have wanted to flee, but didn't.